THE DIFFERENCE of a DARCY

A PRIDE AND PREJUDICE VARIATION

TIFFANY THOMAS

For Philip Van Doren Stern
and Francesco "Frank" Capra—
whose creativity helps us all see
the difference we each make in the world
and that it truly is a wonderful life.

Prologue

Darcy House, London—July 30th, 1811

Fitzwilliam Darcy sat straighter in the saddle as the sea breeze tugged at his coat. Ramsgate's rooftops crested the rise before him, and his horse quickened without command. He had made excellent time—better than expected. A smile tugged at the corner of his mouth.

He had told Georgiana to expect him at week's end. Instead, he had finished his work two days early and had decided he would surprise her. It had been far too long since he had seen his sister in spirits as high as they sounded in her last letter. She had written of fresh air, long walks, and piano practice—and while her companion Mrs. Younge had not significantly impressed Darcy at their introduction, the woman had seemed competent enough.

The sight of the townhouse, which was their rented home for the summer, filled him with satisfaction. He dismounted quickly, handing his reins to the groom and ascending the front steps two at a time.

The butler opened the door in surprise. "Mr. Darcy! We were not expecting—"

"No matter," Darcy said as he removed his gloves. "Is Miss Darcy at home?"

"She is in the drawing room, sir. I shall announce you."

But Darcy waved him off, smiling faintly. "No need. I should like to see her expression when she realizes I am here."

He stepped lightly down the hall and pushed open the door.

"Georgie?"

1

His sister looked up—and in the next moment, let out a delighted cry. "Brother!"

She flew to him without hesitation, flinging her arms around his neck. Darcy stumbled back half a step, then caught her with a soft laugh.

"You are in excellent spirits," he said. "It is good to see you, dear girl."

"Oh, you are just in time!" she said breathlessly, her eyes alight with joy. "I have the most wonderful news!"

Mrs. Younge, seated by the window, half-rose. "Miss Darcy, perhaps it is best if—"

Darcy lifted a hand, frowning. "Let her speak, madam. What has you so flustered, Georgiana?"

The girl drew back and clasped his hands, beaming. "I had hoped you would come in time. Now you shall not miss the wedding!"

Darcy blinked. "Wedding?"

"Yes!" Georgiana twirled once, breathless with excitement. "I wanted to wait until you arrived before we eloped, but now we need not delay! Here, I will send a note to Mr. Wickham to let him know the good news."

The name struck him like a blow.

"Wickham?" he repeated, his voice flat.

Mrs. Younge had gone ashen. "Sir—please, allow me to explain—"

"You will remain silent." He turned on her sharply. "Do not move."

The woman's mouth opened again, but a quick motion brought a footman to the door. Darcy's voice was low and cold. "Do not allow her to leave this room."

The man nodded and took his position.

Darcy turned back to his sister. "Georgiana… what madness is this? You cannot mean to marry George Wickham."

She looked hurt. "But why not? He is kind and attentive and speaks of you with such warmth. He said he was certain you would approve. He remembered all the times you played together as boys. Even Father admired him—"

"No," Darcy said, his tone low and dangerous. "Absolutely not."

Georgiana's face crumpled. "Why are you angry? Why should it matter who I marry, if I love him?"

"Because you are not out. Because you are not of age. Because you are being deceived."

"You do not know him!"

"I know him better than you ever could," he snapped. "And there is no world, no fortune, no condition under which I would approve of such a match. He is a liar. A scoundrel. Lowborn filth who preys upon young girls for money and revenge."

Her lip trembled. "That is not true. He said you had a quarrel at university, but he had hoped—"

Darcy's voice rang out like a thunderclap. "You will not see him again."

Georgiana flinched as if struck. "You are cruel!"

"And you are a child," he growled. "A naïve girl being manipulated by a man who does not love you."

Tears sprang to her eyes. "You do not understand. You never try to understand."

"I understand far more than you think."

"You are heartless!" she cried, backing toward the door. "You do not care who I love, you just want to control me! Well, I wish—I wish I did not have a brother at all!"

The words landed like a knife.

Darcy said nothing. He only raised a hand and pointed.

"To your room. Now."

Sobbing, she fled.

Silence crashed down over the room.

He turned toward Mrs. Younge, who stood trembling in the corner. Her hands were folded tightly at her waist, knuckles white. Her composure had slipped—just a little. Enough for him to see the fear beneath it.

"You will tell me *everything*," he said darkly. "Every word. Every meeting. Every note. And God help you if I find even one lie."

3

Her lips parted, then closed again.

Darcy stepped forward. "Do not waste my time with denials."

She swallowed hard. "I—Mr. Darcy, I—"

"Start with how you came to be in my household," he bit out. "Those references you provided—who wrote them?"

Mrs. Younge's eyes flicked toward the door. The footman still stood there.

"I… I was desperate," she whispered. "My last position dismissed me without warning, and I—"

"The references were forged."

She gave a faint nod.

Darcy's nostrils flared. "And how long have you known George Wickham?"

Her gaze dropped. "Since childhood. My mother was his aunt."

"Of course," he muttered. "Nepotism and deception—Wickham's favorite tools."

"I only meant to introduce them," she said, voice rising slightly. "It was George who pursued the matter further. He said… he said there would be no harm in it. That you would come round once the wedding was done."

Darcy's hands curled into fists. "You aided and abetted a planned elopement with a girl not yet sixteen. That is harm, madam."

Mrs. Younge flushed. "I did not know she was so young. And he said—he promised—five thousand pounds. Once the marriage was complete and the dowry settled."

Darcy gave a short, humorless laugh. "Then you are a greater fool than I thought."

Her head jerked up.

"Georgiana's dowry is only released upon marriage *with the approval of both guardians*. Otherwise, she receives only the quarterly interest directly to herself. You would have been waiting a very long time."

The woman stared at him, dumbfounded.

"And Wickham," he added with a sneer, "was *in the room* when my father's will was read. He knew all of this. He lied to you."

Mrs. Younge's face contorted with rage, but it did not last. A heartbeat later, she turned as pale as parchment when he stepped forward again.

"You should be grateful I do not call the magistrate," he said icily. "Fraud. Forgery. Attempted abduction of an heiress."

Her knees nearly buckled. "Please... Mr. Darcy, have mercy, I beg you—"

"Do not insult us both by pretending remorse," he snapped. "The only reason I shall not drag you before the law is for Georgiana's sake. The scandal would be unendurable."

She nodded quickly, trembling.

"You are dismissed at once. If you provide an address, your wages to this day shall be sent to you. *To this day*, mind—there will be no payment for the full quarter."

"Yes, sir," she whispered.

"You will not ask me for a reference. I shall not give one. If I hear your name again in connection with any position as a governess, companion, or teacher—anywhere in England—I shall ensure no respectable family will ever consider you again."

Tears began to fall.

"You have ten minutes to gather your things," he said. "My valet will accompany you to ensure you take only what belongs to you."

Mrs. Younge dipped into a clumsy curtsy and stumbled past the footman.

Darcy stood alone in the drawing room, the fire behind him too weak to dispel the chill that had settled in his limbs.

His sister had nearly been ruined.

And it had all happened under his name. Under his roof.

He closed his eyes and gripped the edge of the mantel. *What would Father say?*

Without looking, he raised his hand and rang the bell with more force than necessary. Within moments, the housekeeper entered wiping her hands on her apron and casting a wary glance at the smoldering fire and the tense set of his shoulders.

"Mr. Darcy, sir?"

"I require Miss Darcy's maid. Immediately."

"Yes, sir." She curtsied and turned to fetch the girl.

Darcy remained by the hearth, pacing twice before forcing himself to stillness. He did not blame the housekeeper or the butler—neither had been of his choosing. The furnished house had come with a partial staff, and he had made only minor additions of his own.

But the maid—Georgiana's personal attendant—had come from Pemberley. She was Mrs. Reynolds' *niece,* of all things. He expected better.

When she entered, he turned sharply. She was no older than twenty, red-cheeked and pale-eyed, with a nervous expression and trembling fingers wringing the edges of her apron.

"You are Sally, Mrs. Reynolds' niece."

"Yes, sir."

He nodded. "You have known my sister since she was a girl."

"Yes, sir."

"Then tell me why you allowed her to believe she might marry George Wickham without my knowledge."

Sally's mouth parted. Her face crumpled.

"I—I tried to stop it, sir. I truly did. I begged her not to agree to it, but she would not listen. She was so happy, and Mr. Wickham was so charming—at least to her."

"And to you?"

The girl hesitated, then dropped her gaze to the floor, flushing. "He would look at me strange-like when Miss Darcy was not in the room.

"Then why did you not sound an alarm? Send for help?"

"Mrs. Younge, sir. She said if I tried to meddle or sent word to you, she would report me for theft and have me arrested."

Darcy's brow furrowed. "Theft?"

Sally nodded miserably. "Said she'd claim I stole a brooch. That it would be her word against mine. I was terrified."

He exhaled harshly and pinched the bridge of his nose.

"My plan," Sally said quietly, "was to wait until Mrs. Younge and Miss Darcy left—I thought I could speak to Mr. Filkins, the butler, or even send an express myself. Or walk to the post if I had to. But I was afraid. If I left too soon, she might… they might go early, and Miss Darcy would be alone."

Darcy looked at her for a long moment.

Sally's chin trembled, but her eyes did not waver. "I am sorry, sir. I know I should have found a way sooner. But I did not want to leave her."

His anger softened—not extinguished, but redirected. He saw now the impossible trap the girl had been caught in. And in truth, she had done the most important thing she could have: she had stayed.

"Thank you," he said at last. "For not abandoning her. That alone may have made the difference."

Sally's eyes filled with tears.

"I am going to give you something," he said quietly, stepping to the escritoire and opening a small case. From within, he removed two crisp five-pound notes.

Her eyes widened.

"This first one is for you, as a way of expressing my gratitude for your loyalty." He extended it, and she reached out with a trembling hand.

"This other is for emergencies *only*," he said. "If ever there is danger again—if Wickham or anyone else returns, if Georgiana is in distress—you will use it to send me word. Any delay could be disastrous. Is that understood?"

Sally took it solemnly, hands shaking. "Yes, sir. I swear it. I'll keep it with me always."

Darcy gave a terse nod. "Good. Now please return to my sister's room and begin packing. We will return to London tomorrow. Tell her nothing of Mrs. Younge for now. I shall speak with her myself later, once she has calmed."

Sally curtsied deeply and slipped from the room. He sat down and the desk, ran a hand through his hair, and began to write.

> *Richard,*
>
> *I know this letter will not reach you in Spain for quite some weeks, but I needed to tell you about Georgiana's experience in Ramsgate. Do you remember my old playmate from childhood? Well, she encountered him here, of all places. Is that not the most strange coincidence? Fortunately, I arrived in time before he departed. It is a pity you could not be here to give him your regards.*
>
> *The companion your mother interviewed was also required to depart, which has greatly saddened my sister. Due to her feelings on the matter, we will be traveling to London as soon as may be. She misses you, and so I believe residing with your parents under your mother's care will be best for her tender emotions.*
>
> *It is so strange to think that she has grown so much and is nearly the age to be married, though I know I hope for a few more years yet before she makes such a decision. It would not do for her to choose poorly because of a young girl's fancy.*
>
> *Please do take care. I will admit that I will be greatly relieved once you have returned to England's shores.*
>
> *Darcy*

He kept the letter vague, just in case it fell into the wrong hands, but he knew Richard would understand its meaning. He wrote the address and summoned a footman to have it delivered immediately. His job complete, his mind returned once more to his sister.

He climbed the staircase to the family rooms with long, clipped strides, his anger only barely kept in check by years of practiced self-control. He stopped before Georgiana's door, knocked once firmly, and called her name.

"Georgiana? May I come in?"

"No!" came the immediate reply, high and sharp through the wood. "You have broken my heart. I will never speak to you again."

Darcy drew a slow breath and let it out through his nose. "I understand that you are upset—"

"You understand nothing!" she cried. "He loves me. And I love him. Why would you be so cruel? Why would you take him from me?"

His jaw tensed. "Because he is a terrible man, Georgiana. He sought to take advantage of you—"

"You always hated him," she interrupted, her voice trembling with fury. "You never gave him a chance. Why do you despise him so much? What has he ever done to you?"

Darcy closed his eyes. "That is not a fit subject for discussion with a young lady, especially one who is not yet out."

"Do not speak to me like I am a child!" she shouted.

"I speak to you as your guardian."

"I wish you were not my guardian!" she shrieked. "I wish you were not even my brother! Then I could do as I pleased!"

Darcy's heart twisted. The words struck deeper than he could admit. For a moment, he said nothing.

When he spoke again, his voice was colder. "We shall not continue this discussion. I expect you to be packed and ready by eight o'clock. We depart for London at first light."

"I will be glad to go," she snapped. "At least then I may return to *my* establishment and be free of your tyranny."

Darcy's voice turned iron. "You shall do no such thing. Mrs. Younge has been dismissed—permanently—and you will not be living alone again."

"I will not live with *you*!" she cried. "You are horrid!"

"I am not offering that option," he said, tight-lipped. "I am a bachelor. You will reside with the Matlocks until a more suitable arrangement can be made."

"I refuse."

"Then you may prefer Rosings. I am certain Lady Catherine would have a strict regimen ready for you within the hour."

There was a strangled gasp—then the thump of something soft being thrown across the room.

"I will never speak to you again!" she wailed.

Darcy's temper snapped.

"Well, then I shall be grateful for your silence," he said, voice clipped. "I would not care to hear such childish nonsense from a girl who bears the Darcy name and is the granddaughter of an earl. You do not know how fortunate you are."

"I *hate* you!"

He stepped back from the door, shoulders stiff. "So be it. I expect you dressed and downstairs at the appointed time. We will leave without delay."

Without waiting for a reply, he turned and walked away, his boots heavy on the stairs. His hands shook slightly as he reached the bottom landing.

Righteous indignation burned through him—justified, he told himself. He had arrived just in time to rescue her. To protect her. To shield the Darcy name from shame.

But behind the anger, beneath the pride, something deeper throbbed.

She had wished he were not her brother.

And part of him feared that, perhaps, she meant it.

Chapter 1

Darcy House, London—December 4th, 1811

Darcy sank into the high-backed leather chair behind his desk in the study of Darcy House. The fire in the grate crackled softly, giving off a steady warmth that failed to settle the agitation in his chest. A thin beam of afternoon light filtered in through the tall windows, catching the gilt edge of a book left forgotten on the windowsill. It might have been peaceful, had he not just returned from White's and a thoroughly unsatisfying luncheon with Charles Bingley.

They had not quarreled, precisely. But Bingley had been restless and melancholy, folding and refolding his napkin with increasing agitation as the soup course went cold.

Darcy had known what was coming before Bingley spoke a word.

"She is the loveliest creature I have ever known," Bingley had said abruptly, with a note of strained defiance. "And I do not care what Caroline or Louisa says. I intend to return to Hertfordshire and offer for her before Christmas."

Darcy had weighed his words with care. "You know I hold Miss Bennet in high regard, Bingley. But I must ask: are you certain of her affections?"

Bingley looked genuinely distressed. "I... I believe so. I *think* so. Do you not?"

Darcy had hesitated. "Her manner is amiable, but I have observed it to be the same with all. It would be... ungenerous to presume too much upon her kindness."

Bingley had faltered, his hopeful smile fading. "Do you truly think she does not care for me?"

Darcy had met his gaze evenly. "I cannot say with certainty. But I know you would not wish to press attentions upon a lady whose feelings are not engaged. That is not in your character."

Bingley had not answered. Not properly. The soup had cooled, the fish dried beneath its sauce, and their conversation limped toward other matters before they both gave it up entirely and parted ways with strained civility.

Now, alone in his London study, Darcy unbuttoned his coat and leaned forward, elbows braced on the desk. His gut twisted uncomfortably. He had done what was best—for Bingley. For Miss Bennet, too, surely. If her affections were not deeply engaged, she would recover in time. If they were… *No, they are not.*

Or is that just wishful thinking? a voice in his head taunted. After all, if Bingley were to marry the eldest, you would often come in company with her sister.

He shoved the thought of Miss Elizabeth away and reached for the stack of letters awaiting his attention. They had been set aside by his man of business and were meant for review before being forwarded on to Netherfield. He glanced at the topmost one—his steward's familiar hand, steady and neat.

> *Sir,*
>
> *The lambing pens are in place, and the eastern pasture has been reinforced as you directed. Mrs. Anstruther has recovered from her fall and sends her gratitude for your gift of wine. The tenant families have been informed of your usual Christmastide gifts, and all anticipate a parcel from Pemberley on the Eve…*

He read on a while, soothed by the simple routine of caring for his home.

Another letter followed, this one from the parson in Kympton, reporting minor repairs to the parsonage and informing him which tenant families still needed help preparing for the winter. Darcy drafted a short note of approval on a half sheet and set it aside.

The next letter in the pile, however, made him groan aloud.

The script was unmistakable: bold, slanted, and underlined with imperious flourish. *Lady Catherine de Bourgh.*

Darcy hesitated a moment before breaking the seal. The wax cracked like a pistol shot in the quiet room. He opened the thick parchment and read, brow furrowing as the lines progressed.

> *Fitzwilliam,*
>
> *Your cousin Anne has taken ill. I do not speak of some trifling ague or a winter cough, but of a malady which may claim her life before the Easter season begins. She grows thinner by the day and takes no nourishment of substance. The physician has confessed that she may not survive the month. You are her nearest kin, and if you wish to see her again in this life, you must come at once.*
>
> *Your uncle's family will not expect you for Christmas; I have already written to my brother. Your sister will be at the Matlocks. You have no excuse to delay. I have taken the liberty of arranging for Mr. Collins to remain in residence at the parsonage through the holiday, should the need arise to procure a common license.*
>
> *I expect you no later than the twenty-third.*
>
> *—Lady Catherine de Bourgh*

Darcy's jaw tightened. So, it was to be this again. He had no desire to spend the holiday in the draughty halls of Rosings Park, tripping over his aunt's schemes and Anne's feeble protests. But the letter struck a note that could not be ignored: if Anne truly was ill, if there was any real danger…

He let out a long breath and looked toward the fire. He would have to write to Georgiana—she would be disappointed, though she would put on a brave face. She had planned to spend the Christmastide with the Matlocks, but they had hoped he might join them at Twelfth Night. Now, it would seem, he would instead be fending off Lady Catherine's lectures and her hints for him to marry his cousin.

If Anne had eyes half as fine as Miss Elizabeth's, or even a quarter of her wit, then marrying her would not be quite so unpalatable.

No—these were thoughts that were best left in the past. Miss Elizabeth was entirely inappropriate as the future Mrs. Darcy.

He reached for his pen, dipped it in the inkwell, and set it to paper.

My dear Aunt—

He paused, then crossed it out.

Lady Catherine—

That would do. With a grim expression, Darcy began to write.

~~*~*

Hertfordshire, December 4th, 1811

Elizabeth's boots crunched softly over the snow-packed lane, her breath curling before her like smoke in the cold morning air. The countryside lay hushed beneath its pale white blanket, trees sheathed in silver and hedgerows dusted like sugarplums. Though her bonnet did little to keep her ears warm, she relished the feel of the brisk air on her cheeks.

Winter does have its charms… especially when one is out of doors and away from talk of marriage prospects.

Tree branches were etched in white, and holly berries gleamed scarlet in the frost. She ought to have been merry. It was the season for it. But her heart felt heavier with every step.

It had been two days since Charlotte Lucas—her steady, pragmatic Charlotte—had paid a quick call, cheeks pink and voice unnaturally light, to share the news of her engagement to Mr. Collins.

Elizabeth had not known what to say. She had said *something*, surely—polite congratulations, expressions of surprise, perhaps even a half-hearted compliment on the match. But it had been difficult to summon any genuine warmth, much less enthusiasm. Charlotte, who had always seemed sensible, if not particularly romantic, had calmly accepted the attentions of *that man*, as though reason could outweigh ridicule, and comfort make up for companionship.

Now, as she trudged the snowy path to Lucas Lodge, Elizabeth found herself more sad than shocked. Sad that Charlotte had felt so little hope for anything better. Sad that the world was organized in a manner that intelligent women were forced to make such decisions.

And sad, if she were honest, that this Christmas—their last together as girls—would be colored by such a sacrifice.

As she gave her name to the maid and was shown into the modest parlor of Lucas Lodge, Elizabeth realized she felt no nearer to peace on the subject than she had before her walk. *Poor Charlotte; to share the rest of her life with such a man.*

Lady Lucas and Maria were seated near the hearth, bent over a basket of mending, their fingers working nimbly despite the chill in the room.

"Miss Eliza!" Lady Lucas greeted her warmly. "Do come in, my dear. Your timing is excellent—we have just stoked the fire again."

Maria gave a cheerful, if slightly breathless, smile. "Charlotte is downstairs helping Cook with the fruit puddings—she will be up directly."

Elizabeth removed her gloves and took the offered seat, unable to entirely suppress a flicker of surprise. *Charlotte in the kitchens?* It was not entirely improper—particularly in a household without a full staff, and Charlotte *would* be marrying soon—but it still gave her pause.

Mrs. Bennet would be horrified.

"My girls? In the kitchens?" she could hear her mother's shrill voice echo in her head. *"They are daughters of a gentleman, not housemaids!"*

A few minutes passed in pleasantries before Charlotte entered, her cheeks pink with exertion and her hands lightly dusted with flour. She wiped them hastily on her apron, but the dusting remained like a ghost upon her fingertips. Elizabeth rose to greet her, noting that her friend's eyes were red-rimmed, though her smile was bright enough to distract anyone not looking too closely.

"Lizzy! You are so good to come in this weather. I hope the snow was not too deep on the lane?"

"Only enough to be pretty," Elizabeth said gently, eyeing her friend. "Though I begin to worry that your cook may be working you to death before you even reach Hunsford."

Charlotte laughed, but it sounded brittle. "It is only Christmas puddings. I must learn to manage such things myself soon enough."

Maria, who had been watching the exchange with barely contained energy, burst out, "Have you told her yet? About the letter?"

Charlotte flushed. "Maria—"

Lady Lucas gave a small sigh and stood. "I shall leave you young ladies to speak privately. Maria, come assist me with the linens."

"But Mama—"

"Now, Maria."

With a theatrical groan, Maria rose and followed her mother from the room, pausing only to shoot a significant look back at Elizabeth.

When the door had closed, Elizabeth turned to Charlotte. "What letter?"

Charlotte sighed and sat. She began pulling at the edge of her apron—an old nervous habit. "Mr. Collins has written. From Hunsford."

Elizabeth nodded. "And?"

"He told Lady Catherine of our engagement."

Elizabeth made a small sound. "I would have thought he had done so already."

"He wished to do it in person. He was eager to share the news with her directly."

"And her ladyship was displeased?"

"Quite the opposite," Charlotte said with a small, almost rueful smile. "She was very approving. In fact… too much so."

Elizabeth tilted her head. "Go on."

Charlotte hesitated. "Lady Catherine insists that a proper lady must be established in her own home *before* Christmastide begins. She believes it sets the tone for the entire marriage. Mr. Collins agreed at once, of course."

Elizabeth's brow furrowed. "You mean to say…"

"The wedding is to take place on the seventeenth," Charlotte said quietly.

"Of *December*?"

"When he returns to Hertfordshire."

Elizabeth stared at her. "But—but that is in two weeks."

Charlotte nodded. "Yes."

"And you had intended—"

"To marry in January. To spend Christmas at home. My last as Miss Lucas." Her voice broke a little on the last word, though she straightened at once. "But Lady Catherine was insistent. Mr. Collins wrote that the arrangements are already in motion."

Elizabeth sat back, absorbing the news. "That is… very sudden."

Charlotte gave a thin, watery smile. "Yes. But I knew, when I accepted him, that my life would no longer be my own."

There was no bitterness in the words, only resignation.

Elizabeth reached for her friend's hand. "I am so sorry, Charlotte."

"I had hoped Maria might accompany me. If we were taking the usual wedding trip, she would be my companion in any case. But my father's cousin is visiting for Christmas, and she is bringing her children. Maria will be needed here to help tend them." Charlotte's voice broke on the last word.

There was a faint creak from the hallway. Elizabeth glanced toward the parlor door just in time to see it open an inch farther.

Maria slipped inside without shame or apology, her eyes bright with excitement. "Well, if I cannot go," she said with the air of someone who has had a marvelous idea, "why not take Lizzy?"

Elizabeth blinked.

Charlotte turned sharply. "Maria—"

"She could," Maria insisted, stepping into the room. "It makes perfect sense. She is your dearest friend, and she is not needed at Longbourn. Jane and Mary will manage the mending, and Kitty and Lydia are not likely to notice one way or another."

"Maria, it is not your place to extend an invitation—" Elizabeth began.

But Charlotte had already turned to her. "Would you?" Her voice was low and earnest. "I would not have asked, but... if you could come, Lizzy, I would be so grateful. It would make it all *bearable*. Truly."

Elizabeth hesitated, caught entirely off guard. "I—well—I must ask my father, of course."

"Of course," Charlotte echoed quickly, but her eyes were already shining with relief. "Only if he agrees."

"I was only trying to help," Maria said, flopping into a chair and reaching for the sewing basket with complete innocence. "Better you than me, anyway. I could not stand being shut up with Mr. Collins all through Christmastide."

Elizabeth opened her mouth to protest again, but the words failed her. There was nothing to say. Charlotte looked so worn and hopeful, and Maria had said aloud what no one else dared.

The matter, it seemed, was decided: to Kent she would go.

Chapter 2

Rosings Park, Kent—December 21st, 1811

The snow had begun again by the time the carriage turned onto the long drive to Rosings. A bitter wind sliced through the trees, piling fresh drifts atop the frozen ruts already carved into the lane. Darcy shifted stiffly, joints aching from the jostling, and tugged his greatcoat tighter about his frame. The lamps were already lit at the great house, glowing faintly through the flurry. It was near dark, though not yet five o'clock.

His arrival was nearly three hours later than intended. A tree had fallen near Maidstone, forcing the post-chaise to take an abominable alternate route. His coachman had cursed under his breath most of the afternoon. Darcy had said little. His mind was already at Rosings—already with Anne.

If she truly is as ill as the letter had suggested...

He stepped down onto the packed gravel, his boots crunching as he crossed the drive. The butler opened the door before he reached it, and he was ushered into the high-ceilinged entrance hall with no more warmth than the winter air behind him. Lady Catherine was already striding down the marble staircase.

"You are intolerably late," she announced, arms folded above the embroidered swell of her gown. "You were expected at four. It is past seven."

"I apologize, Aunt," he said with a bow. "A blockage on the road out of Maidstone delayed us longer than expected."

"No excuse," she said, waving him toward the drawing room. "Anne waited to see you. She was quite determined. But she grew tired, poor thing, and retired just before tea."

Darcy removed his gloves and followed her into the room, catching sight of the same stiff-backed furniture and over-embroidered cushions that had plagued his memory of the place for years. The fire burned hot in the grate, but the rest of the house held the damp chill of old stone and draughty windows.

Darcy frowned. "Is her condition so serious?"

Lady Catherine raised a handkerchief to dab delicately at the corner of her mouth. "It is not as dire as it might have been had you delayed further."

Darcy narrowed his eyes, but said nothing. A roaring fire crackled in the drawing room, but it did little to ease the chill that had settled into his bones.

"She has grown quite ill," Lady Catherine continued. "Delicate. Her appetite is poor, but the physician insists she must avoid all strong emotion. I trust you will not upset her tomorrow."

Darcy bowed his head slightly. "Of course."

"And do not make her speak overmuch," she added, her voice clipped. "You may sit with her. Offer comfort. She is, after all, your intended."

Darcy froze. "My—pardon?"

"Intended," she said again, sharply, as though daring him to object. "It is high time the connection was formalized. You are both of age. There is no obstacle."

"It is not a connection to which I have agreed," he said coldly.

"We can discuss all that when Mr. Collins arrives tomorrow."

He looked at her blankly. *Why does that name sound familiar?* "Mr... Collins?"

"My new rector," she snapped. "I understand he was introduced to you when you were visiting that tradesman friend of yours in Hertfordshire."

A faint image of a tall, heavyset, bumbling man rose in his vision. "I vaguely recall him, yes."

"Well, he will be calling tomorrow with his new wife."

"Wife?"

"Indeed. He returned to Hertfordshire just long enough to fulfill his duty. I had sent him there with every expectation he would choose one of his cousins. The estate is entailed entirely away from the female line, you know. Five daughters—utterly unprovided for. I had hoped he would secure one of them, and I believe he did." She sniffed. "Though not the eldest, unfortunately. Perhaps the second. They were married last week."

A chill swept through Darcy, far colder than any he had suffered during the long, snowbound ride. His racing pulse thundered in his ears.

"The second?"

"It might have been the third. I have no idea."

"Do you know her name?" he asked carefully.

She glared at him over her cane. "Mrs. Collins."

"I mean her given name."

"Certainly not. I have never even laid eyes on the lady. One woman is as good as another, I imagine. I gave him strict instructions on what qualities he should look for when choosing amongst his cousins."

Darcy stared into the fire, every muscle rigid. The flames blurred before his eyes.

Elizabeth.

He had thought her safe. He had thought her too clever, too discerning to ever accept a man like Collins. She had turned him down—had she not? At the Netherfield ball, she had danced with him only out of obligation. She had mocked him afterward with a glint in her eye.

And yet—if her family's situation were truly desperate… if she had been made to feel it her duty…

His mind reeled. *He* had made Bingley question Jane's affections.

Perhaps she had come to believe comfort was more valuable than compatibility. Perhaps she had given up waiting for anything better.

A dull ache bloomed in his chest.

Elizabeth… the wife of such a man.

He could not bear it.

"Excuse me," he said abruptly. "The journey has left me fatigued."

Lady Catherine waved him off without lifting her gaze. "Breakfast is at nine. Be punctual."

He escaped to the corridor, passed the portrait of the late Sir Lewis without a glance, and climbed the stairs two at a time.

It was only once his valet, Bates, had left and the candles were extinguished that he sat on the edge of the bed, hands folded beneath his chin, and whispered the truth aloud to no one.

"I left her."

~~*~*

Elizabeth had never before felt so thoroughly a guest and so thoroughly out of place.

It had been two days since she arrived at the parsonage, and though she had taken pains to be cheerful and helpful, the awkwardness of the situation had already begun to settle into her bones. She had never in her life spent such intimate time in the company of a newly married couple—and she hoped never to do so again.

The wedding breakfast, at least, had taken place at Lucas Lodge, which spared her the exquisite discomfort of being beneath the same roof as Charlotte and Mr. Collins on their wedding night. But the next morning, her friend had fetched her with a blush and a forced smile, and Elizabeth had done her best to return both with equal civility— though the words *maidenhood* and *Mr. Collins* had no business occupying the same thought at once.

She had not known where to look as the carriage drove them southward. Charlotte's contented composure clashed strangely with Mr. Collins' constant preening, and Elizabeth could not decide which was worse: the cloying boasts of the husband or the resigned serenity of the wife.

She could not blame Charlotte, not really. Her friend had made a practical choice. And Elizabeth had agreed to come, had nodded with all apparent willingness when her father gave his consent.

But now, walking down the stairs of Hunsford Parsonage, she felt keenly how very *not* at home she was.

Mr. Collins had been effusive in his eagerness to show off the house, pointing out every chair, every servant, every stick of furniture that Lady Catherine had either provided or approved. He had, with unmistakable satisfaction, paused before the fireplace in the drawing room to mention how *this very hearth* might have belonged to another, had circumstances aligned differently. He even hinted, with a sanctimonious smile, that *some ladies* knew not their own best interest.

Elizabeth had smiled as one might at an overfed cat, said nothing, and blessed heaven when he left shortly after to present himself to his patroness.

Once he was gone, the house felt lighter.

Charlotte, free from her husband's hovering presence, decided to tour the home again, properly this time. They met the maid-of-all-work—a shy girl with red cheeks and capable hands—and the cook, a middle-aged woman who doubled as housekeeper and greeted Charlotte's arrival with something like audible relief. It was clear the staff had not quite known what to expect in a mistress, and the discovery that she was practical, composed, and nothing like her husband was received gratefully.

Together, the ladies walked through the modest gardens, now dormant beneath frost. They inspected the hen coop, visited the kitchens, and reviewed the linens. Elizabeth listened with real pleasure as Charlotte began to speak of routines and improvements, of how the small parlor off the back would be made her private sitting room.

"It appears to be the quietest part of the house," Charlotte said, half-smiling as she pushed open the door. "I believe I shall move a few of my books and keep my correspondence here. Mr. Collins may have his study, and I… I shall have this."

Elizabeth turned slowly, taking in the small square room with its single window overlooking the hedgerow. "It is an excellent idea. You deserve a space of your own."

Charlotte flushed. "I hope my husband will approve."

The day passed in relative ease, broken only by Mr. Collins' return before dinner. He burst into the parlor flushed with success, announcing that they were all invited to Rosings on the morrow for the formal presentation of *his wife* to Lady Catherine de Bourgh and her daughter—and, as he added with particular pomp, to a *nephew of her ladyship, presently visiting Rosings, though he could not say which one, for she had several.*

"One of the sons of her brother the earl, no doubt," he declared. "Or perhaps her late sister's eldest child. Such fine connections, and always gracious to her humble servants. Her ladyship said nothing of the holidays, but I suspect a Christmas dinner or musical evening shall be proposed in the coming days."

Elizabeth listened with a composed expression, noting silently that Charlotte appeared rather less enthused than her husband. It was a strange kind of triumph, to be dragged before Lady Catherine only days after one's wedding, but it was clearly what Charlotte had expected.

When the clock struck nine and the lamps were trimmed, Elizabeth excused herself early, pleading fatigue from travel and cold weather. In truth, it was not weariness that sent her upstairs but a quiet desperation to escape the subtle, unbearable reminder that Charlotte and Mr. Collins now shared a bedroom.

She took her candle and book, settled into the small chamber they had given her—plain, but tidy and warm—and tried to lose herself in *Evelina*. The prose was charming, the heroine witty, but her eyes would not still. They kept returning to Longbourn, to Jane's soft, sad smiles, to the empty place where hope had once sat.

This was to be her Christmas: a parsonage in Kent, a pompous clergyman, and a strained silence. No Gardiners. No bustling children. No candlelit drawing rooms filled with music and cheer.

Only duty. And Charlotte.

She turned the page with a sigh and pulled the coverlet tighter. *Perhaps tomorrow will be better.*

~~*~*

Elizabeth followed Mr. and Mrs. Collins up the long, winding path to Rosings. Her shawl—thick and warm, woven by her Aunt Gardiner two Christmases past—was wrapped tightly around her shoulders, and she was very glad she had thought to bring her sturdiest boots from home.

The wind bit at her cheeks, and the sky hung gray and heavy with the promise of more snow. It was not terrible weather for walking, but neither was it entirely suitable for a visit to a baronet's widow and her delicate daughter.

Elizabeth's eyes narrowed just slightly as she stepped over a patch of icy gravel. Surely, if Lady Catherine wished to make a proper impression upon her new rector's wife, she might have thought to send the carriage.

But then again, Lady Catherine de Bourgh did not appear in company to please—only to be pleased.

At least from what I gather based on Mr. Collins' information.

She watched as Charlotte leaned slightly toward her husband, murmuring something that caused Mr. Collins to straighten proudly and quicken his pace. There it was again—that curious, subtle influence her friend had begun to exercise. A word here, a gentle correction there. Charlotte was learning how to manage him, how to steer him without ever letting go of his reins.

From a practical standpoint, the match made perfect sense. Charlotte was nearly seven and twenty, plain, prudent, and without fortune. Mr. Collins was absurd, yes, but he also had a living, a patroness, and no vice except pomposity. Already the parsonage was beginning to run smoothly under Charlotte's quiet governance. She would make it her own.

But I could never have borne it, Elizabeth thought, her breath rising in white clouds. *Not for all the patronesses in Kent.*

If Mr. Bingley had not come to Netherfield—if Jane had been unprotected—might her mother have pressed Mr. Collins upon her instead? A chill crept through her not caused by the weather.

Thank heaven for Mr. Bingley. *He will return soon. I know he loves her—there was admiration for her in all his looks.*

As they reached the front steps of Rosings, Elizabeth glanced up at the towering façade. The great house loomed pale and still behind a veil of frost, its columns trimmed in icicles, the windows glowing faintly with candlelight. A footman admitted them without ceremony.

Inside, the entrance hall was grand but unwelcoming, all marble and echo. The butler took their wraps with cool efficiency, and a maid stood nearby with slippers for them to wear, as their boots were caked in mud and snow.

Elizabeth unpinned her shawl and smoothed her hair quickly, suddenly wishing the walk had been shorter. A few snowflakes clung to her lashes. She turned to speak to Charlotte—only to find that her friend had paused by the mirror to adjust a loose curl at her temple.

Elizabeth found herself suddenly at Mr. Collins' elbow as they crossed the threshold into the drawing room.

"Mr. and Mrs. Collins," the butler intoned. Then, with only the faintest pause, "And guest."

Elizabeth stopped mid-step.

Mr. Darcy.

Her eyes widened before she could help it.

There he sat, in the opulently decorated room, perfectly composed, in a dark coat and buff waistcoat, watching her with unreadable intensity. His gaze swept over her once—briefly, sharply—and then returned to her face.

Something flickered there.

Elizabeth's breath caught.

Mr. Collins was already bowing and speaking effusively. "Lady Catherine, Miss de Bourgh," he intoned to the elderly woman seated regally beneath a portrait of the late Sir Lewis and the frail looking young woman next to her. "If I may have the incredible honor of presenting to you—my wife, Mrs. Collins."

Lady Catherine's eyes turned to Elizabeth, who opened her mouth to correct the assumption, but Charlotte stepped forward at that moment, joining them at last with a small, steady smile.

The mistake was not addressed.

And Mr. Darcy continued to stare at her.

~~*~*

Darcy rose with the others when the butler announced the parson and his party.

"Mr. and Mrs. Collins... and guest."

He did not hear the final words.

His eyes had locked on the young woman walking just behind Mr. Collins. She stood with elegance, her figure unmistakably familiar beneath a plain but well-cut spencer. Her cheeks were pink from the cold, and a dusting of snow clung to the dark curls peeking out from beneath her bonnet.

Elizabeth.

The shock landed like a blow to the chest.

It could not be. It *should* not be.

But there she was—standing beside Mr. Collins as the idiot beamed and bowed and proclaimed, "Lady Catherine, if I may have the incredible honor of presenting to you—*my wife, Mrs. Collins.*"

The words cracked through Darcy's skull.

No!

He felt the floor sway slightly beneath him, though he did not move. His breath came short, but he forced it steady. Years of practice kept his face impassive, his shoulders square.

His eyes never left hers.

She looked surprised—just for a moment. Not alarmed. Not ashamed. But surprised to see *him*, seated so calmly beside his aunt, as though *he* were the specter, not she.

27

And then another woman entered. A second figure, smaller, with her hair in a tidy bun tucked under a cap, smiling quietly. She took Mr. Collins' arm and gave Lady Catherine a composed curtsy.

Darcy blinked.

Who…? What…? She looked vaguely familiar, and Darcy could faintly remember Elizabeth speaking with her on several occasions in Hertfordshire. It was she who urged Elizabeth to play one evening at a dinner party.

Lucas Lodge… Miss Lucas… Charlene? Cherise?

His heart gave a sickening twist of relief—and something close to mortification.

Lady Catherine was now greeting the *actual* Mrs. Collins with a blend of scrutiny and condescension. Mr. Collins had not clarified, and Elizabeth had not corrected.

Of course she would not—not here, not in front of the room. She is too refined for that.

Yet Darcy had believed it. For a full minute, he had believed it.

But Elizabeth was *not* married. Not to Collins.

He nearly had to sit—he felt a bit faint. *What a strain on my nerves*, he thought, then flushed slightly at realizing he sounded exactly like Elizabeth's mother in that moment.

Lady Catherine narrowed her eyes at the unfamiliar face beside the Collinses and pursed her lips. "What is this? I trust, Mr. Collins, that you have not returned with *two* wives."

Elizabeth's eyebrows arched slightly. Mr. Collins turned red to the tips of his ears.

"No—no indeed, your ladyship!" he spluttered. "This is—this is Miss Elizabeth Bennet, my cousin. She has been so good as to accompany us from Hertfordshire and spend the holiday at the parsonage."

"Your cousin, and yet not also your wife's sister?" Lady Catherine's gaze narrowed at the sniveling man. "Does this mean you did *not* marry one of the daughters from whom the estate was entailed?"

Darcy stiffened.

28

"I—I did not," Mr. Collins confessed with a nervous glance toward his wife.

"I gave *specific* instructions, Mr. Collins," Lady Catherine snapped. "You were to mend the injury done to the Bennet ladies by uniting the estate and family through marriage. That is what a conscientious clergyman would do. That is what I *expected*."

Mr. Collins gulped and looked—inexplicably—at Elizabeth, who was now frowning and looking at her friend in concern.

What the devil is going on?

Chapter 3

Elizabeth was *not* amused.

At first, it had been nearly comical—stepping into the drawing room of Rosings and finding its mistress every bit as imperious, overbearing, and self-satisfied as Mr. Collins had breathlessly described. Elizabeth had expected grandeur, hauteur, and some degree of foolishness from Lady Catherine de Bourgh.

But she had not expected this.

To speak so, she thought furiously, *in front of me. In front of Charlotte.*

Elizabeth stood rigid beside her friend, her hands folded tightly in front of her to keep from clenching them. Charlotte's face had paled; her chin quivered just slightly despite her best efforts. Mr. Collins, for his part, looked as though he might sink into the floor.

And Lady Catherine went on blithely, tearing through them all with the precision of a blunt axe. "You were to mend the injury done to the Bennet ladies by uniting the estate and family through marriage," she declared. "That is what a conscientious clergyman would do. That is what I expected."

Elizabeth's vision blurred at the edges. It was not merely offensive—it was monstrous. She glanced toward Darcy, still standing stiffly in front of the chair nearest the hearth, only to find him watching the entire exchange with an unreadable expression.

His features were still, almost grim.

Of course, she thought bitterly. *He must be just as disgusted as his aunt. How dare the lowly parson marry a woman of his own choosing and not that of his patroness?*

Her cheeks flamed.

Charlotte looked on the verge of tears.

And Mr. Collins—of all people—was gaping at her.

Elizabeth's fury snapped into place like a well-fitted glove. If no one else would speak, she would.

She stepped forward, her voice clear and composed. "He did propose to one of his cousins, your ladyship," she said evenly. "Sadly, she declined."

The silence that followed was absolute.

Lady Catherine blinked. Mr. Collins let out a strangled sound, part cough, part whimper. Charlotte's breath hitched audibly beside her.

Elizabeth did not waver.

Lady Catherine recovered first, her features tightening into a mask of affronted dignity.

"She *declined*?" she repeated, as if the word itself were offensive.

"Yes, your ladyship," Elizabeth said with perfect calm. "It was not a good match."

Across the room, Darcy stirred slightly, but Elizabeth refused to look at him. She could feel his gaze pressing at the edge of her vision like an itch she would not scratch.

"She would rather remain a burden on her family," Lady Catherine said with a sneer, "than secure a respectable living and provide for her future?"

"It was not, I believe, the living she objected to," Elizabeth replied. "Nor the security. Rather, the two people were so different in character that the match would not have been a happy one."

Mr. Collins gave a soft wheeze, his color shifting toward puce.

Lady Catherine turned a withering glare upon him. "You did not tell me any of this."

"I—I did not believe it relevant, your ladyship!" he squeaked. "The refusal was most unexpected—and swiftly followed by my second proposal—to Miss Lucas—who, of course, accepted me at once!"

Charlotte flushed deeply but said nothing. Elizabeth felt her own temper start to burn again. She had to look somewhere else, anywhere to calm her feelings, and so she glanced—just briefly—at Darcy.

He was still watching her.

No, not watching—*studying*. His brow was slightly furrowed. His posture was tense, but not hostile. Confused, perhaps. And if she were not mistaken, troubled.

What right did *he* have to look troubled?

Turning her attention back to Lady Catherine, Elizabeth said, "And I can assure you that all of my sisters and I are very happy that our dear friend will one day be the mistress of Longbourn."

Lady Catherine's mouth tightened into something between a grimace and a sneer. Mr. Collins blinked rapidly, uncertain whether he had just been complimented or shamed.

Charlotte looked as though she might either cry or fall to the floor. Elizabeth reached out and took her friend's hand. "Charlotte—that is, Mrs. Collins—is a good woman with a kind heart and practical nature. She will make Mr. Collins a much better wife than any of my father's daughters could have."

She felt Charlotte squeeze her hand tightly. The room was silent as the occupants all watched Lady Catherine closely for a reaction.

Darcy, though she did not dare look again, shifted slightly on his feet.

Lady Catherine's fan snapped open with unnecessary force.

"Well," she said at last, voice cutting, "I suppose *some* women must be content with what their temperament and circumstances allow. Though I cannot approve of disobedience in daughters."

"No more can my father," Elizabeth replied sweetly. "Which is why he will not force any of us to marry against our inclinations."

Charlotte stirred beside her. It was subtle—but Elizabeth saw it. The flicker of gratitude in her downcast eyes. The faint lift of her chin.

Lady Catherine, apparently deciding she had been insulted but unable to isolate the particulars, waved her hand again. "Very well, then. Why are you all standing about? Take your seats. Where is the tea? Why has it not yet come?"

The assembled party began to shift and murmur with renewed stiffness. Mr. Collins scrambled toward a chair as if fearing he might be accused next. Charlotte followed more slowly, her composure returning by degrees, though her hands still trembled slightly as she reached for her gloves.

Elizabeth sat last of all, choosing a place near the hearth—but not beside Mr. Darcy.

He had not moved since Lady Catherine's dismissal. Still upright. Still silent. His gaze was not on her, but she felt it nonetheless.

He was no longer watching her with disapproval. That had been her first assumption—of course it had been, after that scene. But now she wondered.

Was he surprised? Offended?

Ashamed of his aunt's ill-breeding?

She shook the thought away. It hardly mattered. Whatever Mr. Darcy's opinion, it was no concern of hers.

The door opened at last, and the tea tray arrived, carried by a footman with an expression carved from marble. He placed it on the low table and retreated at once. Another maid followed with a plate of pale, dry biscuits.

Lady Catherine made a great show of inspecting the tray before motioning for Charlotte to pour. "Come, Mrs. Collins, show me what manners your mother has taught you."

Elizabeth bit the inside of her cheek.

Charlotte served the tea with quiet dignity. Elizabeth took her cup with a polite nod, then sipped in silence as Lady Catherine began what could only be termed as an inquisition.

"So, Mrs. Collins," her ladyship began, lifting her own cup with exaggerated care, "you have been mistress of the parsonage for—what? Two days?"

"Yes, your ladyship."

"Hmph. And have you found the kitchen tolerable? The last cook I sent was not a complete fool, but she had a tendency to oversalt the sauces. I trust you have corrected this."

Charlotte inclined her head. "Mrs. Trant seems quite capable. We have not yet had occasion to judge her sauces, but the morning rolls have been excellent."

"You must not allow her to bake unsupervised," Lady Catherine warned. "She is given to laziness. You will need to rise early, of course—no later than six—and make yourself acquainted with every inch of that kitchen. The firebox in particular must be scrubbed weekly."

Charlotte murmured her agreement, her tone serene.

Lady Catherine continued without pause. "Have you begun your inventories? You must count the linens yourself, not merely take the word of the staff. And you are keeping a proper housekeeping book?"

"Yes, your ladyship."

"You must make note of every farthing. If you require a format, I shall send you a copy of Miss Jenkinson's. Her method is not elegant, but it is thorough."

Elizabeth took another sip of her tea, managing not to choke. Across from her, Miss de Bourgh sat in silence, blinking slowly at nothing in particular.

Lady Catherine went on. "Have you rearranged the furniture? You must not. The sideboard in the dining room must remain as it is—Sir Lewis had it placed precisely for the light. You will find the right-hand drawer tends to stick, but it must not be forced. The key is to press slightly to the left as you pull."

Charlotte gave a gentle smile. "I shall remember, ma'am."

"And the servants," Lady Catherine added, "must never be permitted to sit while polishing silver. It is the beginning of idleness. I insist upon it."

Elizabeth stared into her teacup, forcing her features into bland attentiveness. She dared not look at Charlotte, for fear she would either laugh or weep on her friend's behalf. It was a masterclass in maternal tyranny masquerading as magnanimity.

She let her gaze drift—just momentarily—toward Mr. Darcy.

He had not spoken a word since they sat. His posture remained formal, but his expression… not quite indifferent.

He looked as if he were taking notes. Or making calculations. Or perhaps attempting not to intervene.

Good, Elizabeth thought with some venom. *Let him sit in silence and listen to what his noble relations think is the proper lot of a married woman.*

Lady Catherine had launched into a new subject—the conduct of the maids—and Elizabeth prepared herself to endure what she was sure would be a tedious evening.

~~*~*

Darcy stood before the mirror in his dressing room, slowly knotting his cravat for the second time. The first attempt had been too tight; the second was now too loose. He had retied his neckcloths with perfect efficiency since he was fifteen—but tonight, his fingers seemed foreign.

He scowled at his reflection, then gave up and let the valet finish the task.

His thoughts were elsewhere, circling back again and again to the drawing room, to Elizabeth Bennet, to everything that had unfolded that afternoon.

It was not just the shock of seeing her again—though that had been enough to set his blood thrumming in his ears. It was not even the disorienting moment when he thought she might be Mrs. Collins.

No—it was what happened after.

It was the way she had stood her ground beneath the weight of his aunt's sneering remarks, her chin lifted, her tone calm. She had not flinched, even as Lady Catherine berated Mr. Collins for his matrimonial failure, nor as she was interrogated about her sisters, her fortune—or lack thereof, and her family connections.

She had simply… spoken. Clearly. Firmly. Truthfully.

Darcy adjusted his cuffs. His brow furrowed.

He was ashamed of his aunt. Truly ashamed. For all her insistence on breeding and lineage, Lady Catherine had displayed all the delicacy of a fishmonger in a rainstorm. To say such things in front of a newlywed! In front of her guests! In front of Elizabeth.

He had seen Elizabeth's eyes flare in defense of her friend. Had seen her temper held in check by sheer will and civility. No shrill retort, no simpering submission—only poise.

He found himself wondering if Charlotte Collins had heard those same accusations before. If she had known what sort of reception awaited her when she accepted the parson's hand.

He doubted it.

And then… there was Elizabeth's role in it all.

She had refused Mr. Collins.

That had struck him like a thunderclap.

He had not known of the entailment on Longbourn—not in detail. The estate was of modest size, and he had paid it little heed. But now, understanding that her family's home would pass to another line, that her father had no male heir, that her situation was precarious—and still, she had refused a man who could offer her security?

He was silent a long moment, staring at the carved edge of the dressing table.

Was she waiting for me to return? he thought suddenly. *Is that why she refused Collins?*

It had been foolish to leave Hertfordshire so abruptly—but his motives had been good. He and Bingley had both been in danger: Bingley, from a loveless marriage, and himself, from bewitching eyes and an ill-bred family.

Still… she had teased him so freely at Netherfield. She had stayed near him while her sister recovered. She had challenged him, danced with him, argued with him. Her flashing eyes and playful smile even as she shred him to pieces with her wit.

How could she not have been waiting for me to speak?

He suddenly felt like the worst of villains.

He had left her. Left her to explain herself to her family. Left her to endure another Christmas unmarried. Left her to face the possibility of becoming *Mrs. Collins* because he could not distinguish his own pride from her value.

And still—*still*—she had remained true.

She would not have rejected the offer of security from her cousin… *not unless she hoped for* me.

He felt a rush of something like resolve.

He would not let her suffer any longer. He would not allow her to question, to wonder, to wait. He would propose—at once. Tomorrow, if the opportunity arose. Christmas Eve, at the latest.

He would make her his wife.

And he would make her happy.

~~*~*

The fire in the blue parlor at Rosings crackled softly the following evening. The tea service had been cleared away, though Lady Catherine remained stationed like a general at her usual post. Mr. Collins had found a footstool and was attempting to recount a secondhand anecdote about the Bishop of Norwich. Charlotte sat listening with admirable patience.

Elizabeth stood near the instrument, already regretting that she had acquiesced to Lady Catherine's demand that she "entertain the room." The pianoforte at Rosings was better tuned than the one at Longbourn, but the room itself had all the warmth of a marble mausoleum.

She rifled through the sheet music on the piano and discovered a faded copy of a little German piece she had learned from her aunt Gardiner years ago. It was sweet and not terribly long: precisely the sort of thing one could offer without inviting criticism for either ostentation or indolence.

When she finished the first movement, Mr. Darcy stepped forward.

"May I turn the pages for you, Miss Bennet?"

She looked up in surprise and wariness.

"If you wish," she said lightly.

He stood beside her as she began again. For a few moments, neither spoke.

It was maddening.

She had been trying, since yesterday, to make sense of his presence, of his odd expressions, of that intense gaze he seemed to fix on her whenever he thought she would not notice. But now—standing so near, watching the sheet music with dutiful solemnity—he seemed not at all inclined to speak.

Very well, then. *She* would.

"You must miss your friend Mr. Bingley," she said softly, keeping her eyes on the keys. "I know the neighborhood in Hertfordshire grew quite fond of him."

There was the briefest pause. Then: "Indeed? That is kind of you to say."

Elizabeth's fingers faltered for half a note, but she recovered. "Yes. I believe his return is still hoped for by many."

"I doubt it," Darcy said. "He has no real reason to return. His sisters prefer the society in town, and the lease at Netherfield was never a permanent one."

She stopped playing.

Darcy looked at her in question.

"I beg your pardon," she said, turning the page unnecessarily. "My hands were cold. They have gone stiff."

But it was not cold. It was fury.

Of course. *Of course.* Mr. Bingley had not simply drifted away. He had been *guided* away—steered, no doubt, by the same man who stood beside her now, polite and inscrutable, speaking of Jane's heartbreak as though it were a trivial matter.

He had done it. She was sure of it now.

He had separated them.

She pressed on through the remainder of the piece, though she could barely see the notes. When the final chord faded, she rose at once and curtsied.

Lady Catherine gave a reluctant nod. "Adequate, I suppose. You really will never play well unless you practice, Miss Elizabeth."

Elizabeth murmured her thanks and returned to her chair, barely hearing anything around her. Darcy had resumed his seat without comment and stared at her. She determinedly avoided his gaze, focusing her attention on Lady Catherine giving Mrs. Collins instructions about calls to pay the following morning.

She could not even look at him.

The walk back to the parsonage was cold and quiet. Charlotte spoke only once—something about the quality of the orange marmalade—and Elizabeth mumbled a vague reply.

She went to bed early, pleading a headache.

But it was not pain that kept her awake. It was fury. White-hot and slow-burning.

He *did* it.

He took Bingley away. He made Jane suffer. And not for some noble cause, not even for *Bingley's* sake—but to preserve his own sense of superiority. To spare himself the embarrassment of a connection to trade, to a family with silly sisters and little fortune.

And he calls himself a gentleman.

She turned in her bed, pulling the blanket higher, and wished—truly wished—she had never come to Kent.

~~*~*

Darcy leaned against the carved mantel in the east drawing room, a brandy warming slowly in his hand. The fire crackled low, casting flickers of gold across the wood paneling and gilded frames. A clock chimed somewhere down the hall—ten, perhaps.

There had been no time to speak privately with Elizabeth that evening at tea. His aunt had monopolized the entire conversation, and quickly whispering in Elizabeth's ear as she played the piano was far less than she deserved.

No, if he wished to speak with her alone, he would need to go to the parsonage the following morning while the Mr. and Mrs. Collins were out.

For once, he was glad for his aunt's officiousness.

Lady Catherine had gone on about calling cards, cakes, and the correct distance to stand from a drawing room hearth. Darcy had barely heard any of it; he had been watching Elizabeth.

She had not looked at him once since the moment at the pianoforte. Not during the tea, not even when he passed her cup. Her hands had been steady, but her mouth—so often animated—had been tight. Restrained.

Perhaps it was nerves. Or surprise. Or modesty.

She could not have known what he meant to do.

He would go early. Not so early as to seem improper—he would not insult her dignity with a clandestine call—but soon enough that he might not be leaving her waiting any later than he should.

He had once imagined proposing to her in a great hall, with flowers and candles and witnesses who understood her worth.

Now… he would settle for a warm fire, a quiet room, and the chance to speak his heart at last.

Darcy exhaled and stepped away from the mantel.

Let others question. Let his aunt fume. Let the world call him proud or precipitate or mad. He would *not* let another day pass in silence.

He rang for his valet.

Tomorrow, he would speak.

Tomorrow, she would be his.

Chapter 4

Hunsford Parsonage, Kent—December 24th, 1811

The door shut behind Mr. and Mrs. Collins with a clatter and a cloud of snow-dusted wind. Elizabeth watched through the parlor window as they made their careful way up the lane, Charlotte steadying herself with one gloved hand on her husband's arm. The parson's voice wafted back to her on the wind, echoing in the cold until the door latch clicked properly into place.

Peace. At last.

Elizabeth turned from the window and wrapped her shawl a bit tighter around her shoulders.

"I could come," she had said earlier that morning, when Charlotte made mention of their calls to several of Lady Catherine's most venerable neighbors. "I do not mind the cold."

But Mr. Collins had immediately turned crimson. "Certainly not! I must insist, Cousin Elizabeth, that you remain here. We shall not risk another scene like the one at Rosings. It would be most improper were you again mistaken for my wife."

Elizabeth had blinked. "I did not imagine Lady Catherine found it improper at all. She seemed quite in favor of the notion, as I recall."

Charlotte gave her friend a reproving look as Mr. Collins blustered something about appearances and reputations and the dignity of the cloth.

"Of course, sir," Elizabeth said repentantly.

And that had been the end of it.

Now, she only shook her head and gave a dry little laugh.

Married to him, she thought, giving an exaggerated shudder as she passed the mirror in the hall. *No. I was certainly right to refuse.*

The parsonage seemed unusually quiet. No barking orders from Mr. Collins, or calm reasoning from Charlotte. Elizabeth padded down the narrow hallway toward the cozy back room the new Mrs. Collins had claimed for herself—the little parlor with the view of the garden and the well-worn armchair by the hearth.

The fire was already lit. Charlotte had ordered it so that morning, anticipating her return with red cheeks and frozen fingers. It crackled merrily in the grate, casting long shadows against the polished table and half-unpacked crate of books.

Elizabeth let herself sink into the armchair and closed her eyes.

For a moment, she imagined herself back at Longbourn.

The Gardiner children would be tying ribbons to the stair banister, arguing over the best location for the paper stars. Lydia would be laughing somewhere near the front hall, hanging mistletoe over every doorway she could reach, just in case any officers be inclined to call.

Elizabeth flushed slightly as one officer's image came to mind. *Lieutenant Wickham… would he attempt to catch me under one?*

Eyes still closed, she allowed herself the luxury of imagining the scene: a sly, playful smile and a scandalously chaste kiss on the cheek, his lips brushing against her skin. Her stomach fluttered a little at the thought. *If only old Mr. Darcy had never had a son,* she thought idly, *then Mr. Wickham could marry as he pleased. He could have his inheritance. He could—*

Her smile faded.

Jane.

Her thoughts, like smoke, always curled back to Jane. To the pale, tired eyes that had refused to sparkle even with Christmas so near. To the heart that had been, perhaps, quietly broken—thanks to the man who haunted Elizabeth even now in Kent.

Mr. Darcy.

Her fists clenched in the folds of her shawl.

He had done it. Had separated them. Had torn something lovely and full of promise for the sake of his own prejudices. How many lives had he altered with a few well-placed words? How many hearts had he dismissed in pursuit of his own comfort?

She gave a bitter sigh and opened her eyes.

And blinked.

A knock—gentle, but firm—sounded from the front of the house. A moment later, the maid's hesitant voice: "Miss Bennet? You have a caller."

She frowned. "*I* have a caller? Who is it?"

"Mr. Darcy."

~~*~*

Darcy stood in the front entryway, hat in his hands. Now that he was here, he was suddenly anxious. Realizing he was twisting the brim and destroying its shape, Darcy took a deep breath and forced his hands to still.

"If you will follow me, sir."

He followed the maid down the narrow corridor and into a small sitting room.

"Mr. Darcy, miss," the girl whispered.

"Thank you, Hannah."

Elizabeth nodded at the girl, who bobbed a curtsy and disappeared through the door, which she left ajar. Darcy debated leaving it open but decided it would be best to have privacy for the conversation. It would not do for a servant to listen at the door, then run to Lady Catherine with the news of his proposal before he had even returned to Rosings.

No, she had best hear the happy news from me directly.

He focused his attention on Elizabeth, who had risen to her feet upon his entrance. "Mr. Darcy," she said in a cool voice, "this is certainly a surprise."

The tone startled him slightly, and he faltered. "I… I hope I do not intrude."

She remained standing. Her hands were loosely clasped before her, and though her expression was polite, it held no warmth.

He tried not to let that unsettle him. She was guarded. Of course she was. A gentleman did not show up unannounced to a lady's drawing room in hopes of declaring himself without producing some measure of confusion.

"I had hoped for a moment to speak with you privately," he said, gesturing faintly toward the chair across from hers. "May I?"

Her eyes widened. "Of course."

He sat. She did the same. The fire crackled between them, and for a long moment, neither spoke.

Then he began.

"I find it difficult to know where to start." He glanced down, then back to her. "Perhaps it would be best to be direct."

Her gaze did not falter.

"I have come," he said, "to ask you to be my wife."

He paused—not for effect, but because the words themselves held weight enough to steal his breath.

"I cannot pretend this decision was made without difficulty. I struggled—sincerely—against the many disadvantages of such a match. Your family's situation... your relations... even your mother's behavior at times..." He trailed off, then pressed forward with resolve. "But despite every rational objection, I find myself unable to conquer my feelings. I love you."

Elizabeth did not move.

Interpreting her silence as shock, he leaned closer, encouraged.

"I am not blind to the disparity in our situations, Miss Bennet. My connections, my income, my obligations—they all speak against such a union. Were I to consult only reason, I would not be here. But I cannot be silent any longer. I cannot fight it."

He gave her the barest smile. "Against my judgment, my family's expectations, and every possible consideration of propriety—my heart has chosen you."

Something flickered in her expression, but it wasn't the joy he expected to see. Still, he pressed on. "I cannot forget you. I do not want to forget you. I have watched you—at Netherfield, and here—and I cannot help but admire your honesty, your wit, your conviction. You are unlike anyone I have ever known."

Her fingers tightened slightly over the arm of the chair.

"I am aware," he added quickly, "that your connections may be considered a disadvantage. But I no longer care." He stood and crossed the space between them, taking her hand in his. "Miss Bennet, I offer you my heart. Marry me."

Another silence followed.

Darcy waited.

Elizabeth drew a breath, then said, "I am sorry, Mr. Darcy. But I cannot accept." Her voice was calm. Quiet. And colder than the frost outside.

Wait… what?

~~*~*

Even as she said it, Elizabeth scarcely believed the words had come from her own lips.

Her heart was racing. Her hands, damp and cold, gripped the fabric of her gown where it pooled in her lap. She had not expected this—not *this*. She had expected perhaps another stilted conversation, a silent stare, another moment in which he observed her like some curious insect beneath glass.

But this?

He had *proposed*.

He had walked into this room and asked her to marry him, in the same tone one might offer a lady the last of the fish course. Earnest, yes—but laden with conditions. An apology and an insult, offered side by side like wine and vinegar.

He was still standing before her, stunned, as if *he* had been struck.

"I—I beg your pardon?"

Elizabeth folded her hands in her lap and looked down at them. "No."

"No?" he echoed, like a man who had tripped and could not quite comprehend the ground was no longer beneath him.

Her shock was beginning to bleed into something else now—something hot and rising in her chest. How dare he stand there and look *injured*? Had he expected her to thank him? To fall to her knees in gratitude for being chosen—by a man who could scarcely keep the disgust from his voice even as he asked for her hand?

"No," she said again, more firmly this time. "I do not accept."

Darcy drew back half a pace, like a man finding himself unexpectedly in a duel.

"You astonish me," he said at last.

She laughed—short, sharp, bitter. "I assure you, the feeling is mutual."

He flushed and frowned at her. "I do not understand."

"It is a simple enough word, Mr. Darcy; a mere two letters of the alphabet, and only one syllable. Although, I understand from a reliable source that you prefer words of four syllables, so perhaps I shall tell you that I am disinclined to acquiesce to your request."

When he did not respond, Elizabeth stood. She was unable to remain seated while he loomed above her, still too tall and too self-possessed for a man who had just proposed as if she ought to be *grateful* for the humiliation. Her sudden movement force him to take a few steps back.

"May I ask… *why*?" His voice was strangled, but she could not bring herself to feel any sympathy for him.

"I cannot accept a man who makes it plain he sees my family as a disgrace, who considers my connections a burden to be borne. Do you expect me to thank you for overcoming your revulsion in order to offer me your hand?"

He looked genuinely startled. "I meant no insult—"

"No? '*In spite of my family*,' I believe you said. '*Despite every rational objection.*'" She smiled thinly. "What poetry. You have insulted nearly every person I hold dear, and you expect me to thank you for it."

Darcy's hands curled at his sides. "My feelings are sincere. Do you not feel the honor—or, at very least, the comfort—of knowing the strength of my regard in order to overcome such formidable obstacles?"

"You speak of affection, Mr. Darcy, but your words reek of condescension. And worse still, worse than your pride, is the damage you have already done to those I love."

"I spoke only what is true," he said stiffly. "You cannot pretend your family has no—"

"Do not *dare* finish that sentence," she hissed. Her voice rising, she added, "You have separated my sister from the only man who has ever shown her *true* affection, and not just admired her for her beauty. You have caused her to suffer. You have interfered—without invitation, without justification—and you have the audacity to stand before me and ask for my hand in the same breath."

He looked as though she had slapped him. Perhaps she had. Not with her hand, but with the truth. Her fingers itched to make contact with his face.

"I did what I thought was best," he said hoarsely. "Bingley—he—"

"Was in love with her," Elizabeth said. "And you knew it."

They stared at one another, the fire hissing between them.

"You hate me," he said.

"I did not before," she said, "but now I cannot help but wish you had never been born."

She turned away, gripping the edge of the mantel as if to steady herself.

Behind her, the silence was deafening. Outside, a bird trilled in the hedge. The fire snapped once in the grate.

But there were no footsteps. No words.

Then the door opened and closed again.

Elizabeth stood still for a long moment, then let out a breath through her nose. Her hands were cold. She pressed them to her skirts and sat slowly back down in the chair by the fire.

He had proposed. With all the gravity of a man bestowing a title.
And now he was gone.

She stared into the flames, too furious to be triumphant.

~~*~*

Darcy scarcely knew how he reached the gate leaving the parsonage.

The lane was thick with frost, but he felt none of it. His gloves were on, his greatcoat buttoned, but his whole body felt raw, exposed, like the wind had sliced straight through his ribs and stolen the breath from his chest.

She had refused him.

Not with hesitation. Not even with regret.

Flatly. Completely. As if the very idea of becoming his wife was *offensive.*

"I cannot help but wish you had never been born."

He flinched again at the memory. Those words would echo for a long while, he suspected.

Each step toward Rosings felt heavier than the last. He was not certain how long he had wandered the park's outer edge before the house came into view. The windows glowed with candlelight, the scent of roast goose wafted faintly on the night air. Somewhere within, the silver was being polished, the punch set out. Lady Catherine believed in formality—even at Christmas.

Christmas. His steps slowed. This was supposed to be a happy time of year, filled with goodwill and cheer.

And yet the woman he loved despised him.

He swallowed hard and climbed the steps to Rosings' front door. The footman at the door opened it quickly, and Darcy stepped inside, shoulders hunched against the warmth.

"Mr. Darcy, sir—Lady Catherine requests your presence at once."

Darcy gritted his teeth. *Of course she does.*

He passed his hat and gloves to the servant with numb fingers. "Inform her that I am indisposed."

"Sir?"

50

"A headache," he said sharply. "And a matter of business that requires my attention. I will not be coming down."

The man blinked. "Yes, sir."

Darcy turned without waiting and climbed the stairs two at a time, not stopping until he reached the sanctuary of his bedchamber.

Once the door was shut and locked behind him, he leaned back against it, letting the weight of the silence settle over him.

It was Christmas Eve.

He had thought—he had *truly believed*—that this night would mark the beginning of his life with her. That she would say yes. That he would write to Georgiana with joyful news. That he would finally feel… settled.

Instead, he felt hollow. Like he had been carved out.

It was worse than Ramsgate.

That moment—that *other* moment—had been terror and fury. A nightmare. But this? This was… personal. This was *rejection*. He had opened his heart—awkwardly, yes, and perhaps not with the finesse of a practiced courtier—but openly nonetheless.

And she had thrown it back in his face.

With a trembling hand, he rang for his valet to bring up a tray, then crossed to his writing desk and pulled out paper and ink.

If she had misunderstood him—if she had judged him wrongly—it was not too late to set it right. He had been too blunt. Too proud. The fault, if he were being honest, might partly be his.

He uncapped the ink and began.

Miss Bennet,

You must allow me to explain—

He stopped. Crossed it out.

You have, perhaps, been misled—

No. Too condescending.

My intentions were honorable—

He crumpled the sheet and threw it into the fire.

Another. Another attempt.

Too cold. Too desperate. Too angry.

He wrote until his hand cramped, until the hearth was glowing with the ash of failed confessions. Page after page blackened and burned, curling at the edges like scorched petals.

At last, he shoved back from the desk and stood, breathing heavily.

Ink would not suffice. That much was clear. She may even refuse to read it. Refusal, it seemed, was in her nature.

Very well, I shall know how to act.

As the words would not come to his pen, then he would speak to her once more. Calmly. Firmly. As a gentleman.

She would see sense—she *must*. She would be made to understand how deeply she had wronged him. How ungrateful and rash her judgment had been.

She would regret it. He was certain of it.

He sat heavily on the edge of the bed, chest still heaving with the last embers of humiliation.

Tomorrow, then.

He would speak to her tomorrow.

And when she finally saw her error, he would forgive her.

Eventually.

~~*~*

Darcy had not expected to sleep.

He lay for hours staring at the ceiling, his mind a snarl of wounded pride and gnawing confusion. Her words rang repeatedly in his ears—not just the refusal, but everything that followed.

You speak of affection, Mr. Darcy, but your words reek of condescension…

You separated my sister from the only man who ever showed her real affection…

I wish you had never been born.

He told himself she was wrong. She had misunderstood. She had misjudged him.

And yet—he had no peace. When sleep finally came, it came poorly.

Darcy awoke the following morning, on Christmas Day, with a start. He was drenched in a cold sweat, his heart hammering against his ribs. For a moment he could not tell where he was—the dim winter light filtering through heavy curtains, the faint scent of coal smoke, the muffled clatter of servants below.

He pressed a hand to his eyes. The dreams still clung to him like cobwebs.

In one, Bingley had stood before him in the drawing room at Netherfield, eyes blank, his usual warmth gone. "You have ruined my life," he had said, over and over, each repetition flat and expressionless. Jane had appeared behind him, pale and thin, eyes full of accusation and sorrow.

"Why would you do this to me?" she had whispered.

Then Georgiana—sweet Georgiana—crying out to him from Ramsgate, but instead of relief at his arrival, she only lamented his coming. You think you know best," she had sobbed. "You *always* say you know best. You never let us choose. Without you, I should have been free—"

Anne was next to appear before him. "My solitude is all your fault, Darcy. If not for you, my mother would have allowed me the freedom to marry as I pleased."

And then his father, stern and distant, seated in the library at Pemberley. "You have ruined all of them, Fitzwilliam. Oh, why must I have had such a son?"

At the end of it all, Elizabeth. Not mocking this time. Not furious. Only standing at a distance, her eyes dark and sorrowful. "Everyone would be happier if you had never been born."

He had woken with a strangled sound and found himself alone, the embers of the fire dying low.

Now the light was gray, seeping around the edges of the curtains. His head ached. His mouth was dry. Every attempt at righteous indignation from the night before had withered; the pages he had consigned to the fire seemed childish, his vow to "set her straight" absurd.

He sat up slowly, swinging his legs over the side of the bed. His cravat hung limp over the chair where he had thrown it. He stared at it for a long time, feeling oddly hollow.

Perhaps she is right, he thought dully. *Perhaps I am nothing but a meddler. Perhaps I ruin everything I touch. Bingley. Georgiana. Cousin Anne. Even... even Elizabeth.*

He rubbed a hand over his face.

It was Christmas morning. He should have been at Pemberley or at Matlock with Georgiana, presenting gifts and seeing her smile. Instead, he sat alone in a cold room at Rosings, unwanted, unloved, and rejected.

Maybe it would be better if I had never been born.

The thought startled him, but it stayed.

He stood abruptly and crossed to the window, pushing aside the heavy curtain. Outside, the fields were blanketed in snow. A weak sun struggled through clouds, sending pale shafts of light across the white expanse. The hedgerows stood like dark stitches against a seam of silver.

He needed air.

Chapter 5

Darcy dressed quickly and slipped from his room, avoiding the main staircase. Servants moved about with trays and candles, preparing for his aunt's Christmas breakfast. He left through a side door, pulling his greatcoat tight against the biting wind.

The snow crunched beneath his boots as he walked down the path toward the edge of the woods, head bent. He had no clear destination. Only a vague thought: that a walk might clear his mind, or at least make the echo of Elizabeth's words recede.

Maybe it would be better if I had never been born.

He turned the words over again in his mind as he reached the stream at the far edge of Rosings Park—the same little grove where he had so often gone to escape his aunt's lectures. The water trickled under a thin crust of ice, dark and cold, like a vein of glass running through the snow.

Darcy picked up a stone and turned it in his gloved palm absentmindedly. All around him, the woods were quiet. The snow was undisturbed but for his own footprints.

He felt cold clear through.

It was not only the rejection. Not only her words. Though those had cut more deeply than he could admit—not even to himself. No, it was something more corrosive still: a slow, crawling doubt that he usually kept buried deep.

He wondered again if everyone he cared about might indeed have been happier without him. *I have ruined everything,* he thought miserably.

Bingley. Jane.

He had believed—truly believed—that Jane Bennet was indifferent. Her manner was quiet, her expressions mild. But now… now he remembered the way her face lit up when Bingley entered a room. The softening of her voice when she spoke his name. The hope that had flickered—genuine, if restrained.

Had he misread it?

Had he destroyed her happiness out of arrogance?

His stomach twisted. He could see Bingley's expression now, the last time they spoke. *"Do you truly think she does not care for me?"* his young friend had asked.

He had hesitated. And lied.

He swallowed hard. His throat burned.

And Georgiana. Wickham.

That betrayal still stung—but worse was the memory of her crumpled letter, her pale cheeks, the way she would not look him in the eye for weeks. She had trusted him. Trusted him to protect her. And he had been so intent on shielding her from disgrace that he never once asked what she wanted.

He looked down at the stone in his hand. His fingers were stiff with cold.

Everything felt wrong. Off-kilter. Broken.

He had tried to act with honor. With good sense. He had told himself his choices were just—admirable, even.

But what if they were just proud? Just self-serving? Just… blind?

"I tried," he whispered. His voice sounded strange in the stillness.

No one answered.

The snow creaked beneath his boot as he shifted his weight. The cold was in his teeth now, in his bones. He should go back. He would be missed.

But would you really *be missed?* The taunt rose from the back of his mind. *After all, the only person who would express any dismay over your absence only values you as a husband to her daughter.*

And so he lingered, allowing the black despair to swirl around him, permeating every fiber of his being until his chest ached.

The pressure was unbearable. He gripped the stone tighter, feeling it bite into his palm. Overcome with anguish, he let out a guttural scream and hurled the stone into trickling water, the sound of shattering ice echoing amongst the snow-covered trees.

Falling to his knees, he buried his face in his hands. "I wish I had never been born!" he said aloud, his voice rough and strange in the stillness.

The words tore from him louder than he had intended. They rang across the empty grove, sharp and desperate. No sooner had they left his mouth than the air changed.

It was not the wind. There *was* no wind. The trees stood still, their branches heavy with snow. But something moved—an invisible ripple, like the world had inhaled and forgotten how to exhale.

Then—without footstep, sound, or warning—a figure stood across the stream.

Not a man. Not quite.

The man—if he *was* a man—looked entirely out of place. His hair was pale as frost, though not from age. His eyes—green, sharp, not quite human—glinted with amusement. His clothing was fine, though foreign in cut, and shimmered faintly as though the light bent around it.

"Well," said the stranger, voice lilting and amused. "That can be arranged."

Darcy stumbled back a half-step, breath catching in his throat. "What? Who…who are you? Where did you come from?"

The peculiar man quirked an eyebrow. "That is the most interesting thing I have heard all winter," he said, ignoring Darcy's question. "So you wish you had never been born, do you?"

Darcy's pulse pounded in his ears. "I did not— That is to say, I—"

"Oh, you did," the man interrupted, cheerful as ever. "Loudly. With feeling. And you meant it. I must say, it has been *ages* since I heard a wish like that made with such conviction. It called me."

He stepped lightly across the stream. Not onto the bridge—onto the water itself. The ice held beneath his boots without a sound.

Darcy instinctively took a step back.

"I did not call for you," he said stiffly.

"You did not need to. Wishes are louder than prayers, and much easier to grant."

The man's eyes glittered.

Darcy's breath misted in the cold air. "What is your name?"

The stranger smiled. "Names are very powerful things. But for your sake, let us say I am—hmm…" He tapped a finger to his lips. "A courier. A guide. A... seasonal gift."

"You are mad."

"I hear that often," he said, entirely unbothered. "But you, Mr. Darcy—you are *obsolete*. Or will be, shortly."

Darcy's stomach dropped. "What do you mean?"

"I mean," the man said lightly, "that you wished to have never been born. And so I have removed you."

"Removed—?"

"From the story. From the equation. From everything." The man's smile widened, but his eyes turned sharp. "You shall walk for a time, but none shall know you. No one will remember you. No one will miss you. You will see the world as it would be… without Fitzwilliam Darcy."

Darcy stared. "You cannot possibly—"

"Oh, but I have," the man said simply. With that, he looked past Darcy—just over his shoulder—and winked.

Darcy stiffened. He turned, confused, following the line of the stranger's gaze.

Elizabeth.

She stood half-concealed by the trees, her eyes wide in disbelief, her breath forming clouds in the cold morning air. Her hands were clutched in the folds of her cloak, her bonnet askew as if she had come in haste.

She had heard.

He opened his mouth to speak—but before he could form a word, something shifted behind him.

He spun back.

The stream was empty. The ice untouched. Snowflakes fell in silence, and the woods were still.

The man was gone.

Not a trace. Not a footprint.

Darcy stood frozen, heart pounding in his ears, the world suddenly too quiet.

Elizabeth remained motionless beneath the trees, staring not at him—but at the empty space where the stranger had stood.

She had seen him too.

So it had *not* been madness.

It had been *real*.

Darcy turned fully toward her. "Miss Bennet—" he began saying, but the expression on her face caused him to pause.

Not anger.

Not confusion.

Wonder.

And perhaps—if he were not mistaken—something like fear.

~~*~*

Elizabeth Bennet awoke on Christmas morning in no festive spirit at all.

Her head ached. Her mouth was dry. And her mood was, in every possible respect, abominable.

She had slept badly, tossing and turning beneath too-heavy bedclothes, her mind churning with every word of Mr. Darcy's astonishing, offensive proposal.

He had come to the parsonage. On Christmas Eve, no less. Uninvited. And asked for her hand in marriage as if doing her a *favor*, a great *honor*.

Despite every rational objection…

She threw back the bedclothes with unnecessary force.

If there had been a less gracious way to propose, she could not imagine it. And then to look wounded when she refused him— *wounded*! As though *he* were the one insulted!

59

She did not even wait for the maid to light the fire. She dressed swiftly in the dim morning light, wrapped herself in her thickest shawl and cloak, and crept downstairs, boots in hand. The floorboards creaked beneath her feet, but neither Mr. nor Mrs. Collins stirred.

Good.

She needed air.

Within minutes she had pulled on her boots and slipped out the kitchen door. The snow had stopped in the night, but the clouds hung low and heavy. The world was white and silent, and the biting air hit her like a tonic.

She tramped toward the grove near the stream behind Rosings. Her cheeks burned from the cold, and she welcomed it. It cleared her head.

But not her anger.

"You speak of affection, Mr. Darcy, but your words reek of condescension."

She muttered the words once more under her breath, half-wishing she *had* slapped him just to see the look on his face. Her hands curled into fists inside her muff. Why had he proposed at all? Why now, after weeks of silence and aloofness? After encouraging Bingley to leave, after humiliating her sister?

"Perhaps," she said aloud to the trees, "you truly *do* believe no woman in England could resist such a prize."

Just then, she heard a scream.

It was raw and guttural, nothing like the polite voices of Rosings or the occasional calls of gamekeepers. It tore through the frosty air like a wounded animal.

Elizabeth froze.

For a heartbeat she thought she had imagined it, but then came another sound: a violent splash, the crack of ice splintering.

Her heart lurched. *Did someone fall into the stream?*

Knowing the water was nearby, she ran in its direction. Her breath came in short, sharp clouds as she ducked under tree branches. The snow clung to her hem and soaked through her gloves, but she paid it no mind. She had never heard a sound like that before—not from an animal, not from a man.

Reaching the edge of the path that opened into the small grove near the water, she paused for breath, eyes scanning the area for someone in the water.

Instead, all she saw was Darcy, kneeling on the bank. His shoulders were tense, his coat dusted with snow.

What? Is he the one who shouted, or is he assisting someone?

Before her mind could catch up with the sight in front of her, she heard him speak—low, ragged, his voice scraping against the silence.

"I wish I had never been born!"

She gasped—too loudly, but Darcy did not hear.

Because the air had changed.

A sharp gust swept through the clearing, and snow danced upwards instead of down. The trees did not move, yet the wind curled unnaturally around them.

And then—without a sound—a man appeared across the stream.

Not a man. Not quite.

Elizabeth's heart stuttered. She stumbled back a pace and ducked behind a tree trunk before peeking around at the strange vision.

The figure shimmered faintly, as though the light could not decide how to strike him. His hair was pale, his eyes unnaturally green. His coat was fine, cut in a fashion she had never seen. He stepped out onto the stream, but instead of crashing through the thin ice, he merely walked on top of it.

What sort of magic is this?

She saw Darcy take a step back, and she clutched the tree trunk to keep herself steady.

The stranger smiled. "That," he said, "can be arranged."

She stared, shocked into speechlessness, as the two men spoke, holding one of the most bizarre conversations she had ever encountered. The odd man finished by telling Darcy that he had been removed from the equation.

Before she could process what that statement even meant, the stranger smiled and shifted his gaze—looking directly at her and winked.

Elizabeth gasped, and Darcy turned. Their eyes met, and his face made his bewilderment clear. "Miss Bennet?"

He said her name like a question, like he doubted the reality of her presence. Over his shoulder, the fae—for what else could he be?—gave her a small smile.

And then he was gone.

Completely.

There was no sound, no shimmer, no burst of light—only the hush of snow and the low creak of the trees.

The stream was still. The broken ice had frozen over again, smooth as glass. The footprints that had marked the bank were filled in.

Darcy stepped forward, staring at the place where the figure had been.

"I—he was just—" He turned back toward Elizabeth, his voice strangely hollow. "Did you see him?"

Elizabeth opened her mouth, then closed it again.

She looked at the spot where the fae had stood. Then back at Darcy. She nodded.

"…Yes," she said softly. "I saw him."

"Miss Bennet?" Darcy's voice was uncertain. "Can you… *see* me?"

A short bark of nervous laughter burst from her lips. "Yes, Mr. Darcy, I can."

"Ah, well… it is just that he said he had *removed* me…" His voice trailed off.

They stood in silence. Somewhere far off, a bird called once, then fell silent. At length, the cold pressed in, through her layers, and she shivered slightly.

Drawing her cloak more tightly around her, she cleared her throat. "Mr. Darcy," she said, her voice uneven, "what just happened?"

Darcy looked utterly undone. His eyes searched the grove as if he could will the stranger back into being.

But the grove gave no answers.

She watched in silence as he swallowed hard.

"I… do not know, Miss Bennet."

~~*~*

Darcy stared at the frozen stream, then at Elizabeth, then back again.

None of it made sense.

His heart pounded hard in his chest, the cold air burning his lungs. The strange man—apparition—was gone. The woods were quiet again. Snow drifted lazily through the boughs above.

Did that really just happen? Or am I hallucinating?

The shock on Elizabeth's face told him that if he did, indeed, imagine it all, then Elizabeth was similarly afflicted. He turned toward her, trying to speak, but no words came.

She looked as shaken as he felt.

"I—" he began, then stopped.

Elizabeth blinked, rubbed her gloved hands together for warmth, and gave a shaky laugh. "I do not suppose… do you often find woodland spirits in Kent?"

Darcy let out a breath, startled into the ghost of a smile. "Not in my experience."

They stood a moment longer, uncertain.

At last, Elizabeth broke the silence again. "Do you think this is all a dream?"

Darcy hesitated. "If it is, it is a very cold one."

That drew a small, breathless laugh from her, and something in his chest eased slightly. He nodded toward the path.

"Come," he said. "Let us walk back. Christmas Day has yet to begin, and I would rather face it with dry boots."

She nodded, still pale, and fell into step beside him.

They walked in silence for some minutes. The snow muffled their footfalls, and the air smelled of pine and smoke. Darcy felt his mind begin to clear—or perhaps simply retreat. What had happened, what he had said, what he had *wished*—it was too large to make sense of now.

He glanced sidelong at Elizabeth.

She was frowning slightly, as if lost in thought. Her arms were folded tightly across her chest.

"How… how much did you hear?" he asked quietly.

Her head turned. "All of it, I believe. Your wish, and everything the… the fae said."

He nodded once, accepting the descriptive title, and they walked on.

They had nearly reached the bend in the lane—the one that curved just before the parsonage came into view—when the faint sound of wheels on gravel reached them.

A carriage. Drawing up to the house.

Darcy narrowed his eyes.

It was a phaeton—high and elegant—and it came to a halt just before the gate.

Lady Catherine's phaeton.

And beside it stood—

His heart stopped.

Elizabeth.

Or a woman who looked *exactly* like her.

But it was not the Elizabeth beside him.

This woman wore a modest lace cap tied primly beneath her chin, her gown plain and proper. She stood stiffly beside Mr. Collins, whose gloved hand rested possessively on her arm.

Her expression was not smiling. Not at ease. It was tight. Controlled. Her chin was slightly raised, her mouth pressed into a line. She looked—Darcy realized with a sick jolt—like someone determined to *endure*.

He acted without thinking. His hand shot out, grasping Elizabeth's wrist, and he pulled her back from the bend, back into the shelter of the trees.

She stumbled, half turning on him. "Mr. Darcy—!"

He hushed her with a sharp motion, finger to his lips. "Quiet."

Her eyes flashed in protest, but he pointed through the hedgerow. "Look."

She hesitated, then leaned forward, peering around the brush. Her eyes widened. All color drained from her cheeks, and she clamped her mouth closed.

Darcy's heart hammered. He could hear the blood in his ears, the faint crunch of snow as Mr. Collins guided the other Elizabeth toward the parsonage door, her figure so achingly familiar in every line of it and yet wrong—utterly wrong.

He felt Elizabeth's sleeve trembling beneath his fingers.

"What kind of madness is this?" he whispered, the words escaping before he knew he had spoken them.

Elizabeth merely shook her head dumbfounded, and he gripped her arm more tightly. The cold pressed in, and the snow fell softly, and still they crouched there, silent.

"What do we do?" he asked in a whisper.

Chapter 6

Elizabeth did not answer. She only stared, frozen at the sight of *herself* on the arm of Mr. Collins, wearing the lacy cap of a married woman.

"Come," Darcy said at her side, "we must hear what they say."

He took her arm, and she allowed him to pull her along, crouching low along the hedgerow until they reached the narrow path that edged the garden wall. Elizabeth knelt beside Darcy in the cold, her heart thudding in her ears. From that vantage point, they were able to see through the branches at the conversing trio.

The voices came clear.

"…and I will not have her called *Lizzy*," Lady Catherine was saying in a clipped, cutting tone. "Such a name is vulgar. A woman of dignity uses her proper Christian name. I was never *Kate*. Or *Cathy*. I would have slapped any servant who tried it."

There was a pause, then a hesitant voice—her voice, but not hers. Quieter. Smaller.

"My sister is called Kitty…"

A sharp rustle, and Elizabeth winced as she saw *her* arm being squeezed tightly by her… husband. Mr. Collins's voice was low and urgent. "That will do, my dear."

The sound of his voice made her skin crawl.

There was a strained silence before Collins spoke again. "May I inquire, your ladyship, after the health of your daughter? Will she be coming for Christmas tomorrow?"

Lady Catherine sniffed. "Mrs. Rothley," she said, disdain in her tone. "No, I have not seen her since her wedding. I still cannot believe she has been wed to an old baron's son. Heir to nothing, I am afraid—but it was all she was fit for. And even that she has bungled."

"Oh dear," Mr. Collins murmured.

"She has not quickened," Lady Catherine said flatly. "Six months, and still no sign. Her physicians say she is too delicate. I believe the weakness must be from the de Bourgh side. She takes after her father, poor girl."

There was the clatter of a cane against gravel, and Elizabeth held her breath. Darcy's sleeve brushed hers as he leaned closer. She did not look at him. She could not.

Lady Catherine gave one final harumph, then: "See that your wife improves her curtsy. And for heaven's sake, do not let her speak in public until she learns to mind her tongue."

"Of course, your ladyship." Mr. Collins opened the front door. "Come, my dear," he said. "You must rest before dinner. It would not do to appear fatigued when next her ladyship calls."

Elizabeth watched the other her—still stiff, still silent—step inside.

The door shut. Then came the sound of retreating footsteps, the crunch of carriage wheels, and silence.

Snowflakes drifted down in hushed rhythm, settling on cloaks and hedgerows alike. Neither she nor Darcy moved.

Until suddenly—he did.

Without a word, Darcy surged to his feet and turned, striding swiftly away down the lane in the direction of the departing phaeton.

~~*~*

Darcy's boots slipped slightly on the snowy gravel as he climbed the lane at speed. His mind spun. His breath came in quick clouds.

She had been there. Elizabeth—yet not Elizabeth—ushered into the parsonage like a stranger in her own life. Her mouth had not smiled. Her eyes had not danced. And Lady Catherine—his aunt—had treated her with the same disdain she reserved for any poor relation barely elevated above servitude.

The phaeton was just cresting the hill, its wheels dragging through the snow.

"Lady Catherine!" he called.

The driver turned, startled—but made no motion to stop.

Darcy broke into a jog. "Lady Catherine de Bourgh!"

At last the phaeton jerked to a halt. The horse snorted and stamped. Lady Catherine turned her head sharply.

The door swung open.

Darcy reached the carriage and planted one gloved hand on the side. "Aunt, what is happening here?"

Lady Catherine stared at him, then frowned. "Do I know you?"

He blinked. "What?"

Her eyes narrowed. "Who are you? What business do you have addressing me with such familiarity?"

Darcy reeled. "It is I, Fitzwilliam Darcy. Your nephew."

Lady Catherine sat straighter in her seat, fury overtaking confusion. "I have no nephew."

"You do," he said, heart thudding. "You must! My mother was Anne Fitzwilliam, your sister."

Her lips curled into a sneer. "My sister had one child: a weak, foolish girl who shamed the family and ran off with a fortune hunter this year. We do not speak her name."

"No... no, that is not—" He faltered. "That is not how it happened."

Lady Catherine raised her cane and rapped it against the inside of the phaeton. "Driver, take us on. And see this lunatic off before I summon the constable."

The footman descended from the back, warily eyeing Darcy.

"My lady—"

"Drive."

The driver flicked the reins, and the phaeton lurched forward. The footman hesitated only a moment before climbing back on.

Darcy stood, stunned, the snow falling thickly around him now.

A soft voice behind him broke the silence.

"Mr. Darcy."

He turned to see Elizabeth—his Elizabeth—standing right behind him.

"You ought not have done that," she told him.

He opened his mouth, closed it again. "She… she did not know me."

"I know." Elizabeth's voice was low. "She did not appear to recognize me, either." Her eyes searched his face, then flicked up the lane after the retreating carriage.

"I hesitated at first," she continued. "I was afraid to be seen. What if she thought I was the other… me?" She swallowed. "But you looked so… I was afraid she might call someone to arrest you."

"She thinks I do not exist," he said bitterly. "And Georgiana. Dear God in heaven…"

Elizabeth was quiet for a moment. Then she reached out and laid a gloved hand on his sleeve.

"I know you exist," she said.

He looked down at her hand, the only warm thing in the world, and rested his own hand over top. "This is madness."

"Well, at least there is only *one* of you in this reality," she said lightly. "I am not entirely certain about having a twin, even if no one recognizes me. Especially if she is resigned to that… fate."

"Apparently, my absence from Netherfield compelled Mr. Collins to offer for you."

She laughed, and he looked at her in confusion. "Oh, he offered for me even with you there. Did you not hear the story?" she said, her eyes dancing with mirth. "I simply refused him."

Darcy winced. "Ah, yes. I had forgotten." *Well, she clearly did not make the refusal because she was waiting on me. I wonder why my presence altered her decision, then.*

His musings were interrupted when she shivered violently. He looked around, startled to realize that the sun was already beginning to set. "It will be dark soon, and then we will be in very real danger of freezing to death."

"But where can we go?" she asked

Darcy pondered a moment, then said, "There is an abandoned hunting lodge further into the woods. It is never used... at least, no one ever went there when I... when I existed. That would be the best place for solitude while we consider our next steps."

Elizabeth gave a weary nod, tugging her shawl closer around her shoulders. "Lead the way, then. Unless your mysterious stranger appears again to offer directions."

Darcy's mouth twitched despite himself. "He seems to prefer dramatic exits. I doubt he will be of much help."

They stepped cautiously from the edge of the trees, careful to keep well away from the parsonage. The light was fading fast now, the low winter sun casting everything in silvery blue. Elizabeth's skirts dragged through the snow, the hem heavy with the damp, and Darcy noted again how pale she looked.

The couple did not speak for several minutes. The path through the woods was barely visible under the fresh fall, but he remembered it well. He had walked it dozens of times during his previous visits to Rosings—always alone, always when he needed to clear his mind. It was odd to tread it now with someone beside him. Even more odd that it should be her.

"Do you think... do you think that Jane is dead? Or my father?"

He startled. "I beg your pardon?"

"I simply cannot imagine a scenario in which I would have accepted Mr. Collins's proposal, unless there was a danger to my family. But if my father were dead, why would Mr. Collins be at Hunsford instead of Longbourn?"

He glanced sideways. "I do not know. It is difficult to tell what laws govern this... place."

She gave a sharp little laugh. "I am not certain if there are *any* laws that govern it."

Darcy shook his head. "This morning, I had plans to write you an apology. To explain myself better. I thought I had simply made a poor proposal."

"You did," she said dryly. Then, a moment later, "But… not so poor as Mr. Collins did the morning after the Netherfield ball."

His lips quirked again, briefly. "I suppose I should take that as comfort."

Another few minutes passed. The trees thickened. Their breath clouded before them, and Elizabeth's pace slowed slightly. He offered his arm without comment; she took it without protest.

At last, the hunting lodge appeared through the branches: a small, weathered structure of gray stone and shuttered windows, half hidden beneath an overgrown pine. The door stood crooked on its hinges, but it opened easily enough with a firm shove.

Inside, it was dim and chill. But it was dry.

Darcy went to the hearth and began clearing out the old ashes while Elizabeth crossed to the single bench along the wall and sank onto it.

"I do not suppose you have matches in your coat pocket?" she asked hopefully.

"As a matter of fact," he said, pulling a small tin from his inner pocket, "I do."

She blinked. "Why on earth do you carry matches?"

"I am a man. I have pockets. If you had pockets, you would carry necessities as well."

She gave a soft, reluctant laugh.

Darcy struck one and set it to the old kindling, fanning it gently until the fire began to take. It would not burn long—there was only a small stack of split logs inside, and he doubted anyone had replenished it in years—but the light was steady and the heat blessedly real.

They sat in silence for a while, watching the flames.

Then Elizabeth said, almost idly, "So… you wished you had never been born. And now we are here."

He did not answer right away.

At last, he said, "It was said in despair. But it was meant."

She looked over at him.

He did not meet her eyes. "I realized… I realized that I have done nothing but bring harm. To Bingley. To Georgiana. To you."

"You did not harm me," she said softly. "Not really."

He glanced at her, startled. But she was watching the fire.

"You offended me," she added, "but you did not *ruin* me or my life. Not like this... this world has done."

"If this world even exists," he said. She looked at him questioningly, and he smirked. "It is entirely possible that we have simply gone mad."

"If we are mad, then at least we are not alone in our lunacy. I would much prefer being unrecognized and with you than actually having married Mr. Collins."

"What other explanation is there?"

She was silent. "The fae. He told you that you had been removed. Perhaps... perhaps he somehow had the power to actually do it."

He turned away from her and ran a hand through his hair. "Removed from what? Time? Memory? My family does not know me, you are apparently married, and that—that—was not Rosings as it should be."

Elizabeth wrapped her arms around herself. "Then we are somewhere else entirely. Some... other version of our lives."

"No." Darcy shook his head. "Not ours. Mine."

She looked at him sharply. This time, he met and held her gaze. "This... whatever this is... it began with *my* wish."

"Do you truly wish you had never been born?"

When he did not answer, she asked, "Why?"

"Why?" The word burst from his lips. "Because *you* said it! The woman I love told me she wished I had never lived."

"But you were angry, not distraught."

His shoulders slumped. "Only at first. But when I awoke this morning, my heart was broken. I realized then that my actions had done the same to my friend, and to your sister—and even to mine. All I could think was how much better their lives might have been without me."

Elizabeth's brow furrowed. "You truly believe that?"

He stared into the fire. "I did. At the stream I believed it with all my heart."

A log shifted, sending a small shower of sparks up the chimney. The light flickered across her face, softening her expression.

"And now?" she asked quietly.

"I do not know," he admitted. "Part of me still thinks it must be true. And yet…" He glanced at her, then quickly away. "And yet here you are. You could have walked away. But you did not."

Elizabeth's lips curved faintly—though it was not quite a smile. "Well, it was that or freeze to death. My options were limited."

Her face grew serious, and she leaned over and placed her hand on top of his. "I spoke in anger yesterday, Mr. Darcy. I was offended, and my pride was wounded. I apologize."

He let out a soft breath, almost a laugh, though it caught in his throat. "You are far more forgiving than I deserve."

For a moment neither spoke. The wind whispered against the shuttered windows. Somewhere in the distance a branch cracked beneath the weight of snow.

Then Elizabeth straightened a little. "If your wish brought us here," she said slowly, "then perhaps it can also return us."

Darcy looked at her, startled.

"Or at least," she went on, "we can learn what must be done. If this is a glimpse of the world without you, then perhaps you were meant to see it."

"To what end?" he asked hoarsely. "To punish me?"

"Or to teach you," she said softly, "and as I have been included in this magic, to teach me as well."

Darcy stared at her for a long moment, the firelight catching in his dark eyes. He wanted to believe her. He wanted to believe this nightmare might have a purpose. But outside the snow continued to fall, soft and relentless, and the world beyond their little fire felt cold and strange and vast.

At length, he noticed Elizabeth smother a yawn—and a shiver. The fire had burned lower, casting longer shadows on the stone floor. Darcy glanced around the small hunting lodge, dismayed by how little comfort it afforded. One cot, narrow and worn, occupied the corner. A simple bench, where Elizabeth sat, lined the opposite wall. That was all.

He stood with a sigh and reached for the door. "I shall fetch more wood."

She did not protest, though he noticed her huddling deeper into her shawl.

Darcy stepped out into the cold and returned quickly with as much dry timber as he could find in the lean-to behind the lodge. He stoked the hearth into a more vigorous blaze and dusted his hands off before turning to her.

"You should take the bed."

Elizabeth looked up from where she sat on the bench, her expression unreadable. "It is hardly large enough for you to stretch your legs across," she pointed out. "I shall be quite comfortable here."

"You will not," he said firmly. "You are tired, and chilled, and you are a lady. I am not so far gone as to forget the dictates of civility."

She tilted her head. "You would be most uncomfortable."

"I am already uncomfortable," he said dryly. "Your comfort is more important."

Elizabeth gave him a look. "And what of the fact that there is only one blanket?"

Darcy hesitated. The fire's warmth would not last through the night. The stone floor would grow bitter, and frost would surely creep in through the cracks in the walls.

She drew a breath and looked away. "It is only... for warmth, of course."

His brow furrowed. "I beg your pardon?"

Her cheeks turned scarlet. "The bed," she said, her voice low. "If we both used it. And the blanket. It would be far warmer than... than freezing separately." She kept her gaze firmly on the hearth. "We need rest. And clear heads come morning."

Darcy stared at her, stunned. "I could not—Miss Bennet, I could not possibly presume—"

"You will not be presuming anything," she said, lifting her chin. "You may be quite certain I am not making an improper offer."

The blush that flamed across her face belied her composed tone, but she held firm. "Besides," she added, with a glance toward the cot, "as I am already seated here on the bench, you would have to move me bodily if you intend to lay claim to it alone."

Darcy opened his mouth, then closed it again.

"Unless," she said calmly, folding her hands, "you intend to behave ungentlemanly after all?"

He made a strangled sound that might have been a laugh. "You are a most provoking woman."

She arched an eyebrow. "Is that a yes?"

"It is a surrender," he muttered, and moved to bank the fire.

They prepared in silence—Darcy moving stiffly, deliberately not looking at her as he laid the blanket flat across the narrow cot. She removed only her boots and outer layers, setting them near the hearth to dry. He did the same.

She was already curled beneath the blanket when he turned back. With great care, he lowered himself onto the other side, staying as close to the edge as possible. The cot creaked ominously.

For a moment, neither moved.

Then her elbow brushed his. "Apologies," she murmured.

"No, forgive me," he said at once. "I did not mean to—"

Her foot accidentally bumped his shin.

"I swear I am not doing this on purpose," she muttered.

"It is entirely my fault," he said, trying to keep his voice steady. "I should have—"

She turned slightly, her shoulder touching his. He drew in a sharp breath.

"This is not how I envisioned us sharing a bed for the first time," he muttered.

She stilled.

Darcy closed his eyes. "Forgive me. That was inappropriate."

There was a long silence.

Then she giggled.

It was soft and unexpected and made something in his chest unclench.

"You forget," she whispered, turning her face toward him, "that I am the woman you once declared to be only tolerable. I believe I am more surprised by this situation than you."

He groaned. "Will I never be allowed to forget that?"

She laughed again—quiet, breathless, half-delirious with fatigue. "Can you imagine the look on Miss Bingley's face if she could see us now?"

That did it.

Darcy barked a laugh, low and surprised, and Elizabeth stifled another giggle in the blanket.

They lay there, shaking with silent mirth, pressed shoulder to shoulder by necessity, and for a few moments—just a few—the strangeness of the world outside was forgotten.

Eventually, the laughter faded into stillness. Her breathing slowed. His eyes grew heavy.

And together, side by side, they drifted into sleep.

Chapter 7

Elizabeth awoke slowly the morning after Christmas, cocooned in warmth. The fire still crackled gently in the hearth, its orange glow flickering behind her closed lids.

The maid must have stoked it without waking me. That was kind of her, to be so quiet.

A soft weight rested across her waist, solid and warm, and the steady sound of breathing close to her ear told her she was not alone.

For a moment, she thought Jane had come to her side in the night, as she sometimes had when they were children—seeking comfort or warmth on a particularly cold winter's evening.

But then she shifted slightly, and the body pressed against hers was not soft and slender like Jane's.

It was firm. Hard, even. And the arm across her waist was heavier than Jane's—and distinctly… hairier.

Her eyes flew open.

Memory flooded in like icy water: the grove, the duplicate version of herself, the strange fae man, and Mr. Darcy—who now, unmistakably, lay beside her.

Every muscle went taut.

She dared not move. Not yet. Perhaps, if she kept very still, he would remain asleep and she could extract herself with dignity. Her breath slowed, and she kept her limbs perfectly still, feigning slumber.

And then, with the slightest shift, the arm lifted.

Darcy stirred beside her, drew a breath, and withdrew.

She heard the rustle of cloth as he rose from the cot, the soft creak of his boots on the floor. Then a gentle pull of the blanket, tucking it more securely around her.

Her eyes fluttered open just in time to see him shrug on his coat and slip outside.

The door thumped closed behind him.

Elizabeth exhaled.

She sat up slowly, brushing back her hair and glancing around the cabin. It looked no different by morning light—still dim, still bare—but the fire gave it an air of something close to comfort. Her thoughts, however, were far from settled.

We need a plan.

She wanted—needed—to return to Longbourn. To see her father. To discover if Jane had fared better in this strange version of the world. Her imagination painted terrible images: her sister alone, abandoned, her heart broken. Or, worse still, married to someone wholly unsuitable.

But perhaps—perhaps!—if she had married Mr. Bingley... *that* could be why Mr. Collins chose Elizabeth instead of Jane.

She felt a sudden, wild pang of hope.

Surely Mr. Collins marrying *her* signified something good for Jane, did it not?

The door opened again, letting in a blast of cold air—and Darcy, his arms full of wood.

He set the logs by the hearth and turned toward her. "How are you feeling?" he asked.

At that exact moment, her stomach gave a loud, unmistakable growl.

Her face flushed crimson.

Darcy blinked, then gave a wry smile. "Ah," he said gently. "I believe I have my answer."

She tugged the blanket up a bit more and gave him a sheepish glance. "Food is not the only necessity at present," she said in a near-whisper. "There is... also the matter of a chamber pot."

His eyes widened slightly, then darted to the far corner of the room where a dusty bucket sat beside a coil of rope and a rusted lantern. "I can step outside," he said quickly, already reaching for the door.

"Thank you," she murmured, mortified.

He left her alone, and she made quick use of the bucket and donned her clothes from the day before. When she was finished, she wrapped herself again in the blanket and carried the makeshift chamber pot outside, where Darcy was pacing the edge of the clearing.

"*I* will clean it," she said at once, before he could offer.

"You should not—"

"Please allow me to maintain some dignity," she said firmly.

He bowed slightly and looked away.

Elizabeth scrubbed it out with handfuls of snow, then placed it discreetly near the edge of the lodge.

When she returned, the fire had been stoked again. Darcy stood near the hearth, arms folded.

"We cannot remain here," he said without preamble.

"I agree," she replied, brushing her hands dry on her skirts. "We will freeze—or starve. Besides, there is nothing to be learned here."

He nodded. "Where do you suggest we go?"

She sat on the edge of the cot. "I believe we must begin with Longbourn."

His eyebrows lifted.

"Surely your absence from Netherfield, along with my having married Mr. Collins, means that your friend must have offered for my sister. At least, I hope that is what happened."

"And if it is not?"

"Then at least we may learn something more of this world. If my family is there… if they remember me." She paused. "You will likely wish to go to London. To check on your sister."

His face darkened slightly. "Yes, although she may be at Pemberley if… if she is married."

"We will need funds," she said. "Do you have any with you?"

81

Darcy reached into the inner pocket of his coat and withdrew a coin purse. "Fortunately, yes. And I always carry a sovereign sewn into my coat lining."

Elizabeth gave a small smile. "Then we may avoid starvation. I have some, as well—about three pounds tucked into the hem of my dress, and some coin in my sewing roll."

Together, they retrieved their coins and counted: fifteen pounds in Darcy's purse, and just over fourteen shillings between the two of them hidden in various folds and linings. Enough, perhaps, for food, for travel—for something.

"I admit," Darcy said ruefully, "I have no notion what things cost individually. Purchases are made for the household in bulk."

"A loaf of bread and a pound of cheese may cost a shilling or so," she said. "If we are careful, we can make that food last a day or even two."

He nodded. "And a public coach is usually one shilling per mile, divided amongst the passengers."

"It is nearly fifty miles to Longbourn," she said, frowning. "Too far to walk."

"We can travel by public coach," he assured her. "If we can reach the posting inn at Hunsford or Westerham, we might secure passage north."

"And what shall we say if anyone asks who we are?"

He hesitated, then said, "Would you be opposed to traveling as a married couple? It would invite less scrutiny."

She felt her cheeks flushing and strove to keep her voice calm. "Perhaps we are William and Beth Smith. We can be new friends of Mrs. Collins who are traveling, and we have been asked to call on her family."

He stared at her for a long moment. Then he gave a soft laugh. "Beth Smith," he said. "That may take some getting used to."

She flushed, but her chin lifted. "We have been through stranger things."

"Yes," he said quietly, "we have."

And then neither spoke for a while—both thinking of what they had left behind, and what they might be walking toward.

~~*~*

The road was half-frozen beneath their boots, the snow hardened overnight into a crust that crunched underfoot. Darcy walked a step behind Elizabeth at first, watching the movement of her cloak as it brushed through brittle hedgerows.

He *should* be thinking about their plan. About coin and carriages and destinations. About the utterly fractured reality they had woken into.

But he was really doing instead was thinking of that morning.

Of warmth. Of her soft breath against his collarbone. Of the peaceful, nearly unimaginable moment when he had opened his eyes to find Elizabeth Bennet—*his* Elizabeth—curled beneath his arm like something precious and unguarded.

Her curls had tickled his chin.

For the briefest instant, he had not remembered anything amiss. It had felt natural. Right. His arm around her waist. The quiet of morning. The faint scent of lavender and firewood.

Then memory had come crashing back. And shame with it.

And yet—even now, even with the weight of uncertainty pressing in on all sides—he could not regret those hours spent in her presence. To have her near, without artifice or performance, was something he had never dared imagine. And yet it had happened. And she had laughed with him, even teased him, just before sleep had claimed them both.

He cleared his throat and lengthened his stride to match hers.

They reached the posting inn—a narrow, soot-smudged building on the edge of the village—and stepped inside. The warmth hit them like a wave, along with the scent of stale ale, fried onions, and damp wool.

Darcy moved to the counter while Elizabeth waited by the door. The thin, balding man behind the desk looked up at his approach. "Happy Christmas, governor."

"Happy Christmas," Darcy replied automatically, his surprise evident. *I had forgotten yesterday was Christmas.*

"One-way to Meryton, Hertfordshire, please," he continued, retrieving a handful of coins from his coat. "Via public coach. Two seats."

The man scratched at his stubbled chin. "Coach to Meryton departs in half an hour. It's the only one today, seeing as it's Christmas. There's a stop in Town first, o'course. All northbound goes through London this time of year."

Darcy blinked. "London?"

"Aye. Long Acre in Covent Garden."

Darcy stepped back, glancing toward Elizabeth. She raised a brow.

He motioned toward the door. "Excuse us a moment."

They stepped into the cold again, and Darcy exhaled a breath that steamed in the frosty air.

"If there is a stop in London…" he began.

"…we could see my aunt and uncle."

He paused, his train of thought lost with her interruption. "I beg your pardon?"

"Mr. and Mrs. Gardiner—my mother's brother and his wife. They would welcome us, I am sure."

"Even on the day after Christmas?"

"Oh!" Elizabeth's expression told him she had entirely forgotten about the holiday as well. "They may not be there, then. Usually they come to Longbourn. Although, if they were there for my—" she grimaced "—wedding, then they may be back in London already. My uncle cannot leave his business for long, and my young cousins do not enjoy travel from their home."

"Ah, yes, well… I suppose we could stop by and see. I had thought to go to Darcy House. My father kept a small safe in the study, hidden under a floorboard. I was the only one who knew of it." He looked at her seriously. "If it has not been emptied, it might give us enough to last as long as we need."

Elizabeth was quiet for a moment. "It is a risk."

"I can be discreet."

84

"But what if someone sees you? What if they... they call the constable?" Her expression twisted with anxiety.

Darcy felt a pang at that. That she would worry for him—even now, after everything he had done—softened something in his chest. "We shall stop at the Gardiners' first," he said. "If they remember you, they may let us stay. Then I will go to Darcy House after dark."

She hesitated, then gave a reluctant nod. "Very well."

His lips twitched. "Besides... it would be rather difficult to explain how *Mr. and Mrs. Smith* came to possess the key to a townhouse in Mayfair."

Elizabeth smirked. "I suppose *Mrs. Smith* will have to work on her husband's humility."

He chuckled under his breath. "A lost cause, I fear."

They turned and returned to the inn, handing over their coins and receiving two slips of paper in exchange. Then, bundled and breathless, they boarded the waiting coach.

Darcy let Elizabeth ascend first, then followed, ducking low beneath the curved roof. Inside, the cabin was dim and close. Two passengers already sat in the opposite corner: an older woman with a lace cap and a narrow-eyed boy with a satchel on his knees.

Darcy sat beside Elizabeth, his shoulder brushing hers, and for the first time since waking, he felt a thread of something steady.

A direction. A plan.

London first. Then Longbourn. Then—whatever else this strange new world required.

He glanced sideways at Elizabeth.

She was staring out the frosted window, her lips slightly parted, her breath fogging the glass. One hand was braced on the seat beside her.

She looked brave. Determined. And lovely.

He turned his face toward the window, lest he say something foolish.

The coach jolted into motion.

~~*~*

By the time the hackney drew to a stop before Gracechurch Street, Elizabeth's heart was pounding so loudly in her chest that she was certain Darcy could hear it.

The familiar row of tidy brick homes, the polished knocker on the painted green door—everything looked just as it should. And yet... nothing felt right.

Darcy stepped out first and turned, offering his hand to help her down. His gloved fingers closed gently over hers, steadying her as her boots met the cobblestones. He was quiet, but she saw his eyes flick over the modest yet well-kept houses, taking in the neat curtains, the swept steps, the faint scent of roasting chestnuts from somewhere down the lane.

She did not miss the slight lift of his brows.

Not disapproving. Surprised.

Elizabeth held her head high and rang the bell. A maid opened the door and showed them into the sitting room. They walked into the room, and there stood her aunt. Not changed in the slightest—still with that smooth, elegant brow, the composed smile, the gentle manner of speech that had always soothed Elizabeth as a child.

"May I help you?" Mrs. Gardiner asked, polite but reserved, her gaze taking them in with a flicker of curiosity.

Elizabeth's throat closed. *She does not recognize me, either.*

Darcy stepped forward. "Pardon the intrusion, madam, especially on Christmas day. We are William and Beth Smith, traveling north. We hoped to stop briefly and pay our respects. Your niece—Mrs. Collins—spoke warmly of you when last we saw her."

Elizabeth could have kissed him for the ease with which he delivered the lie.

Mrs. Gardiner blinked, her expression warming just slightly. "Mrs. *Collins*? Oh... yes, of course. Lizzy. Do come in and be seated, please."

Elizabeth stepped in from the hall and immediately felt a wave of memories rush over her—the scent of lavender polish, the familiar creak in the stair, the tall cabinet filled with Aunt Gardiner's china. It was all the same.

Except that no one knew her.

The awareness settled heavily on her shoulders.

Darcy's expression was unreadable, but she could see him glancing around with restrained interest—at the clean lines of the entryway, the quality of the drapes, the quiet elegance of the Gardiner home. He had clearly not expected such genteel refinement in Cheapside.

Elizabeth felt a flicker of grim satisfaction as she settled onto a comfortable chair near the fire.

Mr. Gardiner came into the room behind them, and introductions were repeated. Mrs. Gardiner rang for tea, and a plate of buttered biscuits accompanied the warm drink.

"You say you met Lizzy? How is my niece?" Mrs. Gardiner asked.

Darcy and Elizabeth exchanged glances. "She seems to be settling," Elizabeth replied cautiously. "Of course, we only just became acquainted with her…"

Her voice trailed off as she realized the awkwardness of having to describe herself as a stranger would. Darcy, clearly sensing her disquiet, quickly said, "She seems to be very kind, and I think the parish will flourish under her care."

Mr. and Mrs. Gardiner beamed. "You say you are heading north, though, did you not?" Mrs. Gardiner asked. "What part, if I may ask?"

"Derbyshire," Darcy replied. "A small town called Lambton—you may not have heard of it."

"Why, I certainly have!" Mrs. Gardiner exclaimed. "I am from Lambton, you see, though I have not been there in many years."

"Oh?" Elizabeth's voice was noncommittal. "My husband's sister lives there. It is my first time to travel this far, and I hear it is quite lovely."

Mrs. Gardiner's expression softened at that. "It is. I spent much of my youth there. I am sorry to say it has changed considerably, though."

Elizabeth's hand tightened around her teacup.

"Oh?" Darcy asked, his tone light but attentive.

Mrs. Gardiner leaned slightly forward. "It used to be so peaceful— a good school, a thriving village. But in recent years… well. The estate passed to Miss Georgiana Darcy, you know, but her uncle managed it for her. Then she eloped with the steward's son—Wickham, I believe his name was."

Elizabeth's heart stopped. She glanced quickly at Darcy. He had gone very still.

Mrs. Gardiner went on. "They say he was charming, at first. The whole county thought him delightful—handsome, well-mannered, quick with compliments. But after the wedding, the truth emerged. Selfish. A gambler. He has nearly drained Pemberley dry. Many of the tenants have left. And Lambton itself... we had thought to visit again this summer, perhaps even go walking in the Peaks, but it is no longer the sort of place I would bring my children."

Elizabeth forced a smile. "That is... very sad to hear."

Darcy's hands were folded tightly in his lap, and she knew without looking that his jaw was clenched. She cleared her throat. "Thank you for the tea. We should let you get back to your day. We have not yet secured lodging for the night."

"Oh, but do stay," Mrs. Gardiner said at once. "Surely you are not setting off again without dinner? And... and if it is not too bold of me— well, we have a guest room. You are very welcome to it."

Elizabeth hesitated, her heart caught between gratitude and ache.

How many evenings had she passed in this house? How many quiet conversations, how many nights helping the children into bed, how many long walks with her aunt down Cheapside's less-traveled lanes?

And now... she was a stranger.

"That is very kind of you," she said softly. "We would be most grateful—"

"But I am afraid I have a commitment this evening that will keep me out quite late," Darcy interjected. "I should hate to have my comings and goings disturb your peace, especially on a holiday."

"Oh," Mrs. Gardiner blinked. "Well, of course, we understand. But you must at least let us feed you before you go."

Elizabeth forced a smile. "We would be honored."

Mrs. Gardiner brightened. "Wonderful. Then I will see what can be managed—something warm, at least. And perhaps a bit of cheese toast for the road."

She bustled off toward the kitchen with her husband following behind, leaving Elizabeth and Darcy alone in the parlor.

Elizabeth looked at him. "We have not the funds for an inn; at least, not a respectable one."

"But here we will be noticed, scrutinized. We do not have a trunk or even a satchel with belongings. Besides, what if the worst occurs, and I am arrested for theft this evening?" Darcy shook his head. "It could be disastrous for your uncle's business to be associated with a criminal."

"I see your point," Elizabeth said with a sigh of resignation.

He nodded once. "The longer we wait, the more the risks multiply. If there is anything left at Darcy House, I must find it before someone else does."

Her eyes narrowed slightly. "Then I am coming with you."

He opened his mouth to object, but she lifted a hand. "To keep watch. Or create a distraction. Besides, you wish me to remain at an inn, alone?"

He sighed, but there was no heat in it. Only weary admiration.

"As you wish… Mrs. Smith."

They exchanged a look—half anxious, half amused—and sat back in silence, listening to the muffled sounds of supper being prepared in the kitchen. Mrs. Gardiner returned a few minutes later with her husband.

"Cook will have something ready for you soon. You can take it with you."

"You are very good," Elizabeth responded. "Thank you for your kindness, especially on Boxing Day."

Mrs. Gardiner smiled, her expression touched with something almost wistful. "Of course. I only wish we had more time to get come to know you better."

Elizabeth swallowed past the sudden tightness in her throat. "So do I." She forced a smile, "But you never know—you might easily tire of us once the novelty of our acquaintance has ended."

"That sounds like something my niece would say," Mrs. Gardiner said, and Elizabeth was horrified to see her aunt's eyes misting somewhat.

"You mean Mrs. Collins?" Darcy asked, and Mrs. Gardiner nodded in response.

"She is the first of our nieces to marry," Mr. Gardiner explained, "And it was a bit unexpected. We have always viewed our Lizzy and her sister Jane as our own daughters, and—as with any change in life—there is a sense of sorrow."

"I understand perfectly," Elizabeth said, "and I can tell that she feels the same about the two of you."

Her own eyes welled with tears, and she felt Darcy reach out and place a hand on her shoulder. She looked at him gratefully and was startled by the depth of feeling in his eyes. For a long moment neither of them looked away; the air between them seemed to hum with unspoken understanding—of shared loss, of recognition, of something neither dared to name.

Then Mrs. Gardiner gave a soft, embarrassed little laugh that broke the spell. "Look at us, weeping over nothing. Ah, here is a basket from the kitchens."

Elizabeth rose and took it from her aunt, her heart still unsteady. They made their farewells and wished one another a happy Christmas, then Elizabeth forced herself to walk out the front door and back out into the strange, new world she inhabited.

Chapter 8

Darcy adjusted the weight of the basket in his lap as the decrepit hackney jolted forward, its wheels creaking in protest against the uneven London stones. Beside him, Elizabeth sat with her hands folded tightly atop her reticule, her gaze fixed on the window though the glass had already fogged over from their breath.

For several minutes, neither of them spoke.

Then she said softly, "You are very quiet."

He looked down at the leather strap holding the basket closed. "I am thinking."

"That," she murmured, "is always a dangerous thing in your case."

He almost smiled. "I am thinking," he repeated, "of how strange it must have felt for you to sit across from people who have known you your whole life, only to find they have no idea who you are."

"It was more difficult than I anticipated," she said in a shaky voice. "I wished for nothing more than to throw myself into my aunt's arms and tell her everything."

"You are quite close to them, then?"

"Yes," she whispered. "Mr. Gardiner is my mother's brother, and Jane and I have spent many a month in their home over the years."

He raised his eyebrows in shock that the fashionable, refined man he had just met was *Mrs.* Bennet's relation. On seeing his expression, Elizabeth gave a watery laugh. "Did you expect them to be vulgar?"

He hesitated. "No. Not vulgar. But…" He trailed off.

"But what?" she prompted.

"I had heard they lived in Cheapside. I… assumed a certain tone would accompany such an address."

Her mouth curved faintly. "And now?"

He turned to look at her fully. "Now I see they have more warmth, more refinement, and more natural grace than half the drawing rooms of Mayfair. Good company has less to do with address than I might have thought."

She blinked, clearly startled.

He exhaled slowly and added, "Your aunt is a remarkable woman."

Elizabeth smiled, but it was a subdued smile, touched with something more fragile.

He continued, "It was strange, though. Sitting across from her, hearing her speak of you, yet knowing she spoke of someone else entirely."

"Yes," Elizabeth said, her voice quiet. "I kept waiting to feel comforted. And instead… it felt like mourning."

Before he could respond, the hack came to a halt. Darcy stepped out first and offered his hand. Elizabeth took it, her fingers cold in his.

They stood before the gates of Darcy House.

Or what remained of it.

The shutters were bolted. The door chained. No lights. No staff. The windows were boarded over.

A metal placard hung beside the gate:

Property of Crown Bank of London

Auction Pending

A paper notice flapped damply underneath it.

Darcy stared in shock, a cold, hollow ache forming in his chest, his hands clenching into fists. The house looked… abandoned. Stripped of dignity. As though it had died and no one had noticed.

Elizabeth stepped closer. "I am sorry," she whispered, her hand tightening around his arm.

He swallowed, a lump having formed in his throat. "This house has been in my family for generations. Since the reign of Queen Anne."

She tilted her head, studying him. "Do you think the safe you mentioned is still in there?"

"I believe so," he said. "It was built into the masonry—my father's doing. The staff did not know of it, and Georgiana—*my* Georgiana—was also unaware of its existence."

She eyed the ramshackle building. "Do you think it safe to go in?"

"I doubt anyone lives there now, and it was solidly built. Even if it has been neglected for a year or so, the worst danger should be no more than dust and cobwebs."

"Perhaps I should go in with you, then."

"No." His voice was firm. "I need you to wait outside, to keep watch. I will go inside alone."

"But—"

"*Mrs. Smith*, you will wait under the lamppost. Keep your cloak drawn about your face. If anyone comes, or if I do not return in ten minutes, you must leave at once. Return to your aunt and uncle's."

She looked far from satisfied, but she nodded. With a wry smile, she said, "I will do my best to look disinterested, not anxious. No one suspects a woman who is bored."

Reluctantly, Darcy removed her hand from his arm and approached the entrance. The snow muffled his steps as he approached the chained gate. He pressed his gloved hand against the iron—cold, unyielding—and stared up at the house that had once been his sanctuary.

"Not anymore," he muttered, glaring down at the brass D on the knocker that was now tarnished green from neglect.

With a glance over his shoulder at Elizabeth's form beneath the lamplight, he removed his set of keys from his greatcoat pocket. Fortunately, it still fit the gate, which meant it would also be able to open the door. *At least Wickham's laziness is good for something.*

The gate creaked open with a protesting groan. Darcy stepped inside, boots crunching through the icy drift that had accumulated on the front steps. The massive door loomed dark above him, and though the key turned easily in the lock, it took all his strength to shove it open.

The hinges shrieked.

He winced and paused, listening—but no voice answered, no hurried footsteps came to investigate.

The house was still. Empty.

Darcy stepped into the entry hall and pulled the door closed behind him. The familiar scent of oak and lemon oil was gone. In its place was the sharp tang of mildew and cold stone. The air felt hollow, as though the very walls were holding their breath.

He did not light a lamp—there was no need. His steps were sure, his path etched in memory. The soles of his boots echoed too loudly on the marble floor.

To his left, the grand staircase curled upward into darkness. He looked away.

Georgiana had once tripped down those steps in slippers too large, laughing as the governess gave chase. He had caught her at the bottom. She had thrown her arms around his neck.

He turned his face toward the corridor and walked on.

Past the music room withs its door ajar, a sheet of music left yellowing on the floor.

Past the salon where his mother once read aloud, her voice lilting over a novel, her hands busy with embroidery. The fire had always been lit there. Always.

Now the hearth was dark. The ashes long cold.

He reached the study.

This door was closed, as it had always been in his father's time. Darcy placed his hand on the latch, hesitated—and pushed it open.

Dust motes swirled in the beam of gray light filtering through the cracks in the shuttered window. The old desk stood sentinel by the fireplace, its surface covered in a fine film of neglect. Books sagged on the shelves. A pair of gloves lay curled and brittle beside an empty brandy decanter.

He stepped inside, closing the door behind him.

His breath misted faintly in the air. He went to the far corner of the room, knelt, and reached behind the false panel of the wainscoting.

The latch stuck—swollen from cold or damp—but after a moment it gave way. The panel creaked open, revealing a narrow cavity.

There, nestled inside, was the old iron strongbox.

He drew it out with both hands and set it on the desk.

There was no lock. His father had always said that anyone who knew of its existence had no need to pick a lock—they were trustworthy.

Darcy opened the lid.

His heart clenched.

Inside were several small bundles of pound notes wrapped in oilskin, their edges slightly curled with time. Sovereigns glinted dully beneath a folded bank ledger. He exhaled sharply—it was more than he had hoped for. More than enough for the next steps.

But it was the envelope beneath the ledger that caught his eye.

For a moment, his breath caught.

It was familiar—his father's handwriting. Bold. Precise.

He reached for it—but as he turned it over, his stomach turned to ice.

The envelope was blank.

No name. No direction. No "To my son, Fitzwilliam."

It had once been there. He was certain of it. He had seen that envelope, years ago, after his father's passing. But now... nothing. Only silence and parchment.

He opened it with trembling hands.

Inside was a single sheet of paper. Also empty.

Nothing written. No signature. No parting wisdom.

No acknowledgment.

His throat burned.

He shoved the envelope aside and turned back to the bundles of money with renewed urgency, wrapping several in an oilcloth and slipping them into the inner pocket of his greatcoat. The sovereigns he transferred to his purse. When he rose, it was with clipped, purposeful movements.

He was not angry, exactly.

But he was no longer stunned.

He understood now.

This world had not only moved on without him—it had been rewritten. He had never inherited this house. He had never been born to receive that letter. His father had never known him.

He was a shadow in someone else's story.

Darcy closed the lid of the strongbox, returned it to the panel, and shut it with finality. A speck of dust fell from the ceiling.

He paused one last time, surveying the room. The air felt colder now. Still hollow.

No trace of him. Not even a ghost.

He turned on his heel and strode for the door, the weight of the stolen money heavy against his ribs. The familiar scent of dust and aged wood followed him like a ghost as he unlocked the latch and eased the door open—

A shriek split the air.

High. Frantic.

Elizabeth!

The sound pierced straight through him. His breath caught—then he was moving.

He flew down the front steps, boots sliding on ice-slick stone, his greatcoat billowing behind him. The iron gate clanged as he wrenched it open, the chain long-since rusted through.

She wasn't under the lamplight.

He whirled toward the alley beside the neighboring townhouse, then the opposite curb, panic flaring hot in his chest.

"Elizabeth!"

Another cry—this time muffled. Closer.

He ran.

~~*~*

Elizabeth drew her cloak tighter around herself and shifted her weight from one foot to the other as she watched Darcy disappear into the townhouse. The street was nearly empty, save for the occasional hackney rattling past or the distant clip of hooves on cobblestone.

It was not yet late, but the winter dusk had fallen quickly. The air carried that sharp, metallic chill that foretold snow, and each breath she exhaled hung before her like smoke.

She rubbed her gloved hands together and tried not to think of how alone she looked—one solitary figure standing beneath a lamppost outside a shuttered townhouse.

Everything about the day had been strange beyond comprehension. *No—the past two days.*

The magic—if she could call it that without being guilty of heresy—had turned her life upside down. Her family altered beyond recognition. Herself doubled. And at the center of it all, Fitzwilliam Darcy—who should have been the very last man in England she could ever trust—was now the only person she could.

Her lips curved faintly despite herself. *How absurd.*

Not two days ago on Christmas Eve, she had despised him. She had thought him proud, intolerant, cruelly judgmental. And yet—there had been no cruelty in the man who shared his blanket with her in that freezing lodge. There had been no arrogance in the man who trembled when he realized his sister might be lost to ruin.

There was something raw in him now. Stripped bare. Vulnerable.

And how well he had hidden it before!

She felt a pang of guilt as she thought of her own words—the furious declaration that she wished he had never been born. It had been said in anger, and now it had become true in some unfathomable way. *She* had set this madness in motion.

A wave of remorse washed through her, cold and heavy.

Footsteps echoed along the street.

Elizabeth turned her head slightly. A man was walking from the corner—well-dressed, his hat pulled low, his greatcoat swinging with each confident stride. A gentleman, by all appearances. He passed her at first without so much as a glance.

But then he stopped.

He turned.

His eyes caught hers under the lamplight, and something in his expression shifted—an assessing, interested look that made her stomach twist.

He retraced his steps. "Happy Christmas," he said, his tone too smooth. "Cold evening.

Elizabeth inclined her head politely but said nothing.

"You should not be standing out here alone," he went on. "Pretty little thing like you."

"I am waiting for someone," she replied, her voice firm.

"So I see." His gaze lingered on her cloak, her boots, her hands. "I would have thought you had found warmer company by now."

Her pulse quickened. "Sir, I think you mistake me."

"Oh, I do not think I do," he said, his smile tightening. "No lady of breeding would be out here unchaperoned after dark. So tell me the truth, sweetheart—how much?"

She recoiled, heat and fury flooding her face. "You are mistaken," she said again, more sharply. "I am not—"

His expression hardened. "Then what are you? A servant? A tradesman's girl playing coy?" He stepped closer, his breath thick with brandy. "You would not stand out here if you do not want attention. Perhaps you are waiting for it."

"Let me go," she said, but her voice trembled.

He caught her wrist. "No need to pretend."

"Unhand me!"

Her protest only made him sneer. "Hush. You will wake the neighborhood."

He tugged at her arm, dragging her a few paces toward the darker side of the street. Panic surged up her throat. She tried to wrench free, but his grip was iron.

"I said let me go!"

He jerked her harder. "You'll thank me once—"

She screamed.

The sound tore through the quiet street, echoing off the shuttered houses.

The man's hand clamped over her mouth, but she bit down—hard. He swore, stumbling back, and she twisted away, gasping for air as she let out another shriek.

Then another sound—a door flung open, bootsteps pounding against the stone.

"Elizabeth!"

Darcy's voice.

Relief surged through her chest, too great to speak. She turned toward the sound, and there was Darcy: coat unfastened, hair wind-tossed, face pale with fury.

Her assailant stepped back, eyeing the approaching figure warily.

Darcy was taller, broader, his stride full of purpose. The gentleman's narrowed gaze flicked over Darcy's shoulders, his fists, his eyes. He scowled.

"Tch," the man muttered, shaking out the hand she had bitten. "Keep your woman under better regulation."

Elizabeth stiffened in outrage, but the stranger had already turned and strode away, muttering to himself as he disappeared into the shadows.

Darcy reached her side. "Are you hurt?"

She shook her head. "No. No, I am only..." She pressed her trembling hands to her midsection. "Startled."

He exhaled, long and uneven, and then—without waiting—he gathered her into his arms.

She gasped softly against his shoulder, but did not resist. The warmth of him pressed through her cloak and into her skin, thawing the fear that had frozen her limbs. His gloved hand cradled the back of her head as though she were something precious.

"You are safe now," he murmured into her hair.

She shut her eyes for just a moment.

Then, lifting her face to his coat buttons, she asked, "Were you successful?"

He leaned back slightly, enough to meet her eyes. "Yes. The hiding place was untouched. I found more than enough to sustain us for…" he hesitated. "Enough for several weeks, if need be."

A breath of relief escaped her lips, and she sagged a little in his embrace. Her body still shivered despite the fire in her cheeks.

Darcy noticed at once. Without a word, he drew her even closer, wrapping his arms more snugly about her as though to ward off every remaining chill in the air—and in her heart.

"Come," he said softly, his voice low and steady at her ear. "Let us find a coaching inn for the night."

And she nodded. This time, she did not let go of his hand.

~~*~*

The sign above the coaching inn creaked on its rusted hinges as the wind pushed against it. "The Ox and Crown," it read—weatherworn but respectable, with a warm yellow glow in the windows and a promise of privacy in the narrow alley just off Fleet Street.

Darcy pushed open the door and held it for Elizabeth, whose cheeks were still blotched with cold and alarm. She stepped inside without a word.

The innkeeper looked up from behind the counter. "Evenin'. Happy Christmas. Room?"

"Happy Christmas. Yes." Darcy pulled out a few coins from the small purse he had tucked in his coat. "One room. For myself and my wife."

Elizabeth glanced at him sidelong, but said nothing as she removed her gloves. The innkeeper accepted the coins without scrutiny and nodded briskly.

"Hot water?" he asked, looking them up and down.

"If you please. We have been traveling for quite a while. And—" Darcy paused, then added, "—could you send a girl to the nearest clothier or dry goods shop, if there is one open on Boxing Day? We require a change of garments. Something plain and serviceable for a lady of my wife's size and—" he dared one glance at Elizabeth, "—excellent taste."

"And for you, sir?"

"Anything respectable. Coat, shirt, trousers."

The innkeeper called out for Meg, a gangly, red-cheeked girl who appeared from the back room. Darcy handed her several coins and gave instructions, watching as she nodded eagerly and disappeared into the night.

Their room was on the second floor. Small, but clean. A narrow bed with a quilt, a basin stand, a hearth already lit with a cheery fire. Elizabeth disappeared into the washroom with a murmur of thanks as a maid arrived bearing a steaming pitcher of water.

Darcy waited outside, standing in the corridor with one hand pressed against the wall. His body ached with fatigue, but his mind would not rest.

The scene at Darcy House haunted him.

That home—*his* home—had been like an extension of Pemberley. He had taken it for granted, walked its halls in boyhood, read by its library fire as a young man. And now it was gone. Sold off to satisfy another man's debts.

Wickham.

His jaw clenched. If Georgiana had truly married him—willingly or otherwise—then the implications went far beyond empty coffers. She would be vulnerable, isolated, perhaps even mistreated.

But what could he do? He was no one. Not in this world. He had no legal authority. No brotherly claim. He could not even gain entrance to his own house.

He thought of the safe in the study and the money he had collected from there. At least Wickham had not known of that. A small mercy.

Wickham.

But Georgiana…

He closed his eyes, his fist tightening against the wooden frame. Memories of Christmases in the past flooded through his mind.

Georgiana at seven years of age, her curls tied with a red ribbon as she shyly presented him with a drawing of a lopsided gingerbread figure she had made herself. She had clung to his waist when he praised it, her eyes bright with pride...

A bright Christmas afternoon, teaching her to skate on the frozen lake on the front lawn of Pemberley, her laughter ringing across the ice as he steadied her hands. She had declared it the happiest day of her life.

The year that Georgiana had insisted upon giving every servant a gift she had sewn herself. The stitches were crooked and the ribbons mismatched, yet the entire household had worn them proudly for her sake.

One Christmas morning when she had crept into his chamber before dawn, whispering that she feared Pemberley would forget about Christmas due to their father's illness. He had carried her down the stairs in his arms to show her the decorations.

The first Christmas after their father's death, when Georgiana had slipped her small hand into his and asked if they would still hang Father's favorite holly wreath. He had promised her they would, even though the sight of it nearly broke him.

But then the image of that man grabbing Elizabeth next appeared in his mind. The sound of her cry; he had never felt terror like he did in that moment. Not even when he had arrived at Ramsgate and saw Georgiana pale and trembling as Wickham fled.

But this time, he had nearly been too late. Not by hours, but by seconds.

He would never forget the look on Elizabeth's face when he reached her. Or the fury that had surged in his chest. Or the way she had trembled in his arms.

He exhaled through his nose and forced himself to calm.

They could not go to Derbyshire. Not yet.

Elizabeth's family mattered as much to her as Georgiana did to him. He saw it in every line of her face when she spoke of Jane. Of Mr. Bennet. Of her sorrow at being forgotten.

And Hertfordshire was on the way.

He would go with her. Help her discover what had changed. What could be set right. Perhaps, if they could understand the rules of this strange world—this twisted echo of their lives—they could find a way to reverse it.

Behind the door, he heard the sound of water pouring and fabric shifting.

Soon it would be his turn.

And after that... whatever waited next.

Chapter 9

Elizabeth stirred as pale morning light filtered through the thin curtains of the coaching inn. And just as the morning before, she awoke with a warm arm draped across her waist.

Darcy.

Sometime in the night, his arm had crept around her waist and held her gently as they both succumbed to exhaustion. Now his breathing was even and deep behind her, his presence a steady warmth that spread through her like the sunrise on Oakham Mount.

She lay still, eyes open, watching the light shift along the wall. It was not unpleasant. In truth, it was… comforting.

How strange.

Last night came back in fragments: washing with the hot water Darcy had ordered before she even asked, changing into the new shift he had sent the maid to fetch, and him slipping into the bed beside her—once again, at her insistence.

The chair near the fire would be just as uncomfortable as the floor, she reasoned.

Besides, she trusted him to be honorable. He had not once looked at her with anything but courtesy. Not even in their close quarters.

But the reality was she felt safest with him sleeping at her side. Her cheeks warmed slightly as she remembered him whisper, "Happy Christmas, Miss Elizabeth" before they both fell into a deep sleep.

This is probably the strangest Christmas ever… well, save the first one.

She bit her lip in consternation. She had been wrong about Darcy in Hertfordshire… so very wrong.

She had judged him. For his pride, his reserve, his bluntness. She had clung to that remark at the Meryton assembly—*not handsome enough to tempt me*—as if it were proof of his character. She had wielded it like a sword, never once questioning whether her own pride had made her blind.

Darcy had misconstrued Jane's motives, but she had done the same with regards to him. It was not so different, and she could not fault him for not realizing Jane was guarded when she did not see it in him.

She shifted slightly, trying not to wake him. But his arm withdrew at once, and a moment later he was sitting up behind her, clearing his throat softly.

"Good morning," he said, his voice a bit hoarse with sleep.

"Good morning," she replied, keeping her gaze on the sliver of light beneath the door.

He stood and moved to the basin, pouring water to wash his face. She remained in bed for another moment, uncertain how to broach what she now knew she must say.

They dressed in relative silence, both moving with the ease of routine and weariness. When they emerged downstairs, the innkeeper had already arranged for a light breakfast and summoned a coach. The fare was paid from Darcy's recovered funds, and the public coach—bound for Hertfordshire—was set to depart within the hour.

As they waited in the yard, watching their meager luggage loaded atop the coach, Elizabeth turned to him.

"Mr. Darcy."

He looked down at her, brows raised slightly.

She drew a breath. "I believe I owe you an apology."

His eyes searched hers. "For what?"

"For… my behavior. When you proposed." Her cheeks warmed, but she pressed on. "I was angry—righteously so, I thought—but I now see I was just as guilty of presumption as you."

His mouth opened slightly, but he said nothing.

"I judged you on very little, and I clung to that judgment far too long. I thought I knew your character, but I see now I did not. Not truly."

Still, he did not speak. His gaze was steady but unreadable.

"I am sorry," she said quietly. "Truly."

After a long pause, he replied in a voice just above a whisper. "You were not wrong in everything you said, Miss Bennet. But... thank you. It means more than you know."

She gave a small nod, unsure what else to say.

The coachman called for passengers to board, and they climbed in without another word. The other occupants precluded any further conversation, and that was just as well.

Elizabeth settled beside him on the bench, staring out at the rooftops as the carriage jolted into motion. The passing scenery caused her thoughts to shift from the man beside her to their destination.

Longbourn. What will we find there?

She had spent the last day imagining possibilities, but none settled easily. Why had she accepted Mr. Collins in this version of the world? What could have driven her to such a fate?

Only one answer made any sense: to save her family.

Has something happened to Papa?

The thought struck hard in her chest. If he had been ill—if he had *died*—the urgency for security would have been greater than she had ever known. And she, in her grief and desperation, might have bowed to it. If he were gone, there would have been no support, even if she had wished to refuse Mr. Collins.

She bit her lip. *Please*, she thought silently, *please let him be well.*

And Jane... where was Jane?

She had not seen her at Rosings, nor heard her name. She had searched the Gardiners' faces for some reference, some mention, but there had been nothing. No indication of a wedding. No talk of London visits. No sign of the gentle sister who had always steadied her.

Had Jane married? Perhaps to Bingley? Or did this world's Elizabeth marry Mr. Collins to protect Jane from a lifetime of misery? After all, if Darcy's absence somehow prevented Bingley from going to Netherfield, then Jane would have been the one being thrust at their cousin.

The carriage jolted over a stone in the road, and Elizabeth blinked against the window. The landscape outside was becoming more familiar, and she knew it would not be long now until she had answers.

She exhaled and drew her shawl more tightly around her shoulders.

Whatever they found at Longbourn… she would face it.

And she would not face it alone.

She turned her gaze to the man beside her. Silent. Steady. His presence—once a source of stress and frustration—was now the one constant in an unfamiliar world.

He must have sensed her watching, for he turned to meet her eyes. For a moment, neither spoke. The warmth in his gaze startled her—gentle, reassuring, a silent promise that whatever lay ahead, he would not leave her to face it alone.

Across from them, one of the other passengers—a man with thinning hair and a self-important air—cleared his throat and leaned slightly forward. "Forgive me, miss," he said pompously, "but your face seems familiar. I cannot help but think—have we met before? Perhaps in London?"

Elizabeth blinked. The cadence was uncanny. If she closed her eyes, it could have been Mr. Collins himself.

Before she could find a polite response, Darcy spoke with quiet firmness. "My wife's face is often remarked upon, sir. But I assure you, she is quite singular."

The man gave a startled blink, muttered something unintelligible, and sat back with a sniff. The woman next to him leaned forward slightly and said with a cheerful smile, "You two make such a handsome couple. Newlyweds?"

Elizabeth opened her mouth, unsure how to respond—but Darcy's voice came smoothly and without hesitation. "Yes. Just a few days ago."

"Oh, how lovely," the woman cooed. "Still in the honeymoon phase."

Elizabeth caught the twinkle in Darcy's eye, and before she could stop herself, she murmured beneath her breath, "Let us hope it lasts longer than the wedding night."

Darcy coughed once—violently—and turned to hide a grin.

She pressed her lips together, trying not to laugh. The other passengers took no notice. The coach rattled on toward Meryton.

But between Elizabeth and Darcy, the warmth lingered.

~~*~*

The village had not changed.

That was Darcy's first thought as the coach rolled into Meryton's square: the streets narrow and uneven, the buildings weathered but clean, the small shops clustered like hens in a roost. The late December wind stirred the last brown leaves in the gutters and carried the mingled scent of chimney smoke and yeast from the bakery.

And yet, everything had changed.

He descended first and turned to offer his hand to Elizabeth. She accepted with quiet poise, but as her boots touched the cobblestones, he saw the flicker of hesitation in her eyes. Her gaze moved slowly over the familiar lane, as though each building were a test of memory.

She smiled faintly at a woman crossing the square—a friendly, open expression that faltered when the woman looked her way with confusion, nodded politely, and moved on.

Darcy saw it clearly this time. The moment Elizabeth's heart squeezed behind her calm expression.

He fiercely wished to be able to do something, but what comfort could he offer when the universe itself had conspired to replace her with another?

They made their way to the inn Elizabeth suggested. A small sign above the tavern door creaked in the wind: *The Boar and Barrel*. Hardly elegant, but it would do. He requested a private room and signed the register as *Mr. and Mrs. William Smith*, handing over the money without flinching.

They climbed the stairs and set their modest belongings down. The bed was narrow but clean; the hearth cold, but well-stocked. It would do.

"It is too late for calls," Elizabeth murmured as she peeked out the room's single window. "They will be at dinner… or preparing for it."

Darcy nodded. "Tomorrow, then."

She turned from the window, her brows knit in thought. "But if we were to walk the village now… perhaps we might hear something."

A ghost of a smile tugged at his mouth. "You intend to eavesdrop?"

"I intend to shop," she said archly. "If the townspeople insist on speaking freely in front of paying customers, well—that is hardly our fault."

They bundled against the cold once more and stepped back into the narrow street, passing modest households already shuttered against the dusk. The bell over the door gave a cheerful jingle as they entered the milliner's shop. The scent of lavender and starch lingered in the air, and bolts of muslin and ribbon-lined shelves painted a far prettier picture than anything Darcy had seen in recent days.

Elizabeth moved with ease through the narrow aisles. This was her world—one he had once dismissed too quickly. He watched her trail her fingers across a roll of sky-blue ribbon, then turn to the older woman behind the counter with a warm smile.

"Good afternoon," she said. "I was last in Meryton some months ago, visiting family. I thought perhaps I might find a new bonnet ribbon while we are in town."

The shopkeeper—pleasant-faced, with a fraying lace cap and shrewd eyes—offered a polite smile. "You have the look of someone familiar," she said. "But I can't quite place you."

Elizabeth's smile flickered. "I am an… acquaintance of Elizabeth Bennet's."

"Ohhh," the woman said, brightening. "Longbourn—of course! Miss Elizabeth married the parson from Hunsford, did she not? Fine young woman. Bit quick with her tongue, but clever. You a cousin, then?"

Elizabeth paused, then dipped her head. "Something like that," she said softly. "I recently came from seeing her in Kent. I must say, it was… quite a shock for me."

"As it was for all of us." The woman lowered her voice with evident delight at the opportunity for gossip. "Most of us thought it would be the eldest to marry first—Miss Jane, you know. Such a beauty. And everyone saw how Mr. Bingley—he's the man who let Netherfield—how he looked at her."

Darcy kept his expression carefully neutral.

"But then he up and left!" the woman went on. "Day after the ball, just packed up and went, he and those sisters of his. Never said goodbye proper. Not a word to anyone, not even Miss Bennet. Left all the servants without a quarter's notice, too."

"I had not heard," Elizabeth said, her voice barely above a whisper. "And Miss Bennet?"

The woman's lips pinched in sympathy. "Heartbroken, poor girl. It was all over town. Faded to nothing, they said. Still hasn't quite recovered, though she puts on a brave face."

Darcy stared down at his gloves, his jaw tight.

"As for Miss Elizabeth—Mrs. Collins now—well, no one expected her to accept the man, especially seeing how she turned him down the first time."

"She did?" Elizabeth gasped.

The noise called the attention of two women stood near the back of the shop. "Talking about Miss Lizzy's wedding again, are you?" one of them asked.

"Yes, I was just telling the lass here that it came as a shock."

"*I* was not surprised," the other woman said. "It was a good match for the Bennets, and I told Sir William as much the other day. And he agreed, you know. Said it had all the hallmarks—solid connection, respectable living, and just enough beauty to keep a man pleased."

"Pray, excuse me."

111

Darcy watched in consternation as Elizabeth bolted from the store, causing the women to frown after her.

"Please forgive my wife," Darcy said. "She has not been feeling well lately."

To his surprise, the women exchanged knowing glances. "She will be right as rain in a few weeks," one of them said. "The first few months are always the most difficult."

Confused, Darcy merely thanked them and paid for ribbon before following Elizabeth out into the cold evening air.

He spotted her a few paces away, standing stiffly at the edge of the street near the lamplight, her back to the door. Her posture was straight, but her arms were crossed tightly over her chest, and even from behind, Darcy could see the tension radiating from her.

He approached quietly. "Elizabeth."

She did not turn. "I know it was not real," she said, her voice low and tight, "but to hear them speak of me that way. As though I were some… prize to be assessed for practicality. '*Just enough beauty to keep a man pleased.*'" Her hands clenched under her arms. "I would almost rather they had called me plain."

"I told them you were unwell, and they said you would be well in a few weeks." He hesitated. "I confess I do not understand why they said the first few months are always the most difficult."

She let out a sharp burst of laughter. "They must think that I am… increasing."

Darcy could feel heat flood his cheeks, and she laughed again before saying, "I must say, *that* is certainly not a rumor I have had to endure before."

He smiled faintly. "You bolted quite dramatically. I suspect they are crafting an entire backstory for us as we speak."

She gave a weak giggle, then quieted again, her gaze drifting down the lane toward the familiar curve that led to Longbourn.

He followed her line of sight and said gently, "It is late. Shall we return to the inn?"

"Perhaps we could visit the bookseller first?" she asked. "It would be nice to have something to do this evening. Mr. Reid keeps quite a large selection of chapbooks, in addition to the usual expensive tomes."

The idea of reading together in bed with a warm fire in the grate stirred something unexpectedly tender in Darcy's chest.

He coughed lightly, schooling his voice. "That sounds... pleasant."

She glanced at him sidelong, her brows arched in amusement. "Pleasant? From you, Mr. Darcy, that is practically a sonnet."

His lips twitched. "Then allow me to wax rhapsodic. Nothing would give me greater joy this evening than acquiring a worn pamphlet of overblown verse and sharing it aloud before a crackling fire."

Elizabeth gave a small, delighted laugh. "Careful, or I shall begin to think you enjoy poetry."

"I enjoy *you* enjoying it," he said, almost without thinking. She looked at him, her expression softening. For a long second, neither of them moved.

Then she nodded and turned down the lane. "Come, sir. I believe Mr. Reid closes at six."

Darcy followed, the chill evening suddenly not quite so cold. The air smelled faintly of chimney smoke and pine, and beside him walked a woman whose smile warmed more than any fire. A false world, perhaps—but one in which he was beginning to feel strangely alive.

As they entered the bookshop, the scent of old paper and pipe smoke wrapped around them like a memory. The shelves, overfull and lovingly disorganized, ran almost to the low ceiling beams.

Elizabeth smiled, her fingers trailing lightly across the spines of well-worn volumes as she wandered down a narrow aisle. Darcy followed her silently, his eyes scanning the titles: treatises on botany, volumes of poetry, tattered novels printed in small batches and passed from hand to hand.

Near the counter, two voices drifted to them—soft enough not to be intended for eavesdropping, but loud enough to carry nonetheless.

"My aunt is here," Elizabeth said in surprise.

Darcy looked over and saw Mrs. Philips at the counter, bundled in a thick shawl and chattering away with a man he could only surmise to be Mr. Reid.

Mrs. Philips gave a cackling laugh, the sound carrying across the nearly-empty shop. "She turned him down at first, you know. Poor Mr. Collins left the room with his tail tucked, according to Kitty and Lydia. But then her mother made her see reason."

Mr. Reid's voice was tight as he responded, "But you must admit, madam, that Mr. Collins is far below your niece with regards to intellect. If you ask me, I would have said she would marry someone with the sense to keep up. Someone who could match her wit."

Mrs. Philips let out a sigh. "She always was clever. Too clever, some would say. That tongue of hers—"

"She was a sharp one, Miss Lizzy. Came in every fortnight like clockwork, always asking after the latest essays or travelogues. Had more opinions on Cowper and Barrow than most educated gentlemen I have met."

Darcy felt a rush of something fierce and bright surge in his chest at that, but he made no sound.

"Better a foolish parson's wife than a spinster," retorted Mrs. Philips, shaking her head. "We cannot always marry poets and princes, Mr. Reid. And if Mr. Collins is a bit pompous, well, Lizzy will manage him. She always had a way with words. If you ask me, it is Jane you should feel sorry for, abandoned like that."

"Ah yes," Mr. Reid said with a note of distaste. "That Netherfield fellow… he was in here once or twice. Smiled a lot. Did not read."

"That is the one."

"Pity," Mr. Reid muttered. "Miss Bennet seemed quite taken with him. And he with her."

"Precisely! It was nearly a certainty, you know. All the town expected it. But there was no proposal—nothing but smiles and calls—and then he was gone. Gone!"

"Quite rude of him."

Mrs. Philips sighed. "We all thought so. The whole household packed up and left overnight. No farewells, no explanations—and none of the usual settlements. It was obvious then that Elizabeth needed to accept Mr. Collins after all, to secure the family's future."

There was a pause. Then Mr. Reid added more quietly, "I hope Miss Lizzy finds some peace. She deserved... well, something more."

Darcy could feel Elizabeth go very still at his side. He stepped slightly closer to her—not touching her, not yet—but just near enough that she could feel his warmth.

After a long moment, she turned back toward the shelves and selected a slim volume of Cowper's poetry.

When they approached the counter to make their purchase, Mr. Reid greeted them with a polite smile and made no mention of the conversation. Elizabeth asked after a pamphlet or two, her voice light. If he recognized her, he gave no sign.

When they stepped out into the cold again, Darcy reached gently for her hand to put on his arm and repeated his earlier question. "Shall we return to the inn?"

She nodded. "Yes. I think I have learned quite enough about my reputation for one evening."

As they walked back through the darkening village, Elizabeth asked softly, "Do you think she—my other self—was truly so different from me? Or do you think I could have become her... under the right circumstances?"

Darcy considered. "I think you are the same woman. But placed in a world with fewer choices."

She was quiet for several steps. "Perhaps. Or perhaps she was wiser than I. She accepted security, stability. And I—" she looked up at him, eyes troubled— "I rejected it all. Even you."

He stopped. "Elizabeth—"

She shook her head. "No. I do not regret refusing that proposal, Mr.... *William*. But I do regret... not seeing *you*. Not who you truly are, the man I have come to know the last few days."

Darcy could only look at her—this woman who had haunted his thoughts, challenged his pride, and now walked beside him in an impossible world.

As they reached the top of the stairs to the hall that led to their room, he reached for her hand. And this time, he felt her fingers curl into his without hesitation.

The touch was light, but it grounded him more surely than the floorboards beneath their feet.

Nothing more was said as they entered their room. The fire Darcy had arranged earlier glowed in the hearth, casting flickering shadows against the walls. Their meager supper of cheese and bread, the remnants of the hamper from Mrs. Gardiner, remained mostly untouched on the side table.

Elizabeth removed her bonnet slowly and crossed to the fire, her silhouette calm but reflective. Darcy lingered by the door, her earlier words still echoing in his mind.

I do regret... not seeing you.

He swallowed. "Elizabeth."

She turned, and the light danced in her eyes.

He took a slow step forward. "You see me now?"

She smiled, small but real. "Yes. I do."

A long silence fell between them; not heavy, but full of something unsaid.

Then she sat on the edge of the narrow bed and looked at the books they had purchased, the stray curl escaping her braid as she reached for the volume of poems.

"Do you think the other me ever reads to her husband?" she asked lightly.

Darcy gave a quiet laugh. "If she does, I suspect he does not understand half of it."

"Then perhaps he and I are well matched."

He crossed the room and sat beside her. "But not well suited."

She looked up at him.

"No," she said softly. "No, I cannot imagine finding contentment being married to *him*.

Time seemed to pause in that moment. Though no declaration was made nor kiss exchanged, there was an understanding that settled between them like the firelight.

They were no longer strangers in a strange world.

They were together in it.

Chapter 10

Elizabeth stirred beneath the heavy coverlet, warm and drowsy in the early light. The familiar scent of woodsmoke lingered from the hearth, and something firmer than a pillow cradled her head—something that rose and fell in a slow, steady rhythm.

Darcy.

As she had the prior two mornings, she awoke and realized their positions had shifted from polite distance to something far more intimate during the night. Her back was tucked snugly against his chest, one of his arms curled protectively around her waist, anchoring her in place. His breath stirred the hair near her temple. There was no awkwardness in it. Only warmth. Comfort. As though they had always begun the day this way.

She did not move, did not wish to disturb him. She simply lay still, letting her mind drift over the events of the past few days.

Was it truly only three days since he had come to the parsonage at Rosings? Since he had made his ill-fated proposal and she had torn his pride to shreds? Since the fae—or angel, or whatever it was—had granted that terrible wish and erased him from the world?

And yet here they were, side by side in a narrow bed in a modest inn in Meryton. A false husband and wife in a world that no longer remembered them.

It ought to have been awkward.

It was not.

It felt like a lifetime—and yet, impossibly, like no time at all.

She smiled faintly and closed her eyes again, imagining what it might be like to wake like this every day. In this bed. *With him.*

The thought surprised her—but it did not frighten her.

He is not the man I thought him, she admitted silently. *And perhaps I am no longer the woman I thought I was, either.*

Their breakfast was simple—the remnants of the hamper from the Gardiners—and the time soon arrived that they could leave for Longbourn. The weather was fair enough, with gray clouds and a brisk wind, though there was nothing in the skies that appeared threatening. Elizabeth donned her gloves as they stepped out from the Boar and Barrel, and she began walking down the familiar footpath towards Longbourn.

Darcy matched her stride without comment. They walked in companionable silence, the village slowly waking around them, chimneys puffing soft trails of smoke into the sky. A few shopkeepers swept their thresholds. A dog barked somewhere in the distance.

It is strange, Elizabeth thought, *how natural it feels to walk beside him now. How easy.*

She glanced up once to find him watching her from the corner of his eye, and they both smiled.

"I never imagined," she said softly, "that I would one day return to Longbourn in the company of Mr. Fitzwilliam Darcy."

His mouth twitched. "Neither did I. Let us hope your family is not too shocked by your presence—or mine."

She smiled. "As friends of the new Mrs. Collins paying their respects, I daresay we will be invited to tea."

But as they passed the hedgerow near Lucas Lodge, the wind picked up. A low rumble of thunder growled in the distance, and within moments the sky broke open.

It was not a gentle rain, but a deluge—soaking and wild, pouring down in sheets that blurred the path and plastered Elizabeth's cloak to her frame. She squealed and ducked her head, gripping the sides of her cloak. Darcy immediately shrugged out of his greatcoat and held it above them both, tugging her closer beneath its span as they ran.

They dashed toward the familiar iron gate of Longbourn, her half-laughing gasps rising over the roar of the rain. Her slippers slipped on the muddy path, and Darcy's arm caught her around the waist, steadying her.

"There!" she cried, pointing to the small outbuilding that sheltered the garden tools. He nodded, and they ducked beneath its shallow overhang, breathless and dripping.

Elizabeth pressed a hand to her bonnet, which had gone thoroughly askew, and looked up at him.

He was soaked. Rain streaked through his hair, water ran down the side of his jaw, and his cravat was utterly ruined. For a moment, they simply stood there, catching their breath, rain pounding the thatched roof just inches above their heads. Their hands still clasped.

But he was grinning.

So was she.

"I believe," she said, breath hitching, "that your greatcoat is no longer the fashionable item it once was."

"My valet will quit in protest," he teased. "That is, if I still employed one. Alas, *Mr. Smith* has not the funds nor the station to be a man of leisure."

They stood beneath the arch, the rain slapping down just beyond their shelter, and for a moment neither moved. As she continued looking up at him, she noticed once again just how tall he really was. The amusement on his face revealed a dimple in his cheek that she had never noticed before.

His eyes held hers, dark and full of something that made her breath catch in a different way. His hand was still at her waist. Her fingers still clutched his coat.

He was very close. Close enough that she could see the raindrops on his lashes. Close enough that she could feel the heat of his breath, warming the space between them.

Her heart beat strangely in her chest—too fast, too full.

His eyes flicked to her lips, which parted instinctively. She did not move.

He bent slightly, as if—

"Hoy there!"

The voice startled them both. Elizabeth jumped and turned.

Thomas, the gardener, stood a few paces off beneath his own caped cloak, holding a sack of potatoes and watching them with mild interest. His brows lifted high on his head, but he said nothing.

Elizabeth coughed, stepping hastily back from Darcy's embrace.

"Can I help you, ma'am?" Thomas asked.

"We… were caught in the rain," she said, unnecessarily. "We—we are here to call on the Bennets."

He grunted and pointed them toward the front. "Best use the main door. Mrs. Hill will see you in."

"Thank you," Darcy said with his usual gravity, though his ears were visibly pink.

They followed the path around to the front door, Elizabeth's heart thudding far too quickly for the chill. She tried to smooth her skirts and pin her bonnet more securely, but it was a losing battle. She looked like a drowned cat, and their wet boots squelched with ever step.

Darcy rapped smartly on the door. Within a moment, the bolts turned and the door cracked open to reveal Mrs. Hill, the woman who functioned as both housekeeper and lady's maid. She looked them both up and down with a faint pursing of her lips.

"I… apologize for the intrusion," Elizabeth began with as much poise as she could muster. "We are friends of the new Mrs. Collins, traveling north. She suggested we might pay our respects at Longbourn if our journey allowed."

The housekeeper's face softened at once. "Oh, bless you. Of course, of course. You poor things, caught in that mess." She stepped aside and ushered them in. "You'll want towels and the fire, no doubt. I'll see to it. Come in, come in."

Elizabeth crossed the threshold with a strange twisting in her chest, blinking at the familiar surroundings—so unchanged, and yet it felt as if years had passed since she last crossed the threshold.

She was home—and yet not home.

Darcy's shoulder brushed Elizabeth's as he stepped in behind her, somehow giving him strength. From down the hall, he heard footsteps and the unmistakable sound of Mrs. Bennet approaching.

"Oh! Oh, my dear heavens!"

Darcy turned just in time to see the woman sweep into the entryway, all flustered affection and fluttering hands. Mrs. Bennet stopped short at the sight of them, her eyes widening at their soaked garments and dripping hair.

"You poor souls! You are drenched! Hill, where are the towels? Fetch them at once! Come—come in, come in—don't stand there puddling on the floor!"

The years melted away in an instant. Darcy felt as though he was a child again, being fussed over after falling in the stream next to the dairy at Pemberley. But this was not his mother, and he was receiving warmth not as a child, but as a guest.

Still, the embrace of Mrs. Bennet's concern was oddly comforting, even in its unfamiliarity.

"We are very sorry to trouble you, madam," Elizabeth said, curtsying. "I am—my name is Beth Smith, and this is my husband, Mr. William Smith. We are new friends of your daughter, Elizabeth. Mrs. Collins told us we must call if our travels brought us through Hertfordshire."

Mrs. Bennet's face transformed from fussing to beaming. "Well! How very thoughtful of her. Oh, she is quite the mistress now, our Lizzy—Mrs. Collins, I mean," she added with a fond laugh. "I always said she would do well in marriage. So clever! Such a sensible girl."

Darcy had prepared himself for shrill nerves and empty flattery, not a flurry of towels and genuine welcome. He gave a polite bow in acknowledgment of the introduction.

Mrs. Bennet took in his height, his broad shoulders, and his noble bearing with increasing delight. He felt his cheeks begin to warm slightly at her frank appraisal.

"Well, I must say, you are a fine-looking pair! Quite fine, indeed." She did not wait for a response. "You must come sit by the fire—Hill, the parlor, and for mercy's sake, the hearth! Jane! Jane, where are you? Come help me see to our guests!"

"I assure you, madam," he said, "we do not mean to disturb your household, especially the day after Boxing Day." He looked around at the housekeeper, who was efficiently directing a maid to stoke up the fire.

"Oh, nonsense!" Mrs. Bennet flapped a hand. "No trouble at all. As my brother did not come for Christmas this year, we gave the servants yesterday off instead of today. And a good thing, too! My nerves cannot bear to see good people soaked through! You must dry yourselves and take something hot. Hill, tea, if you please, and perhaps that broth Cook had left over."

Darcy found himself steered into the sitting room, familiar to him from his prior calls, and yet now strange in being received with such warmth. Elizabeth took a plain wooden chair nearest the hearth. Darcy remained standing her side until Mrs. Bennet insisted he sit as well.

"Never mind the upholstery, dear. I daresay it could use a cleaning anyway."

He had once dismissed her as frivolous and fawning—yet she treated him now with the same unreserved kindness she had once shown Bingley, and without any hope of advantage.

It was humbling.

If a sodden stranger arrived at Pemberley—especially on Boxing Day, of all days—claiming acquaintance with Georgiana, he might offer them dry garments. But they would be shown to the kitchens, not his drawing room.

"Oh, but what dreadful weather," Mrs. Bennet continued without pausing for breath. "Hill says it came on quite sudden—did you get caught very far down the lane?"

"We had just passed Lucas Lodge," Elizabeth replied, accepting a towel and blotting her face. "It struck before we could reach shelter."

Mrs. Bennet tsked and bustled to adjust the fire screen. "Well, I am sure you must be frozen. Poor lambs. So, tell me—how did you meet Mrs. Collins?"

"I was visiting Kent recently, where I encountered Mr. Smith." Elizabeth gave Darcy a fond smile, and he nearly forgot it was all a pretense. "One thing led to another, and... well, here we are, newly married as well."

"Oh, that is wonderful! And how is my daughter? I imagine she has taken to her duties quite well. She always was a bright one."

Darcy's heart wrenched as he saw the flash of pain in Elizabeth's eyes. "Yes," she managed to say. Darcy could hear the slight hitch in her voice. "Indeed. She... seems to have settled in."

"Such a good match," Mrs. Bennet said, settling herself on the edge of the settee with the air of one entirely satisfied with her own foresight. "So very suitable. Of course, we always thought the eldest would marry first—our Jane is such a beauty—but it was not to be."

Darcy watched as Elizabeth arched a brow over a fine eye. "No?"

Mrs. Bennet's face pinched ever so slightly. "Mr. Bingley—he is the gentleman who let Netherfield last autumn—he left rather suddenly, you see. Quite shocking. Everyone thought... well..." She fluttered her fingers vaguely. "But no engagement was ever announced. And a young lady must be sensible, must she not?"

She smoothed her skirts. "Mr. Collins had been disappointed, of course, when Lizzy first refused him—silly girl! But then when he turned his sights towards my Jane—who was heartbroken and pining after Mr. Bingley—Elizabeth changed her mind. I daresay the matter was settled quite practically."

Darcy gripped his teacup, fighting to keep his expression neutral. *So even with my absence, Mr. Bingley still abandoned Miss Bennet and Netherfield. It was not entirely my fault.*

"Jane," Mrs. Bennet continued, "has not been quite herself since. She rarely goes out. But she is the gentlest creature—she bears things with such grace." Her voice dropped. "Though I do worry. She grows thinner by the day."

Elizabeth frowned in concern at her mother, and—for a moment—Darcy wished he could kiss her cares away. He was also surprised by Mrs. Bennet's sincerity. There was no lamenting the loss of Bingley's fortune, but rather genuine concern over her daughter's emotions.

He had believed her to be coarse, and often she was—but in warmth, in welcome, she far outshone many women of higher rank.

Certainly more than Lady Catherine ever has.

"Ah! Here she is now. Jane, darling! Where have you been?"

Darcy stood before he realized what he was doing, and then Elizabeth's sister entered the room.

Jane looked very much the same—elegant, fair, her features lovely as ever. But Darcy saw the difference at once. Her smile, though immediate, did not reach her eyes. Her figure, though graceful, seemed frailer. And there was something heavy in her expression—something quiet and pained.

Elizabeth shifted, and he could tell that she longed to run to her, to embrace her and hold fast and tell her everything would be well. *That is how it will feel for me with Georgiana, I imagine.*

Instead, Darcy said with careful gentility, "It is a pleasure to meet you. Mrs. Collins spoke so fondly of her sister."

Jane glanced at her mother, then back at Elizabeth. "You are... friends of Lizzy's? You seem familiar somehow, but I am not certain..." Her voice trailed off.

Darcy felt the ground shift slightly beneath his feet as Elizabeth replied, "Yes, I met her when she came to the Hunsford parish."

Bowing, Darcy added, "We were passing through and wished to pay our respects. Your mother has been most kind."

"Did you, perhaps, bring a letter from her? Correspondence of any kind?"

Unprepared for this question, Elizabeth looked at Darcy, who shook his head. "No, I am afraid our schedules did not allow time for that. We were not even sure if we would come here as we journeyed. I am taking my wife north to Derbyshire to meet my sister."

"Oh, I see."

Darcy had not thought it possible for Jane to appear more subdued, but the light in her eyes dimmed further still. The silence that followed stretched a beat too long before Mrs. Bennet clapped her hands. "Well! I daresay you have had enough talk—come, let us see if Cook can spare a few biscuits for our guests. And perhaps a dry gown for Mrs. Smith. I daresay you are of a size with Lizzy. Jane, could you fetch one from your room?"

That Mrs. Bennet's cheer extended so easily to a married couple of modest name and damp boots made him feel a fool for the pride he had once placed in lineage alone. He had always believed himself generous. Civil.

But perhaps his civility had been more arrogance than kindness.

Jane hesitated, her gaze lingering on Elizabeth. But then she turned obediently and went upstairs. Mrs. Bennet frowned at Darcy, looking him up and down. "I would offer you something of my husband's to wear, sir, but I am afraid that you are much taller than him."

"That is… very generous of you, madam, I thank you for the offer, but I am quite alright."

"Perhaps one of the manservants has something… I will have Hill ask."

Before Darcy could protest, Mrs. Bennet bustled from the room. As the door shut behind them, Elizabeth sank slowly back into her chair, heart pounding.

"There is something very wrong with Jane," she whispered to him.

~~*~*

Every part of Elizabeth's body thrummed with anxiety. There was something wrong—she knew it with certainty. Jane's smile had been too thin, her voice too still. Whatever had happened, it weighed heavily on her sister's heart, and Elizabeth's own heart ached with the need to understand it, to fix it.

Before she could decide what to do, however, Jane reappeared in the doorway.

"If you will come with me," she said softly, "you can change in the guest chamber."

Elizabeth rose at once. "Thank you."

Darcy inclined his head. "I shall remain here until your return."

She followed Jane up the familiar staircase, her hand brushing the smooth wood of the banister she had once slid down as a girl. Everything looked the same—the gilt-framed landscapes, the threadbare runner, even the faint creak on the third stair—but the warmth of home felt distant, like something glimpsed through glass.

Jane led her to the guest room at the end of the hall. The fire had been recently stoked, the curtains drawn against the storm's gray light. As soon as the door shut behind them, Elizabeth turned.

Her sister's composure faltered the moment they were alone. The gown—which Elizabeth recognized as one of her own—trembled slightly in Jane's hands. Elizabeth took it from her sister and set it on the bed. Jane began to excuse herself, but Elizabeth asked her to remain and help her with the buttons in the back.

"Now, Jane," Elizabeth said gently as the final button was secure, "your sister has confided much in me about you."

Jane froze. Her eyes widened in sudden panic.

Elizabeth blinked, confused by the reaction. She softened her voice still further. "I can tell you are troubled. Please, will you not tell me for yourself? It did your sister much good to confide in me, and I think you will find the same."

Jane's throat worked soundlessly. Then, with a small, broken sound, she set the gown on the bed and pressed her hands to her face.

"Jane!" Elizabeth exclaimed, rushing forward, but her sister was already shaking with sobs—quiet at first, then deeper, the kind that came from long restraint.

"I am so ashamed," Jane choked. "So very ashamed. I did not mean for any of it—oh, my dear Lizzy. My poor, dear sister. I never wished it to end this way."

Elizabeth knelt beside her, though her heart was pounding. "End what way? Dearest, you are trembling. Tell me—whatever it is, you must tell me. It will ease your heart to speak of it."

Jane drew a ragged breath, lowering her hands at last. Her face was blotched and wet, her blue eyes shining with anguish.

"I cannot bear it any longer," she whispered. "I feel so guilty, just so guilty for everything that has happened to her. To Elizabeth. She should never have had to marry him. It was my fault. All my fault."

Elizabeth hesitated, her pulse roaring in her ears. "What do you mean, your fault?"

Jane swallowed hard, tears slipping silently down her cheeks. Her voice was barely audible.

"I am with child."

Chapter 11

Elizabeth's breath caught. For a long, stunned moment, she could not speak—could not move.

Jane bowed her head into her hands once more, and the room filled with the quiet, wrenching sound of her weeping.

Fortunately, this allowed Elizabeth time to gather her composure and remember that she was supposedly not hearing this for the first time. She moved up to sit near Jane on the bed and began to rub her back soothingly.

"It is alright," she said hoarsely. "You are not alone."

Jane shook her head miserably. "You do not understand. You *cannot* understand."

"Tell me, then."

"It began at Netherfield," Jane whispered at last, her voice thick with shame. "After I fell ill and remained to recover. He was so attentive… so kind. Not just in company, but in private. And after a few days, he… he began to speak of marriage. Not formally, you see, but in the gentlest ways… of gardens and furniture and London seasons."

Elizabeth's heart ached. So much like the man she had seen with her own eyes—charming, soft-spoken, sincere in all appearances. A man who once needed Darcy to steady him toward honor.

"I believed him," Jane went on, her voice breaking. "I *wanted* to believe him. And one evening… he came to my room. To check on me, he said."

Elizabeth looked down, trying to maintain the calm of someone who already knew this—but it was harder than she expected. Her hands clenched in her skirts.

"It was foolish. I know it now. I should not have let him in. But at the time—it felt like a promise. A future. I did not even realize what was happening until it was over."

Blushing slightly, Elizabeth did her best to remember that in this world, she was a married woman and not an innocent maiden.

"I had no reason to think—" Jane's breath hitched. "Two weeks later, I began to feel ill again. My courses did not come. I thought it might be stress, or lingering effects of my cold. But then the ball came, and I could feel it—something was *changing*. I told him that night. I pulled him aside and said the words as quietly as I could."

Elizabeth's eyes stung.

"He looked... surprised. Frightened. Almost angry. He said we would speak more the next day. But there *was* no next day. He was gone. The whole house was gone. No word. No letter. Nothing."

Clenching her fists, Elizabeth seethed with anger. *How dare he! How could he trifle with my sister and disappear without so much as a word?*

"And then," Jane whispered, "I heard that Lizzy had rejected Mr. Collins. And I thought, if I married him, it would protect us. My shame could be hidden under the guise of a marriage. But then—" She gave a shaky breath. "Lizzy convinced me otherwise."

"Why?" Elizabeth asked, even though she already knew.

"Because she thought Mr. Bingley would return." Jane's voice cracked. "She... she thought if I got engaged to Mr. Collins, I would be trapped—and if Mr. Bingley returned, it would be too late. The worst thing, she said, would be for Mr. Bingley to come back to Netherfield and me be unable to accept him."

"So she sacrificed herself."

Jane gave a miserable nod. "She was so certain, and I believed her. I *wanted* to believe her. So, I let her marry him, let her sacrifice herself. She told Mr. Collins she had changed her mind."

"And you agreed to this."

Jane looked up at Elizabeth with eyes full of shame. "I did not have the heart to stop her. I did not truly believe Mr. Bingley would return, but I desperately *wanted* it to be true. He promised to be back by Christmas, but the day after the wedding, I received a letter from Caroline Bingley."

"Oh? What did she have to say?"

"She said that they were quite happy in London, and she listed all of the different parties and events they had planned for the holidays."

"So, he is not returning." Elizabeth bit her lip to keep from venting her spleen about faithless lovers and their pernicious sisters. "What is the plan now?"

"Lizzy said for me to go to the Gardiners in a few months. She said she could convince Mr. Collins to do the lying in at their home instead of Hunsford, and she would claim my child as her own. But now she is gone. Her life is ruined, and all because of my selfishness, my weakness."

Elizabeth drew in a long breath and placed her hand gently over her sister's. "You were not weak," she said. "You were frightened. And you were trying to do what you thought was best."

"I feel so... so *dirty*," Jane whispered. "And Lizzy—she walks through the house with Mr. Collins on her arm, and Mama praises her for being dutiful, and all the while she is covering for *me*. She will never have a chance to find happiness or love."

"She loves you," Elizabeth said, her voice thick.

"I do not deserve it," Jane whispered. "I have ruined her life."

Elizabeth swallowed against the knot in her throat. "None of this is about what we deserve. It is about what we do next."

Jane let out a sob, and Elizabeth wrapped her arms around her and held her close. They stayed like that for several moments, silent except for the soft crackle of the fire and the sound of Jane's quiet, broken breathing.

When Elizabeth finally spoke, her voice was steady again. "Whatever happens next, you will not face it alone."

Jane only nodded, pressing her face into Elizabeth's shoulder.

Outside, footsteps passed faintly in the corridor. The house carried on as if nothing had changed.

But Elizabeth knew, without doubt, everything had.

~~*~*

A few minutes after Elizabeth disappeared with Jane, the housekeeper came to the parlor where Darcy waited. He gratefully accepted the servant's garments—a modest but clean pair of trousers and a soft linen shirt, clearly belonging to one of Longbourn's taller footmen. His own clothes were handed off to a scullery maid, who promised they would be dried by the kitchen fire. As he changed in a small side room off the back hall, he was thankful for the relief from damp fabric clinging coldly to his skin.

The fit was not perfect—he lacked a cravat, and the waistcoat hung awkwardly from his shoulders—but it was warm and dry, and he reminded himself that vanity had no place in his current position. He was not Mr. Darcy of Pemberley, heir to generations of wealth and pride. He was William Smith, traveler, friend to a country parson's wife.

When he returned to the front parlor, he found the fire now blazing high and a fresh pot of tea laid out on a tray. A moment later, Mrs. Bennet herself bustled in, cheeks pink with effort and satisfaction.

"There now! Much better, sir, you must feel more like yourself." She plumped a cushion beside him and poured him a cup of tea without waiting to be asked. "It is a pity we hadn't a waistcoat that fit you better, but you wear it well, if I may say so."

Darcy inclined his head. "You are very kind, madam. I am indebted to you for your generosity."

"Nonsense. I would do no less for any friend of Lizzy's." Her voice warmed on her daughter's name, and Darcy felt a pang—of gratitude, of shame. He had once dismissed this woman as foolish, loud, and grasping. She was still all of those things—but she had also offered him her fire, her food, her finest guest chair, and even the use of her household's wardrobe, without hesitation.

The front door creaked open. Voices rang out.

"Oh, Mama, it *poured*! Aunt Philips gave us each a handkerchief to wear like a cap!"

"And Lydia danced in the puddles—Mama, you should have seen it."

The door burst open and three young women—drenched and full of noise—tumbled into the hall. Mary, Kitty, and Lydia. Darcy had seen them before, of course, in another life. But never quite like this.

"Oh!" Lydia exclaimed, skidding to a halt as she caught sight of him. "Who is *that*?"

"Lydia!" Mary hissed, but it was too late.

Mrs. Bennet smiled proudly. "This is Mr. William Smith, a friend of Lizzy's. He and his wife have come all the way from Kent."

Upon hearing that the handsome stranger was married, the younger two girls lost all interest in him entirely and turned their attention back to their mother.

"Oh, Mama, you simply *must* come to Meryton tomorrow," Lydia said, shaking out her damp shawl. "Captain Carter has grown a most dashing mustache, and everyone says it makes him look positively foreign."

"Lieutenant Denny has a new pair of boots," Kitty added. "They were a Christmas present from his mother. And there is a new officer—Lieutenant Saunderson. He is *very* tall. Taller even than—" She glanced back at Darcy, then lost her train of thought.

Lydia giggled. "Denny bowed to *me* first, even though Mary King was *clearly* angling for it."

Darcy said nothing, but he listened closely, brow faintly furrowed. There was no mention of Wickham, and yet the girls' breathless delight in the society of officers—young men they scarcely knew—was enough to concern him.

Their enthusiasm was not malicious, but it was naive. Reckless. They tossed around names and flirtations as if they were lace ribbons or sweets. He wondered how many of those men—Captain Carter, Lieutenant Denny, and this new Saunderson—had ambitions no greater than cards, drink, and dalliances with foolish country girls.

Then, quite suddenly, Lydia spun toward him and asked abruptly, "Are *you* an officer?"

Darcy blinked, caught off guard. "No, I am not."

"Shame," Kitty muttered, flopping back into her chair. "You would look quite fetching in a red coat."

He felt the tips of his ears begin to burn. "I confess," Darcy replied, inspiration sparking, "that I am rather glad I never joined the army."

That got their attention. Kitty leaned forward. "Why?"

Darcy folded his hands together, schooling his tone into that of idle conversation. "Because most officers, despite the polish of their uniforms, are not sons of gentlemen. They are often laborers or servants, hired by those of higher birth to fill the ranks. Men with little means and less conscience."

Mary looked up from her copy of what appeared to be *Fordyce's Sermons*, nodded vigorously. "I have tried to tell them as much."

Darcy continued, his voice even. "They often fall into gaming and debts. Some take liberties with women's reputations. And the pay is meager—fifty to a hundred pounds a year, before expenses. Most cannot afford a servant, let alone proper housing. And when children come…" He looked toward the window as if considering. "There is rarely enough to go around."

Kitty and Lydia both looked stricken. "Fifty pounds?" Kitty whispered. "That is less than my pin money!"

Darcy nodded solemnly. "Your cousin, Mr. Collins, has a living worth three hundred pounds a year. That does not include the patroness' generosity, nor the garden and poultry he might sell for profit."

Mary cleared her throat. "And surely a man of God is more admirable than a man of war. The former serves the soul, while the latter only follows destruction."

"Quite so," Darcy said, bowing slightly.

The younger girls were quiet after that.

A creak came from the hall, and Mr. Bennet's dry voice rang out. "Bravo, sir. You have silenced my girls on the subject of officers more thoroughly than anyone else could have done. And I do not even know your name."

Mrs. Bennet turned, beaming. "Mr. Bennet, this is Mr. and Mrs. Smith. They are friends of Lizzy's!"

Mr. Bennet's gaze settled on Darcy. His eyes twinkled with mild interest—but at the mention of Lizzy, something behind them dimmed. "Indeed? A friend of Lizzy's," he repeated softly.

Before Darcy could respond, the door opened again. Jane entered, trailed by Elizabeth.

The sight of Elizabeth, her hair still slightly damp, her expression sober but composed, settled something in him. She looked toward him, and he read the message in her eyes: *Later*.

Mrs. Bennet clapped her hands. "Your clothes are still damp, I am afraid. Hill says the clothes will take another hour at least to finish drying by the fire. Why not stay to dinner?"

Darcy hesitated. "We are very grateful, madam, but we had not intended—"

"Oh, nonsense!" she cried. "You will catch your deaths walking back after dark, especially on unfamiliar roads. The carriage can take you. You must stay. It is only mutton, but it is hearty."

Mr. Bennet nodded from the hearth. "The lady has made up her mind, Mr. Smith. You would do well to yield."

Darcy glanced at Elizabeth, who gave a slight nod. "Then we thank you most sincerely."

After some further bustling and the announcement that dinner would be served shortly, Darcy turned to Elizabeth. "May I take you for a short walk in the garden? We have sat far too long in coaches of late."

Kitty let out a laugh. "Then you truly are Lizzy's friends! She walks every day, even when it snows."

Mrs. Bennet waved them off with a smile. "Mind you do not track mud when you return—and do not get wet again!"

The rain had passed, leaving behind a sky of silver clouds and damp air that smelled of moist earth and fallen leaves. Darcy offered Elizabeth his arm, and she took it without hesitation.

They passed through the garden gate and walked in silence down the damp stone path.

When they were far enough from the windows, Elizabeth said quietly, "Jane is with child."

Darcy stopped short.

"It happened at Netherfield. He—Bingley—he seduced her. Promised marriage. And when she told him she was expecting… he left."

A cold fury settled over Darcy's shoulders. "I never saw any sign that he was a rake, never suspected that he would trifle with an innocent maiden. If I had known, I would have never befriended him. How could he—"

"You *prevented* him from acting on his weaker impulses," she said softly. "I imagine your friendship steadied him. But without you… he strayed."

Darcy's jaw clenched. "Then I am to blame for both. For misjudging your sister—and for this terrible wish, causing me to fail in guiding my friend."

"No," Elizabeth said firmly. "You are not to blame. We each have responsibility for own actions, even Jane."

"What will they do now?" he asked.

"When I—the other me—rejected Mr. Collins, Jane considered accepting him. But when I—that is, the *other* me—bother! This is all quite confusing."

"I think I can follow," Darcy said with a cheeky smile, attempting to lighten her mood. "I *do* have more understanding than your husband, *Mrs. Collins...*"

She sniffed in mock affront, then sobered and continued, saying, "Well, when *I* discovered Jane's plan and its cause, I still thought Mr. Bingley might return, and I did not wish for Jane to be trapped. So, I accepted Mr. Collins, in order to give Jane time to wait for her beau, and I would offer a chance for escape if he did not come back."

"And he has not."

Elizabeth shook her head. "No. The plan is for Jane to go to the Gardiners, and the other me will join her there and pass the child off as her own."

There were tears in Elizabeth's eyes as she spoke the last. Without thinking, Darcy reached for her hand and pulled her into his arms. He did not speak.

He did not need to.

He knew her heartbreak, for it mirrored his own over Georgiana's marriage to Wickham.

"Would you like to remain?" he asked. "To assist your sister? I can continue to Pemberley on my own."

As soon as the words left his mouth, he wished he could snatch them back. His heart froze at the very idea of being parted from her.

Even now—just the thought of journeying to Derbyshire without her by his side, without her steady voice and fierce gaze—left him feeling unmoored.

But he would never ask her to choose between him and her sister.

Not when he knew what it was to fear for someone you loved.

Elizabeth was looking at him, her eyes glimmering with unshed tears. He did not want to go without her.

He wanted her to say no.

To say she would come with him.

To say that they would face whatever came next—together.

But before either of them could speak further, the door to the house creaked open.

"Dinner is served!" came the call, cheerful and oblivious.

Elizabeth turned her head toward the voice, then looked back at Darcy. "We can speak more on the subject later," he whispered in her ear, leaning down.

She gave him a small nod.

Wordlessly, he offered his arm. She took it, and together, they stepped back inside.

~~*~*

The dining room at Longbourn was just as she remembered it—dimly lit with tall tapers, the scent of roasting meat and rosemary thick in the air. A steaming joint of mutton rested proudly at the center of the table, flanked by potatoes, stewed apples, and a loaf of brown bread. It was modest fare, but hearty, and to Elizabeth it felt achingly familiar.

They took their places, and Elizabeth found herself seated across from Darcy. Mr. Bennet took his customary chair at the head of the table, while Mrs. Bennet presided opposite him, fluttering napkins and directing Hill with exaggerated graciousness. Jane sat beside her mother, a pale shadow of the sister Elizabeth remembered, though she still offered soft encouragements to Kitty and Lydia as they chattered on.

And Darcy—dear heaven, Darcy—was... *smiling*.

Not that stiff, barely-there smile he used when nodding at society acquaintances, but a real, unguarded expression of amusement. His eyes sparkled as he listened to Kitty's retelling of a spoiled pudding at Aunt Philips's, and he even let out a short laugh when Mr. Bennet quipped about a neighbor's prize pig being smarter than the man who owned it.

Elizabeth could only stare. She had never seen him like this. Not at Rosings. Not even at Netherfield.

He was at ease. Relaxed. Human.

And her heart—already too full from the day's revelations—twisted painfully.

If things had been different—if this were the true world, and they had come together not through magic or misfortune, but choice and affection—would he have sat here beside her, proud and certain, as her betrothed?

Would she have watched him tease Lydia with dry wit and exchange thoughtful glances with her father across the table?

Could this have been their future?

The ache of it almost made her miss her own laugh when he raised a brow and offered her the last bit of stewed apple with a silent *"Shall I?"* She nodded and smiled, and he passed it to her with a faint smirk, as though they had been married ten years and this was merely another evening meal in a life shared.

But it was not. None of it was real. And the laughter around the table, though genuine, could not erase the truth: her family did not know her.

As Jane quietly declined another helping and looked down at her plate, Elizabeth's thoughts turned once more to her sister. Should she remain? Should she stay behind and help Jane bear this burden? There was a strong sense of duty in her heart—after all, what kind of sister would abandon her in such a moment?

And yet...

The very idea filled her with dread.

Staying would mean accepting this new reality. Settling into it. Making it her own.

And she could not—*would not*—do that.

To stay would be to surrender. To believe that this strange new life, where she was married to a man she barely knew and her sister carried another man's child in secret, was permanent.

No. She would not give up hope. Somewhere—*somehow*—there must be a way back.

In any case, there was already a solution for Jane—Mrs. Collins would claim the babe as her own. If Elizabeth chose to remain at Longbourn to help Jane, there would be too much danger of her being discovered in her lie. She had never *actually* met Mrs. Collins, and as soon as Jane met that woman at the Gardiner's home, everything would unravel.

Besides... the idea of parting from Darcy left her far more unsettled than she dared admit. He was the one person in this world who knew her—truly knew her. The only one who shared her memories, her past, her pain.

To leave him behind would be like stepping into darkness without a lantern.

She glanced at Darcy again, watching the way he engaged Mr. Bennet in quiet conversation about land use and crop rotation. His intelligence was evident, but so too was his restraint. He asked questions. He listened. He offered observations rather than declarations.

He is a good man, she thought, with a ripple of awe.

Not only principled, but *influential*. She had seen it now with her own eyes—how his friendship had steadied Bingley, tempered him, perhaps even kept him from becoming the kind of man who would seduce a gentlewoman and abandon her at the first sign of consequence.

Darcy had not even realized the impact he had on his friend. His influence was subtle. Steady. Guiding.

But powerful.

He could be arrogant—yes. And brusque. And absolutely dreadful with strangers.

A smile curved her lips.

But beneath it all, he was loyal. Decent. Kind.

She had been so blind to it before. She had not understood what kind of man he truly was. And now that she did, she could feel the truth blooming within her like a fragile flower uncurling in the cold.

She was starting to fall in love with him.

She lowered her gaze to her plate, startled by the force of it.

Yes. She was falling in love with Fitzwilliam Darcy, and no amount of rain or magic or broken timelines could undo that.

Chapter 12

The meal passed more quickly than Darcy expected, and far more pleasantly. Elizabeth had smiled, laughed, and even teased him once when he dropped his spoon, and though his retort had been mild, the way her eyes crinkled at the corners made his heart twist with something dangerously close to contentment.

But all too soon, it ended.

Hill brought back their dried clothing—wrinkled and still a touch damp, but warm from the hearth—and they changed once more before taking their leave.

Mrs. Bennet all but wrapped them in blankets for the carriage ride back to the inn, pressing leftover biscuits into Elizabeth's hands and calling after them with cheerful insistence that they *must* come again at the end of their journey on their way back to Kent.

Darcy could not remember the last time he had been bade farewell so warmly.

He climbed into the hired carriage behind Elizabeth, settled across from her, and shut the door as the driver clicked his tongue and turned the horse into the lane.

The silence was immediate.

Elizabeth looked out the window. Her profile was blurred by the glass, which was misted from the warmth of their breath meeting the cold outside.

Darcy folded his hands and stared at them.

He wanted to speak—to say something to ease her pain, ask what she planned. Whether she would remain.

But he knew well that there was nothing he could say to calm the hopelessness in her eyes. In any case, words would not come. His chest was too tight about what she might say.

What if she turned to him, serene and resolute, and told him that she must stay at Longbourn—that her duty to her sister outweighed all else?

Could he fault her for it?

What if she says yes? What will I do if she wishes to remain here?

Could I leave her?

The thought hollowed him out. He had only just found her—truly found her—and now he might lose her again. And not to time or magic or some inexplicable twist of fate, but to choice. Her choice.

And he knew it must be hers.

So, he stared down at his hands and said nothing, watching her from the corner of his eye as she gazed out the window. The sound of hooves and wheels over gravel filled the space between them. He heard her sigh once, but she did not look up.

When they reached the Boar and Barrel, the innkeeper greeted them at the door with a genial nod. "Evenin', sir. Will you be wantin' the room a third night, or just this one more?"

Darcy hesitated. He glanced toward Elizabeth—but she was already climbing the stairs, her skirt gathered in one hand, her head slightly bowed.

"May I let you know in the morning?" he asked, unsure. Would Elizabeth wish to remain in Longbourn to try and find a way to help her sister in this world? Perhaps they could find work and remain in the area, but how much influence could they really have? Especially with Jane leaving so soon.

The man nodded. "Aye, that's fine."

Darcy gave a tight smile and handed over a coin before slowly climbing the stairs and lingering outside the door. He knew Elizabeth would need time to freshen up and change for bed.

When he finally entered their room, the fire had already been stoked and Elizabeth was lying on her side beneath the covers, her back to the door. A few stray tendrils of hair clung to her cheek. She had changed into the shift he had purchased for her in London. Her form beneath the blanket was still, her breathing steady—but not the steady rhythm of sleep.

No, she was awake.

He undressed quickly, laying his clothes out over the chair near the fire to finish drying. Then put on his nightdress and slid into the narrow bed beside her, careful not to touch her. Careful, as always.

But his mind was a roaring thing, far too loud for sleep.

Minutes passed. Her breathing did not change.

Finally, he spoke. Quietly. "I enjoyed dinner tonight."

There was a pause.

"Really?" Her voice was soft, surprised.

He turned his head slightly on the pillow to look at her silhouette in the dark. "I did."

She said nothing.

"Your family was... animated," he added, a smile tugging at one corner of his mouth. "But genuine. Warm. I had thought them only noisy before, but I see now... they care for one another. Deeply."

Elizabeth was still quiet, and he did not expect a reply.

"I used to think," he continued, "that good breeding and polished manners were the marks of superiority. That a composed drawing room reflected a superior household. But I have dined with earls whose tables were silent as tombs. I have been welcomed by ladies of status whose kindness would not extend past the parlor doors."

He swallowed.

"Tonight was different. And it has made me... consider how easily I dismissed things I did not understand."

Still, she did not speak.

His hands curled into the sheets beneath the blanket.

"If you wish to remain," he said carefully, "to assist your sister—I would understand. We could find work..." he trailed off helplessly.

Her breath caught.

He stared up at the ceiling, every muscle tense, his heart pounding as if he had just run from Longbourn again in the rain.

She said nothing.

Not yet.

And so he waited—his entire world poised on the hinge of her silence.

~~*~*

Elizabeth was touched by Darcy's offer. It was thoughtful. Kind. So very like him to consider her feelings—her obligations—even when he must be anxious to return to Derbyshire and to whatever remnants of his life remained there. That he would offer her the chance to stay with Jane... it spoke of selflessness. Understanding.

And yet—

It surprised her.

The truth was, the idea of remaining behind had not even occurred to her. This Jane, tender and dear as she might be, was not *her* Jane. This was not *her* world. It was another Elizabeth who had grown up in this house, who had made choices and forged bonds and accepted a man she had once rejected. It was not Elizabeth's responsibility to untangle those decisions, nor her place to remain in someone else's life.

But Darcy...

Darcy did not exist in this world. And yet, Georgiana was still his sister.

Alone.

Abandoned.

Then, unbidden, a small voice crept into her mind:

He is being polite.

The thought struck like ice.

Why would he want to stay in Longbourn? Was he allowing chivalry to over-rule his own desires? Or was it something worse?

She thought back on the evening and her heart squeezed painfully. Her family had been—she knew it—exuberant. Overwhelming. Loud and ridiculous and lacking in all the refinements his own circle possessed. Her mother had spoken of marriage markets as though they were horse fairs. Kitty and Lydia had fluttered over men in red coats

146

like moths to flame. Jane—poor Jane—had been revealed in all her heartbreak and shame.

What must he think of them? Of me?

By the time he had entered their room, she had already changed into her nightdress and lay facing the wall, curled on her side, uncertain. She listened to the rustle of fabric as he undressed, the creak of the mattress as he lay down carefully behind her, keeping that same respectful distance.

And still, she could not sleep.

Perhaps it had all become too much for him. Perhaps he had offered her the chance to stay because it spared him the discomfort of telling her that he had no wish to continue together at all. Not when her family was so clearly beneath his notice. Not when he now saw what she truly came from. He could wait until she was settled in Longbourn, perhaps even in a position in her family's home, and then simply disappear, without any pangs of guilt or remorse.

And if Jane's condition had appalled him... if it confirmed every prejudice he had ever held about her family's morals...

She felt him, still tense, beneath the covers and longed to speak, but she did not know what to say.

Because she knew what *she* wanted.

She wanted to be with him, whatever that meant. She wanted to remain by his side, to face whatever came next as a pair. It felt so obvious, so *right*—and yet now, uncertainty gnawed at her.

Had she misunderstood? Had she misread his warmth, his patience, his laughter?

What if it was all in my imagination?

The idea struck like a cold wind. That perhaps the comfort between them had been no more than kindness. That his gaze—so often steady and soft—had been only pity. That when he offered to stay in Longbourn, close to her family, it had not been out of care, but as a step towards being free of her.

She closed her eyes tightly, pressing her fingertips against her brow, trying to will the fear away, to will sleep into claiming her. But the silence between them was unbearable. It throbbed like a bruise on her heart.

She wished he would speak—say something, anything—but perhaps he already had. Perhaps his silence *now* was an answer she had no wish to hear.

So, she lay still, trying to steady her breathing, knowing he was just inches away—and fearing he might already be a world apart.

Her breath trembled. A knot formed in her chest—thick and aching. She could not take it anymore.

Turning just slightly toward him, her voice barely above a whisper, she asked, "Do you want to go on…without me?" Her next words came out in a breathless rush. "You have no obligation to me. This world, this reality, it is meant for you to understand, not for me. I do not want to hinder you."

The silence that followed felt endless.

And then—low and ragged—came his answer.

"No."

The word was strangled—rough with something unspoken. It cracked through the darkness like lightning and sent something sharp and bright flooding through her chest.

"No?" she asked, hopeful.

"No," he repeated.

She turned toward him fully then, rolling onto her side to face him. He was already looking at her—his expression stark in the faint moonlight that filtered through the curtains.

"That is not what I want either," she whispered. "I want… I want to go with you, wherever this magic takes you. I just want to *be* with you."

Please.

The words hung there between them—barely breathed, yet weighty as a vow.

His gaze dropped to her mouth. Hers flicked to his.

They were close. So close. The heat between them felt tangible, a pull that thrummed in the air and settled in her skin. His breath mingled with hers, warm and uneven. Her lips parted. She could feel his tension, the hesitation in his stillness.

She waited.

Would he kiss her?

Would I let him?

The question barely had time to form before she knew the answer. She *wanted* it. Ached for it. And yet—beneath the yearning, a sliver of fear curled in her stomach.

She had seen what passion had cost Jane—and that was in a house with chaperons and her sister in the next room. One wrong choice, one moment of weakness, and a woman's life could be altered forever.

Could she truly trust her own judgment in this private, intimate room?

Her pulse pounded as he leaned in, his face close enough now that his nose nearly brushed hers.

She held her breath.

Then—slowly, gently—his lips touched her forehead.

Not her mouth, but somehow that did not matter.

The kiss was soft. Gentle. Reverent.

He lingered there for a moment, his breath stirring her hair, and then he pulled back just enough to whisper:

"Good night."

She closed her eyes, her heart aching with something fierce and unfamiliar.

"Good night," she murmured in reply.

And though no more words passed between them, though the space between their bodies remained chaste, she could not remember the last time she had felt so *seen*.

So safe.

So wanted.

Sleep did not come easily.

But when it did, it was with the ghost of his kiss still pressed to her skin.

~~*~*

Darcy lay on his back, utterly still, as if any movement might shatter the moment, causing to him to awaken from the most beautiful dream. His heart was hammering in his chest with such force, he feared Elizabeth might hear it.

Eventually, though, her breathing changed—it was slow and deep, and he knew she had drifted off to sleep.

But he was still awake.

His lips still tingled from where they had met her skin—just above her brow, where a few damp strands of hair curled from the heat of her head on the pillow. The taste of her lingered, though it had not been a kiss of passion.

It had been adoration. Restraint. A vow unspoken.

But oh, how he had wanted more.

When she had turned to him and said she did not wish to stay—when she had chosen him—him—his chest had felt too small for the swell of emotion that surged within it. For a brief, breathless moment, the ache and fear and longing of the past three days had vanished, replaced by a single, radiant truth:

She wanted to stay with him.

Her softness next to him, the catch in her breath, the shift of the pillow as she turned her face towards him—everything told him she wanted him, wanted the kiss as much as he did.

And he had nearly done it.

But he had not.

He *could* not.

To do so would have been to cross a boundary he was not willing to break. Not with her. Not when he valued her so deeply. Not when her trust in him was something he had earned—slowly, painfully—and might shatter with a single moment of weakness.

She was not *his*. Not truly. Not yet.

And more than that, he could not allow the ache in his chest—or the pull of her nearness—to cloud what mattered most. Her dignity. Her safety. Her *future*.

He thought of Jane Bennet. Of Bingley's abandonment. Of a kind, gentle girl burdened with a shame that should never have been hers.

No, he told himself again. *Not like that. Never like that.*

But if he kissed her now—truly kissed her—he would not stop at one taste. Not when they were alone. Not when the bed was already shared. Not when the barriers between them had fallen so completely.

And she deserved more than that. They both did.

He would kiss her—properly, fully, joyfully—when they were no longer suspended in uncertainty. When he could lay his whole heart before her and know it was wanted. When he could love her without restraint or fear of shame.

It could wait until she bore his name—truly, not in pretense. When they had a place to call home. When the uncertainty of the future was gone. When the world, whichever world they found themselves in, recognized them as one.

And what world *was* this?

His joy was tempered, as it always was, by the strangeness of their reality. They still did not know how long the magic would last—if it was even magic at all. What if they married in this life only for the spell to break? What if *only one* of them returned? What if children came, and they were ripped apart.

What if this world was the true one now?

The questions circled his mind, too numerous, too heavy.

But even with all the uncertainties, one truth remained steadfast and clear: he loved her.

And when they were together for the first time—truly together—he wanted it to be without fear or shame or regret. No secrets, no hesitation. No borrowed names or altered realities.

He wanted to give her everything.

Our first kiss—our first proper kiss—should not be stolen in the dark, in a borrowed bed, as guests in a stranger's inn.

It should be in a time and place of *their* control. Undeniable. Unforgettable.

Because she was not just some fever dream born of magic and longing.

She was *Elizabeth*.

And she was becoming his whole world.

He exhaled slowly, forcing his body to remain still as he listened to her breathing soften beside him. Sleep, for him, was a long time coming.

But for the first time in years, it was not fear or loneliness that kept him awake.

It was hope. And love.

Chapter 13

Elizabeth awoke to the soft creak of the shutters and the faint orange glow of dawn spilling across the floorboards. For a moment, she did not move. Darcy still lay beside her, his breathing deep and even, his hand mere inches from her own. The night's words echoed in her mind—his confession, her choice, the press of his lips to her forehead like a vow whispered in the dark. She felt it still, the warmth of that kiss lingering on her skin like a secret.

She turned slowly toward him, taking in the relaxed lines of his face in sleep. So rare, that expression—unguarded, almost boyish. A version of him few had likely ever seen. She found herself studying him as if to memorize him: the faint crease between his brows, the tousled hair curling at the temples, the dark lashes that cast soft shadows over his cheeks.

She let the moment linger until his lashes fluttered, and his eyes opened.

He blinked at her. "Good morning," he murmured, voice rough with sleep.

"Good morning," she whispered back.

And just like that, the spell was broken.

But it was not lost.

They rose and dressed, the silence between them companionable now rather than strained. After a light breakfast brought to their room—Darcy had seen to it before she had even risen—they stepped out into the crisp morning air to begin their journey northward.

From the village of Meryton to the county border near Bakewell was no short jaunt. Darcy estimated it would take at least five days with good roads and hired post-chaises, perhaps longer if the weather turned. The route stretched nearly two hundred miles, threading north through Northamptonshire and the Midlands before finally reaching Derbyshire.

As the coach rumbled along the unfamiliar turnpikes and coaching inns rolled past the windows, Elizabeth felt the landscape shift—flattening into open farmland, the hills of her childhood giving way to the northward climb. The rhythm of the carriage was steady, almost lulling, and for a time they sat in silence, each wrapped in their own thoughts.

At the next stop to change the horses, the only other occupant of the public coach disembarked and did not return. Elizabeth and Darcy were left to themselves, and the only sign that they were not in a private conveyance was the worn upholstery beneath them and the groaning springs that creaked at every jolt in the road.

And because of their privacy, she could no longer contain the question gnawing at her.

"Mr. Dar—*William*," she said carefully, "may I ask you something… uncomfortable?"

He turned from the window, brows lifting slightly. "You may ask me anything."

She twisted her hands in her lap. "It is about Mr. Wickham."

His entire posture stiffened.

"I only—being back in Meryton made me think of him. Of the stories he told. The… the living that was promised to him. That he claims you denied."

Darcy's jaw tensed. "I see."

"I only mean—" she faltered, seeing the storm brewing behind his eyes. "I believed him, once. Not any longer, of course. But I think I should like to understand the truth."

There was a silence—longer than she expected, heavier than she could bear. Darcy's expression was unreadable, and he looked away from her, his gaze fixed on the passing landscape beyond the window. The countryside blurred past in shades of brown and gray, but Elizabeth hardly saw it. The quiet between them seemed to stretch, sharp and uncomfortable, until it filled the whole of the carriage.

Her stomach tightened. The warmth and certainty she had felt the night before—his tenderness, his kiss, the promise in his voice—slipped away like sand through her fingers. He was angry. Truly angry.

As the seconds ticked by, she sat rigidly, her hands folded tightly in her lap. She told herself she did not mind the silence. It was just a question. A simple inquiry. Perfectly reasonable.

But the longer he said nothing, the more her confidence withered. Her thoughts, so calm and certain that morning, began to churn. The security she had felt—his kiss on her forehead, the warmth in his voice, the way he had looked at her—suddenly felt fragile. Remote.

A prickle of discomfort stirred in her chest. She had never liked being left to guess at another's thoughts. And from him—of all people—it felt intolerable.

She shifted slightly. Why was he so angry? Why would he not speak?

The silence pressed down, too close, too loud. A flicker of resentment sparked low in her gut, catching her by surprise.

"I am sorry," she said at last, too quickly. Her voice was sharper than she intended. "It was presumptuous of me."

"No," he said, his voice low and tight. "It was not. Only… Wickham is a difficult subject for me. He always has been."

"I see."

The tone of her voice made it clear that she did *not* see. He hesitated a moment longer, then exhaled and turned back toward her.

"You are right to ask. And I promised you honesty."

She waited, hands still tightly clasped.

"We were raised almost as brothers," he began quietly. "His father was my father's steward. A good man—steady, intelligent, loyal. When George was born, his mother died in childbirth. A tragedy. She had been a serving girl, but bright and warm-spirited. My father felt it a great loss."

Elizabeth blinked in surprise.

"My father—" Darcy paused, rubbing his gloved thumb against the edge of his seat. "He had always longed for a large family. He had a brother, younger by a few years, who died in his twenties of a fever while on the Continent. I think that loss marked him more deeply than he ever said aloud. So when I was born, and it became clear that my mother could not bear many more children—" his lips tightened—"he saw something of his brother in Wickham. The mannerisms, perhaps. A resemblance. And so he did what he thought best."

Elizabeth tilted her head. "What was that?"

"He had George brought to Pemberley," Darcy said. "Not just as the steward's son. As my companion. We shared tutors, toys, mischief. My father insisted he be educated as a gentleman. My mother hated it. She thought it encouraged entitlement—and she was right. But my father... he saw George as a second son."

"Was he kind, as a boy?"

"Charming," Darcy said bitterly. "Always charming. But selfish. Calculating. He would borrow my books and lose them, break my toys and charm me into silence. He would lie to my parents, and if caught, say it was a misunderstanding. And somehow, I was always the one being scolded for lacking generosity or warmth. My father thought me cold. In truth, I was exhausted."

Elizabeth said nothing. Her fingers loosened their grip, slowly.

"Even as we grew older," he continued, "George knew how to twist affection to his advantage. At university, he gambled away every allowance he was given. My father helped him again and again, even promising him the living at Kympton, despite his lack of interest in the Church. After my father died..." his voice dropped, "...I could not, in good conscience, bestow a parish upon a man who mocked religion and drank himself insensible before lectures."

"And then?" Elizabeth asked softly.

"He demanded money instead," Darcy said. "I gave it to him. Three thousand pounds."

Elizabeth looked down at her lap, guilt roiling in her chest.

"I believed him," she said quietly. "Every word."

"I know," Darcy said, his voice gentler now. "It wounded me, but... I can hardly fault you for it. Wickham is a gifted liar. And I was proud. Silent. I let you believe it."

"I was prejudiced against you," she admitted, her voice barely above a whisper. "I saw what I wanted to see."

He reached for her hand. "If you can forgive me for my pride, I can forgive you for your prejudice."

Her lips curved faintly despite herself.

"Besides," he added, "I am the one who made the foolish wish that brought us here, all because I condemned your family without truly knowing them. So perhaps we both are equally guilty of poor judgment."

The rest of the day passed in quieter reflection. The road north unfolded like a ribbon of history—each milestone another marker of a shared past neither of them remembered, and yet one they were rewriting together.

And that night, when they stopped at a modest inn near Leicester, and Darcy gently touched the small of her back as he guided her inside, Elizabeth knew with quiet certainty that she was exactly where she wished to be.

By his side.

Wherever the road led next.

~~*~*

The next day dawned gray and cold, the air damp with the threat of rain. The inside of the hired coach was warmer than the wind outside, but not by much. They sat close, huddled in their cloaks, their thighs brushing now and then with the movement of the carriage.

They had crossed the boundary into the next county that morning, and the countryside had begun to change—greener, hillier, with fewer villages and more miles between.

Elizabeth studied the scenery for a while, but her mind was elsewhere.

Darcy had asked after her family. He had spoken kindly of Jane. He had even endured Mrs. Bennet with an admirable degree of composure.

It was time she did the same.

She waited until the driver's voice called down about the next change of horses, then looked over at Darcy.

"What is your sister like?"

He blinked, clearly surprised by the question. "Georgiana?"

She smiled slightly. "Unless there is another secret sister you have yet to mention."

That coaxed a faint smile from him, but it faded quickly. He looked down at his gloved hands, laced loosely in his lap.

"She is sweet," he said after a long pause. "Shy. Too shy, I think. She always has been. Gentle, eager to please, but…" He trailed off.

"But?"

"She finds the world overwhelming," he said simply. "People, especially. Other girls."

Elizabeth waited, giving him space.

"When she was younger, I thought it was only that she needed to be socialized," he continued quietly. "Our father died when she was eight. There was no mother. Just Fitzwilliam and me. Two bachelors—one always away with the army, and one buried in estate ledgers and mourning. I… I did not know how to raise a young girl."

There was no self-pity in his voice—only quiet resignation.

"I sent her to school. It is what my aunts advised, and it was what I knew. I thought it would teach her the rules of society, give her friends. A place to belong."

His jaw tensed slightly.

"But it did not. She did not thrive. She withdrew further. The other girls… they were not kind. Not cruel, exactly—but they saw her shyness as weakness. Some mocked her. Others ignored her. I visited once and found her pretending to be asleep to avoid going down to breakfast."

Elizabeth's heart ached.

He looked over at her then, his expression bleak. "I took her home the next day. I thought—" He exhaled. "I thought perhaps a smaller setting would suit her better. My aunt Matlock recommended a companion. A Mrs. Younge."

At the name, his features darkened.

"She was charming in society. A widow, genteel, with good references. I thought Georgiana liked her. Perhaps she did, at first."

Elizabeth sensed the shift—heard the bitter edge creeping into his voice.

"I left them in Ramsgate while I returned to London. I thought it a harmless way for her to enjoy the sea air while I attended to business." He looked away. "It was a mistake."

"What happened?" Elizabeth asked softly.

He stared out the window for a long moment. "Wickham found her there."

Her breath caught.

"Mrs. Younge was not what she seemed. She and Wickham had known each other for years. I believe they plotted it together, waiting for their opportunity. But I stopped receiving any letters from her. I thought she was, perhaps, still despondent, so I decided to surprise her... and instead found her about to elope"

Elizabeth sat up straighter. "Good God."

"I arrived just in time." His voice was low and hard. "He had convinced her that they were in love, that they must flee before I could stop them. I found her with her trunk already packed, planning to leave that night."

"Did you confront him?"

"Not in that moment—he was not present. Instead, I sent my sister to her room and fired Mrs. Younge. When I checked on Georgiana, she was angrier than I had ever witnessed before. My quiet sister was fire and rage. She did not believe me until she heard it from his mouth herself."

Elizabeth gasped and put a hand to her mouth. "The poor girl."

Darcy pressed his lips together. "He was so cruel, denying everything, saying it was all Georgiana's idea and that he never loved her. She wept through the entire exchange, and after I drove him from the house, she begged me not to tell anyone." His mouth twisted. "Not because she feared disgrace—but because she blamed herself."

Elizabeth's fingers tightened in her lap. "She was fifteen, and he was a grown man."

"She turned sixteen two weeks later."

The carriage rocked over a rut in the road. Neither of them spoke for several moments.

At last, Elizabeth said, "He is a monster."

Darcy looked over, startled. Something in her voice—fierce and raw—seemed to move him.

"You were right," she said, more quietly. "I believed his story in Meryton. I thought you had robbed him of his living. I thought him wronged and you proud."

His eyes flicked away, and she hung her head. "I am ashamed of it now."

"You had reason," he said. "I gave you no cause to think otherwise."

"But still—"

"I told you," he said gently, "we are equal in our misjudgments."

She searched his face—serious, composed, with just the faintest hint of sorrow lingering behind his eyes.

"I wish I could tell her it will be all right," Elizabeth said softly. "That she will not always feel this way. That someone will see her, truly see her, and treat her kindly."

He nodded once and looked out the window.

"I will do whatever I must," he said, almost to himself. "Even if we are trapped in this world, and she does not know me. I will find a way to help her."

Elizabeth watched him, her throat tightening.

And in that moment, she saw not the proud man who had once insulted her at a ball, nor the stranger thrust into her journey by some inexplicable force of fate.

She saw a partner. The one man in the world who was the most suited to her in disposition and talents, in understanding and temper.

And her heart knew it.

~~*~*

Darcy sat quietly as the coach rattled onward, the conversation with Elizabeth still echoing in his mind.

She had asked him—gently, curiously—about Wickham, and instead of answering her with the clarity and honesty she deserved, he had bristled.

He had not meant to. Truly. And yet, the instant she had spoken Wickham's name, something had curled in his chest: a hot, acidic knot of memory and shame and fury—and the words had left him more harshly than he intended.

And she had recoiled.

Not dramatically. Not with wounded pride or anger. No, it was subtler than that. A stilling of her hands. A quick blink. A quiet retreat into herself.

But he had seen it.

And he had hated himself for it.

She had only wanted to understand. Of course she had asked. And why should she not have believed Wickham back in Meryton? Darcy had done nothing to recommend himself—nothing to refute Wickham's lies—nothing to make Elizabeth trust him over a charming man with a tragic tale.

And yet she had apologized. Felt shame. Looked at him with those wide, regretful eyes and spoken words he never thought he would hear from her lips.

"I am sorry… It was presumptuous of me."

Not just an apology. A wound cloaked in frustration. He had heard the flicker of hurt in her tone, the defensive edge. And he had deserved every syllable of it.

He had apologized, of course. Tried to explain. But the truth was, he hated the man so much, and had done for so long, that any mention of

161

him was like pressing against an old bruise that had never properly healed. Wickham had been at the center of too many of his failures— failures of judgment, of trust, of protection. Failures that had cost people Darcy loved more than they would ever know.

And now… Elizabeth.

He had hurt her with his tone, and that knowledge unsettled him more than he could admit. He was not used to caring how others perceived his mood. His family, his tenants, his peers—they respected him, they obeyed him, but they did not expect tenderness.

Elizabeth did not expect it either. And yet, somehow, he wanted to offer it to her. Freely. Without reserve.

She made him want to be better. Even when she challenged him. Especially when she challenged him.

He shifted slightly in the seat, glancing across at her. She was staring out the window, one gloved hand resting lightly against her chin. Her expression was thoughtful, quiet. No trace of judgment remained there. Just… empathy. Understanding.

She had listened as he spoke of Georgiana. Not with pity, but with purpose. With fire. When she had called Wickham a monster, something in Darcy had loosened—some old, tight place in his chest that had never quite relaxed.

She sees it now, he thought. She understands. And still she is here.

The coach hit a rut, jostling them slightly. Elizabeth turned to steady herself, her shoulder brushing his. He did not move away.

No, she is not the same woman who dismissed me in Kent. And I am not the same man who walked away from her, determined never to look back.

He wanted to reach for her hand. Wanted to tell her again how sorry he was for the sharpness in his voice. But instead, he simply said, "Thank you."

She looked at him, puzzled. "For what?"

"For asking about my sister."

Elizabeth's brow furrowed softly, but she nodded once. "She matters to you. I wanted to understand."

He gave a faint smile. "You are very good at that."

The carriage rocked on, and this time, silence fell not from discomfort, but from something far more fragile and precious.

Trust.

Chapter 14

The next two days passed more quietly.

After the storm of confessions and tensions surrounding Wickham and Georgiana, it seemed an unspoken truce had settled between them—not one of avoidance, but of reprieve. As if they had agreed, without words, that there was more to discover from that history than old wounds and painful truths.

And so, they talked.

Not of magic, or vanished identities, or ruined reputations—but of childhood mischief and peculiar relations, of foolish school pranks and pet goats and near-drownings in lily ponds. As other passengers came and went, Elizabeth sat at Darcy's side, whispering stories of her youth.

It began with her telling the tale about Kitty's ill-fated attempt to ride a neighbor's pony sidesaddle—a venture that ended with a broken fence, a broken bonnet, and a broken courtship with Mr. Long's son, who never quite recovered from being kicked in the shin at the tender age of thirteen.

Darcy laughed. Not politely—not with the reserved, careful chuckle he had once given her in Kent—but openly. Freely. It changed his whole face. And it made Elizabeth's heart flutter in a way she tried not to examine too closely.

Not in a shared, public coach, that is.

She then went on to share stories of Sunday games with her sisters, of treks to Oakham Mount, of hiding books behind embroidery frames to escape her mother's lectures on lace and propriety.

"You must not think too poorly of us," she said, lifting her chin with a wry smile. "Though I grant you, Longbourn is rarely quiet."

"I have no objections to noise," Darcy said, and his eyes glinted. "When it comes with such entertainment."

She arched a brow, then launched into another tale—the infamous incident of Mary and the poetry book. Mary had composed an original sonnet for Easter and insisted upon reading it aloud before the entire parish over supper. Elizabeth had attempted to spare her family the embarrassment by feigning a coughing fit halfway through the second stanza, only for Lydia to shout, "Lizzy is faking it!" and pour a cup of water over her head to test the theory.

"I imagine the sonnet continued?"

"To the bitter end," Elizabeth replied, deadpan. "Though Papa excused himself early. I am still not sure if it was to laugh or to weep."

Darcy covered his mouth with a gloved hand, visibly shaking.

She described Longbourn in summer—the way the roses grew wild around the kitchen door, how Mary insisted on practicing her pianoforte during thunderstorms because she believed the lightning added drama.

And how Lydia once claimed to have seen a ghost in the west field.

"My youngest sister often woke in the middle of the night to go downstairs and sneak biscuits and other treats from the kitchen," Elizabeth said, doing her best to repress her mirth. "She looked out the window on her way down, and there was a pale specter moving across the west field by moonlight."

"What did she do?" Darcy asked, intrigued by this wholesome view of the lively youngest Bennet daughter.

"She roused the entire house in alarm. Mr. Hill fetched his blunderbuss. But it was only the milk cow, poor thing, who had managed to snag a sheet off the line. It was draped across her horns like a death shroud."

Darcy gave a quiet, helpless laugh. "I do not know what is better— the ghost cow or the poetry."

"Oh, just wait," Elizabeth said, warming to her subject. "One time, Mama insisted that Kitty debut her new cap at Lady Lucas's garden party, even though I told her the feathers made her look like a goose.

But Mama said it was *fashion-forward*, and then of course it rained, and the feathers matted straight down her face. Lydia started quacking."

He shook his head, smiling with disbelief. "You exaggerate."

"I do not. Jane tried to help by offering her bonnet, but the damage was already done. Charlotte could hardly speak for trying not to laugh, and Mr. Lucas asked if we had brought a new breed of domestic poultry with us."

Darcy's laughter faded into something softer. "You... you remember everything so vividly."

She paused. "Of course I do. This is my whole world."

Her voice broke slightly on the last word. *Will I ever regain my family again?*

~~*~*

Darcy looked down at his *wife* with a feeling of awe. There was no boast in Elizabeth's voice. Just quiet affection. It made something stir in his chest—something that longed for warmth like that.

What would life at Pemberley have been like with so many siblings and a warm, loving family?

She went on to tell him about the time she read all of *Robinson Crusoe* aloud to Jane during a week of fevers—and changed the ending so that Crusoe married Friday and opened a lending library on the island. "She was nine and crying about Friday dying. I could not bear it."

Darcy blinked. "You rewrote *Crusoe*?"

"With a happy ending. Naturally."

"I cannot tell if I should be impressed or appalled."

"Both," she said sweetly. "You will learn that about me."

He smiled again, then realized he had probably done so more in the last week than in his entire life.

Later still, she told him how her father had once gifted her a volume of Shakespeare's comedies for her thirteenth birthday. It was the only time he had remembered her birthday without her mother's prompting.

"I read *Much Ado* first. And I decided then and there that I would never marry anyone who did not at least *attempt* to banter with me."

"High standards," Darcy murmured.

"You have not yet heard what happened to Mr. Poole a few years ago," she said with mock severity. "He told me that girls had no head for Shakespeare. I challenged him to a sonnet contest. He fled the next day."

Darcy pressed a hand to his heart theatrically. "Remind me never to slight the Bard in your presence."

"Oh, you are quite safe," she said lightly. "You read. You laugh. And you have not yet compared me to a summer's day, which is frankly the dullest of all options."

"I shall aim for something more original, then." He met her gaze. "You deserve it."

The air shifted.

Just slightly.

Not enough to change the tone. Not enough to make either of them look away. But something had passed between them—an understanding. A recognition.

I want this kind of joy for the rest of my life, he thought.

The moment ended when they stopped once again for a change of horses and a few minutes to stretch their legs.

Once they had resumed their places side-by-side in the carriage, Elizabeth said playfully, "Now that you have heard all of my stories, Mr. Smith, it is only fair that you return the favor. What was growing up like for you?"

"Not nearly as interesting as your upbringing," he said. "It was, in comparison, quite dull. I was not raised among ghost cows and feathered tragedies."

She smiled. "No, I imagine Pemberley is quite devoid of poultry mishaps—too dignified and highbrow to be otherwise."

"There was a peacock once," he admitted to her delight. "My father purchased one from a collector in Bath. It screamed outside the nursery window every morning for a week. My mother declared it a harbinger of doom and made the steward sell it to the vicar."

Elizabeth laughed. "That is not so very far from my world."

"No," he said after a moment. "Perhaps not."

His heart leaped when she reached out to touch his knee. "I wish to hear everything," she said in a serious voice.

And so he told her about Pemberley. About climbing the stone bridge as a boy and leaping into the river, much to the horror of his nursemaid. About stealing apricots from the glasshouse and blaming the footman, then confessing with such guilt that the entire staff forgave him at once. Of sneaking into the library at night to trace his fingers along the spines of forbidden books by candlelight.

And did you read them?" she asked, amused.

"Some," he said. "But mostly I liked the smell. The heavy, dusty scent of old bindings and dried ink. It made me feel… important, somehow. As though knowledge were a secret I was about to uncover."

Elizabeth smiled. "I think I would have liked young Master Darcy."

"I think he would have adored you."

That silenced her—but not unpleasantly. After a few moments, she smiled brightly and said, "Tell me about your Grand Tour."

He blinked, surprised. "How did you—?"

"Well, you *are* a wealthy young man in England… and I believe you mentioned it during that first dinner at Rosings."

He huffed a laugh. "Ah. Yes. That dinner. I should thank you for that, by the way."

"For what?"

"For not stabbing my aunt with your fork."

"I was sorely tempted."

He smiled faintly and looked down at his hands. "I went when I was twenty years of age. You are quite correct. It is a tradition of sorts— my father had done the same. My cousin Fitzwilliam went before his commission. I was meant to spend four years abroad in France, Italy, Greece. But then Napoleon had other plans."

Elizabeth nodded soberly.

"So, I revised my course. I went north instead. The Low Countries, some of Germany, then to Denmark and briefly to Sweden. It was cold. Uncomfortable. But beautiful. Austere. I wrote pages and pages about the architecture. I thought I might collect art, once." A beat. "I never did."

"What happened?"

He was quiet a long moment, letting the memories flood over him. Then: "A letter came. My father had been thrown from his horse."

Her smile faded. "Oh."

"I returned at once, but he had already passed."

Tears filled her eyes. "I am so sorry."

Darcy's eyes drifted to the window. "He was a complicated man— not prone to strong emotion. At least, not with me. But I admired him greatly. I thought I had years more to learn from him. Instead, I was left with a large estate, a grieving sister, and more responsibility than I felt equipped to bear."

She reached for his hand, unthinking. He did not pull away.

"You were only twenty-three," she said gently. "That is a great deal to carry."

He looked down at their joined hands, as though startled by the comfort it offered.

"I made mistakes," he said quietly. "A great many."

She said nothing, waiting.

"Georgiana was twelve. She hardly knew me. I had been away at Cambridge, then abroad. I tried to manage her like a steward— dutifully, distantly. I listened to my aunts. I sent her to school. I thought... I thought it was what she needed."

Elizabeth's brow furrowed.

"She hated it," he said simply. "She never said so in her letters, but she came home thinner. Quieter. She started writing poems with endings that never resolved. Just faded out."

The image hurt. Elizabeth gripped his hand tighter. "And that is when you sent her to Ramsgate."

"Yes," he said in a rough whisper. "The worst mistake of them all."

170

"You saved her," Elizabeth countered, her voice low but firm. "That matters more."

They sat in silence for a while after that, the rhythm of the road lulling them both into quiet thought.

Eventually, the mood lightened again—almost imperceptibly. He told her a fond story about Fitzwilliam falling off a donkey in Germany and swearing in five languages while village children applauded.

"You and your cousin are quite close, it seems."

"He is my most cherished friend," he replied. "You would love him... well, in our world, at least. I am not certain who he would be here. Everything is so changed."

"You have had a great impact on those in your life."

"I suppose," he said, looking down at his hands.

Perhaps she realized that he was close to breaking, for she deliberately turned the topic of conversation with a light voice. "I have never been anywhere."

Grateful for the reprieve, as his eyes were suspiciously wet, he asked, "Kent was your first time away?"

She nodded. "Unless you count visiting my Aunt and Uncle in Cheapside. Which I do not."

"You ought to," he said gently. "London is a worthy destination. And your uncle is a man of great sense."

"He is," she agreed. "But it is not the continent. I have never seen the Alps, or the sea, or even a castle beyond what I have read in Mrs. Radcliffe's novels."

He looked thoughtful. "Would you like to?"

"To what? Travel?"

He nodded.

Elizabeth exhaled. "More than anything. I have always longed to see the world. But Papa never cared for exertion or expense. He preferred his books and his fireside—and I understand. He has every right to be content. But I always hoped... perhaps one day."

Darcy's eyes flicked toward the window. The pale, wintry landscape passed by—bare trees, sheep huddled against hedgerows, snow-patched fields under an iron sky.

"You never know," he said. "You may marry a man with the means to travel."

"I care more about his character than his pocketbook," she said, "and it would not matter if we remained in England our entire lives, so long as we are together."

Darcy was quiet for a moment, watching the frost-glazed trees blur past the window. Then, almost casually, he said, "Perhaps his affairs will make it possible. For example, I have an estate in Scotland I try to visit every other year."

He held his breath, waiting for her response.

~~*~*

Elizabeth's heart fluttered. Her breath caught, though she tried to cover it with a slight laugh. "Is that so?"

He turned toward her, a half-smile on his lips—but his eyes, they were intent. "It is remote, and often wet, but the mountains there are green and ancient. The lochs are still as glass, and the sky feels closer, somehow. I think... I think you would like it."

Their eyes met and held.

Warmth bloomed in her chest, spreading outward until her fingertips tingled. It was not the promise itself, not even the place, but the way he said *you*. Like he was already picturing her there. Like he wanted her there.

She said nothing at first. She could not. The feeling swelled too large to be named. But then, softly, she replied, "I think I would, as well."

And though nothing more was spoken, the quiet between them was rich with possibility.

Together felt like more than a word.

It felt like a future.

~~*~*

They reached the posting inn near dusk, the light fading quickly beneath a sky heavy with clouds. It had not snowed that day, but the threat of it hung in the air, and Elizabeth was glad for the warmth of the fire as they stepped into the modest common room.

Their dinner was a simple affair—thick mutton stew with crusty bread, and a small pot of weak tea that tasted faintly of smoke. She did not mind. She was far too tired to be particular.

They spoke little over the meal, both weary from the road and, perhaps, from the undercurrent of anticipation that neither dared give voice to. Tomorrow they would reach Lambton. Tomorrow the strange, uncertain future would finally become the present.

Their room was no different than the others they had shared— narrow bed, drafty window, a worn hearth with a crack in the mantle. But it was private, and it was theirs for the night. Elizabeth changed into her nightdress while Darcy tended to the fire, then slipped beneath the blankets and turned to face the wall.

He joined her shortly after, careful as always to keep his body a respectful distance from hers, though she felt the dip of the mattress as he settled beside her, the faint shift of the bedclothes, the comforting sound of his breath just behind her ear.

For a while, there was only silence.

And then, softly, he said, "We will reach Lambton tomorrow."

She blinked in the dark, her fingers curling around the edge of the blanket. "Oh?"

"I know," he said, his voice low. "It feels as though we have lived a thousand lives since we left Kent. But the journey is nearly done."

She turned slightly, just enough to glimpse his profile in the firelight. "Do you have a plan?"

He hesitated. "I do."

She waited.

"I cannot simply arrive at Pemberley's gates and announce myself. Not if they do not recognize me, and there is no evidence to suggest that they would. Such an arrival would invite chaos… suspicion. And if Georgiana has been harmed, it could place her in even more danger."

Elizabeth's throat tightened. "So, what will we do?"

"Lambton is close—less than five miles from the estate. And the inn there is small, but decent. We will stay a day or two, ask careful questions. Most of the townsfolk have family at Pemberley: cousins, uncles, siblings. I hope we may learn something of the household's state."

"That is clever," she said quietly.

He gave a faint, humorless chuckle. "I am desperate. But thank you."

"What is our story?"

"That we are newly married," he said, "and that I grew up in the area. I wished to show you my childhood home on our wedding journey. Pemberley has always welcomed visitors. It is not uncommon for tourists to request a walk through the gardens or a view of the house. If nothing else, I hope to gain entry that way."

Elizabeth nodded, though her heart had begun to pound. They were so close now. And yet what lay ahead felt vast, unknowable, and heavy with consequence.

Darcy exhaled, long and quiet, and the bed shifted again as he turned to face the ceiling. She could sense his unease.

"Are you worried?" she asked.

He did not answer at first.

"Yes," he admitted at last. "More than I care to say."

She reached across the space between them, her hand finding his beneath the blankets. Their fingers twined without effort.

He did not speak again, and neither did she.

But they held each other's hands until sleep claimed them both.

Chapter 15

The sun was sinking low in the sky on the couple's fifth day of travel. As the carriage grew dim, Darcy drew back the curtain. He leaned forward slightly toward the window upon noticing that they were cresting the final hill. His heart tightened at the first sight of Lambton.

It was nothing like the village he remembered.

As a child, he would run to Lambton from Pemberley nearly every day during the horse-chestnut season. There were the occasional visits for a penny's worth of barley sugar from the grocer's wife, or to purchase a new pair of riding gloves. Then, as a young man, he had accompanied his father on Thursdays to settle accounts with shopkeepers—his father always insisting they pay what was owed, even in the leanest seasons. "A gentleman's reputation," the elder Mr. Darcy had said, "rests as much on his honesty in trade as in blood."

But now...

The main street stretched ahead in weary silence. Shutters hung crookedly on half the buildings, paint peeling from cracked window frames. The milliner's shop was boarded up, the butcher's door ajar with no sign of trade within. The bakery where he used to buy currant buns as a boy was closed, and even the church spire in the distance, once the loudest and warmest corner of the green, was cold and still.

A few townspeople shuffled past with downturned eyes, faces drawn tight with suspicion or fatigue. The village had not merely quieted—it had withered. As though prosperity had turned its back and taken the sun with it.

Darcy sat back, stunned.

How could so much damage and decay occur in just a year under Wickham's control?

Beside him, Elizabeth said nothing, but he saw her glance out as well. Her hand tightened in her lap.

The coach pulled into the yard of the King's Head Inn—a modest but well-kept establishment in his memory. But even here, signs of decline were evident: the sign was weather-faded, the cobbles were cracked, and the windows were fogged with soot and grime

A young man—not the innkeeper Darcy had known—emerged to greet them and help with their bags.

He was wiry, with tousled hair and sleeves rolled to the elbow, a linen cloth slung over his shoulder. He wore a smile, but it was tired, and his boots bore more cobbler's patches than polish.

"Afternoon," he said, reaching for the door as Darcy stepped down. "You have the look of travelers needing food and fire. Welcome to the King's Head."

Darcy inclined his head politely. "Thank you. We should like a room for the night—quiet, if you please. And a meal, if it is not too much trouble."

"No trouble," the man replied, glancing at Elizabeth with a flicker of curiosity before waving over a stable boy. "We have mutton stew this evening, and I will have a fire going in the front parlor. Cold day for travel."

Darcy nodded once, then, after a pause, casually said, "I came here many years ago, as a boy. The innkeeper was a Mr.… Wilton, I believe was his name. He had a fondness for putting a bit of flour in the stew."

The man chuckled. "That he did. Always said it kept his constitution firm." He extended a hand. "He was my uncle. I am Samuel *Whitlow*."

Darcy shook it. "Ah yes, that was it. A pleasure, Mr. Whitlow. Is your uncle well?"

"He is, thank God—retired now. Sold the place to me a few years back and moved down to Sheffield to live with my aunt." Samuel's smile dimmed slightly. "Did not have much choice, really. Once business started drying up…"

He trailed off, then cleared his throat and gestured toward the door. "Come in, sir. Ma'am. You will find the hearth warm while you wait for the maid to assure the room is in readiness."

Elizabeth murmured her thanks as they stepped inside. The inn's main room was clean but dim, the scent of smoke and stewed meat lingering in the air. Darcy brushed off the chill from his coat and looked around.

"It is… quieter than I remember," he said after a moment.

Samuel nodded, busying himself with the registry. "It is that. Lambton is not what she was."

He did not elaborate.

Darcy signed the book and passed it back. "We have come to see the area. My wife has never been this far north before. I grew up nearby."

"Ah," Samuel said, glancing up. "So, you are local?"

"In a manner of speaking."

Samuel hesitated. "You would not have family at… Pemberley, would you?"

Darcy's heart beat once, hard. "I did."

The man's eyes flicked between him and Elizabeth. "Well," he said carefully, "you will find things… changed. Since old Mr. Darcy passed, it has been different. Village too."

Darcy waited, letting the silence stretch. Eventually, Samuel exhaled and leaned on the desk.

"Folk used to depend on that estate, you know. For trade. Employment. There was always a coach or cart in the street. Always coin changing hands. But after the funeral… nothing. The young lady—Miss Darcy—was sent off, and the house sat empty. Staff left one by one. Took goods on credit, promised payment once the will was settled."

Darcy's stomach turned as Samuel looked down at his hands.

"But many of the stewards and housemaids all disappeared. Left their tabs unpaid and no answers to be had. Then came word that Pemberley would close up altogether. Mr. Darcy had no son, you know, and folk said he never recovered from the loss of his wife."

Darcy's throat constricted.

"But what about his daughter?" he managed.

The innkeeper gave a sad shake of his head. "Too young to manage such a house. And when she went to live with her mother's kin—the Matlocks." His mouth twisted slightly. "Poor girl. Never looked happy. Then… well, they tried to marry her to some doddering old duke, if gossip is true."

Elizabeth stiffened beside him.

"She ran off instead. Eloped to Gretna with the steward's son. Whole thing caused a scandal." He paused, eyes scanning the room as though to ensure they were not overheard. "Now the house is open again, but not many dare go near it. The young master drinks too much, and they say the young miss is often seen weeping in the garden. Wearing the same gown every day. A bad business, that."

Elizabeth gasped softly, and Darcy swallowed hard, his hand clenched behind his back. "Thank you, Mr. Whitlow. You have been very helpful."

The man looked at him curiously, then softened. "I did not mean to cast gloom over your visit, sir. We do not see many travelers these days. But if you knew the old master… I daresay he would be glad to know someone remembered Pemberley in its glory days."

Darcy nodded once, then took Elizabeth's arm as the man said, "I reckon that the room is fit now. If you will follow me."

The couple followed the innkeeper upstairs in silence. Darcy could feel Elizabeth giving him glances beneath her eyes, but he kept his gaze focused on the steps.

"Here you go, sir, madam," he said, opening the door and gesturing into the room. "I will send a maid up when supper is ready."

"Thank you, Mr. Whitlow," Elizabeth said when Darcy did not speak. "We are grateful for your hospitality… and for the information."

Darcy wordlessly pressed a coin into the man's hand. Mr. Whitlow bowed in gratitude, then left the room, closing the door behind him.

Looking around, Darcy was relieved to discover that the room was clean, albeit modest and worn at the edges. The fire had been laid but not lit, so he wordlessly set about striking the flint. Once his task was complete, he crossed the room to the narrow bed in the corner. It creaked under his weight as Darcy sat down heavily upon it, staring at the bare, plank floor.

Elizabeth hung her cloak neatly over the chair near the hearth. When she turned and saw him still sitting there, his back bowed, his eyes cast low, she came to stand beside him.

Darcy had not yet removed his gloves. He was not entirely certain he could even move his fingers.

Sitting carefully down beside him, Elizabeth softly said, "It is worse than you imagined."

He nodded, unable to lift his head. "Much worse."

For a long moment, she said nothing. Then she reached over and placed her hand over his. "I am so sorry."

He shook his head. "You have nothing to be sorry for."

"I meant—for what you saw. For what has become of the place you love."

That struck something deep within him, and he closed his eyes.

"I knew it might be changed," he said. "But I thought… I thought it would be smaller, perhaps. Or unfamiliar. Not this." His voice grew ragged. "Not hollow. Not broken."

She gave his hand a small squeeze. "Would you like to go back out into the village? Speak to some of the shopkeepers as we did in Meryton? Perhaps they can tell us more."

He drew a shaky breath. "I am not certain I wish to know anything more. I think I have heard enough for now."

"Of course." Elizabeth nodded, her brow furrowed in sympathy. "Do you have an idea of what we shall do tomorrow?"

He lifted his eyes at last and met hers. "Pemberley once offered tours," he said slowly. "It is a grand estate, and my father—our father— believed it wise to permit public days, like Chatsworth or Blenheim. We charged nothing for entry, but donations to the tenant charities were welcome. I had thought… I had hoped… we might gain admittance that way."

"And now?"

"Now I do not know. With Wickham in possession…" His voice trailed off.

Elizabeth sat back on her heels. "Then perhaps we find another way."

He offered her a tired smile. "What other way is there?"

She tilted her head thoughtfully. "We could try to obtain positions in the household. A maid and a steward's assistant, perhaps. Or I might serve in the stillroom."

Darcy blinked. "You cannot be serious."

"I am perfectly serious."

"You would *work* at Pemberley? In *service*?" His eyes widened, a flush rising to his cheeks. "Elizabeth, that is not— I could not ask that of you."

"You did not," she said simply. "I offered."

"But—"

"You forget," she interrupted gently, "that while I am a gentleman's daughter, I come from a much humbler estate than yours. At Longbourn, we do not have so many servants that we can afford idleness. I have often acted as my sisters' maid, helping them dress or do their hair, and I have spent more than a few mornings in the kitchen when someone was ill and I wished for breakfast, or the fire had gone out in my room and I was too cold to wait for help."

She gave him a wry smile. "I assure you, the idea of labor does not offend me—especially if it means aiding someone in need. Besides, in this world, I am a married woman with no money and no connections. I cannot afford to be proud."

He flinched. "Still, I cannot abide the thought of you—"

"It is not forever," she said. "And it is not for just anyone. You care for your sister. And I care for you. That is all the reason I need."

The words hit him like a blow to the chest. For a moment, he could not speak. He simply stared at her—this remarkable woman, who had once rejected him with righteous fury and now offered to toil in a stranger's kitchen for the sake of a sister she had never met.

She looked away then, her cheeks coloring faintly. "Besides," she added in a lighter tone, "if your fear is that I end up in the kitchens, you need not worry. I can make a respectable biscuit—and I promise I shall only poison Mr. Wickham."

He stared at her in astonishment, uncertain whether to laugh or be alarmed. Fortunately, a soft knock at the door spared him from determining whether she was a talented cook—or a budding murderess.

"Remind me to never anger you," he muttered as he crossed the room and opened the door.

He heard her giggle behind him as he looked down at a young girl of around ten years. "My father said that supper is ready. He wishes to know if you would like it to be brought up on a tray for a farthing."

"We will come down directly," Elizabeth said from behind him.

Below-stairs, they ate their meal in silence, side by side on a bench by the fire. The stew was hot, if plain, and the tea weak enough to see the bottom of the cup through it. But it filled the aching hollow in his stomach, and Elizabeth's presence at his side helped ease the one in his heart.

As they returned upstairs, Darcy held the candle while Elizabeth undid her braid and changed behind the screen. He stared into the fire until she slipped beneath the covers.

Then he changed quickly and slid in beside her, careful not to disturb the blanket.

But he could not sleep.

Not tonight.

He lay on his side, facing the wall, and listened to the wind howling outside the shuttered window, but rest would not come. The smell of smoke from the hearth was faint, mixing with the scent of lavender from Elizabeth's hair.

He had hoped—so foolishly hoped—that coming here would feel like a homecoming. That he would find something familiar, some piece of his former life preserved.

Instead, he found ruin, all because he had never been born.

And in his absence, everything had suffered.

His mind spun with fears and doubtsHe had no notion if all was truly lost—if his home, his sister, his very purpose in life had been swept away by one foolish, selfish wish. Had he ruined the lives of hundreds by vanishing from their memories? Were his tenants, his servants, the entire village of Lambton suffering because of his pride and thoughtless words?

But worst of all—had he lost Georgiana?

It was unbearable. Every image of her—her bright eyes, her timid smile, the way she clung to his hand when she was small—rose before him like ghosts.

He had failed her.

And the knowledge of that failure carved him open.

He shut his eyes against the pain, but it surged up behind his ribs. Would he ever see her again? Would she know him? Or had he consigned her to misery, abandoned in a cold world without protection, without affection?

The weight of it pressed on his chest, relentless and suffocating. Guilt churned in his stomach until he could scarcely breathe, and the pain gathered behind his eyes like a storm. He fought against it, swallowing hard, willing the tears away—but it was no use. Like a dam that had cracked beyond repair, the sorrow surged forward.

He bit the inside of his cheek, trying to stop the tears he felt gathering. He would not cry. He was a man—he had always controlled himself, always borne pain in silence. He had grieved for his parents behind closed doors. He had buried his doubts about Georgiana's care for years. He had held back every sign of weakness since he was twenty-one and the weight of Pemberley fell on his shoulders.

But now... now, the burden was too great. The cracks splintered, and the storm broke loose.

His throat tightened, and his chest began to shake. He pressed a fist to his mouth, but a single sob escaped before he could stifle it. Another followed, raw and unbidden. He turned his face deeper into the pillow, desperate to muffle the sound, but it was no use.

Then, he felt it —a touch. Gentle. Steady.

Elizabeth's hand, resting on his shoulder.

He froze.

A thousand instincts screamed at him to turn away, to bury his shame, to apologize for his weakness. But he could not speak. Her fingers remained—firm, warm, unafraid.

And that was what undid him.

Her tenderness.

Her presence.

The fact that she did not recoil, but leaned into his pain.

Tears slid hot and fast down his cheeks. His shoulders trembled. His chest ached with the force of it, as if his body could no longer contain the despair.

He wept.

He wept like a child lost in the dark.

And still the tears came.

He wept for Georgiana—raised by the cold earl and his equally frigid wife, stripped of music and laughter and sunshine, her spirit dimmed by duty and disdain.

He wept for his tenants, their livelihoods in shambles, the shops shuttered, the homes falling to ruin—for the men who had once tipped their hats with pride, and the women who had smiled from garden gates.

He wept for the steward's son, for the young man with the crooked, carefree grin who had turned into a monster, drunk and cruel and unchecked.

He wept for the butler who had once carried him on his shoulders, for the maid who would sneak him sugared plums, for the horse groom who taught him how to ride.

He wept for Lambton, for Pemberley, for everything his ancestors had built.

He wept for his father—who had died without a son. Who had died never knowing he *had* one. Who had once believed in honor and duty, and whose legacy was now nothing more than shuttered windows and unpaid debts.

He wept for the man he had been. For the pride that blinded him. For the bitter wish that had brought all this to pass.

He wept for Elizabeth, for the world she had lost, for the burden she now carried beside him with such grace.

And somewhere, buried deep beneath it all, he wept for the fear that none of it could ever be put right.

That even if they reached the house, even if they found Georgiana…

It might already be too late.

Time became meaningless. The ache in his chest surged and surged, hollowing him out.

Slowly, silently, Elizabeth drew close and wrapped her arms around him, burying her face in the space between his shoulders, holding him with such quiet strength that it stole his breath.

The weight of his guilt did not vanish—but it lightened, eased by the steady cadence of her breathing at his back.

The jagged ache in his chest dulled where her cheek pressed into his back.

Her nearness did not fix what had been broken—but it reminded him that all was not lost. That he was not lost.

She was there. With him. Still.

In spite of his weakness.

The rhythm of her breathing and the safety of her arms began to still the storm inside.

Her palm stayed firm over his heart, a silent promise that she would not let go.

He closed his eyes, and for the first time in what felt like days— perhaps longer—his mind did not race with worries and concerns.

Instead, the images of Lambton faded. The hollow eyes of shopkeepers, the shuttered doors, the ruined fields… they receded like a nightmare before the morning light.

And in their place was only her—soft, steady, warm.

As he lay there, basking in the warmth of her body against his, sleep crept in at the edges of his thoughts, slow and heavy.

His limbs, tense for so long, began to uncoil.

The last thing he knew was the hush of her breath on his neck, and the memory of her voice saying, "*I am here. All will be well.*"

Chapter 16

The early light had only just begun to shine through the curtains when Elizabeth's eyes opened the following morning, washing the dingy walls in a pale gray glow. She blinked slowly, the heaviness of sleep still clinging to her limbs.

The memory of the night before washed over her in quiet waves.

His anguish had come without warning, as sudden and fierce as a storm tearing through the branches. She had not known what to do, not at first. It had been dark. Quiet. And then, from beside her, the sharp sound of a breath caught. Another. A choked sob that he tried—and failed—to suppress.

He had turned from her, burying his face in the pillow, shoulders drawn taut with effort.

She had hesitated, not wishing to call attention to his tears and embarrass him, as she imagined would be the case with most of the opposite sex.

Not that I have slept beside many weeping men.

But she had sisters. She had seen the trembling of a mouth that wished to hide its hurt. The stiffness of a body fighting to keep control.

She had known, and she could not remain still.

Her first touch had been hesitant—just her hand, resting lightly on his back. He had flinched. For the briefest second, she nearly withdrew it, fearing she had only deepened his distress. His breath caught and then quickened as his grief intensified, his frame wracked with sobs.

So she had come closer. Slipped her arm around him, her cheek pressing softly to his shoulder, her fingers splayed over the ribs that still shook from the force of his grief.

And there, in the quiet dark, she had held him.

Prayed for him.

Willed, with every fiber of her being, that some of the ache in his chest might lift.

Now, in the stillness of morning, her own eyes stung with tears.

She had never imagined he could break so completely.

Always he was composed. Controlled. Sharp-witted and strong-jawed and, yes, occasionally overbearing—but never this.

Never undone.

Was it only exhaustion? she wondered. Not merely from the physical toll of five days in a carriage, but the emotional weight he bore.

The loss of Pemberley. The failure to protect his tenants. The uncertain fate of Georgiana.

She sighed softly, her gaze drifting over the worn ceiling above them.

She needed to rise. Her bladder was making its needs increasingly known. But she remained where she was, unwilling to disturb him.

Not when he needed rest so badly.

Instead, she closed her eyes again, listening to the soft rhythm of his snores, and let her thoughts drift into quiet prayer.

Dear God... please. Ease his burden. Give him peace, even for a little while. Let today bring clarity. Let it bring hope. Let us do what we came here to do.

Let him know he is not alone.

After some minutes, her body gave her no further grace. She bit her lip and exhaled, her need to rise growing too insistent to ignore.

Easing back slowly, one inch at a time, she did her best not to disturb the man sleeping beside her. She moved with the same care one might give a skittish colt—cautious, gentle, and without sudden motion.

But just as she slipped from beneath the coverlet, his breathing hitched.

He stirred. She stilled at once.

After a long, suspended moment, he merely turned his face slightly into the pillow, murmuring something incoherent, and settled again.

Blessed reprieve.

She hurried behind the folding screen where the chamber pot waited, then splashed her face from the pitcher with what little water remained. Her fingers trembled slightly as she wiped her hands on the towel and caught sight of herself in the mirror. Her reflection looked far older than the girl who had left Longbourn for Hunsford only a few weeks prior—worn not by time, but by emotion.

And yet... her eyes held something steadier now. Something resolute.

When she returned to the bedside, Darcy was awake.

He did not speak at first, only met her gaze with a quiet that was somehow more meaningful than words. There was no mention of the night before. No acknowledgement of his tears or her embrace.

But something had shifted.

She saw it in the way he looked at her—as though she were something solid. Safe. A lighthouse on a storm-beaten shore.

"Good morning," he said softly, voice still rough with sleep.

"Good morning."

The simplicity of the greeting, the civility of it, was somehow more intimate than anything they might have said.

He sat up slowly, stretching out the stiffness of a poor mattress and days of travel. She turned to busy herself at the basin again, allowing them both the small dignity of pretense.

Soon after, they shared a modest breakfast of toasted bread and weak tea in the inn's small dining room. The innkeeper's wife brought it with a tired smile and a murmured hope for finer weather.

It had snowed in the night—only a dusting, and already melting— but the morning remained grey and heavy. The kind of cold that settled deep in one's bones.

Still, Darcy seemed better. Not cheerful, but upright. Ready.

"So," Elizabeth said lightly, sipping her tea, "what do two vagabonds do on the morning after their arrival in a near-abandoned market town?"

He glanced at her over the rim of his cup. "I believe they walk five miles to a ruined estate on the off chance it remains open to tourists."

She laughed, and the sound warmed her own heart.

"I suppose we could have simply asked someone in town," she said, "but where would the romance be in that?"

"Indeed," he said with dry amusement. "Not nearly as dramatic."

He hesitated, then set his cup down.

"I do not wish to overburden you, Elizabeth. The walk is a long one. If you prefer to rest—"

She waved a hand. "Mr. Smith," she said archly, "have you forgotten what an excellent walker I am? Even Miss Bingley was forced to admit my accomplishment, and as you well know, she was usually my severest critic."

His smile came slowly—genuine, if still touched by fatigue. "Very well. But if you expire from exertion, I shall take no blame."

"None at all," she said. "I shall simply haunt you until your dying day."

"Comforting."

She tilted her head, her eyes twinkling. "As ghosts go, I daresay I would be more charming than most."

"Of that I have no doubt."

They rose together then, gathering cloaks and gloves, preparing for the cold outside. Their footsteps echoed down the stairs and out into the street, past shuttered shops and empty windows.

The road to Pemberley lay ahead.

And though the path might yet end in heartbreak, Elizabeth could not help but feel a quiet thrum of anticipation in her chest.

Darcy was beside her.

They were walking together.

And that, at least, was something.

~~*~*

They left Lambton just after breakfast, the air cold enough to nip at Darcy's ears, though the sun made a valiant effort through the clouds.

Elizabeth walked beside him, her cheeks pink with wind and exertion, her pace brisk despite the many miles ahead.

Darcy had not expected to feel nervous.

But as the road curved away from the village and into the countryside he knew so well, tension crept into his limbs. The road had more holes than he remembered, and the hedgerows more wild. Yet the shape of the land had not changed.

It still knew him, even if those who lived upon it did not.

"I imagine you traversed this road often?"

Elizabeth's question broke through the silence. He nodded. "As a child, I used to visit Lambton with my parents—my father particularly valued the weekly visits. He believed in paying accounts promptly and ensuring the Pemberley estate supported the town's merchants."

She hummed her approval. "Wise of him."

Darcy allowed himself a small smile. "He thought it dishonorable to do otherwise. Lambton was thriving then. One of the larger market towns in the north, though still far smaller than Meryton, to be sure."

"Is this Pemberley land already?" Elizabeth asked, craning her neck to look at the gentle hills.

"Nearly. The home woods begin just beyond that bend. The house sits within a natural bowl, surrounded on three sides by hills and trees."

"I cannot wait to see it," she said. "It sounds like something out of a novel."

He smiled at that. "You will find no ruined towers or tragic abbeys. My mother insisted upon symmetry."

"As any woman of sense would."

Their pace slowed as the trees thickened and the land sloped more steeply. Here was the stone wall he had scaled as a boy to pick blackberries. There, a twisted oak he had once named Wellington for its sturdy limbs. The past tugged at him with every step.

"This is the home wood," Darcy said softly. "We are close now."

"Is it a large estate?" she asked.

Had it been anyone but Elizabeth, he would have refused to answer. Knowing her curiosity stemmed from genuine curiosity rather than mercenary ambition, he instead softly said, "Ten miles around."

She whistled softly. "Many trails, then. That would satisfy even my unladylike fondness for walking."

"In time, I could show you every one."

He had not meant it as a promise, but once said, it lingered between them.

He cleared his throat. "My father used to walk the boundaries with me. Once each spring. He said a man should know what he owns. And who depends upon him."

"How many families live here?"

The fact that she cared more for the people of Pemberley than its grandeur warmed his heart. "In total? here are nearly two hundred tenant farms under Pemberley's care, some upwards of a hundred acres each."

Her eyes widened. "Two hundred? That is—far more than I imagined."

"Most are generational. Sons inherit from fathers. The families know every stone and stream on their plots. I grew up knowing their names, their crops, their worries. My father saw to it that I understood—truly understood—that we are not masters of the land. We are its stewards. Its servants."

He glanced away, the memories too sharp for a moment.

"He used to say that owning land is not about wealth. It is about weight. Every roof, every field, every child born to a tenant—those are ours to protect. And ours to fail."

Elizabeth was quiet, absorbing his words.

"Even though we were not close—I was too serious for him—he taught me about duty. I struggled to understand how he could spend so much time with me, but not really see me."

She gave him a sympathetic look. "Much like my own mother."

He nodded. "By the time I was fifteen, I understood a little better. He was teaching me to see the land not as property, but as people. Their harvests, their debts, their weddings and baptisms and burials. All of it flowed back to Pemberley. He *wanted* me to be serious about those under my care."

"That is a great deal to carry," she murmured.

He met her gaze. "It is. But it is also a privilege. Or it should be."

Her expression grew serious. "You miss it."

"I miss it every day," he admitted. "I do not know what we will find when we arrive."

They walked in silence for a few minutes more, the trees thickening as they approached the woods.

"I had thought Longbourn large," Elizabeth said after a time. "But it is barely twelve tenants. Most under twenty acres. My father... he manages well enough, but he rarely visits them. He says it is their land to work, and if they need something, they will come to him."

Darcy said nothing for a moment. "I know many others who believe similarly, but I realized that if you closely at their estates, you begin to see the cracks."

"Cracks?"

He nodded. "When one stops walking the fields, one forgets the names of the children. When one forgets the names, one forgets the needs. And when one forgets the needs, the land suffers. Or worse— the people do."

Elizabeth looked at him, her brow furrowed slightly. "You take your duty seriously."

"Duty is what remains when all else fades," he said quietly. "My father may not have shown me much affection, but he showed me that. If my name is forgotten, if my fortune disappears—what I owe to Pemberley and her people remains."

She reached over and touched his hand, briefly. "They are fortunate to have you."

He looked down at her fingers, warm against his. "I do not exist in this place. I do not know if they are cared for with the same diligence here, but I cannot imagine they are."

Conversation paused as they continued their journey, the trees thickening and the air growing cooler beneath the canopy. The road curved gently uphill, lined with mossy stone walls and the scent of damp leaves. Somewhere above them, birdsong echoed faintly in the bare branches.

Darcy's hand clenched at his side.

Each step felt heavier now. He could not tell whether it was dread or longing—perhaps both—but the familiar path wound like a memory beneath his feet.

"We are nearly there," he said softly as they approached a large hill. As they crested the rise, the trees thinned—and suddenly the world opened.

There, nestled in the distant hollow, lay Pemberley. He smiled slightly upon hearing Elizabeth gasp at his side.

Its stone façade stood proud against the backdrop of hills and bare trees, the great house reflecting the winter light with a pale, solemn dignity. The lake stretched before it, glassy and still, the reflection marred only by reeds left uncut at the edges. Behind the house, the slope rose gently into familiar forests, *his* forests.

"It is beautiful," Elizabeth whispered. "Not proud or grand in an artificial way. It looks like it belongs."

He swallowed, pride and pain mingling. "My mother insisted it remain so. She loved the hills."

As they descended the slope, however, the illusion began to shatter. The closer they came, the more clearly the signs of neglect showed themselves.

Weeds grew between cobblestones where gardeners should have passed. Hedges bulged untended, and the outer fences sagged. Where there should have been activity—stableboys, undergardeners, footmen preparing for the day's visitors—there was silence.

Darcy's step slowed. His breath caught.

Elizabeth touched his arm. "Whatever we find, we face it together."

He nodded, but his chest ached. The house loomed larger now, but it no longer seemed like a place of comfort.

At the outer gate, they paused.

"The main door?" she asked gently. "Or the back entrance?"

"I… do not know."

She offered a half-smile. "One offers tea. The other offers work. I know which one I prefer."

"We had determined to seek a tour of the estate, but if we later decide we wish to work here…" his voice trailed off.

"I did not think of it that way," she replied.

"Nor did I until this very moment."

They stood in silence, staring at the house for several moments.

"Let us try the servants' entrance," Darcy said at last. "It may give us more options."

She nodded, and without letting go of his arm, stepped with him through gate.

The side path crunched faintly beneath their feet—gravel overgrown with moss and stray grass. The farther they walked, the more the silence pressed in around them.

Darcy had not taken the servants' entrance in years. Not since boyhood, when he used to sneak down for a bannock or a honeyed apple, favored by the kitchen maids and scolded in equal measure by the cook.

Back then, the kitchen had been the heartbeat of the house—always hot, always loud. Even in the earliest hours, one could count on the thrum of activity: scullery maids at the pump, pots clanging, the warm scent of bread and boiling broth, the crackle of the great hearth, the ever-present rhythm of a house alive with purpose.

But now—

He pushed open the door, and the hinges groaned. The scent of damp stone greeted him first, musty and chill.

They stepped into shadow.

The kitchen was cold. Still. Silent.

No bread. No fire. No scent of stewing meats or fresh herbs hanging from the beams.

A few pots hung from their hooks, dull with dust. A chopping board lay forgotten on the long worktable, and a basket of root vegetables in the corner had begun to soften and rot. The great iron hearth, once the roaring heart of Pemberley, sat empty. Dead.

His chest tightened.

There should be ten people here. At least. Preparing for midday. Baking, boiling, braising. Someone humming a tune. Someone barking orders. The dog curled beneath the hearth waiting for scraps.

Now there was nothing. Only silence and the echo of a life that had once pulsed so vibrantly through these walls.

Elizabeth stood close beside him, her gloved fingers brushing his sleeve.

"I am so sorry," she whispered.

He could not answer.

His jaw clenched, and he swallowed the sharp ache rising in his throat. He had feared to see the neglect outside—but this? This lifelessness?

It was grief. As if a dear friend had passed in his sleep and none had noticed.

He stepped forward slowly, his boots echoing against the flagstones. Elizabeth remained at his side, her presence steadying. She said nothing, only matched his pace as they passed through the scullery and into the narrow hallway beyond.

He turned left, navigating by memory. Past the butler's pantry. Past the linen room. The air was stale here, like a house that had not drawn breath in weeks.

The familiar door stood half-open ahead.

The housekeeper's room.

He hesitated, heart pounding. The carved nameplate was still affixed to the wood, its lettering a little dulled.

He pushed the door open gently.

The room was small but tidy. A cup sat on the desk, half full of long-cold tea. A list of linen inventories lay on the blotter, alongside a keyring and a small stack of household accounts. The hearth here still held the faintest trace of warmth.

And a woman sat behind the desk, looking down at a ledger.

A flicker of hope surged. He exhaled, tension bleeding from his shoulders, and said softly, with quiet relief—

"Mrs. Reynolds."

Then froze.

He had spoken without thinking.

He was not Fitzwilliam Darcy. Not here. Not now.

Elizabeth's head turned toward him sharply, eyes wide.

Darcy's breath caught.

What have I done?

Chapter 17

The woman behind the desk startled slightly, her brow furrowing as she looked up from the household ledgers.

"Do I know you?"

Out of the corner of her eye, Elizabeth saw the look of panic on Darcy's face. She stepped forward and schooled her expression into a polite apology.

"Forgive us, ma'am. We presumed you were Mrs. Reynolds—someone in Lambton gave us that as the name of the housekeeper here at Pemberley."

"I see. Yes, I am Mrs. Reynolds." Her eyes narrowed, and she leaned back slightly in her chair. "Who might you be?"

"My name is Beth Smith, and my husband is William. We arrived in town only yesterday." Elizabeth offered the lie as smoothly as she could. "We are newly married and traveling through in search of occupation. My husband grew up in this area as a boy, and he wished to show me how beautiful it is."

The older woman's sharp gaze shifted to Darcy, who bowed his head respectfully.

Elizabeth continued, "We had heard that Pemberley was once open to visitors, but when we arrived, we saw the state of things... well, we thought perhaps there might be work available instead."

"Work?" Mrs. Reynolds echoed, folding her hands together. "I am afraid the estate is not what it once was. There is no coin to pay new hands—not even old ones, half the time."

"That is no trouble," Darcy said quickly. "We would be willing to work for room and board alone."

Mrs. Reynolds looked skeptical. "You would work for food and a roof with no questions asked? For a place you have never been? With no assurances of safety or pay?"

Elizabeth offered a rueful smile. "We understand a thing or two about difficult households. And we do not know yet how long we shall remain in one place. We have reasons to move on eventually, but for now…" She lifted one shoulder. "A quiet position, even temporary, would suit us well."

The housekeeper's eyes narrowed again. "You are not… fleeing anything, are you?"

"No!" Elizabeth said quickly. "Nothing of the sort. We simply…" She hesitated, then added, "We are waiting to hear about an opportunity. But until then, coin is low, and we would rather earn our keep than drain what little we have left."

Mrs. Reynolds was quiet a long moment, eyes passing over each of them in turn. Her expression remained wary—but gradually, something in it shifted.

"Well," she said slowly, "I cannot say why, but I believe you. I would not usually take such a chance, but there is not much left to lose. All the valuables have long been sold off, so it is not as though you can make away with the silver."

Darcy inclined his head. "You are wise to be cautious."

"Hmph. Cautious does not keep a house running. Willing hands do."

She rose from her chair, eyeing them both with a touch more curiosity than suspicion now. "What can you do?"

Darcy glanced at Elizabeth, allowing her to answer first.

"I can perform duties as a lady's maid," she said. "Hair, dressing, sewing. I can cook a few simple meals. Nothing elaborate, but I know my way around a kitchen."

Mrs. Reynolds' eyes brightened a little. "Mrs. Wickham would appreciate a lady's maid. She has struggled without one. The girl has not been properly turned out in months."

Elizabeth gave a slow nod, heart hammering.

"And you, sir?"

Darcy stepped forward. "I can serve as a footman, or assist with work in the gardens or stables if needed."

Mrs. Reynolds looked him up and down. "You are tall enough, I will give you that. Too refined for mucking stalls, but we all do what we must."

She turned back toward the desk. "I will find you a small chamber. You will share, I assume?"

Elizabeth's throat tightened slightly, but she nodded. "Yes, of course."

Mrs. Reynolds opened a ledger and made a brief note. "You may begin tomorrow. If you are of a mind to prove yourselves useful today, Cook could use help preparing supper. And the scullery is always in need of hands."

Elizabeth offered a smile. "We are happy to begin today, but we will need time to walk back to Lambton to retrieve our belongings."

The housekeeper pursed her lips. "Can either of you ride?"

"I can," Darcy said, stepping forward.

"Then you may use a horse from the stables. Tell John that Mrs. Reynolds said to put you on Nelly." Once Darcy nodded his understanding, Mrs. Reynolds continued. "Go now. Your wife can begin her duties in your absence."

"Thank you, Mrs. Reynolds." Elizabeth's voice displayed her sincerity.

Mrs. Reynolds' gaze was sharp but not unkind. "Whatever brought you here, I hope you find what you are looking for. This house could use a little hope."

Elizabeth swallowed and offered a quiet, "Thank you."

Beside her, Darcy said nothing, but his hand brushed hers as they turned to follow the housekeeper through the narrow hallway back to the kitchens.

"This is where I leave you," the housekeeper said once they reached the large stone room.

Darcy nodded politely, and Mrs. Reynolds disappeared back down the passageway. Before they entered the room, however, he gently caught Elizabeth's arm and drew her back to him.

"Are you truly all right with this?" he asked softly. "Working here, I mean. Living like this."

Elizabeth tilted her head. "Do I seem unwell with it?"

"That is not an answer."

She smiled faintly. "I said I was willing, and I meant it. I am not afraid of a little hard work."

Darcy still looked troubled. "It is not just the work. It is everything. The deception. The uncertainty. I hate the thought of you scrubbing pans or—God forbid—hauling chamber pots."

Elizabeth placed her hand lightly on his chest. "I am not afraid, William. I told you before: I have lit my own fires and tended my own sick sisters. I know what it is to be useful."

The sound of his first name leaving her lips felt strange, but she could tell it affected him. He reached up, covering her hand with his.

"You should not have to be," he told her.

"And yet," she said with a small smile, "I want to be. Especially here. Especially for *you*."

His hand tightened around hers briefly, and she saw it again—that storm behind his eyes. Worry. Pain. Determination.

"I will return as quickly as I can," he said quietly.

Elizabeth nodded. "Go. I will be fine."

He hesitated only a moment longer, then released her hand and turned down the corridor.

Elizabeth inhaled deeply, steeling herself. Then she stepped into the kitchen.

The room was quiet, save for the ticking of a wall clock and the faint hiss of the low-burning stove. No pots bubbled. No footmen stood at attention. The wooden tables were mostly bare, save for a few stacked bowls and an empty pitcher.

A door creaked open behind her.

Elizabeth turned as a middle-aged woman entered through the side door, shaking droplets of water from the hem of her apron and carrying a basket of eggs. Her graying hair was hastily pinned, and her expression was one of mild irritation as she muttered to herself.

"Had to go gather them myself," she said, placing the basket on the nearest table. "Don't mind the hens, but hate the scullery work. I was meant to be baking, not chasing down hens in the cold."

She looked up suddenly, eyes narrowing at the sight of a stranger in her kitchen.

"Who in heaven's name are you?"

Elizabeth offered a quick curtsy. "My name is Beth Smith. Mrs. Reynolds sent me to speak with you. My husband and I have been taken on to help."

The woman snorted, wiping her hands on her apron. "Help? With what?"

"I can cook a little," Elizabeth said quickly. "And I am quite good at following directions."

The cook's expression remained wary, but not entirely unfriendly. "Well. If you can peel carrots and keep your nose out of the pies, we will get along well enough."

"I shall do my best."

The cook looked her up and down once more, then grunted and reached for a knife. "You may call me Mrs. Wells."

Elizabeth smiled faintly. "It is a pleasure to meet you, Mrs. Wells."

"Well, we'll see about that. Grab a bowl and start with the carrots."

Elizabeth rolled up her sleeves and got to work.

~~*~*

The stable yard smelled of damp hay and manure, familiar and grounding. Darcy let the quiet surround him as memories flooded through his mind: his first time on a horse, his father at his side; Georgiana's expression on receiving a pony for her birthday; feeding his new steed an apple.

None of those occasions existed anymore.

As he rounded the corner, he stopped suddenly and stared in shock as a grizzled old man lifted his head from shoveling the muck. His frame was stooped with age and labor, his face deeply weathered, his once-dark hair now silver at the temples. But the eyes—sharp, dark, and tired—were unmistakable.

"Bates?"

Darcy's former valet squinted. "Aye?"

Emotion surged in Darcy's chest.

The stablemaster squinted in the half-light. "Do I know you, lad?"

Darcy composed himself quickly. "Forgive me. I... Mrs. Reynolds told me to come find you, for work."

Jonathan grunted. "Well, I am John. Who might you be?"

"I am William...William Smith. My wife and I have just been hired on to work."

"Only work here is horses and hay," said Bates, holding out his pitchfork.

Darcy hesitated. "Mrs. Reynolds said I could ask for Nelly to ride into Lambton, to retrieve our belongings first."

"Well, there's the saddle," Bates said, pointing at the tack.

"Yes, thank you," Darcy replied, his voice low.

Darcy turned to the saddle, and silently watched Bates return to his work. He had only been five years of age when his father had hired Bates to serve as his son's valet. The son of a loyal tenant and sharp as a whip, Bates had more in mind for his future than a farm, and yet here he was, mucking out the stalls. George Darcy was a master who took great satisfaction in helping those beneath him succeed.

To see the man who had so meticulously cared for Darcy for more than twenty years—indeed, he had almost been like a second father to him—scooping muck in the stables was painful to witness.

Darcy saddled the old, but gentle work horse, and mounted.

With the mare's steady gait beneath him, he made his way toward the inn. The sun had dropped low in the sky, casting long shadows across the frosted road.

I cannot believe that Christmas was less than a fortnight ago. It feels as though an eternity has passed since I was at Rosings… believing Elizabeth would accept my attentions.

He winced at the reminder of his pride and conceit. How certain he had been that his wealth, his consequence, his desire alone were enough to justify a proposal—and her acceptance. He had thought himself so generous—so noble—for loving a woman beneath him. And he had believed, truly, that she would be flattered by his notice.

But now…

Now, she walked beside him as an equal, and not because of his status or station. She had seen him undone—afraid, weeping, exposed—and had not turned away. When she smiled at him now, it was not the tight, mocking curl of a woman barely tolerating his company. It was soft. Real. And when she looked at him, she did not merely see Fitzwilliam Darcy of Pemberley.

She saw *him*.

And that knowledge steadied him as he finally arrived in Lambton on the old nag who looked to be as old as Darcy was himself.

The innkeeper looked up from his ledgers when Darcy entered, his eyebrows lifting with interest.

"You are back earlier than I expected," the man said, leaning forward. "Find what you were after at Pemberley?"

Darcy hesitated. "We have accepted temporary employment on the estate."

The innkeeper's brows rose higher still, then knit with worry. "Workin' up at Pemberley, are you? That is... well, I hope it is a short arrangement. Depends on how long George Wickham stays gone, I suppose."

Darcy's jaw tightened. "Away from home, is he?"

"For now," the innkeeper said warily. "Out on business, or debauchery—depends who you ask. But mark me, sir, best watch out for your wife when he's back. Pretty little thing like her would not stand a chance against him. That man is not right. Charming, aye, but poison all the same, and with a fierce temper when he does not get what he wants."

Darcy clenched his teeth at the man's description of Elizabeth, but the concern on the innkeeper's face was sincere, not leering.

"Thank you," Darcy said at last, pressing the coins into his hand. "For the warning."

With his saddlebags secured, he swung back into the saddle and rode toward Pemberley. The wind bit at his coat and collar, but it was the weight in his chest that chilled him most.

What have I brought Elizabeth into?

~~*~*

The ride back to Pemberley was long and cold.

By the time Darcy unsaddled Nelly, his hands were stiff and aching. The moon had begun its slow rise over the distant ridge. He offered quiet thanks, his voice hoarse, and as he made his way back toward the servant's entrance, boots crunching on the frozen gravel.

Warmth and light spilled from the kitchen windows, a welcome contrast to the chilled dusk.

Inside, Elizabeth turned at once. Her expression softened with visible relief and she motioned him to a chair at the servants' table.

"It is not much," she said, brushing a loose curl from her cheek as she set a plate before him. "But it is warm."

It was more than he expected.

The meat pie was plain, the crust uneven, but the scent made his mouth water. A thick slice of bread, a bit of crumbly cheese, and an apple completed the meal.

"Thank you," he said quietly.

She gave him a small smile and returned to the hearth, where she was wiping a low shelf near the stove. The cook looked up from peeling onions and gave him a sharp nod.

"So. You are the husband, then."

Darcy straightened slightly. "I am."

"When you have finished eating, fetch some water. There's a pail in the corner."

Darcy bowed his head slightly in acknowledgment and dug into his meal, savoring each bite. The food was simple but nourishing, and the presence of Elizabeth in the same warm room made it feel more than sufficient. As he worked through the pie, she came to sit beside him, her sleeves still rolled.

"Mrs. Wells is not half as frightening as she first appears," she said in a low voice. "But she does not suffer laziness. I suspect I shall not have much time for sitting for quite a while."

He gave a dry smile. "Have you met anyone else?"

She shook her head. "Only Mrs. Wells and Mrs. Reynolds, though I have seen signs of a few more maids. It is remarkably empty here."

At that moment, the kitchen door opened, and Mrs. Reynolds entered with her ledger tucked under one arm.

Darcy rose at once. The housekeeper gave him a brief nod, then turned to Elizabeth.

"I have spoken with the mistress," she said. "She would be glad of assistance in the morning. You are to help her dress and bring up a tray for breakfast. If she does not answer when you knock—which is likely—you are to try again after ten."

Elizabeth curtsied. "Yes, ma'am."

Mrs. Reynolds gave a satisfied nod and swept back out the door without another word.

The silence she left behind did not last long.

Mrs. Wells snorted from her place by the hearth. "That tray will do no good. Hasn't eaten proper since she fell with child."

Elizabeth stilled. Darcy froze, his spoon halfway to his mouth.

The cook noticed. "Aye. Poor thing. Scarcely more than a girl, and no mother to guide her. Left all alone with a husband not worth the name."

She clicked her tongue and returned to her onions, as though she had not just delivered a blow to both their hearts.

Darcy could not breathe.

Pregnant. Georgiana.

His sister was to bear a child.

He met Elizabeth's gaze across the table. Her eyes were wide, stricken.

Neither spoke. They finished their meal and completed their remaining tasks in silence. The air was heavy with unexpressed thoughts.

Elizabeth washed the dishes while Darcy fetched the pail and carried water in from the pump. Mrs. Wells directed them with gruff efficiency, setting oats to soak for the morning and barking orders about wiping down the table legs before bed.

By the time the last towel was hung and the final bowl dried, both of them ached in every limb.

They climbed the stairs side by side, neither speaking until they reached the small, cold chamber Mrs. Reynolds had assigned.

The bed was narrow. The blanket thin.

But it was clean.

Darcy sat on the edge to remove his boots, then stood aside so Elizabeth could do the same.

They said little as they readied for sleep. Too much had changed in a single day. Too many thoughts filled their minds.

When at last they lay down—shoulder to shoulder in the narrow bed—it was Elizabeth who turned to him, laying a hand gently over his heart.

"I am so sorry," she whispered.

Darcy swallowed, his throat tight.

"I was not here to protect her," he said hoarsely.

She made no reply, only reached for his hand beneath the covers and laced her fingers with his.

They lay like that for a long time, two hearts beating in the dark.

And though sleep came slowly, when it did, it found them together.

Still holding on.

Chapter 18

The light was still dim when Elizabeth awoke, the early dawn casting only the faintest hue of silver across the modest chamber. For a long moment, she lay still, listening to the even sound of Darcy's breathing beside her, steady and warm. He had not stirred once in the night, which she hoped meant he had found some small measure of peace.

She had not.

Pregnant.

Elizabeth closed her eyes against the thought of a young girl—nearly the same age as Lydia—alone in this crumbling house, bearing a burden she should not have had to carry alone.

Rising from the bed, she winced as she stretched out her stiffened muscles. She dressed quickly in the dim light, pinning up her hair without the aid of a mirror and washing with the cold water left in the basin. The morning chill clung to the stone walls and tile floor, biting at her skin, but she ignored it.

As she reached for her shawl, Darcy stirred. His hand searched the space where hers had just been. When he found only emptiness, he blinked and sat up.

"You are leaving?"

"We should be up now," she whispered. "I am to fetch Georgiana's tray, and you will have chores as well."

His expression tightened at the name, but he nodded, swinging his bare legs over the side of the bed with a yawn.

Elizabeth flushed at the sight and escaped into the corridor, making her way silently to the kitchens. Her footsteps were muffled by the worn flagstones. Mrs. Wells was already at the stove, stirring a pot with one hand and balancing a tray with the other.

"There you are," she said without turning. "Mistress's breakfast. Bread, weak tea, porridge. Not that she'll touch it. Where is your husband?"

"Mr. Smith will be along shortly." Elizabeth stepped forward and accepted the tray. "I will take this up to Geor—to Mrs. Wickham now."

"She will not say thank you," Mrs. Wells warned. "Mind you, she is not cruel. Just… quiet. As if she is somewhere far away."

"I understand."

"She is still a lady in spite of her age. Remember that."

"I shall."

Elizabeth turned to leave, but Mrs. Wells added, "And if she sends you out, do not take it personal."

"I will not."

The tray felt heavier than it ought to as Elizabeth made her way through the winding corridors. Mrs. Reynolds had given her a tour of the house last night, making particular mention of Mrs. Wickham's rooms. *East wing, second floor. Door at the end of the corridor.*

 She was grateful for the forethought; she would have been lost otherwise. The house had always loomed in her imagination—majestic, warm, proud. And now it was still majestic… but quiet. Wounded.

Like its mistress.

She reached the door and gently knocked on it with one knuckle.

For several moments, there was only silence. Eizabeth was about to turn to go, when a faint, dull voice said, "Enter."

Elizabeth entered with slow, steady steps, adjusting the tray in her arms. The room was sparsely furnished—no vanity, no dressing screen, not even a wardrobe. A single chest stood in the corner, and the hearth had only the faintest glow of embers, as if no maid had entered to stir it up again for the morning.

And there, in the narrow bed under a faded quilt, sat Georgiana.

Elizabeth's breath caught.

The girl—no, the young woman—was a shadow of what she imagined. Her figure, once likely elegant, was now slight to the point of frailty, making her rounded belly all the more prominent beneath the loose folds of her nightgown. Her hair hung in limp waves around her thin face, and deep shadows bruised the skin beneath her eyes. Her hands clutched the edge of the quilt, knuckles white.

Elizabeth forced a gentle smile. "Good morning," she said softly. "I brought your breakfast."

Georgiana did not reply.

The girl looked at her for a long moment—her eyes pale and wary. Then, slowly, she turned her head toward the window again.

"I am not hungry."

"I understand. Just the tea, maybe? The biscuits are very good this morning."

No answer.

Elizabeth approached slowly, set the tray down on the nearby table and stood back.

"I am here to help you dress, if you wish it," she said.

"I do *not* wish it," said Georgiana tersely.

Elizabeth nodded, but wasn't sure what to do next.

"Just go." Georgiana said, but there was more misery in her tone than fury.

Elizabeth curtsied and slowly backed out of the room feeling defeated. She hesitated only once, just beyond the threshold, listening for any movement from within—but there was none. Only silence, heavy and impenetrable.

She closed the door as softly as she could.

The disappointment settled in her chest like a stone, though she had expected nothing different. Still, it hurt—to see a young woman looking so hollow, so withdrawn, and to be powerless to ease it. She had not appeared to be angry. Only… lifeless. Apathetic.

For the remainder of the day, Mrs. Reynolds put her to work cleaning rooms that had not seen use in years.

"There have only been a few of us here since the house was reopened," the housekeeper explained. "A handful of maids is not enough to get a house like Pemberley in readiness very quickly."

Thick dust coated the furniture like a second skin. Cobwebs hung in forgotten corners. Elizabeth worked with care, though her mind remained half in that upstairs chamber, replaying the brief exchange again and again.

That night, as she once again collapsed into bed beside Darcy, she was too exhausted to do anything. Neither was able to speak a word before sleep claimed them.

The next few mornings passed in much the same manner. Elizabeth would rise early, fetch a breakfast tray, and walk it up the narrow stairs to the mistress's chamber. Each time, she knocked softly, entered upon silence, and was met with the same pale, wary eyes.

"I am not hungry," Georgiana would say—or sometimes nothing at all.

Elizabeth never pressed. She set the tray down and offered simple courtesies, then left the room quietly to begin her next assigned tasks, which mostly consisted of cleaning out disused rooms with dust so thick it lay like snowdrifts across the mantels. Mrs. Reynolds gave her a new room each day, and though the labor was wearisome, Elizabeth bore it without complaint.

Darcy she scarcely saw. He was sent to the stables most mornings and sometimes did not come in until long after sunset. Their conversations, when they came, were little more than tired murmurs exchanged over a shared crust of bread before they fell into the narrow servant's bed. His hand would find hers beneath the blanket, their fingers curling together as if in silent reassurance—but that was all.

By the fourth morning, Elizabeth stood at the window of the bedchamber, waiting for Georgiana to speak. The girl had not even glanced at the tray today. Her eyes were fixed on her lap, her thumb worrying at a cracked fingernail until the skin beneath looked raw.

Elizabeth hesitated. "My youngest sister used to do that," she said gently. "Bite her nails until they bled. Mama would scold her, but she never stopped. I think it was her way of holding the worry in."

Georgiana did not look up, but her fingers stilled.

At last! Elizabeth rejoiced at this small acknowledgment of her existence. Not wanting to push the skittish girl, she retreated from the room with a curtsy.

The following morning, as she dusted Georgiana's vanity table, a pale blue ribbon fell to the floor.

"Oh, my sister Lydia would love this shade of blue," Elizabeth said lightly. "Though with her coloring—like mine—it made her look dreadful. She cried for a week, then gave the dress to our sister Jane, who looks more like you, ma'am. It suited her perfectly, and I imagine this ribbon would do the same for you."

Realizing she was rambling, Elizabeth stopped speaking. Georgiana did not reply, but Elizabeth could feel the girl's eyes following her until she left the room.

The next day was when the walls finally came down.

After delivering the breakfast tray, Elizabeth was almost to the door when she heard a quiet voice behind her.

"You have two sisters?"

Elizabeth turned slowly, warmth blooming in her chest.

"Four, actually. I am the second of five daughters."

Georgiana nodded once, almost absently. Her gaze had dropped to the tray again, but her voice came more clearly this time. "I think I would have liked to have had a sister."

The admission hung in the air between them, fragile and precious. Elizabeth nearly cheered for joy—but she checked herself, keeping her hands still against her skirts.

"They can be troublesome," she said with a small smile, turning to the hearth to bring the cold fire back to life. "But I would not trade them for anything. Even when they steal my ribbons and lose my books."

Georgiana tilted her head slightly. "Do you have a brother, too?"

Elizabeth blinked, then shook her head. "No. My mother had five daughters and not a son among us. Which, as you might imagine, she has never quite recovered from." She gave the fire a soft poke with the iron and added kindling. "We do have a cousin, however, who stands to inherit everything. He is quite devoted to his duty. And to his sermons. And to the sound of his own voice."

A sound that could almost have been mistaken for mirth came from the bed.

Elizabeth grinned over her shoulder. "He once spent a full hour explaining to my father why his hens were not laying eggs due to a spiritual failing."

Georgiana's lips twitched. "And was your father persuaded?"

"He fell asleep," Elizabeth replied solemnly, "but it did not stop our cousin from writing a strongly worded letter on the subject."

This time, Georgiana couldn't help herself. She let out a sharp giggle—surprised, unguarded, and so rusty it sounded like it had not been used in years.

Encouraged, Elizabeth moved to the tray and uncovered the bowl with a small flourish. "I snuck a bit of honey into the porridge," she whispered. "Do not tell Mrs. Wells. She thinks her porridge can stand on its own."

She poured the tea, then added as casually as she could, "And I made the bread this morning. Only my third attempt, so if it is terrible, do not blame the kitchen." She held the chair out for her invitingly.

Georgiana glanced toward the plate as if contemplating scaling the alps, then slowly, hesitantly, pulled back the bed covers.

Elizabeth helped her with her dressing gown and guided her gently to the chair. Georgiana took up her spoon and cautiously tasted the porridge. Elizabeth turned away to make the bed, but she kept talking— about the stubborn nature of rising dough, about the weather, about how Mrs. Wells had muttered all morning that the new scullery girl had arms like boiled turnips.

When she turned back, the bowl was nearly empty. It was all Elizabeth could do to keep from clapping her hands in excitement. She could not stop the grin from appearing on her face as she left Georgiana's room with the nearly-empty tray.

The air was warm with steam and the scent of stew for dinner, and Mrs. Wells looked up as she entered.

"Well?" the cook barked. "Left it all again?"

Elizabeth lifted the tray with a grin. "No, ma'am. She ate nearly all the porridge. Even a bit of the bread."

Mrs. Wells gaped. "What did you do? Threaten her?"

"Of course not!" Elizabeth laughed. "We only talked."

Mrs. Reynolds emerged from the hall just in time to hear this and fixed Elizabeth with a sharp look.

"Talked?"

"I may have... shared a few stories. About my sisters. My cousin. Bread."

The housekeeper's eyes narrowed. "You are her maid, not her friend."

Elizabeth straightened. "I understand. But it was not my intent to cross a line... only to comfort someone who seems very much alone."

Mrs. Reynolds was silent for a moment. Then, in a gruff voice, she said, "I ought to scold you for being too familiar."

"Yes, ma'am."

"But it is the first full breakfast she has eaten in months." Her tone softened, just slightly. "So, I will not."

Mrs. Wells harrumphed. "Just do not expect her to eat my stew for dinner. I doubt your conversation is enough to manage that miracle."

Elizabeth smiled faintly as she gathered her apron to begin the next task. "You never know," she murmured. "Small miracles may happen, even here."

~~*~*

Like a dam breaking, once Georgiana began to speak, it was as though nothing could contain her.

At first, it was only a few questions—soft, hesitant things asked as Elizabeth poured tea or fluffed pillows. Within days, she was peppering

215

Elizabeth with inquiries: about her family, her childhood, the weather in Hertfordshire, the cost of London ribbons, the taste of strawberries in June.

It was not idle curiosity; it was thirst—a deep, aching thirst, and Elizabeth's words were water in a parched land.

Each morning, Elizabeth would arrive with the breakfast tray, and each morning Georgiana would be waiting—not always smiling, not yet—but awake, expectant. She allowed Elizabeth to help with her hair, even asked her once if the braid was neat enough, or if it looked foolish. Elizabeth assured her it was beautiful.

Little by little, the days changed.

The first milestone came quietly: Georgiana asked if she might wear a morning gown rather than her nightdress. Elizabeth did not cry, but she had to blink rapidly as she helped her lace it up.

The next day, she asked for the curtains to be drawn. "Just a little," she said. "I do not wish to see the whole world. Only the tree outside."

Another day, she accepted a book from the library. "Something I have read before," she requested. "*Evelina*. So I am not startled by the ending."

Elizabeth brought it to her, and Georgiana smiled at the first page like it was an old friend.

And then, one chilly afternoon, Georgiana surprised them all.

"I should like to go downstairs," she said, not looking at Elizabeth as she said it. "To the sitting room. Only for a short while."

Elizabeth helped her dress and put her house slippers on, then offered her arm to assist. Georgiana clutched it tightly the entire way down the stairs. Her steps were slow, and her breath caught more than once, but she did not turn back.

She lasted only fifteen minutes in the drawing room before she wilted against the cushions, worn out by the effort. But when Elizabeth suggested they return upstairs, Georgiana said, "Not yet," and stayed for five minutes more.

It was the beginning of her return, and the entire household could feel the shift. The few housemaids in residence even smiled kindly at Elizabeth when they passed in the halls.

Elizabeth still scrubbed and laundered and swept. Her hands were raw more often than not, and her back ached by midday. But her heart was lighter. Darcy's quiet glances in the evenings grew warmer. There was a rhythm now to their lives. A shared purpose.

And Elizabeth was grateful for the work. Keeping busy meant she could forget just how much she missed her family. *Poor Jane—I do hope the plan she and Mrs. Collins came up with is proceeding smoothly.*

So, when Mrs. Reynolds asked Elizabeth to help carry coal buckets to the upper bedrooms one morning, Elizabeth nodded and began rolling up her sleeves.

But a soft voice from the stairs interrupted them.

"Mrs. Reynolds?"

The housekeeper and Elizabeth turned in unison, gaping at their mistress, who had never before come downstairs into the servants' area on her own accord.

"Yes, Mrs. Wickham?" Mrs. Reynolds instantly moved to the young girls' side. "How might I be of assistance?"

"I should like Beth to remain with me today. In the sitting room. If… if she is willing."

Elizabeth's eyes widened, and the new scullery maid gasped, though she was quickly hushed by Mrs. Wells. Mrs. Reynolds looked as though someone had suggested feeding the silver to the pigs.

"Beth is a maid, Mrs. Wickham, employed in the scullery," she said slowly. "It would not be appropriate for her to act as your companion."

"But my father was a gentleman," Georgiana said, chin lifting slightly. "And hers was as well."

The words landed like a dropped tray.

Mrs. Reynolds turned to Elizabeth with eyes narrowed in suspicion. "Is this true? You are the daughter of a gentleman?" The skepticism in her voice was clear.

Elizabeth curtsied. "Yes, ma'am. My father was a country gentleman. But I am no longer in that station. I serve where I am needed, and I do not object to the work."

That seemed to soothe the worst of Mrs. Reynolds' concerns, though her brow remained furrowed.

"Even so, the household runs short-handed," the housekeeper told Elizabeth. "I cannot spare your time for idle chatter."

Georgiana blinked quickly. "It is not idle to me. Please, Mrs. Reynolds. There is… there is no one else to talk to. Am… am I not the mistress of this house?"

This last sentence was spoken quickly, and Georgiana immediately shrank back, as if expecting a blow to come from in response to her defiance.

There was a long pause. Mrs. Reynolds looked from one to the other—at Georgiana's pale, imploring face and Elizabeth's respectful calm—and sighed.

"Perhaps," she said at last, "we might strike a compromise, Mrs. Wickham. I truly meant it when I said that rely on Beth to keep this house running. She does more work than three of the other maids put together."

Georgiana's shoulders sank with relief.

"Beth may sit with you for an hour each morning after helping you dress for the day. After that, she will return to her duties. I cannot afford to lose her entirely."

A ghost of a smile bloomed on Georgiana's face. "Thank you, Mrs. Reynolds. That is more than fair."

Elizabeth nodded solemnly. "Yes, ma'am. Thank you."

The older woman gave them one final look—half suspicious, half resigned—then turned and walked back down the corridor.

Elizabeth glanced at Georgiana, who was still standing at the foot of the stairs.

"Shall we?" she asked gently.

Georgiana took her arm. "Yes," she said quietly. "Please."

And together, they stepped into the drawing room. The fire was low, but Elizabeth stoked it. When she turned back, Georgiana was already seated, hands folded in her lap.

"Well, now, Mrs. Wickham—what would you like to discuss?"

The girl slumped in her chair slightly. "I... I am not sure. I have not... that is, I have never..."

Georgiana's words trailed off, her hands twisting together in her lap. She stared at them as if they might somehow finish the thought for her.

Elizabeth sat across from her—not too close, not too far. "That is quite alright," she said lightly. "We may talk about anything—or nothing at all. I am content just to sit with you."

A long pause followed. Then, tentatively: "You have spoken of your sisters before. What... what was it like, having so many people of the family living in the house?"

Elizabeth's heart squeezed. She smiled, soft and genuine. "It is like having built-in friends... and sometimes built-in enemies. A house full of secrets and noise and hair ribbons gone missing. A battlefield one moment and a sanctuary the next."

Georgiana blinked. "I think I would have liked that. Will you... will you tell me about them?"

Elizabeth smiled—then blinked, startled by the sudden sting behind her eyes.

"I do not mind," she said, her voice quieter than before. "Though I ought to warn you—my sisters are all dreadfully silly. Except when they are not."

And then she began to talk of her sisters.

Of Jane's gentleness, and her way of listening without ever judging.

Of Mary's solemn lectures and the way she always misquoted scripture.

Of Kitty's eagerness to laugh—even when no one else was laughing.

Of Lydia's noise, her wildness, her chaos—and her joy.

She told of rainy afternoons squeezed five in a row on the settee, of arguments over bonnets and gowns and lace, of whispered jokes at the dinner table. Of long walks and shared secrets and slammed doors. Of growing up in a house always half-broken and half-full.

And then, without warning, her voice caught. She turned slightly away, dashing a tear quickly from her cheek.

"I am sorry," Georgiana whispered.

"No—do not be." Elizabeth smiled through the blur. "I would rather remember them—even all their maddening imperfections—than forget they existed at all."

A long silence settled between them.

Then Georgiana said, "I think they must have been wonderful."

Elizabeth let out a quiet breath. "They were. They are."

And Georgiana reached, very gently, for her hand.

It was not healing. Not yet.

But it was hope.

And in that moment, it was enough.

Chapter 19

The next morning, as the fire warmed the drawing room and frost silvered the windows, Georgiana surprised Elizabeth with a quiet laugh.

"I have no idea what I am supposed do in society or say in a drawing room," she admitted, fidgeting with the hem of her sleeve. "I know what ladies are meant to—embroider or write letters or discuss the weather—but I never learned *how* to do any of it. I was always in the nursery. Until I was not."

Elizabeth tilted her head. "What do you mean?"

"I went to my aunt and uncle's home after my father died," Georgiana said. "I remained upstairs in the nursery until they could send me away to school. It was a horrible place. Well, the school was alright, I suppose, but it was so very lonely. I was not titled, you see, as most of the girls there were. And I never left, not even on holidays—the earl and countess thought it disruptive."

Elizabeth's heart twisted. "You stayed at school the whole year?"

Georgiana nodded. "Every term. Every holiday. They said it was best for me to stay with my tutors and lessons. But no one wrote. No one visited."

"I am so sorry."

Georgiana's eyes dropped. "I got used to being invisible."

There was silence for a moment, then Elizabeth asked gently, "And what happened when you left school?"

"I was fifteen. My aunt said I needed to begin preparing for my come-out. So, they hired a companion. She was strict. Cold. She cared

221

more about my posture and my curtsy than my thoughts." Georgiana gave a small, wry smile. "I never got my come-out, in the end."

Elizabeth's brows lifted slightly. "Why not?"

Georgiana hesitated, then spoke in a voice laced with embarrassment. "Because I met my husband."

Elizabeth's breath caught, but she kept her expression calm. "Would you… would you like to tell me about it?"

Georgiana's eyes did not lift from her lap. "It was Hyde Park. I was not quite sixteen. My companion had a cold and stayed behind, so I was walking with just my maid and a footman. George Wickham saw me— he recognized me from when I was very young. I did not remember him well, but he said we were great friends once. He was so kind. So handsome."

Elizabeth swallowed, her throat suddenly tight.

"He flattered me," Georgiana said, twisting her fingers together. "He told me I was beautiful. That I deserved better than the life I was living. We… we arranged more walks. He sent me notes through my maid. Sometimes he visited when my aunt and uncle were out. And then one day, he told me he loved me."

Elizabeth nodded, urging her gently to continue.

"He said that if we eloped, I would never have to come out. I could avoid all the pressure and just live quietly with him at Pemberley. He made it sound so perfect." She closed her eyes. "That summer, we went to Matlock for the heat. George followed us there. And one night… we left."

"Left?"

Georgiana nodded. "Straight to Gretna Green. It took two days. The first night, we shared a room. He was very kind. Polite. He kissed me once, and then let me sleep. I thought—" She broke off and shook her head. "But the next day, after the marriage… he was different."

Elizabeth's stomach clenched.

"He took me to the inn," Georgiana whispered, "and he was not gentle. At first it was… pleasant, I suppose, but then I was frightened.

He was loud. Demanding. He said it was his right now. That I belonged to him."

Tears welled in her eyes.

"And after that, all he spoke of was money. That he was master now. That he would finally have everything he deserved." She let out a bitter laugh. "But when we returned to Matlock, my relatives shut the doors in our faces. They would not see me. The earl said I had made my choice and was no longer his responsibility."

Elizabeth wanted to scream.

"They told him the dowry was inaccessible until I turned twenty-one. He was furious. Said I had tricked him. That I was a worthless waif. He drank half the way to Pemberley and ranted the rest."

She looked up, her voice hollow.

"And when we arrived... the house was musty, nearly empty. He disappeared within a week. Took what coin he could find. Said he was going to London. I have not seen him since."

Elizabeth reached over slowly, placing her hand over Georgiana's trembling fingers.

"You did not deserve any of that," she said quietly.

Georgiana did not reply—but she did not pull away.

And that, Elizabeth thought, was something.

~~*~*

That evening, after the house had quieted and the last chores were done, Elizabeth climbed the narrow stairs beside Darcy. Their feet were heavy with fatigue, but her thoughts were still tangled in the conversation from earlier that day.

Once inside their small, shared chamber, Darcy lit the single taper candle near the washbasin while Elizabeth unlaced her bodice and hung her gown. The routine was familiar now—quiet, careful, companionable. But tonight, she sensed something stirring beneath the surface of it all.

She waited until they were both beneath the thin coverlet before speaking.

"Georgiana told me about how she married Wickham today," Elizabeth said softly into the darkness.

Darcy shifted beside her, his body stiffening. "She did?"

"She said he was kind at first. That he kissed her once, and nothing more, the night before they married. But after…" Elizabeth swallowed hard. "After, he changed. She was afraid."

Darcy's jaw clenched. She could feel the tension radiating from him.

"I want to kill him," he said, his voice low and shaking. "I want to find him and rip him apart. But what angers me more—what shames me—is that I did not react much better when it happened at Ramsgate."

He rolled onto his back and stared at the ceiling.

"She was just fifteen. And I—I was so full of pride. So angry. I barely heard her explanation. I was too busy being horrified at what might have happened. I accused her of being reckless. Of being foolish. But I never told her *why*. I just said how disappointed I was in her."

Elizabeth turned toward him, her hand seeking his beneath the covers.

"I was just as bad as Wickham because I was supposed to love her, and instead I just made her feel ashamed."

"Knowing girls of that age, I imagine it did not go well."

"She screamed at me," he continued, voice thick. "Told me that she wished I had never come. That she wished she did not have a brother." He let out a shaky breath. "I have never forgotten it."

Elizabeth's heart ached. "And then I told you that I wished you had never been born."

Darcy turned his head slightly. A beat of silence passed.

"You did," he eventually whispered in a voice rough with emotion.

"I did not mean it," she whispered. "I was angry. But I should not have said it, no matter how angry I was."

She reached up and cupped his cheek, a day's bristle scratchy beneath her palm. "You did not deserve it. Not from your sister. Not from me."

He started to object, but she placed her finger gently against his lips.

"No. Listen to me. You were wrong about many things—so was I. But you have always tried to protect the people you love. You are a good man, Mr. Darcy."

"Not William?" He let out a shaky laugh. "So formal. I would have imagined we were past such things."

"No, not when we are here. Not when that name is not who you *truly* are. But if you insist, I shall call you Darcy… or Fitzwilliam, if you would rather."

His gaze searched hers, and something shifted in his expression—something soft and aching. "Say it again."

She tilted her head. "Fitzwilliam?"

He closed his eyes briefly, as if the sound of it brought him peace. "Yes. That is who I am. With you, I remember."

Elizabeth's hand lingered against his cheek. "Then Fitzwilliam you shall be. You are a good man, *Fitzwilliam*."

He looked away, blinking hard.

"I remind Kitty of it all the time," Elizabeth continued. "You cannot blame others for how you behave. Even when Lydia is at her most provoking—and heaven knows she often is—it is still Kitty's choice to rise above or not."

Her voice softened further.

"I should have remembered that. I let my anger take over. But you did not force me to say those words. That was my choice. And I am so incredibly sorry for the hurt I caused."

Darcy looked at her fully then, his gaze searching hers in the flickering candlelight.

"I forgive you," he said quietly.

Elizabeth nodded. "And I forgive you."

The silence between them was not empty—it was full. Of understanding. Of pain. Of love.

She laid her head on his shoulder, and he wrapped his arm around her waist, pulling her close. For a moment, she thought he might—finally—kiss her, but he did not.

But still, together, they slept.

~~*~*

The next morning, Georgiana was already up when Elizabeth entered the bedchamber with the breakfast tray. The girl's posture was straight in the high-backed chair, but her hands were clenched tightly in her lap, and her face was pale beneath the gentle light streaming through the window.

Elizabeth set the tray down without comment and moved to the window, as she usually did, to draw the curtain just slightly wider. The silence stretched.

Then, in a voice so low it might have been a breath, Georgiana said, "You must despise me now."

Elizabeth turned slowly. "Despise you?"

Georgiana did not lift her eyes. "Now that you know what kind of person I am."

Elizabeth crossed the room and sank into the chair beside her. "And what kind of person is that, exactly?"

Georgiana gave a broken little laugh. "Foolish. Fallen. Weak. I knew eloping was wrong. I did it anyway. I threw away everything for someone who never cared for me."

There were tears forming at the corners of her eyes, but she blinked them back furiously. "I am… I am ruined. You must think me utterly beyond redemption."

Elizabeth reached out and gently laid a hand over Georgiana's trembling fingers. "No. I think you were a lonely girl who was tricked. Who was starved of affection and grasped the first hand that reached toward her."

She waited until the girl finally looked up, her eyes red-rimmed and vulnerable.

"You needed to be loved," Elizabeth continued softly. "And when no one around you who was willing to fill that need—to fill your heart, your soul, your sense of worth—of course you believed someone who did."

227

She exhaled slowly. "People are like buckets, Mrs. Wickham. We all need to be filled—with kindness, respect, love. If no one teaches us how to fill our own, or how to protect it... someone else will come along and pour in whatever they like. Even poison."

Georgiana swallowed hard, her lip quivering.

"You are not ruined. You are wounded. But wounds can heal."

Elizabeth gave her fingers a gentle squeeze. "So no, I do *not* despise you. I think you are very brave."

A long silence followed. Elizabeth could see the thoughts behind the girl's eyes—the shame, the fear, the desperate hope that perhaps, just perhaps, she might not be cast out entirely.

But then a knock came at the door, and Elizabeth glanced at the clock.

"I must go," she said gently. "Mrs. Reynolds will be waiting."

Georgiana gave the faintest nod, her eyes fixed on the folded napkin in her lap.

Elizabeth stood and crossed to the door—but just before she left, she paused and looked back. "You are not alone anymore, Mrs. Wickham."

There was a brief silence. Then, in a voice barely above a whisper, the girl said, "Could you... could you call me Georgiana?"

Elizabeth blinked. Her heart twisted at the tentative hope in the girl's voice. Smiling sadly, Elizabeth replied, "I am afraid Mrs. Reynolds would not approve."

Seeing the girl's face fall, she added, "But I believe I might safely be able to call you Mrs. Georgiana."

The girl's eyes lifted, wide and bright, and she nodded vigorously. "Please. I do not wish to hear my husband's name."

"Very well, Mrs. Georgiana. I shall see you in two hours in the drawing room."

Elizabeth dipped a curtsy, then left the room with brisk steps—her heart full, her mind racing. She took a hasty meal in the kitchen, then set to work, polishing a hallway mirror and sweeping the upstairs landings. Once her morning duties were complete, she splashed cold water on her face, straightened her apron, and returned to the drawing room.

She found Georgiana already seated in her usual chair near the fire, a folded shawl draped neatly in her lap. The girl looked up as Elizabeth entered—no smile, but no fear either. That was progress enough.

"I have been thinking," Georgiana said, her tone hesitant but curious. "You spoke this morning of... of learning to fill one's own bucket. How does one do that?"

Elizabeth's brow lifted, pleasantly surprised. "There are many ways. Little things, mostly."

She sat down across from her. "For some, it is sewing—something useful or beautiful. You could mend linens or embroider a handkerchief."

Georgiana looked thoughtful.

"Or music," Elizabeth added. "You might play the pianoforte or arrange a tea tray just as you like it. You might even design a table or practice a new language—anything that brings order or joy to your day."

Georgiana's lips parted slightly. "French? Or Italian?"

"I am not fluent," Elizabeth said with a soft smile, "but I know enough to muddle through."

Georgiana looked toward the window, her expression quietly alight.

"I like that idea. Of filling the day with... small things. Things that are mine."

Elizabeth nodded. "That is the best place to begin."

Georgiana turned back to her, her gaze steadier than it had been in days. "Then let us begin. Today."

The days that followed brought a quiet but steady transformation. As Georgiana found small ways to fill her hours—sorting linens, reviewing old piano sheets, even threading a few careful stitches into a baby's cap—her shoulders gradually lost some of their tension. The hollowness in her voice softened. Her gaze no longer fell to the floor quite so often.

And yet, the silence that settled after their morning chats still clung to Elizabeth's thoughts. There was so much Georgiana did not know. So much no one had prepared her for.

One chilly afternoon, as they sat in the drawing room and the fire snapped softly in the hearth, Elizabeth reached across the workbasket and gently asked, "Have you made many things for the baby yet?"

Georgiana looked up in surprise. "Made?"

"Clothes. Blankets. Perhaps a bonnet or a gown?"

The younger woman blinked. "I... no. I have no idea what is needed. Or how to begin."

Elizabeth gave her a warm smile. "Then that is the perfect place to start. A few small things, perhaps. Sewing is like writing love into fabric. It gives you time to think... to hope."

Georgiana glanced down at her lap, fingers twisting the edge of her shawl. "But I do not have anything. No patterns. No cloth. Not even old things to rework. And this is not London—there are no shops nearby. Not that I could pay for anything, even if there were. And my jewels..."

She stopped abruptly. Her lips pressed into a thin line.

Elizabeth said nothing for a moment, then reached for a length of thread. "In my family's home, we kept things in the attic. Old gowns of my mother's. Toys we outgrew. Furniture that was unfashionable, but still strong and sound. I wonder... might Pemberley have something like that?"

Georgiana's brow furrowed. "I do not know. I never thought to ask."

"Mrs. Reynolds might," Elizabeth said. "She has been here a long time. She may remember what was put away."

With sudden purpose, Georgiana reached for the bell. A moment later, Mrs. Reynolds entered the room, her expression alert.

"You rang, ma'am?"

Elizabeth nearly smiled at the address—Georgiana still seemed surprised by it.

"Yes," Georgiana said softly. "Do you know if there is anything stored in the attic? Any clothing? From when my mother was alive?"

Mrs. Reynolds blinked. "The attic?"

She stepped farther into the room and looked from Georgiana to Elizabeth, her expression unreadable. Then her eyes widened.

"I quite forgot," she murmured. "It has been more than fifteen years. After your mother passed, the master had so many things removed—furniture, baby clothes, even her favorite books. He said he could not bear to see them. I suppose he locked them away, and I never thought of it again."

Georgiana's hands curled into the folds of her gown.

"Could we... see them?" she asked tentatively.

"Not today," Mrs. Reynolds said gently. "The light is going already. But if you wish, I shall have the attic opened tomorrow."

Georgiana nodded, and Elizabeth saw something flicker in her eyes that had not been there before.

Hope.

"I think I shall go lie down," she said softly, rising to her feet.

"Would you like help?" Elizabeth offered, rising as well.

Georgiana shook her head. "No... thank you. I am all right."

She left the room, her step slow but unshaken.

Elizabeth lingered only a moment longer before slipping out a side door in search of Mrs. Reynolds. She found the older woman in the main hall, consulting a list of repairs with one of the housemaids.

"Mrs. Reynolds?" she asked softly.

The housekeeper turned at once. "Yes, Beth?"

Elizabeth hesitated, then lowered her voice. "Forgive me, but... I wondered. Is there a midwife nearby? Someone trustworthy?"

Mrs. Reynolds's expression sobered. "You think she is near her time? She is still so small.

"I do not know. I do not believe even she knows how far along she is," Elizabeth admitted. "But from what she has described—and what I have observed—I should guess she is five months gone. I expect she will feel the quickening soon. I think it would be wise to have someone examine her, to make sure everything is progressing as it should."

The housekeeper sighed. "Aye, that sounds about right. I can send word to town—though Lambton is not what it once was."

"If not a midwife, then perhaps a parson's wife nearby?" Elizabeth asked hopefully. "Someone with knowledge, even if informal?"

Mrs. Reynolds's mouth pinched into a tight line. "Not likely. The living at Kympton was given by the Earl to the son of a crony. The young man never comes near the place, and there is no money to hire a curate. The parsonage stands empty."

Elizabeth stared. "But… what do people do? For worship? For guidance?"

"They do without." Mrs. Reynolds looked tired. "There are no Sunday services. No regular marriages. No baptisms."

Elizabeth's voice sharpened with concern. "Then what about Georgiana? What about her churching?"

"I had not thought that far ahead," the older woman admitted. "Perhaps we can pay a rector from a neighboring parish, but it will cost more than we have to spare."

Elizabeth frowned. "It is disheartening to think that men of the cloth have grown so—so transactional."

Mrs. Reynolds gave a bitter chuckle. "The world has changed, Beth. Or perhaps it has only settled into what it always was, beneath the surface."

She grew quiet then, gazing up the staircase toward the west wing.

"It used to be different here. When the old mistress was alive. There was music. Light. Care." Her voice turned wistful. "But after she passed, and there was no son to inherit… the master gave up. Slowly. Quietly. Until there was nothing left."

Elizabeth followed her gaze, her throat tightening.

Then she reached out and gently touched the woman's arm.

"There may be nothing left," she said softly. "But there is something now. Someone. And soon there will be two."

Mrs. Reynolds did not reply.

But she gave a faint nod.

Chapter 20

Elizabeth stood bundled at the back door, her shawl wrapped tightly around her shoulders, waiting with an eagerness she tried not to show too plainly. When Darcy emerged from the stables, wiping his hands on a cloth, she could not help the smile that broke across her face.

He returned it—wry and warm. "Shall we escape while we still can?"

Their paths rarely crossed now—at least not for long. A quiet brush of fingers when passing one another in the hallway, a tired smile across a supper table, a whispered goodnight before collapsing into sleep. But this afternoon, by some miracle of scheduling or grace, they had both been given the same half-day.

They stepped into the winter chill together, their boots crunching lightly over the frozen earth. The air was sharp, but the sun shone low and golden through the bare trees. The landscape had softened slightly since their arrival—some of the worst weeds and brush had been cleared by his hand and others', though the estate still bore the marks of neglect.

They walked slowly toward the woods beyond the lower meadow, saying little at first. But as the distance from the house grew, so did Elizabeth's words.

"She asked for another book," she said, voice bright with pride. "And she wore a different gown today. I found it buried beneath a stack of blankets in the wardrobe. She even let me style her hair in a new way."

Darcy stopped walking. He turned toward her, his eyes full.

"I do not know how to thank you."

She shook her head. "It is not necessary."

"It is. Elizabeth, you have done more for her in a fortnight than anyone else could in a year. I… I could not have hoped for someone more perfect for her." A pause. "Or for me."

The words landed between them like a breathless secret.

She looked up at him, surprised—and deeply moved.

He cleared his throat, gaze drifting to the horizon. "I have been thinking," he said, more quietly now. "If… if we are stuck here, if this becomes our life—could you be happy like this? At Pemberley, I mean. As we are now?"

Elizabeth exhaled, her breath a cloud in the air. "I do not know. This life—it is difficult. Exhausting. But it is also meaningful. Helping Georgiana has been… incredibly rewarding."

He nodded, but his shoulders slumped slightly as he waited.

"But," she continued softly, "I do miss my family. Jane. Papa. My sisters. Even Mama's fretting and Lydia's wild behavior." Her voice caught. "And I do not know if I will ever see them again, not as their sister."

"I am sorry," he said, the words low and pained. "I never meant—"

"You must not apologize," she interrupted gently. "I do not blame you for what happened. You could not have known." She looked away, her throat tightening. "But I do wonder when, or even if, the angel—or spirit or fae, whatever he was—will decide we may return. He said 'for a time.' But what does that mean?"

He was silent.

When she looked at him again, his expression was so forlorn that it struck her like a blow.

"I did not mean to sadden you," she said quickly. "Truly. I only wonder."

He nodded, but his eyes were shadowed.

"I would rather think on things that give me pleasure," she said, with more cheer than she felt. "Helping Georgiana gives me that. As does walking with you. Talking to you. Coming to know you, even if we are like two ships passing in the night."

His mouth quirked. "More like two ships crashing in the night," he said dryly. "And sinking into a snoring slumber."

She giggled, the sound bright and welcome in the crisp air. "That is not very romantic."

"No," he agreed, "but it is accurate."

They shared a smile, quiet and full of something that felt very close to love.

The wind picked up then, sharp and sudden, tugging at Elizabeth's shawl.

"We should head back," she said. "It will be dark soon—and colder still."

He offered his arm, and she took it without hesitation.

As they turned toward the house, the shadows lengthening behind them, she realized that though nothing about their situation was certain, this—walking beside him—felt like the surest thing she had known in weeks.

~~*~*

Darcy drove the fork into the frozen earth with more force than necessary, the chill of the late January morning stinging his fingers even through the worn leather of his gloves. His breath came in visible puffs,

He had already broken the handle of one spade this week, and John—he still could not get used to thinking of his former valet that way—had fetched another one with a severe look and muttered comment.

This made him grateful for the current silence, and he paused for a moment to pull off one glove, flexing his fingers.

Calluses had formed along his palms, hardened ridges where smooth skin had once marked the hands of a gentleman. His shoulders ached with the familiar soreness of work—not the fleeting strain of fencing or the controlled posture of a mount, but the slow, relentless weight of repetition. His coat, once tailored precisely to his frame, now tugged too tightly across the upper arms. And his breeches, though belted snugly, had begun to hang looser at his hips.

He studied his hand, the reddish lines at his knuckles, the dirt lodged under his nails despite his best efforts. These were not the hands of a man raised to govern estates and sign ledgers from behind polished desks.

These were the hands of a man who worked.

He ought to have felt ashamed. His aunt would have sniffed and called him a drudge. His uncle would have wondered how far he had fallen. Even Bingley, good-hearted as he was, might have raised a brow at the stains on Darcy's cuffs.

But Darcy was not ashamed.

No—there was a strange pride in these marks. They were proof. Proof that he was not merely surviving, but shaping, changing. Doing what had to be done. These hands had helped mend the stable roof. They had cleared weeds from the kitchen beds and turned compost piles and fed livestock when John's old knees gave out.

He was no longer only master in title. He was servant, too—and better for it.

If only it were enough.

He glanced toward the manor, its chimneys smudging the sky with pale smoke. Somewhere inside, Elizabeth was reading to Georgiana or showing her how to piece together a tiny baby gown from salvaged scraps. If anyone had asked him, months ago, what transformation looked like, he would have spoken of fortune, marriage, reputation.

Now he knew better.

It looked like ribbons sewn into old muslin. It sounded like laughter coaxed from silence. It felt like warmth blooming in a drawing room that had long been cold.

All around him, the orchard slept beneath a shroud of frost—gnarled pippin trees stretched brittle limbs toward a gray sky, their roots blanketed in mulch to keep the worst of the cold at bay. Brassicas clung to life in stiff rows nearby—cabbages, cauliflower, sprouts. At the far end of the garden, under warped panes of glass, parsley and lettuce pushed bravely through the soil in a cracked forcing frame. The earth was stubborn. Unyielding.

But he kept at it. Replacing his glove, he adjusted his grip on his tool and once again began to dig at the frozen earth. His knees were damp with the frost through the warn fabric of his trousers, but he ignored the chill.

He had to do *something*.

It had been nearly a month since they arrived at Pemberley—he and Elizabeth, the strangers at the door. A month since they lied their way into service in the house that should have been his birthright. A month since he stood outside his sister's room and realized that she no longer knew him.

And in all that time, it was Elizabeth—always Elizabeth—who had brought light into the place. It was she who coaxed Georgiana to eat, who sat beside her each morning in the drawing room, who spoke gently and cheerfully until that too-thin girl began to speak in turn.

Elizabeth had sewn new gowns from scraps. Helped organize the attic. Spoken to Mrs. Reynolds with respect and the other servants with kindness. Every day she found some new way to ease a burden, to spark a change. She was transforming his sister. His home.

And he—he who had once been master of Pemberley—could do little more than shovel muck, aerate garden beds, and keep the stables from collapse.

He knew it was not about pride—at least, not pride over his former status as one of the wealthiest gentlemen in England. He had left that behind when he bent his back beside her in the kitchens. But as each day passed, a quiet dread unfurled in his chest.

While his absence had made life far worse for the people around him, his current presence had *not* made matters better.

He was here now, but what had changed? What good had he done?

Georgiana was not affected by his presence at Pemberley. It was not he who was able to draw her out, to help her be happy.

If not for Elizabeth…

His throat tightened, and he paused, leaning against the spade and staring out across the frostbitten orchard. He had never imagined a world in which Elizabeth Bennet would willingly live beneath his roof as a servant. And yet here she was—without rank or recognition, without comfort or even certainty—and she had never once faltered. She bore her own grief with grace and turned her strength toward others.

He had watched her from afar these past weeks—watched the way she touched Georgiana's hand, the way she smiled at the cook, the way she still laughed at his jokes, when they had the rare chance to speak.

She was everything good in his world.

But do I mean the same to her?

He exhaled sharply, the breath misting before him. His grip tightened on the handle of the spade, and he raised it high, ready to shove it in the frozen dirt once more.

"Blast!"

The shout came suddenly from across the yard.

Darcy's head snapped up. That was not John's voice. It held none of the tired grumble of the elderly stable hand. Nor was it one of the handful of footmen who still remained—they would not dare raise their voices within earshot of the house.

No. This voice was unfamiliar. And yet, familiar at the same time.

His brows drew together. Who could have come to call? There was no parson. The post had not come in days. Perhaps a tenant? A former tenant, more likely, coming to demand what could no longer be given.

Then he heard it.

Hooves.

Fast. Loud.

Not the heavy plod of a delivery cart or the meandering trot of a farmer's mare—but something sharper. Eager. A stallion. He frowned. The only horse in the stables was Nelly—and she was too old for such sport.

A sharp whinny split the air.

Darcy stiffened. Someone was in the stable. *A thief?*

He dropped the spade and picked up the pitchfork lying near, then rushed forward. His boots crunched over the frost and gravel, his breath tight in his chest. Rounding the corner, he raised his makeshift weapon, half-expecting to find a thief haltering Nelly. His fists clenched. He would defend what little remained of Pemberley if it came to that.

But he stopped short at the sight before him.

It was not a thief.

It was worse.

George Wickham.

~~*~*

The fire crackled quietly in the drawing room hearth, lending warmth to the morning light that spilled across the worn rug and well-scoured floors. Elizabeth sat near the window with a length of pale muslin spread across her lap, carefully pinning one of the repurposed panels from Lady Anne's gowns. Across from her, Georgiana leaned forward in her chair, her own needle poised over a faded infant cap she had unearthed from a forgotten trunk.

The last several days had been spent in the attic, wrapped in dust and memory. They had uncovered a small trove of baby garments—caps, bonnets, gowns no longer than a foot in length. There were bolts of unused cloth and two gowns of Lady Anne's that, though outdated in style, were of fine make and sound fabric. Elizabeth had carefully begun to alter them to suit Georgiana's swelling form, and Georgiana, to Elizabeth's delight, had taken up the work herself with surprising eagerness.

"This one was mine," Georgiana said now, lifting a gossamer blanket with a smile both wistful and proud. "Mrs. Reynolds said I cried endlessly unless I was swaddled in it. She kept it for years in a box with my first lock of hair."

Elizabeth smiled. "A sentimental heart in such a formidable housekeeper. I never would have guessed."

"She can be very softhearted when she thinks no one is looking."

Georgiana folded the gown gently and returned to her stitching. After a long pause, she said, "I do hope this baby is a boy."

Elizabeth glanced up from her work. "Why is that?"

"Because then he may inherit," Georgiana said simply. "He could be the master of Pemberley and stand on his own. If it is a girl…" Her voice trailed off. "A girl will be nothing but a pawn. Like I was."

Elizabeth set her needle aside and leaned forward. "That may be true in part. But even pawns can move. Even within the constraints of our world, you have choices. Not all of them, but some."

Georgiana looked unconvinced.

"You choose to get out of bed each morning," Elizabeth continued softly. "You choose to sew, to speak, to come down to this room. You may not choose everything in your life, but you can choose how to fill your hours. You may decide what books to read, what colors to wear, how to spend your time."

"I used to play," Georgiana said suddenly. "All the time. The pianoforte, I mean. I would sing, too. For hours. But I have not touched it since I married."

Elizabeth's brows rose. "Then I think it is high time you did."

Georgiana shook her head. "It does not feel right."

"Your husband has already taken so much from you," Elizabeth said gently but firmly. "Do not let him take this, too. Do not let him win one more thing."

Georgiana was quiet, her needle still. Then, slowly, she straightened her back and looked toward the hallway.

"Very well," she said. "I shall open the music room today."

Elizabeth smiled with quiet pride. She bent again to her mending just as a sudden noise from outside made her freeze.

Raised voices.

A shout. Then another.

She rose quickly and crossed to the window.

"Oh no," she gasped.

Behind her, Georgiana turned sharply in her chair. "What is it?"

Before Elizabeth could form a reply, the door burst open and Mrs. Reynolds hurried into the room. Her usual calm was nowhere in evidence; her cheeks were pale, her eyes wide with something like fear.

Georgiana stood at once. "What is going on?"

Mrs. Reynolds' voice was clipped and tight with urgency. "It is your husband," she said. "Mr. Wickham. He... he has returned."

~~*~*

Darcy watched in shock as Wickham fought to bring his horse under control. The animal was spirited and barely broken, wild-eyed and frothing, its bridle askew.

It was far too majestic a creature for a coarse man like Wickham.

"Stupid beast!" Wickham bellowed, jerking the reins and lashing its flank with the crop.

The horse reared again in protest, hooves slicing the air. Wickham barely held his seat.

A low grunt of disgust sounded just behind him.

Darcy turned, startled to find John standing at his shoulder, arms folded and jaw clenched.

"Pity the brute was not thrown," the older man muttered under his breath.

Darcy said nothing aloud, but in his heart, he agreed.

They both remained where they were, unmoving, as Wickham cursed and wobbled in the saddle, trying to force the animal into a tight circle.

Then he saw them.

"Oi!" Wickham shouted. "You there! Come help!"

John exhaled sharply through his nose. "If only to spare the beast his lash," he muttered, then moved forward with stiff limbs and a weary sigh.

Darcy remained rooted, spade still in hand, as John approached the horse and caught the reins with practiced ease. The animal huffed and pawed the dirt, but calmed slightly under a steadier hand.

As soon as all four hooves were firmly on the earth, Wickham sneered and slid from the saddle with all the grace of a sack of grain. He staggered slightly as his boots struck the frozen ground, then, with a flourish, he pulled a flask from the inside of his coat and took a long draught.

Foxed.

Darcy's stomach turned. *It is not even midday.*

Wickham wiped his mouth with the back of his hand, swaggered a few steps toward the house, then lifted his voice in a crude bellow.

"Where's my wife? Georgiana! Georgie, my girl!" His voice slurred over the words, and Darcy winced at the unpolished speech from a man who had always prided himself on his gentlemanly behavior. "I'm back, Georgie! Come give your Wickham a kiss!"

Darcy stiffened, fists curling tight around the handle of the spade he had forgotten he was holding. His whole being bristled with fury—but as he took a step forward, John's hand came down hard on his arm.

"Do not," the older man said quietly.

Darcy looked at him, confused and outraged.

"Best not to get involved," John added in a low tone. "You may have been a gentleman before you came here, but you are no longer. Nothing good comes from standing up to a master. Not when you're a servant. Not even to the likes of him. The law is no friend to men in livery."

The words struck Darcy like a blow. He drew a sharp breath and looked down at the worn coat he wore, the trousers loose at the waist, the calluses on his hands. His clothes were homespun. His boots scuffed. To all the world, he was a servant. And if he intervened—

"But, my wife," he said, desperately, "is not just a servant. She is a gentleman's daughter."

John's eyes softened slightly. "Aye. I know. So does Mrs. Reynolds. She will do what she can to protect the girl."

But the grim concern in the man's voice spoke more honestly than his words.

Darcy turned back to the courtyard. Wickham was shouting again, something slurred and incoherent, waving the flask toward the front door.

*If he harms one hair on Elizabeth's head—on Georgiana's—*Darcy thought, his vision blurring with rage, *I will not be held responsible for what I do.*

Chapter 21

Elizabeth stared at the housekeeper in horror before turning to Georgiana, whose face had gone white.

So white, in fact, that for a moment Elizabeth feared she might faint. Her fingers clutched the arms of her chair. Her mouth trembled open. "He... he is here?"

From outside, Wickham's voice rang loud and clear: "Georgiana!"

The girl flinched.

Elizabeth turned to Mrs. Reynolds, who stood stiffly with both hands wringing the corner of her apron. Thinking quickly, Elizabeth stood and crossed the room to Georgiana.

"Quick, Mrs. Georgiana," she said firmly, taking the girl by the elbow. "Let us get you upstairs. You are quite ill, after all, and must remain in your bed for the baby's sake."

Georgiana blinked. "Ill?"

"Yes," Elizabeth said, guiding her toward the door, "with something contagious, perhaps. A stomach ailment. You have been vomiting and are in frequent need of the chamber pot. You are weak. You must stay abed and away from others."

"I—"

"That is perfect," Mrs. Reynolds cut in, suddenly animated. She seized Georgiana's other arm. "Yes, that is exactly right, missus. A dreadful fever. The master will not wish to catch it."

They hurried down the corridor, feet muffled on the worn carpets, just as the heavy front door banged open below with a deafening crash.

Georgiana gasped and stumbled.

"Almost there," Elizabeth murmured, her heart pounding. They made it into the bedchamber, and Mrs. Reynolds immediately moved to the window to pull the drapes shut.

"I will go help—" Elizabeth started, but a desperate grip on her hand stopped her.

"Do not—do not leave me," Georgiana whispered, eyes wide with terror.

Elizabeth turned back, startled. She looked from Georgiana's pale, stricken face to Mrs. Reynolds'.

The housekeeper's expression hardened with sudden resolve. "It is probably best if you stay in the room with your mistress," she said briskly. "You must tend to her, after all."

Elizabeth opened her mouth to object, but Mrs. Reynolds shook her head sharply.

"Mr. Wickham will not care that you are married, Beth," she said, voice low and urgent. "For your husband's sake, you must remain as unseen as possible."

Elizabeth's breath caught. She gasped, horrified—and nodded. "Yes. Yes, of course."

Heavy, uneven footsteps stomped up the stairs.

"In there." Mrs. Reynolds pointed to the small dressing room off the bedchamber. "I will handle him."

Elizabeth darted into the space, heart thundering. She knelt behind the edge of a tall linen press and gently eased the door nearly shut, leaving only the smallest crack near the hinges through which she could just glimpse the room.

Mrs. Reynolds helped Georgiana into bed, yanked her hair down from its careful braid, and drew the covers up to her chest just as the bedchamber door burst open.

"Georgie!"

Wickham's voice was loud—too loud—and thick with alcohol. He staggered in, one arm raised in mock greeting. The stench of spirits wafted into the dressing room, making Elizabeth's stomach churn.

Georgiana whimpered.

Wickham swaggered over to the bed and blinked at her, his lips curling. "What happened to you?" he asked. "You have gotten fat."

Mrs. Reynolds stepped forward swiftly. "It is the babe, sir."

There was a beat of silence.

Then Wickham let out a raucous laugh. "A father! Well, then! I knew I had it in me. Just a few nights of fine work, and look what it got me!" He grinned wide and leaned down, lips puckered.

Georgiana turned her head quickly, gagging.

He drew back sharply, offended. "Do I disgust you now, Georgie? You were not like this a few months ago. As I recall, you were quite eager for my kisses. Is there someone else?" His voice grew harsh, angry. "Is the babe even mine?"

Elizabeth's nails dug into the linen press.

But Mrs. Reynolds was already speaking. "Of course it is yours, sir! Mrs. Wickham has been terribly unwell. The babe made her sick enough, but then she caught a fever—or something like it. Stomach pains. Vomiting and the like. We suspect one of the maids or the tenant children passed it on."

Wickham recoiled.

"Very contagious, whatever it is," Mrs. Reynolds continued smoothly. "She has not left her rooms for two days. We were just about to summon a physician when you arrived."

He sniffed and took a step back. "Well then. I suppose I shall leave you to it, my dear."

He turned without another word and sauntered out, closing the door with a thud behind him.

Elizabeth let out a breath she did not realize she had been holding.

"There," Mrs. Reynolds said at last, voice shaking just slightly. "That should give us a few days, anyway, to decide what to do."

Elizabeth emerged slowly from the dressing room. Georgiana's eyes were wide and glassy, but she was not crying.

"Both of you," Mrs. Reynolds said, gesturing between them. "Stay in this room. I will bring you food, books, whatever you need. No one else comes in. No one else sees you."

Elizabeth nodded.

"Thank you," Georgiana whispered, able to speak at last.

~~*~*

Darcy's arms ached from the weight of the firewood stacked in his grip, but the ache was welcome. It gave him something to focus on—something other than the image of George Wickham striding into Pemberley as if it were his birthright.

With a grunt, he shifted the bundle higher and nudged open the rear servants' door with his boot. The kitchen corridor was warm, the air heavy with the scent of onions and roasting meat—though tension practically crackled from the other end of the hallway.

"Three courses!" came a sharp, aggrieved voice. "Three bloody courses!"

Darcy set the logs down just as Mrs. Wells appeared in the kitchen, red-faced and fuming. A mixing spoon was clutched in her hand like a weapon. She slammed it onto the counter, snatched a copper pot off the shelf, then turned in place as though unsure which indignity to tackle first.

"He has not been here in weeks—weeks—and now he returns like a conquering general, barking orders as if he pays the bills! Cake with his tea, he says! Venison for supper!" She spun back around. "Venison, when we have not had a proper kill since Michaelmas!"

She reached for a bag of flour and slapped it onto the counter.

Darcy stepped forward cautiously. "I can bring in more wood for the ovens, if needed."

Mrs. Wells flinched, then huffed. "Aye, and water too, while you are at it. If he wants cake, the man will get dry bread unless we get the batter thick enough to rise."

Darcy nodded and made to leave again, but just then Mrs. Reynolds appeared in the doorway, a strand of hair coming loose from her bun.

"Do what you can, Mrs. Wells," the housekeeper said without preamble. "With any luck, he will be too sotted by supper to recall half of what he ordered."

Mrs. Wells scoffed. "We should be so fortunate."

Mrs. Reynolds turned to Darcy. Her eyes were sharp, but her voice was low and firm. "Beth and Mrs. Wickham are secure upstairs. For now, we are maintaining the pretense of illness—a stomach ailment, very contagious. That ought to keep him away from them for a few days."

Darcy exhaled slowly, nodding. "Thank you."

"But with your wife confined, I am down one set of hands. I shall need help."

"Of course," he said quickly. "Anything."

"I hope you do not mind some maid's work," she said bluntly. "There is polishing, trays to carry, fires to tend. He will expect the usual service. And I will be... preoccupied with diverting him as much as possible."

"I understand," Darcy said at once. "And... thank you."

"Thank me when it is over," she muttered. Then, after a brief hesitation, she added more grimly, "I am hoping he will tire of country life within a day or two. That is his habit, at least, from what I remember of him. But something in me fears he has returned because he is out of coin—or worse, because he is running from trouble."

Darcy's mouth tightened. "Let us hope trouble does not follow him."

Mrs. Reynolds nodded once, then turned to the cook. "Do what you can, Mrs. Wells. Even if it is stew and a scorched cake, make it look like a feast."

Mrs. Wells muttered something about the devil's appetite, but Darcy was already lifting the wood and heading back to the scullery—eyes sharp, ears alert.

The remainder of the day continued in the same manner. All day long, he found things to polish, trays to carry, fires to stoke, boots to clean. The rhythm of the work helped keep his hands from trembling, but his mind...

His mind would not still.

From the moment Mrs. Reynolds had closed the door behind her that morning, he had not seen Elizabeth once. No shared glances. No whispered asides in passing. No chance to brush her fingers as he passed the dishes at supper.

He was simply *alone*.

And Wickham—Wickham was *everywhere*. Stomping through the halls, slurring orders, knocking over a decanter in the study and laughing as the footman scrambled to clean it. From the murmurs of the kitchen staff, he learned Wickham had already sent for wine twice more and spent a full half hour in the music room yelling at the old piano for being out of tune.

"Even the furniture has abandoned me!" he had bellowed.

Darcy clenched his jaw each time he passed the study. He kept his eyes down, as a good servant ought, but every muscle in his body screamed to turn back and confront the man. To drag him bodily from this house and throw him out into the snow.

But he could not.

Not now.

Not when the cost of being discovered might endanger Elizabeth.

As night fell, he retreated at last to the small servants' room he and Elizabeth had shared since arriving at Pemberley. The bed was neatly made—his hands had done so that morning—but now it looked foreign. Empty. Wrong.

He stood for several moments before sitting down heavily on the edge of the mattress. His hands burned with the effort of the day—blisters forming in new places beneath the calluses he had already earned—but he barely noticed.

He kept staring at the hearth, watching the flame's flicker begin to die.

Upstairs, in the mistress's chambers, Elizabeth lay alone.

Worse—she lay connected to that vile wretch, sleeping only a thin door away.

What if the liquor does not dull his... appetite?

Darcy pressed his fists to his knees.

He considered it—rising, creeping upstairs, and settling just outside Georgiana's chamber door to listen for trouble. He could do it. He *should* do it.

But the maids had been whispering. He had heard the rumor passed between servants' lips with giggles and wide eyes.

"Is it even his child?"

"Did you hear what he said?"

"Maybe it belongs to one of the footmen."

The blood drained from Darcy's face at the thought.

If Wickham found him loitering near Georgiana's door... if he were accused, if Elizabeth were shamed, if Georgiana were further endangered...

He swallowed hard and bowed his head.

No. He must stay away. No matter how much it pained him.

He lay down on the narrow mattress, staring up at the ceiling. The walls creaked. Wind whispered under the eaves. Somewhere a shutter banged loose. And through it all, he listened.

Listened for a cry, a footstep, a scream. If he heard one, he would do whatever was required.

And if Wickham so much as looked at Elizabeth or Georgiana the wrong way—servant or not—he would not be held responsible for what came next.

But no sound came.

At last, near dawn, he drifted into a fitful sleep—his dreams dark and heavy with helplessness. Elizabeth reaching for him, but he could not move. Wickham laughing. Georgiana weeping. Flames consuming the halls of Pemberley as he pounded on doors that would not open.

And still, he slept.

Alone.

~~*~*

The first day passed slowly, like wading through thick, invisible fog.

Though the fire burned warmly in the hearth of the mistress's chamber, neither Georgiana nor Elizabeth could quite relax. Every sound in the corridor—every footstep, creak, or muffled voice—made them flinch. Wickham's drunken shouting earlier that morning had not been repeated, but the memory of it lingered like the scent of cheap port.

Georgiana sat on the edge of the bed, arms wrapped tightly around her knees, while Elizabeth tried to summon calm for them both.

"We need distraction," she declared after several minutes of fraught silence.

Georgiana glanced at her with dull eyes. "From what? My life?"

"From the noise of your thoughts," Elizabeth said firmly. "So here is what we shall do. I will tell you every ridiculous story I can remember from my childhood until you either laugh or tell me to be quiet."

And so she did.

She began with tales of Lydia—falling into a pigpen at age five, insisting she could make gooseberry jam with onions, and once stealing a pair of Lady Lucas's shoes because they sparkled. Then came Mary's failed attempt at writing poetry and Kitty's tantrum over a bonnet that blew into a pond.

Georgiana smiled faintly at the first tale, then chuckled a little by the third, even though she had heard some of them before.

It was not much, but it was a start.

Mrs. Reynolds came in shortly thereafter, her arms full of distractions: books, sewing, and a small tea tray. "Try to keep your minds occupied," she said softly, casting a wary glance toward the locked adjoining door to the master's chambers. "And your ears alert. I will bring supper later."

The hours passed slowly. Elizabeth read aloud while Georgiana worked at mending a small linen gown they had salvaged from the attic—one that had once belonged to Georgiana herself, now destined for the child she carried.

When night fell, the tension returned in full.

Elizabeth moved the chair from the vanity to sit before the connecting door, placing a heavy folio of music atop it for good measure. If Wickham tried to enter in the night, the racket would surely wake them both.

They lay side by side under the bedclothes, both still clothed in case they needed to flee, Elizabeth with her eyes fixed on the dimly glowing embers. Georgiana stared at the ceiling.

"Do you think he will come in?" the girl asked softly.

"I do not know," Elizabeth replied truthfully. "But I do not think he will tonight. He was well into his bottle when last we heard him."

Indeed, not long after, Wickham's unmistakable snores reverberated through the connecting wall. It was crude and vulgar—but oddly comforting. At least while he slept, they were safe.

Georgiana turned toward Elizabeth. "I am glad you are here."

Elizabeth reached across the narrow space and gave her hand a squeeze. "So am I."

And at last, they both slept.

~~*~*

It was midmorning the following day, when the fire in the drawing room finally began to chase away the chill. Mrs. Reynolds knocked softly and slipped inside, holding out a sealed envelope on a salver.

"For Mrs. Wickham," she said with a respectful nod before quickly exiting.

Georgiana blinked in surprise, her embroidery needle halting mid-stitch. "For me?"

Elizabeth leaned over curiously. Georgiana's hand trembled slightly as she reached for the thick envelope. She stared at the family crest impressed in wax, then at the familiar, sprawling handwriting.

"It is from Colonel Fitzwilliam," she whispered. Her hands began to shake even more.

"Your cousin?" Elizabeth asked gently.

Georgiana nodded, eyes suddenly bright with tears. "I— I have not heard from Richard since before—since before I married. I thought…" She swallowed. "He must be so ashamed of me; he could not even bear to write."

255

Elizabeth's heart clenched. "Open it," she said softly. "Read what he says."

With trembling fingers, Georgiana broke the seal and unfolded the thick paper. Her eyes moved rapidly across the page, and after only a few lines, her hand flew to her mouth. Her shoulders began to shake, and the letter dropped into her lap as tears spilled freely down her cheeks.

Elizabeth reached for her hand. "What is it?"

Georgiana could not speak for a moment, only shook her head and handed her the letter. Elizabeth took it gently and scanned the words.

My dearest Georgiana,

I scarcely know how to begin this letter. I sit here with pen in hand, surrounded by the warmth of our family home, and yet I feel as though I am writing to someone I failed most grievously.

I have only just returned to England. My last assignment took me far afield—to a place where post is unreliable, and the world even more so. I did not know. I did not know, Georgie, that you had left Matlock, that you had married, that you had been abandoned, and—God above—that you are now with child. Word of your condition has spread beyond Lambton to even here at Matlock.

Forgive me. Not for what I did, but for what I could not do. For not being here. For not protecting you, as I swore I always would.

I should have been at your side. I should have been there to knock Wickham's teeth in and drag you back home myself.

Instead, I return to hear my baby cousin's life has been turned inside out while I played soldier in some foreign field.

You are not alone, Georgiana. I know that is little comfort now—but I mean it with every part of me. You still have family. You still have me. I will come to you as soon as I am able. If you will have me, I will do whatever I can to set things right—or at least better than they are now.

I am at Matlock recovering from my wounds, so I am only a few hours' ride away. As soon as I can comfortably make the journey, I intend to call on you. If your husband is also at Pemberley, be assured that I will be having words with him about his treatment of you.

I love you, dear girl. I always have.

Yours devotedly,

Richard

Elizabeth blinked back tears as she finished reading. When she looked up, Georgiana was quietly weeping again—but this time with relief.

"I thought he hated me," she whispered. "I thought he was so disappointed in me, that he could not even bring himself to write. That he had washed his hands of me entirely."

Elizabeth shook her head. "He loves you. He was not silent out of judgment, Georgiana. He was silent because he did not know."

Georgiana sniffled and clutched the letter to her chest. "I thought I had no one."

"But you do," Elizabeth said gently. "You have more people supporting you than you realize. You have Colonel Fitzwilliam. You have Mrs. Reynolds. You have me and my husband."

A small, broken laugh escaped the girl. "I do not deserve any of you."

Elizabeth gave her hand a gentle squeeze. "None of us deserve the people who love us. That is what makes it a gift."

Georgiana looked at her, blinking rapidly through tears. "May I write him back? At once?"

"Of course, my dear! You hardly need *my* permission. Remember, you are mistress of Pemberley."

And as Georgiana rose and hurried to find pen and paper, her cheeks still streaked with tears but her posture straighter than it had been in days, Elizabeth offered up a silent prayer of thanks.

Hope, once a fragile ember, now burned a little brighter.

Chapter 22

It had been three days.

Three days of silence, sewing, and stories. Three days of worry and waiting, of watching the door like it might swing open at any moment and bring with it everything they feared. Three days of Wickham roaming the halls like a fox outside the henhouse, and Mrs. Reynolds faithfully delivering trays and diversion to the mistress's chamber.

But it could not last.

By the fourth day, Mrs. Reynolds entered the room with tight lips and a pinched expression. "He is beginning to suspect," she said grimly. "If we keep you shut away any longer, he will come up here himself. And if he finds Beth…"

Georgiana paled visibly.

Elizabeth reached for her hand. "You do not have to sit with him long. Only for meals. After that, return here. I shall be waiting."

It was not enough to make Georgiana brave—but it was enough to make her move.

That evening, she dressed slowly in one of the looser gowns they had altered from her mother's things—soft gray with a darker sash, and a fichu to hide the neckline. Elizabeth helped arrange her hair and offered her a final look of encouragement before she descended.

Elizabeth took the servants' hall down to the dining room, where she stood near the corridor like a sentry. Her hands twisted together in front of her apron. She could not hear the exact words, but she could hear tones—Wickham's voice rising and falling in annoyance, Georgiana's soft and tentative replies.

Darcy passed her several times as he carried dishes in and out, grinding his teeth in an effort to remain silent. Each time he came close, his arm brushed up against hers—not enough to slow him down, but enough to ground her.

The whole household held its breath.

Inside the room, Wickham's mood darkened by the minute. He was irritated by the roast, by the temperature of the wine, by the bread. He muttered about the lack of decent company and barked at Georgiana when she only ate small bites of her food.

By the time the tea tray was brought out, he was pacing behind his chair.

"I have half a mind to drag you upstairs myself," he snapped. "You are my wife, and you *will* fulfill your duties."

There was a pause, and Elizabeth tensed.

Georgiana's voice—shaky but audible—answered at last: "You would not want to harm the baby."

Another pause.

Wickham gave a disgusted scoff. "What does it matter? I prefer a woman who is not ill and simpering all the time, anyway."

And then he was gone.

Elizabeth waited several minutes before she pushed open the dining room door. Georgiana sat perfectly still, hands clenched in her lap, lips pressed into a bloodless line.

Darcy stepped in behind her. "He has taken a bottle and his coat," he said quietly. "He will not return soon."

Georgiana gave a tight nod.

Elizabeth walked forward and touched her shoulder gently. "Come, Mrs. Georgiana. Let us go back upstairs."

Darcy did not speak as they passed him—but as their eyes met briefly, Elizabeth knew they shared the same thought.

This reprieve would not last forever. And something had to be done.

~~*~*

The morning light through the tall windows was soft and grey, falling over the bed where Georgiana sat stitching a length of muslin while Elizabeth sorted through a small basket of ribbons and lace. For now the house was quiet—eerily so. Wickham had returned in the small hours, half-singing and half-cursing, but there had been no further disturbance. Mrs. Reynolds had reported that he still slept off his drink, and so, cautiously, they worked.

Elizabeth glanced at the open door leading to the dressing room, every sense alert though she smiled and spoke lightly.

"Your stitches are improving, Mrs. Georgiana," she said. "At this rate, your child will have a finer layette than any infant in Derbyshire."

A faint blush touched the girl's cheeks. "I only hope there is time enough. I am so slow—"

The words cut off with a small gasp.

The door slammed open.

George Wickham stood on the threshold, his coat unbuttoned, his cravat askew, his eyes bloodshot but alight with something far worse than drink. He leaned against the frame for a moment, surveying the scene, and then his mouth twisted into a smile that made Elizabeth's stomach turn.

"Well, well," he drawled. "No wonder you have been hiding away, Georgie. You have been keeping company with an angel."

He stepped into the room. The scent of stale brandy clung to him.

Elizabeth froze where she stood, her heart pounding. Wickham's gaze fixed on her, roving in a way that made her skin crawl. He came closer—too close—and reached out a hand to trail one finger down the side of her cheek.

"Where have you been hiding this beauty?" he murmured. "I do not recall seeing you before."

Elizabeth forced herself not to flinch, not to recoil, though every nerve in her body screamed at her to move. She folded her hands tightly in front of her and lowered her gaze. "I am Mrs. Wickham's maid, sir," she said, her voice steady only through willpower.

"Her maid?" His grin widened. "A pity. Pretty thing like you should not be wasted pressing gowns and fetching ribbons. Perhaps I can change that."

Georgiana's voice, thin but determined, broke the moment. "Beth is married, sir. Her husband works in the stables."

Wickham's laughter filled the room. "A husband, is it? Then the man is a fool to let you out of his sight. Perhaps he does not... please you as he ought?"

Elizabeth's throat tightened. She took an involuntary half-step back.

"Perhaps," Wickham continued, his tone oily, "you wonder what a real man is like."

Elizabeth's fingers clenched around the sewing scissors in her apron pocket, but before she could speak—or act—the door opened sharply.

"Beth!" Mrs. Reynolds' voice cut through the tension like a blade. "You are wanted below at once."

Wickham turned lazily toward her. "Always taking my toys away, Mrs. Reynolds."

The housekeeper's expression did not change. "I will not say it again, Beth."

Elizabeth curtsied quickly and fled, the pounding of her heart loud in her ears. Only once she was safely in the corridor did she allow herself a breath.

Behind her, she heard Mrs. Reynolds' calm, measured voice: "Perhaps, sir, you might prefer to take your luncheon in the study. I will have it brought at once."

And the door shut firmly between them.

~~*~*

The kitchen was too warm.

Darcy stood by the back table, sleeves rolled, drying the last of the supper dishes. He had just stoked the fire for Cook, who was grumbling over a sauce that refused to thicken properly. The scent of boiling beef hung heavy in the air. Mrs. Wells muttered to herself about overcooked carrots and men who ordered meals like kings without lifting a finger to hunt them.

He was about to ask whether more firewood was needed when the door opened behind him. He turned.

Elizabeth stood there, pale as paper, her hands trembling so badly that she pressed them together to still them. Her eyes darted to Cook, then back to him.

"Beth?" he said softly, stepping forward. "What—?"

"I need a moment," she whispered. "Please."

Darcy nodded tightly and guided her through the scullery and out into the narrow corridor, where the air was cool and still. She leaned back against the wall, breathing fast, her arms wrapped around herself.

He took one look at her face—her wide eyes, the shaken lines of her mouth—and the tight coil in his chest snapped.

"What happened?" he asked, his voice low and urgent.

She shook her head. "He came into her room—Georgiana's room. I think he thought she was alone."

His breath caught. "And you were there?"

"Yes." She still would not meet his gaze. "He—he touched me. My face. He said things. Awful things. About my husband not pleasing me—"

A coldness settled in Darcy's bones. He stepped forward, his fists clenched. "He dared to lay his hands on you?"

She lifted her head, finally looking at him. "He did not hurt me, William."

"I do not care," he snapped. "I will kill him. By God, I will—"

"No!" She grabbed his arm, gripping it hard. "You cannot. You are a servant. He is the master here. If you so much as raise your voice, he could have you beaten or thrown out—or worse. And then what would I do?"

His jaw clenched, his nostrils flaring. "I will not let him near you again."

263

"You will not have to." Her voice trembled, but her eyes were steady now. "I will stay below stairs, or in my room, or with Georgiana. But I will not move about the house without you beside me."

Darcy was still breathing hard, but he nodded. Slowly. "Good. Yes. I will stay at your side whenever I can. And I will speak to Mrs. Reynolds."

"I believe she already knows. She was the one who came in and got me out."

He exhaled through his nose, furious and helpless and aching with gratitude. He reached for her hand and pressed it between both of his own.

"I swear to you," he said quietly, "if he ever tries again—"

"You cannot," she whispered. "Not yet. Not while we're in this world. We will get through this, together."

Her words struck deep. Slowly, he nodded. "Together."

She squeezed his hand once, then let go.

And with only a glance between them, they returned to their places in the quiet war that Pemberley had become.

~~*~*

The next two days passed in a strange, suspended tension.

Each morning, Elizabeth was escorted by Darcy down to the kitchens. He remained near her through every task—hauling coal, polishing woodwork, trimming wick lamps—his presence a constant, quiet shield.

If Wickham left the house, Elizabeth would hurry to Georgiana's side, the two women resuming their quiet projects and conversations in the safety of the drawing room. Georgiana's nerves were frayed, but she tried to hide it behind smiles and stitching. Elizabeth did the same.

It was a pattern—tense, quiet, survivable.

Until the morning it shattered.

Elizabeth was in the upstairs music room, wiping dust from a high shelf while Darcy swept the hearth. The windows were open to let in air, and the scent of coal smoke drifted faintly on the breeze.

Then came the shout.

"Fire!"

Elizabeth's cloth slipped from her hands. Her heart jolted.

Darcy shot upright. "Stay here," he ordered, already halfway to the door. "I will find out what is happening."

He disappeared through the door, leaving her alone. She returned to her work, her thoughts consumed by what could be happening below.

I do not smell any smoke; perhaps it is just something near the stables or in the kitchen.

And then she heard it.

The sound of the latch.

She turned. Too late.

Wickham.

"There you are," he said. "I have been wondering where you were hiding."

Elizabeth's blood ran cold. "Sir, I was only—"

He stepped into the room and shut the door with a deliberate click, his hand twisting the key with a snap. The key vanished into his coat pocket.

"It is amazing, is it not," he said lazily, his lips curling. "how quickly the threat of fire will clear the corridors."

Elizabeth backed toward the window, the air suddenly too thick to breathe, though there was no actual smoke.

"What do you want?" she asked, her voice low and tight, then immediately chastised herself. *Do not provoke him, Lizzy!*

Wickham chuckled. "A moment alone. We have hardly had the pleasure."

"You are drunk."

"And you are lovely," he said, stepping closer. "Even prettier in this light. No need to tremble, little maid. I only want a kiss."

He reached for her with a swaying step, and the scent of brandy hit her like a wall. "I must say," he murmured, reaching out as though to touch her cheek, "my wife has been very selfish. Keeping such a pretty thing locked away."

Elizabeth moved, putting a chair between them. "Do not come any closer."

"Oh, come now." His voice dropped. "Your husband is not here to protect you. And I doubt he is half the man you need."

Her mind raced. The door was blocked. The bell pull was on the far wall.

Her eyes locked on his. "I will scream."

He laughed. "And bring the house down? Why not? Let everyone know how your heart races when I walk into the room."

Her hand found the edge of the side table. "You are a coward," she said, coldly now. "You prey on women because you are too weak to face a real man."

His eyes darkened. "Careful, darling."

"I am not your darling."

She gripped the table. Wickham stepped closer, his hand reaching toward her shoulder—

A sudden sound cut him off.

The crash of wood. A shout. The door behind him burst open with a splintering crack.

"Get away from her!"

Darcy.

~~*~*

Darcy tore through the corridors toward the front door, the cry of "Fire!" still ringing in his ears. If he stood outside, he might be able to see which room had smoke coming from it.

But the moment the frigid air hit his face, however, he realized something was wrong.

There was no smoke.

His eyes narrowed. *No, Wickham would never… would he?*

A cold dread gripped him.

He frantically searched the windows, the irony not escaping him, *hoping* to see flames or smoke, for the alternative was worse.

"Blast!" he swore. "Elizabeth!"

He turned, sprinting back the way he had come.

"William, what in heaven's name—?" Mrs. Reynolds protested as he tore past her in the foyer and made for the room where he had left Elizabeth.

He ignored her.

Skidding to halt in front of the door, he reached for the knob.

Locked.

"Eliza—Beth?" he called, too loudly, panic rising in his chest. "Beth, are you there?"

No reply.

He stepped back and slammed his shoulder into the door. Once. Twice. On the third, it burst open with a splintering crack.

The scene that met him turned his blood to ice.

Elizabeth was pinned between a chair and the wall, her eyes wide with terror. Wickham stood over her, unsteady on his feet, a sickening leer on his face. One hand was extended—reaching toward her cheek. His coat was open, cravat half-untied, and the heavy stench of brandy filled the air.

Darcy saw red.

"Get away from her!" he roared.

Wickham turned, just as Darcy crossed the space and slammed into him, fists clenched. The first blow sent him staggering into the sideboard. The second knocked the brandy flask from his hand.

"You dare touch her?" Darcy snarled, grabbing Wickham by the front of his coat and dragging him from the room. "You dare?"

Wickham shoved back, throwing a wild punch that barely grazed Darcy's jaw—but it was enough to ignite the fury in full. They crashed into the corridor, limbs locked, struggling like beasts. Wickham slipped on the stone floor, nearly going down, but caught himself on a windowsill.

A door creaked open. Then another.

Servants peered out, eyes wide. Mrs. Wells appeared from the kitchen, a rolling pin in her hand. John emerged behind her, having run from the stables with a pitchfork. Mrs. Reynolds stood like stone at the far end of the corridor, face pale, lips pressed into a line.

Georgiana descended the stairs, bracing herself on the banister so as to not lose her balance. "George, what have you done?"

Ignoring his wife, Wickham snarled and shoved Darcy away, panting. Blood dripped from his nose.

"That is it," he spat. "I will have you arrested for assault. You think you can strike your master and walk away from it? You are nothing. A servant."

No one moved.

He turned, pointing at the assembled household. "Go! Someone fetch the constable! Now!"

Not a single footfall answered.

The silence was deafening.

Wickham's eyes darted about the corridor, his bravado crumbling. He looked to Mrs. Reynolds. "You—"

She raised a brow. "I do not take my orders from a man who cannot control himself, especially not if he is so into his cups that he most likely will not remember giving them."

A beat of silence.

Then Wickham barked a mirthless laugh. "Fine. I shall go myself."

He straightened his coat, spitting blood onto the stone floor before casting a hateful glance toward the gathering crowd. "You will regret this," he slurred. "Every last one of you."

No one answered.

He stormed toward the stairs but paused at the bottom of the staircase, where Georgiana stood trembling beside Mrs. Reynolds, her pale hands clutched around the banister.

"And as for you," he sneered, pointing a shaking finger at her, "once I've had my fill of that uppity servant and the maid who thinks she's above her station, it will be your turn to act like a proper wife."

Georgiana flinched violently, tears springing to her eyes.

"You always were a weak, pathetic little thing," he muttered with disgust.

She lowered her head, covering her ears with her hands.

"Maybe I shall be lucky," he drawled, looking her up and down with a cold smile. "Perhaps you'll die in childbirth like your mother did. Then I will be free to find a real heiress."

Georgiana gasped aloud, a broken, strangled sound. Mrs. Reynolds put her arms around her protectively, holding her upright.

Darcy's entire body vibrated with restrained violence. His hands ached, his heart thundered, and his stomach turned with the what-ifs that clawed through his mind. He took a step forward, fury rising—but Elizabeth's hand tightened around his, anchoring him. The tension in her arm betrayed the force it was taking to hold him back.

Without another word, Wickham turned on his heel and stormed out into the cold. A few moments later, the pounding of hooves echoed through the frosted air, fading into the distance.

Only when it was silent again did anyone dare to breathe.

Chapter 23

The foyer gradually filled with murmurs as shock work off. The hushed voices spurred Mrs. Reynolds into motion, and she began barking orders with sharp efficiency, dispersing the servants who had gathered to watch.

"Back to your duties! Cook, tend to the injured. You—fetch fresh linens. You two, clean up this mess before the blood sets in."

Darcy stood unmoving, his fists clenched and chest heaving. Blood pounded in his ears.

Mrs. Reynolds caught his eye. Her voice softened just slightly. "You and Beth—ten minutes. That is all I can spare you. Gather your wits and decide what you are going to do next. Then get out of sight before that wretched man returns."

She gave a sharp nod toward the small cloakroom beside the staircase. Darcy turned and gently ushered Elizabeth inside, closing the door behind them.

It was dark and narrow, barely wide enough for two, and her form pressed up against the length of his body as he closed the door behind them. A thin shaft of light came in through the hinges of the doorframe. The scent of wool and old leather filled the air.

Elizabeth's hand trembled in his.

"I am going to kill him," he said, the words ripped raw from his throat. "I swear to God, Elizabeth—when he returns, I will not hesitate. I will see to it with my own hands."

She flinched at the vehemence in his voice. "Darcy—"

271

"No." He shook his head forcefully. "No, I have had enough. He tried to—he *dared* to lay his hands on you, and I—" His voice broke. "I left you alone."

You were not far. You saved me—"

"I should have been there." He struck the wall with his fist. "I should never have let him near you."

"Darcy—"

"Do not call me that," he said roughly. "That name means nothing here. Nothing. I am no master of Pemberley. I am no brother. No protector. I am only a servant in a world that should not even exist, and I cannot—" His breath caught. "I cannot even keep you safe."

She moved closer, her eyes shimmering. "This is not your fault."

"Is it not?" he whispered. "Everything is broken. My sister, my name, my world. And the one thing—*the one person*—who has made any of this bearable... he nearly ruined you."

Her gaze softened. "But he did not."

He looked away, shoulders shaking. "Only because I reached you in time. What if next time I do not? What if next time he—"

"Then we take steps," she said firmly. "We prepare. We protect Georgiana. We protect each other. But we do not become like him."

"It would be worth it, to rid the world of him."

"I do not believe you."

He let out a bitter laugh. "You do not think me capable of murder?"

"I think," she said slowly, "that you are *capable* of anything. But what matters is not what you *can* do—it is what you *choose* to do."

He stilled at that.

She stepped closer, her hand gently brushing his sleeve. "You are a good man, Fitzwilliam Darcy. You are angry—rightly so. But you are not wicked. You are not cruel. You are not a man who would commit murder in a blind rage."

He closed his eyes.

Her grip tightened. "*No*, Fitzwilliam. I will *not* allow you to kill him."

His shoulders slumped. "How can you even want him alive? After what he tried to do?"

"I know," she said steadily, though her voice was hushed, "and, God forgive me, I *do* wish him dead. But that does not mean we abandon our principles."

"What principles? What honor remains in this twisted world? I wished myself into it—I erased everything I knew. And now I am left powerless to fix it. If I cannot stop him, what good am I?"

"You are *not* powerless," she said fiercely. "You stopped him today. You protected me. You protected Georgiana. That is what matters."

He turned away, his voice rough. "It is not enough. He will come back."

"Then we make a plan. We find a way to stop him without losing ourselves in the process."

Darcy dragged both hands through his hair, wild and unkempt from the morning's chaos. "You do not understand. I *want* to kill him. I want to see his blood on my hands. I do not care about consequences. I—"

"You *do* care," she interrupted, stepping closer. "You care so much that it is eating you alive. But you are not a murderer, Fitzwilliam. You are not a brute. You are a good man—whether this world sees it or not."

"Elizabeth—"

"You would regret it, Fitzwilliam. I know you would."

"Would it even matter? Does this world, this Wickham, even exist? Once we return home, no one would even know."

"*You* would know." She looked pleadingly into his eyes. "This man has already stolen so much from so many. Do not allow him to steal your soul, too."

He stared at her—at the sincerity in her eyes, the gentle defiance in her stance. Her face was pale, but her gaze was steady. She had endured so much, and still she stood here, defending that... that *monster*.

"Then tell me what to do." His voice cracked. "Tell me how to stop wanting to destroy him."

Her hand rose to his face, fingers tracing the edge of his jaw. "You do not have to stop feeling it. You only have to choose to not *act* on it. To be better than he is."

Darcy swallowed hard. The tightness in his chest began to ease—not vanish, but loosen enough for breath to return.

"I want to take you away from here," he said hoarsely. "I want to put you somewhere safe. I cannot breathe, knowing he is near you."

"I know." Her voice was tender. "But you do not have to carry that burden alone."

His eyes met hers, searching. "You forgive me? For letting him get so close?"

"There is *nothing* to forgive." She touched his heart. "You came once you knew. That is all that matters."

He closed the distance between them and held her tightly, his forehead pressed to hers.

"Then I shall never leave you again."

They remained there for several minutes, unmoving, his arms wrapped around her like a man clinging to the last safe thing in a storm. She fit against him perfectly—warm, steady, and alive. He did not want to let go.

If this world were a dream, he wanted to sleep forever.

But reality, as it always did, intruded.

Knock, knock.

"William? Beth?" Mrs. Reynolds' voice was soft, but urgent. "I am sorry, but we must act."

Darcy exhaled, eyes still closed, forehead still resting against Elizabeth's. He opened his mouth to speak, but no words came.

He had no plan.

He had fury. Despair. A desire to protect that bordered on madness. But no strategy, no logic, no idea how to end this nightmare without blood.

Elizabeth lifted her head from where it rest on Darcy's chest, her fingers brushing his arm before turning toward the door and opening it.

Mrs. Reynolds raised an eyebrow at both of them—taking in their drawn faces, the flush on Darcy's cheeks, the quiet fury still simmering in his eyes.

"Well?" she asked.

"I do not have a plan." He hung his head.

"Fortunately," Elizabeth said, her voice calm, "I do."

~~*~*

Elizabeth was still trembling when Darcy pulled her into the closet. The echo of Wickham's voice lingered in her ears—the slurred jeer, the satisfied smirk as he locked the door, the sound of his footsteps as he swayed towards her.

It was confidence of a man certain he could do whatever he pleased and remain unpunished.

It made her physically ill to remember how close he had come.

If Darcy had been a moment later—

She closed her eyes, pressing herself more tightly against Darcy's frame. The thought was unbearable.

And yet, even through the fear, something fiercer stirred within her: anger. Not at Wickham—though he deserved every curse heaven might see fit to rain upon him—but at the injustice of it all.

Here she was, a woman of no fortune, with no family to appeal to and no power in her hands. Darcy, a man of intelligence and strength, was reduced to a servant in his own home. And Georgiana—the mistress of Pemberley—was all but a prisoner within it.

There had to be a way to turn the scales.

But how? He was the master of Pemberley, and they were nothing but servants.

When Darcy said he was going to kill Wickham, a small part of her desperately wished he would.

But only for a moment.

She knew that Darcy was an honorable gentleman. Murder, tempting though it was, would put a blackness in his heart that no amount of love or forgiveness would ever be able to erase.

And so as he spoke of vengeance, her mind raced, desperate for something—anything—that did not end with blood or ruin. And then she remembered.

Georgiana's letter—Colonel Fitzwilliam!

The idea struck her like a spark catching dry tinder. He had written to Georgiana from Matlock, which was only a few hours away. If they could reach him—if he could see what had become of his cousin's household—surely he would intervene. Surely he could do what they could not.

Her lips parted to speak, to tell Darcy of her plan, but then his arms tightened around her, anchoring her to him. The rage and despair that had filled the small cloakroom seemed to ebb with every breath he took against her hair.

For the first time since the fire that was not a fire, she felt safe. Truly safe.

She closed her eyes and leaned into him. The world could wait a little longer.

To her disappointment, a soft knock came all too soon.

"William? Beth?" Mrs. Reynolds' voice carried a weary gentleness. "I am sorry, but we must act. Have you settled on a plan?"

Darcy's negative response only served to harden Elizabeth's resolve. "Fortunately, I have one," she said.

"What are you thinking?" Darcy asked her, a look of trepidation on his face.

Darcy turned sharply toward her, his expression caught between hope and trepidation. "What are you thinking?"

Elizabeth lifted her chin, arching an eyebrow with a faint trace of mischief. "Nothing so dire as you are, I suspect. It involves neither murder nor mayhem—at least, not if we are lucky."

The smallest ghost of a smile tugged at his lips, and she felt her heart ease just a little at the sight.

"It is actually quite simple, really. Georg—*Mrs. Georgiana* received a letter from her cousin, Colonel Fitzwilliam a few days ago."

"Richard?" Darcy asked eagerly, the name escaping him before sense could intervene.

Mrs. Reynolds stiffened, scandal flashing in her eyes. "*Colonel Fitzwilliam* is the son of an earl," she reminded him primly. "And he is on the Continent, if I recall correctly, and of no use to us."

"He is at Matlock, actually, which I understand is only a few hours away by horse." Elizabeth looked at Darcy for confirmation. "He said he would come call on his cousin, and he would like to speak to Mr. Wickham."

As if he could read her thoughts, Darcy said, "I could ride there to retrieve him while you remain hidden."

"Precisely."

Darcy began to move decisively towards the stables, then froze midstep. He turned back to Mrs. Reynolds and asked, "May I use Nell?"

Mrs. Reynolds hesitated, then nodded. "Yes, I think that would be best. If you leave within the hour, you *may* return before nightfall—if fortune favors you. Your wife can stay in the kitchens. There is a small pantry there where she may hide should Mr. Wickham wander below stairs."

"May I see to Mrs. Georgiana, first?" Elizabeth asked. "She must be quite distraught."

Hesitating a few moments, Mrs. Reynolds shook her head. "We should not risk it. He will look for you in his wife's chambers first. Best keep you well out of sight."

"But surely I should be there to help—"

"No!" Darcy and Mrs. Reynolds interrupted in perfect unison.

The sharp echo of their voices filled the narrow room, and for one absurd instant, Elizabeth almost laughed. Darcy's eyes widened slightly in surprise at himself, and the corners of her mouth twitched despite the danger.

"Very well," she said with a small, wry smile. "I see the alliance is formed."

Even Mrs. Reynolds' stern face softened. "Forgive me, my dear, but it truly is for the best. I shall take Mrs. Georgiana to her own chamber and tell anyone who asks that she is still unwell—not that anyone should. You will remain belowstairs until Mr. Darcy returns. I shall have Cook bring your meals, and if he comes down, you are to hide yourself at once."

Elizabeth nodded, sobered again. "And if he returns before the colonel?"

"Then God help us all," Mrs. Reynolds muttered.

Darcy caught Elizabeth's hand, holding it firmly between both of his. "I will come back for you," he said, his voice low and steady, though his eyes betrayed the storm within.

"I know you will."

He pressed her hand once, his thumb tracing the edge of her knuckles, and for a brief, impossible moment, the world stilled—the air, the sound, even her pulse. Then he released her hand and turned toward the corridor.

"Go quickly," Mrs. Reynolds urged. "The longer you linger, the greater the danger."

Darcy nodded once and was gone.

Elizabeth followed Mrs. Reynolds through the servant's passage to the kitchens, where the hearth burned low and the air was thick with the scent of broth and soap. "The pantry will do best," Mrs. Reynolds said, pointing to the narrow door at the far end. "If he comes home, you slip inside and bar the inner latch. If the worst occurs, and he catches sight of you, tell him you are in desperate need of the chamber pot."

Elizabeth managed a weak smile. "So I am to be as contagious as Mrs. Georgiana?"

"That excuse served us once already," Mrs. Reynolds said dryly. "No harm in using it again."

She busied herself with the kettle, pretending to tidy the counter while Elizabeth sat on a small stool near the fire. They both listened for the sound of hooves in the courtyard.

At last, it came—the crisp beat of a single horse galloping away from Pemberley.

Elizabeth pressed her hand over her heart, murmuring a prayer she could not quite form into words.

"God keep him," the housekeeper whispered.

Elizabeth nodded, the sting of tears bright in her eyes. "Yes," she said softly. "And let him bring hope back with him."

There was a moment of silence.

"I will leave you now to Mrs. Wells' company," Mrs. Reynolds said at last. Her duty complete, the housekeeper gave a brisk nod and bustled away. Elizabeth could hear her voice echoing down the passage as she issued orders to some unseen servant, until even that faded into the steady hum of the kitchen.

"Right then," said Mrs. Wells, without looking up from the hearth. She stirred a thick stew, tested the broth with a spoon, and began ladling it into a bowl. "The mistress has not eaten a bite since breakfast, I would wager. I had best take her a tray. Here, you can make yourself useful with this dough. It needs kneading, and I am short on hands."

Elizabeth moved to the worktable, grateful for something to do. She dusted her palms with flour and pressed into the pliant dough, working it over and over until it grew smooth beneath her touch. The rhythm steadied her thoughts. She could almost pretend it was an ordinary day, that Wickham was not out there somewhere, that Darcy was not risking his life and liberty on the open road.

Mrs. Wells was gone for perhaps ten minutes before returning. But she was not alone.

Georgiana followed close behind, her cheeks pale and blotched with tears, her hands twisting the handkerchief she held.

"Please," the girl whispered as soon as she saw Elizabeth. "Please, may I stay here? I cannot bear to be alone in those rooms."

"I thought these might help you be more comfortable, Beth. Oh! Mrs. Georgiana!" The housekeeper stopped short, her eyes widening in surprise. "What... what brings you down here?"

Georgiana rose half from her seat, twisting her hands together. "I could not stay alone," she whispered. "Every sound made me jump. I know it is not proper, but I—"

Her voice broke, and Elizabeth quickly stepped between them. "She was frightened," she said gently. "And she thought, perhaps, that being belowstairs might be safer for a little while."

Mrs. Reynolds' stern features softened, though her brows still drew together in concern. "Safer, perhaps temporarily," she admitted, "but not for long. If he returns and finds you both together... well, it would in actuality be *more* dangerous for Beth."

"Not if he believes we are gone," Elizabeth said, thinking quickly. "Tell him that Mrs. Georgiana fled, and that I went with her to protect her. He will not think to look for us here. No man like him would imagine his wife hiding in the scullery."

Mrs. Reynolds blinked at her, taken aback by both the boldness and the sense of the suggestion. "You would have him believe you fled the house entirely?"

Elizabeth nodded. "Yes. He is proud and careless. If he believes we ran, he will not trouble to search for long."

Mrs. Wells, who had been listening from the stove, spoke up at last. "It does make sense," she said. "If the master thinks his wife has bolted, he will go after her—or drink himself into a stupor. Either way, we gain time."

"They could hide in the stables," Mrs. Reynolds mused aloud.

"No," Elizabeth said quickly. "It is too cold, and the ground is damp. The air would not be good for Mrs. Georgiana." She gave a meaningful glance toward the younger woman's stomach, relieved that Georgiana, still staring at her hands, did not notice. "Here, at least, there is warmth and quiet."

Mrs. Reynolds hesitated a moment longer, then sighed. "Very well. But please, Miss Darcy, promise me you will keep silent." No one seemed to notice the housekeeper's use of her mistress's maiden name.

"I will," Georgiana vowed.

"I have sent John up the hill to keep watch. He is to light a lantern if anyone arrives," Mrs. Reynolds informed them. "I will be keeping watch in the drawing room."

"Thank you," Elizabeth said earnestly. "Truly."

Mrs. Reynolds waved a hand, already turning for the door. "No thanks, only caution. And prayers, if you have any left to spare."

When she was gone, Mrs. Wells looked between the two women and gave a small, resigned sigh. "Well, there is no sense in starving while we wait," she said, filling two bowls from the pot on the hearth. "Eat up, girls—begging your pardon, Mrs. Wickham."

Georgiana startled, then gave a weak giggle. "It is quite all right, Mrs. Wells."

The cook smiled faintly and handed her mistress a bowl, who immediately tucked in. "That is better, my dear. There is no shame in keeping up one's strength."

They ate in near silence, save for the occasional clink of a spoon or the soft pop of the fire. The stew was rich and warm, a small comfort in a day of fear. Elizabeth used a crust of bread to soak up the last of the broth, and when Georgiana looked scandalized by the act, she said with a teasing smile, "It prevents wasting food and makes washing dishes easier."

After a moment's hesitation, Georgiana mimicked her and dabbed the last drops from her own bowl.

Mrs. Wells chuckled, shaking her head. "I wager you gave your mother all sorts of trouble as a girl, Beth."

"You have no idea," Elizabeth said with a smile, though her mind was half elsewhere—listening for hooves, for footsteps, for any sound that might shatter the fragile peace of that small kitchen.

When Mrs. Wells at last glanced toward the clock and frowned, Elizabeth's heart quickened.

"Best settle yourselves in the scullery," the cook said. "If he made decent time, he will be back soon. When he does arrive, Mrs. Reynolds will tell him you have both gone. I will lock the door after you go in. Try to push a barrel or two in front of it, just in case."

With a murmured word of thanks, Elizabeth guided Georgiana through the narrow door. The air inside was cool and faintly scented with soap and coal dust. Together, they arranged the blankets at the wall shared by the kitchen, as it would be warmest. Looking around, Elizabeth quickly dashed out to the kitchen, then returned with a pail.

She caught Georgiana looking at her curiously. "In case we have need of a chamber pot," she explained, causing the younger girl to blush.

Mrs. Wells lingered only a moment more, her weathered face unusually tender. "Keep quiet, girls. Be safe. May angels be with you, and the good Lord protect us all."

Then she closed the door and turned the key.

The soft click of the lock echoed like thunder in the stillness that followed.

Chapter 24

The sound of the lock caused Georgiana to let out a small whimper. Elizabeth looked at her compassionately.

"Here," she said softly, "let us make you comfortable."

She spread one of the blankets upon the floor, folding it over several times until it formed a makeshift cushion. Then she took another and wrapped it carefully about the girl's shoulders. "There. That is a little better."

The scullery was narrow and dim, its single window high and small, letting in only the faintest hint of afternoon light. Rows of shelves lined one wall, and barrels were stacked along the other—some filled with flour, others with salted fish, potatoes, or dried peas.

Elizabeth moved toward them, testing the weight of each one in turn. She tipped them gently, judging which were light enough to move yet heavy enough to serve her purpose.

"Let me help," Georgiana said quickly, starting to rise.

Elizabeth turned at once. "No, no—do not strain yourself. I can manage. Sit and rest."

The younger woman hesitated, then obeyed, her hands clasped over her rounded middle.

"Best keep you and your babe safe," Elizabeth murmured, more to herself than to Georgiana, as she began to roll one barrel toward the door.

After a few minutes' effort, Elizabeth had several of the barrels positioned near the door—enough to hinder any sudden attempt to open it should the lock fail. She straightened, brushing her hands together, and turned toward the small hamper Mrs. Wells had left them.

Inside were two skins of watered wine, a small loaf of bread, a wedge of cheese, a few baked potatoes wrapped in cloth, several dried apples, and a bundle of salted meat. Elizabeth smiled faintly.

"We have enough to camp here for several days, it seems," she said lightly, though the sound of her laughter was brittle.

Georgiana did not return it. Her eyes were wide and glistening in the low light.

Elizabeth knelt beside her and took her hand. "I will do all I can to keep you safe," she promised.

That was enough to break whatever fragile composure Georgiana still held. The girl burst into tears, burying her face in her hands. "Why?" she choked out. "Why are you helping me? How can you not hate me for what I have done? For the danger I have brought upon you? We are practically strangers—why would you risk so much for me? Why not just leave?"

Elizabeth's throat tightened. "Because I would want someone to do the same for one of my sisters," she said quietly. "I have a sister in trouble now—perhaps in very great trouble—and I cannot be there to help her. So I pray that somewhere, someone will show her the same kindness I can show you."

She hesitated, then added softly, "Her name is Jane. She was in love with a man who she thought was honorable. He loved her once, but then he left her behind, and she was left to face the consequences without a husband's name."

Georgiana's fingers brushed the edge of her sleeve, her voice trembling. "I am not sure which is worse—being married to a cruel man, or not being married at all."

Elizabeth smiled sadly. "Both are dreadful in their own way. The world is rarely just to women. My friend Charlotte once said that happiness in marriage is entirely a matter of chance."

"Do you believe that?"

"I used to think not," Elizabeth said, glancing toward the little fire. "But now… I believe chance plays its part, yes—but so do choice and courage."

Georgiana was quiet for a moment, then said, "How can anyone ever trust another enough to marry them? How did you know you could trust your husband—to put yourself in his power so completely?"

Elizabeth drew in a steadying breath, her lips curving into a wistful smile. "Time," she said. "Time, and truth. I misjudged him terribly at first. I thought him proud, arrogant, and disagreeable. At a public assembly, he refused to dance with me—and called me merely 'tolerable.' I thought him insufferable."

Georgiana gave a startled little laugh. "Oh dear. That cannot have gone well."

"No," Elizabeth admitted, laughing softly herself. "It did not. And when he finally confessed his love, I refused him most rudely. But afterward… circumstances threw us together. I began to see him as he truly was. He learned humility, and I learned forgiveness. He admitted his faults, and he changed. When it mattered most, he proved himself dependable, honorable, and sincere. Over time, I came to see the man beneath the pride."

Georgiana sighed dreamily. "That is so romantic. You must love him very much."

Elizabeth felt her eyes sting. "I do," she whispered. "I love him so very, very dearly."

For a long moment, neither spoke. The faint sounds from Mrs. Wells in the kitchen filled the silence between them.

At last, Elizabeth drew the blankets higher about Georgiana's shoulders. "Come now—you must be exhausted. Lie here and rest. When my sisters could not sleep, or had frightening dreams, they would come to my bed, and I would stroke their hair until they calmed. Sometimes I would sing."

She smoothed Georgiana's hair from her damp cheeks, the motion soothing them both. She began to hum—a tune she had not thought of in years, one her mother used to sing on soft summer evenings at Longbourn. The words came unbidden, trembling but sure.

> *Sleep, my child and peace attend thee,*
> *All through the night*

Guardian angels, God will send thee,
All through the night
Soft, the drowsy hours are creeping
Hill and vale, in slumber sleeping,
I, my loving vigil keeping
All through the night.

Elizabeth's voice softened to a whisper, the sound filling the small scullery with peace. Through the small window, faint moonlight streamed in, illuminating Georgiana's face.

While the moon, her watch is keeping
All through the night
While the weary world is sleeping
All through the night
O'er thy spirit gently stealing
Visions of delight revealing
Breathes a pure and holy feeling
All through the night.

Georgiana's breathing began to slow, her lashes fluttering against her cheeks. Elizabeth drew the blanket higher about her shoulders and kept singing, her voice steadier now, the words turning into prayer.

Angels watching ever round thee
All through the night
In thy slumbers close surround thee
All through the night
They will of all fears disarm thee,
No forebodings should alarm thee,
They will let no peril harm thee
All through the night.

She hesitated then, her gaze drifting to the small, frost-rimmed window above them. A single star shone faintly beyond the glass, its light wavering but unbroken. She thought of it as a promise—that somewhere out there, God still saw them.

Though I roam a minstrel lonely
All through the night
My true harp shall praise sing only
All through the night
Love's young dream, alas, is over
Yet my strains of love shall hover
Near the presence of my lover
All through the night

The tune lingered in the still air. Elizabeth's gaze drifted toward the faint line of light beneath the locked door. Somewhere beyond it, Darcy was riding through the cold and dark, and her voice trembled as poured her heart out in song.

Love to thee, my thoughts are turning
All through the night
All for thee, my heart is yearning,
All through the night.
Though sad fate our lives may sever
Parting will not last forever,
There's a hope that leaves me never,
All through the night.

Outside, the wind moaned through the cracks in the stone. But within the little scullery, the two women lay close together, and for the first time in many days, peace—fragile though it was—settled over Pemberley.

~~*~*

Darcy leaned low over Nell's neck, urging her onward with more fervor than the poor beast could easily endure. The mare's breath steamed in the cold air, plumes of white vanishing as quickly as they formed. The road stretched ahead—mud frozen hard as stone, rimed with ice where thin trickles of meltwater crossed the track. Every jolt of the saddle rattled his bones, but still he pressed her on.

"Come, girl," he murmured hoarsely. "We must make better time than this."

The mare flicked her ears, obedient but weary, her stride lengthening only slightly. Each step felt an eternity stolen from Elizabeth's safety. The sun had reached its zenith but already began to sink, throwing long winter shadows across the Derbyshire hills.

He knew these roads—had known them all his life. Yet today, even the landscape felt wrong. The hedgerows seemed lower, the woods thinner, the farmsteads shuttered and silent. Once, this had been his father's land, his home, his charge. Now it was a stranger's country, stripped of its pride and color, and he rode through it like a ghost haunting his own past.

A sharp wind cut through his coat, and he pulled the collar higher, jaw clenched against the cold. His thoughts circled with every hoofbeat.

If he reached Matlock by nightfall, what then? Would they even grant him entry? To them, he was no Darcy—only a servant, grimy and travel-worn, arriving on a half-starved mare with no card of introduction.

And if, by some mercy, he was admitted—would Richard listen? Would he still be the same man, loyal and steadfast, whose laughter had once echoed through Pemberley's halls? Or would he be changed, like everything else in this twisted world—another echo, hollow and unfamiliar?

His hands tightened on the reins, his fingers numb not only from the grip, but from the cold.

If Richard were not himself… if he refused to come… then Elizabeth and Georgiana were alone with that monster.

Darcy's stomach turned violently at the thought.

He could still see her face when he left—the faint tremor in her smile, the quiet courage in her eyes. She had held herself upright, as she always did, though the weight upon her shoulders should have bent any mortal woman.

God, how he loved her for that.

The rhythmic thud of hooves filled the silence. He clung to it—because the alternative was to hear again the echo of Wickham's voice.

The sneer. The slurred laugh.

The sight of Elizabeth trembling.

He pressed a hand against his thigh to still the shaking. The fury that rose in him was almost welcome—it gave him warmth, something to hold onto.

How dare that man exist—how dare he breathe the same air as she did.

But Elizabeth's words came back to him, soft and unyielding:

"*Fitzwilliam,* you *would know.*

If he killed Wickham, no matter the world or the consequence, he *would* know. He would carry that blood forever.

She was right.

He exhaled sharply, forcing the rage down.

Focus. Ride. Do not think of her tears. Do not think of the bruise on her wrist or the terror in her eyes.

Matlock was still hours away. The wind stung his face. The hills rose and fell before him in waves of frost and shadow, and with each mile, his mind swayed between hope and despair.

He tried to pray, but no words would come. Only her name.

"Elizabeth," he whispered into the cold. "Please, God—keep her safe until I return."

The mare stumbled slightly on the uneven ground, and he steadied her, murmuring softly. The brief distraction grounded him. He adjusted the reins and pressed on.

The light was fading now; dusk pooled in the hollows between the hills. Somewhere far behind him lay Pemberley—its chimneys, its darkened windows, and the woman he loved hiding in its depths.

He urged Nell to a canter, ignoring the ache in his shoulders, the sting of the wind in his eyes. If he rode hard, he might yet reach Matlock before nightfall.

And if Richard was still Richard—

If any part of this world still held a shred of mercy—

Then he would not have ridden in vain.

The minutes passed slowly, almost agonizingly so. At last, he road through the front gates of Matlock and directed Nell towards the stable, where he slid down from the saddle. The cold struck him like a blade the moment he dismounted; his cheeks were stung raw and his fingers numb despite the gloves.

Looking around, he was relieved by what he saw. Men bustled about the yard with practiced ease—warm breath steaming in the air, leather boots scuffing, the tidy clatter of harness and tin pails. The stables at Matlock bore the stamp of prosperity: neat strappings, polished tack, and grooms whose coats still held a respectable gloss.

At least the earl still prospers; it will give the colonel more power to be of assistance.

A young groom in a fur cap gave Nell an appraising look and then shot Darcy a filthy stare at the mare's ragged condition. "She looks half-dead, that one," the man muttered, loud enough that Darcy heard it.

"She has done more than is fit for a nag this day," Darcy said shortly. "There is an emergency at Pemberley. Mrs. Wickham sent me."

The groom shrugged and jerked his thumb toward the house. "Best speak to the housekeeper or the butler, then. You will find them faster at the front than hanging about the stables."

Darcy thanked the man and made for the front door, each step crunching on frost. He rapped the knocker with a force born of impatience and fear. The door opened upon an austere visage—a man of brittle courtesy who regarded Darcy's mud-stained form from chin to heel.

The look held no charity.

"State your business," the man said coldly.

"Please," Darcy replied, forcing his voice steady, "I need Colonel Fitzwilliam immediately. There is an emergency at Pemberley, and his cousin requests his presence."

The man's expression did not alter but he inclined his head and closed the door. Darcy was ushered into a broad, warm foyer where the air smelled of peat and polished wood. The warmth of the room was balm, but it only made his impatience crueler.

"Wait here."

Time stretched. Every creak and step sounded like a clock; every idle footman a reprimand to his conscience for not being at Elizabeth's side. At last the door to a side room opened and a gentleman entered, his gait composed, his expression skeptical: Colonel Richard Fitzwilliam. He appeared older than Darcy remembered—tighter in the face, less softened by years abroad—and his dinner dress bore the neatness of military apparel.

Darcy's heart ached as he looked upon the colonel—his cousin, his friend, the man who had once been as a brother to him—and saw nothing but caution in his eyes. There was no flicker of recognition, no spark of the shared memories that had bound their youth. The easy warmth that had always existed between them was gone, replaced by suspicion and distance.

To stand before Richard Fitzwilliam and be met with doubt instead of trust was a wound deeper than pride could bear. It was like gazing into the mirror but seeing no reflection.

"You have come from Pemberley?" Richard asked, blunt and unsmiling.

Darcy inclined his head. "Yes, sir."

Richard's eye took in Darcy's worn clothes, Nell, the smear of road on his hands. "What is your purpose?"

Glancing around, Darcy took in the gazes of the servants that were all fixed on him. "This may be best done in private, sir."

Nodding curtly, Richard turned on his heel and led Darcy to a nearby sitting-room. He closed the door, then turned to look Darcy squarely in the face. "Now what has happened? Who are you, and was is going on at Pemberley?"

"My name is William. Georg—that is, Mrs. Wickham sent me for you."

Darcy cursed himself as Richard's eyes narrowed with lightning speed.

"*Georgiana?* What, pray tell, is the precise nature of your relationship with my cousin."

Darcy gaped, horror at how his explanation might sound tripping through him. "No—no, Colonel—my apologies. My meaning was confused. My wife is her maid, her companion. I have been working in the stables and as a footman. Pray, forgive my clumsy words." He swallowed and tried again. "Let me begin afresh. I am making a muddle of this."

His tongue seemed made of lead, affected by both cold and fatigue. He began haltingly, then faster as the urgency of the truth forced him forward. He told of their employment a month previous; of his wife's work as both scullery and lady's maid, as well as companion to Mrs. Georgiana; of Wickham's drunken return and the threat he posed to Georgiana and her unborn child; of the blow given in a moment of desperate defense; of the threat to fetch the magistrate and the fear that the man's temper might yet yield to worse.

"Did my cousin send a missive with you? Anything to vouch for your character?"

"No. No, she did not. I... I am afraid that the idea of my being doubted did not even occur to us. Time was of the essence, and Mrs. Wickham was understandably quite distraught. Mrs. Reynolds assisted her up to her chambers."

The colonel's scowl deepened. He stood silent for a measured beat, assessing the man before him as if weighing coin.

"You expect me to believe that a stranger ridden hard into my gates declares that my cousin is imperiled, and that you have not thought to obtain a letter, a written word, any confirmation?" he said at last. "It is sudden, and it sounds convenient."

Darcy felt the hot, helpless heat of anger rise. He had no time for diplomacy. He had no parchment of proof because there had been no time for prudence. "Blast, Richard," he heard himself blurt out.

Both men froze. The use of the colonel's Christian name left them astonished—the one at the impertinence, the other at the misstep.

"Honestly, sir," Darcy continued, his voice once again calm, "I do not blame you for your doubts. Wickham is a cad of the worst sort, and if any man has reason to mistrust him, you have seen enough of the Continent to be wise. All I can offer is my oath and urgency. Pemberley needs assistance now."

For a long moment, not a word was spoken. Outside, the wind pressed cold fingers against the windows, and Darcy stood beneath his cousin's searching stare, waiting—heart pounding—for judgment to fall.

Come on, Richard, Darcy urged his cousin internally. *Surely some part of you must recognize me, trust me.*

Chapter 25

After waiting for what seemed to be an eternity, Colonel Fitzwilliam's shoulders eased a fraction. He folded his arms and gave Darcy a long, searching look. "I do not know if what you are saying is genuine," he said at last in a measured tone. "Nevertheless, one does not ignore a plea for protection on behalf of a woman in danger. If you are sincere—and I shall judge that as I may—then I will go."

He hesitated, then added with grim humor, "On the other hand, if this is a trap... if Mr. Wickham has set a snare for me, you will find that I am not easily bested. You will answer to me. Do you understand?"

Darcy felt relief and fear in equal measure. He bowed his head. "Perfectly, Colonel. I will bear any consequence if this is a falsehood. But I beg of you, sir... please, come with haste."

"Very well." The colonel turned to the door as though setting a point to be made. "Give me an hour to gather myself and a small party. I will take my batman and a few of the strongest stableboys."

As the colonel strode from the room, Darcy felt a surge of hope. *Perhaps all can be made right.*

As Darcy waited in the drawing room with the door now ajar, he could see Matlock's front hall slowly began to fill with activity. Footmen and maids rushed to and fro, setting out more candles against the darkening night and closing the house for the evening.

Then, through the din, there was a the distinct sound of the click of a cane on the marble floor.

Matlock—the earl himself. I wonder if he is as cold in this lifetime as he is in mine.

Darcy was not left to wonder long. A rustle of silk announced their entrance as the Earl and Countess of Matlock swept into the room, every line of their bearing proclaiming authority and disapproval in equal measure. The earl's expression was carved in stone—his carriage that of a man well accustomed to deference—and the countess followed like a ship under full sail, her chin lifted, her eyes bright with cold inquiry.

Darcy rose to meet them, bowing low. Their gazes swept over him, assessing him from head to toe. The countess's nose wrinkled slightly, and the earl sniffed disdainfully.

"You are the servant who demanded an audience at this hour?" His silky voice was menacingly soft and smooth.

"I am, my lord."

"You come from Pemberley?"

"Yes, sir."

The earl exchanged a look with his wife. Her lips barely moved, but the faint curl of them conveyed disapproval enough for both.

"And what," she asked, her voice light with disdain, "could possibly warrant a servant disturbing the household of an earl after sundown?"

Darcy's jaw tightened, but he kept his tone measured. "There is an emergency at Pemberley, your ladyship. Mrs. Wickham—your niece—has sent me in haste to fetch Colonel Fitzwilliam. Her husband has returned and poses a danger to her."

The earl's brows rose, and the countess' fan snapped open with a sharp flick.

"My niece?" she repeated. "Mrs. *Wickham*? I had understood her husband to be… unfortunate, but not life-threatening."

"Her situation has grown dire, my lady."

The earl stepped forward, the weight of his scrutiny falling fully upon Darcy. "And why, pray, should I trust the word of a servant whose coat has seen better days and whose face I do not recognize?"

Darcy met his gaze steadily. "Because, my lord, whether you know me or not, your niece is in danger, and every moment we waste brings both her and her child closer to danger."

A heavy silence followed. The countess' fan stilled. The earl studied Darcy a long moment, weighing him.

Whatever he saw there must have convinced him, for he gave a long, weary sigh. "Very well, then. But if this turns out to be folly, you will answer to me for it."

Darcy bowed deeply. "Yes, my lord."

"And if harm comes to son because of my niece's foolishness, then you will answer to *me* as well." The countess punctuated her veiled threat by snapping her fan shut, then turning on her heel and striding from the room. Her husband followed close behind.

Darcy remained in the room, impatiently watching the bustle in the hall as servants passed in hushed agitation. From somewhere deep within the house came the muffled sounds of orders being given, shadowed by the steady tick of the great clock in the vestibule.

When it struck the hour—one solemn chime after another echoing through the hall—Darcy felt the weight of every moment pressing upon him. He had not slept since the night before, and his limbs ached with fatigue. How easily he could sink into one of the chairs by the fire, close his eyes for but a moment—yet he dared not. If he allowed weariness to claim him, the colonel might change his mind, or reason might cool what pity had stirred his heart.

So, he paced the room instead, his steps quick and uneven, his thoughts urging them to hasten. *If only I were myself again,* he thought bitterly. *Then I could be at Richard's side, urging him to move more quickly.*

Of course, if Richard knew me as he once did, then I would not need to beg for his belief, nor wait while he deliberated. He would have been gone before the hour struck.

He turned sharply at the sound of boots in the passage. Colonel Fitzwilliam entered, his coat buttoned and sword buckled at his side. "We are ready," he said shortly.

Darcy followed him out into the chill night air. The courtyard was alive with movement—lanterns swinging, horses stamping against their tethers, grooms tightening girths. Darcy glanced about, seeking the familiar outline of Nell, but she was nowhere to be seen.

"The nag you rode in on was near spent," the colonel said, adjusting his gloves. "She would not see the end of the lane, let alone the road to Pemberley." He gestured to a tall bay whose eyes gleamed with fire beneath the torchlight. "Can you manage something more spirited?"

Darcy's only answer was to seize the reins, swing himself into the saddle, and bring the horse firmly to hand. The animal tossed its head once, then yielded to his command.

Colonel Fitzwilliam's brows rose. "I see you can," he said dryly. Turning his gaze upward, he added, "We are fortunate—the moon is full and the clouds have cleared. It will give us light enough to ride swiftly, though we must take care. The roads are slick with ice from the rain earlier."

Darcy nodded. The air was sharp with the scent of wet earth and horseflesh, the cobblestones glistening like mirrors under the pale light. Without another word, the two men set off, hooves striking against stone as they cleared the gate and took to the open road.

The countryside stretched before them in shadow and silver. Every gust of wind seemed to whisper of Pemberley—of home—and of the woman who waited there in fear. They would not arrive before dawn, perhaps the sixth hour at the earliest, but Darcy pressed his mount onward, his heart a silent, ceaseless prayer.

Please, let Elizabeth be safe.

~~*~*

Elizabeth awoke with a start, uncertain at first what had roused her. The faint clatter of crockery and the low murmur of voices reached her through the half-open door to the kitchen. Dawn's first light filtered dimly through the scullery window, painting the flagstones with a thin, cold gray.

Her neck ached from the angle at which she had slept, half-propped against the wall with Georgiana's head upon her shoulder. The girl still slumbered, her fair hair spread over the folded blanket that served as a pillow. For a moment, Elizabeth simply watched her, relief softening the edges of her exhaustion. Georgiana's breathing was even and untroubled at last.

Gently, Elizabeth eased herself away, careful not to disturb her companion. At once the chill crept back into her limbs, biting through the thin gown she had worn since the day before. The small scullery felt colder than ever, the air heavy with damp stone and the faint smell of ashes from the dead fire.

She moved softly to the corner where a small basin of water and a bowl had been set aside. When she returned, the distant hum of the kitchen had grown louder—the scrape of pans, the thump of a kneaded loaf, and the unmistakable voice of Mrs. Wells giving brisk orders.

Elizabeth moved as close to the door as she could before the barrels impeded her movements. "Mrs. Well?" she called softly.

The noise in the kitchen paused, and Elizabeth could hear the sound of footsteps approaching the door. "Oh, Beth, I wondered if you were awake. It is a wonder if you were even able to sleep at all, you poor lambs. I was just saying to Mrs. Reynolds that I hoped you two did not freeze to death sometime during the night."

Elizabeth managed a faint smile. "We are quite safe, thank you. Has there been any word from my husband or Matlock?"

"None, I fear." The cook's voice trembled slightly. "Johnny never lit the lantern last night—neither your husband nor Mr. Wickham has returned or sent word."

Throat tightening, Elizabeth gripped the barrel on which she leaned. In the hours of half-sleep she had allowed herself to believe that he must be safe by now, that help would already be on its way. But the morning light had brought no certainty. What if something had happened on the road? What if the Matlocks had not believed him—or worse, had detained him for presuming too much? Or—her heart faltered—what if Wickham had found him first?

Before she could ask another question, she heard a loud gasp. "Mrs. Wells?" she called out anxiously. "What is it?"

"Hush, Beth!"

The terror in the cook's tone caused Elizabeth to freeze.

Through the early-morning stillness came the sound of hooves clattering on the loose gravel outside of the kitchen where the path led down to the stables.

"Someone is coming," Mrs. Wells said. "Quick, get as far back into the scullery as you possibly can. The rest of us all know to go to our rooms or to hide; if there is no one in here, then no one can reveal where you are."

Elizabeth's blood ran cold. She turned back into the scullery at once, kneeling beside Georgiana. "Mrs. Georgiana," she whispered urgently, "wake up, ma'am—quietly now."

The girl stirred, blinking in confusion. "Beth? What is it—?"

Elizabeth pressed her hand gently over the girl's mouth and shook her head. Then she lifted a finger to her lips. Georgiana's eyes widened with fear, but she nodded her understanding.

Elizabeth drew her close, pulling the blankets around them both as they crouched against the far wall, doing their best to remain hidden and silent. The scullery was icy; the air smelled of damp stone and ashes, and every sound from the yard beyond seemed to echo against her heart.

The rhythmic drumming of hooves grew louder. Elizabeth held her breath and tightened her hold on Georgiana.

Please let it be Darcy.

~~*~*

The first pale streaks of dawn were just beginning to silver the horizon when Pemberley's great house came into view. The sight, familiar and foreign all at once, stole Darcy's breath. The wide expanse of stone was dim in the early light, its windows dark and shuttered, and a thin mist hung low over the fields like a shroud.

The company guided their horses down the road and along the side of the manor house, where the path split go left towards the kitchen door and right in the direction of the stables. The colonel dismounted and surveyed the silent grounds with a frown.

"Looks like it was not a trap after all—at least, not on the way here," he said grimly. Then turning to Darcy, he added, "I will go in and speak with my cousin. You will remain here until I can verify your story."

Darcy stared at him in disbelief. "You cannot mean to leave me standing here! Not while my wife is in danger. I must go to her—she was being hidden in the scullery."

The colonel cut him off with a raised hand. "You will do nothing of the sort. If what you say is true, and my cousin is indeed in peril, we can ill afford chaos. My men will stay with you. I will see to the rest."

"Sir, please—"

But the colonel was already dismounting, striding across the gravel toward the great front doors. He flung them open and stepped inside, his voice echoing through the silent halls. "Georgiana! Georgiana Wickham!"

Darcy's heart pounded as he listened. No sound came in answer— no footsteps, no startled cry. Only the dull whisper of the wind across the courtyard.

After several long minutes, Fitzwilliam reappeared, his expression grave. "She is not in her rooms," he said tersely. "Where is she?"

Darcy's pulse quickened. "Did you ask Mrs. Reynolds? Surely she would know—"

"I did not see a single soul," the colonel replied. "The house is empty."

A cold dread settled in Darcy's stomach. "Then Wickham has returned," he said hoarsely. "He must have dismissed the staff—taken her—"

He broke off, spurring his horse toward the side of the house, but the colonel's men seized his reins before he could reach the corner. "Easy there," one warned.

"Let me go!" Darcy struggled against them. "Every moment we waste—"

The colonel came round the corner himself, motioning for his men to follow. "We will check the kitchens," he said curtly. "If anyone remains in the house, we shall find them there."

They dismounted and crossed the narrow yard. The kitchen door hung slightly ajar, but the rooms beyond were still and dark. The colonel entered first, pistol drawn, his boots loud against the flagstones.

Darcy waited just outside, straining to hear. "There is no one in the kitchens," the colonel called after a moment. Then, more sharply: "The scullery is locked!"

There was a loud thud, then another shout from Richard. "Jones! Get in here!"

The largest of the footmen obeyed the order immediately, disappearing inside along with his master. A moment later came the sound of wood splintering—then a sharp cry and the crash of broken glass.

Before Darcy could demand what had happened, the remaining men surged forward, weapons drawn. He was pulled along with them through the doorway—and stopped short in horror.

Elizabeth stood at the far end of the room, pressed against the scullery door, her arm raised. In her hand was the jagged neck of a broken wine bottle. At her feet lay Colonel Fitzwilliam, dazed, one hand lifted to back of his head where a thin stream of blood seeped through his fingers.

Every man in the room had turned his sword and gun toward her.

Darcy's blood ran cold.

"Elizabeth!"

~~*~*

The seconds passed like hours as Elizabeth pressed her ear to the scullery door. The sounds outside had grown louder—boots, low voices, and then the scrape of something heavy against the flagstones. Her pulse thundered in her ears.

From the other side of the door came a man's shout, muffled but distinct. "The scullery is locked!"

Georgiana's fingers tightened around Elizabeth's sleeve. "Beth," she whispered, "what do we do? He will find us!"

Before Elizabeth could answer, another voice barked an order—gruff, commanding. "Jones! Get in here!"

A heartbeat later came the splintering crack of wood under force.

Elizabeth's breath caught. There was no time to think. She darted to the shelves, grasping for anything that might serve as a weapon. Her hand closed around the neck of a wine bottle—heavy and smooth beneath her palm.

"Stay behind me," she whispered.

Georgiana's eyes were huge in the dim light, but she obeyed, retreating to the corner.

The pounding at the door came again, louder this time. The wood groaned. Elizabeth scrambled atop a low barrel near the hinges, gripping the bottle tightly. The door shuddered once more, then gave way with a splintering crack, flinging splinters in all directions.

A man burst through, broad-shouldered and shouting, pushing his way past the barrel guarding the entrance.

Elizabeth let out a cry that was half terror, half fury, and swung with all her strength. The bottle came down hard upon his head with a sharp, sickening thud. He staggered backward, crashing into the table before collapsing to the floor.

For one breathless instant there was silence—then the sound of weapons being drawn, and the thunder of boots as others charged towards the broken doorway.

Elizabeth froze in the doorframe, the jagged remains of glass still clutched in her trembling hand, her heart pounding so fiercely she thought it might leap from her chest.

"Do not come any closer," she warned as menacingly as she could, "else I shall hit him again."

She raised her makeshift weapon again high in the air.

"For pity's sake, we are here to help!" shouted the man on the floor. "Stop attacking us, woman!"

"Richard?"

Chapter 26

Before Elizabeth realized what was happening, Georgiana rushed up to her from behind. Elizabeth threw her arm out, preventing the girl from rushing past her.

"No, they have guns!" she cried out. "Stay behind me! I will not let them harm you."

"Georgie?" the man on the floor groaned.

"But it is my cousin," Georgiana protested weakly. "The one who wrote me the letter."

Warily, Elizabeth looked down at the man at her feet. "You are Colonel Fitzwilliam? Then where is Da—where is my husband?"

"Here, Beth."

Elizabeth looked up as Darcy shoved his way through the men standing around in the crowded kitchen. Her shoulders sagged with relief, and she dropped her arm, allowing the broken bottle to fall to the ground amid the shards of glass.

"William, you made it." Elizabeth's eyes filled with tears. "You are safe."

"As are you," he assured her. "The man you have knocked to the ground is, indeed, Colonel Fitzwilliam."

"Oh, I do beg your pardon, Colonel." Elizabeth blanched when she saw the blood streaming through his fingers. "Please, you are injured. I am most sorry. Here, allow me to help you."

She bent down in an attempt to help Georgiana's cousin to his feet, but he waved her off with his other hand.

"My men will assist me," he managed hoarsely, pressing a hand to his temple. He looked around, wincing at the movement. "Stand down, lads. Good Lord—what a blow."

Georgiana once again attempted to get to her cousin, but Elizabeth held her back once more. "There is glass everywhere, Mrs. Georgiana, and you do not have shoes."

"I can carry her," the colonel said. He tried to rise, but staggered. "I can stand—at least, I think I can…"

"No," Elizabeth said quickly. "It would be too dangerous. You are injured."

He gave a short laugh that turned into a wince. "I confess, the world is turning rather more than it ought."

Elizabeth seized a towel from the table and pressed it into his hand. "Here—use this to keep pressure upon the wound. The bleeding seems to have stopped, but you must not strain yourself."

He obeyed without argument, holding the cloth to the gash above his brow. "Then one of my men shall carry Mrs. Wickham."

At that, Georgiana flinched visibly and shook her head, shrinking back toward Elizabeth. Her voice was small but clear. "Please—no. I do not wish to be touched."

Elizabeth glanced from her to the colonel, then spoke softly. "Would you prefer that William carry you instead?"

Georgiana hesitated, then nodded.

The colonel inclined his head. "Very well. Take her upstairs, but mind your footing. The rest of you—two remain here to guard the door, the others see that no one enters Pemberley without my order. Detain any man who attempts it, no matter who he is."

The men saluted and dispersed to their posts.

Darcy stooped and lifted Georgiana gently into his arms. She trembled, but when she saw his face, her fear subsided. The colonel followed slowly, one hand still pressing the towel to his head, the other braced on Elizabeth's arm for balance.

As they ascended, Elizabeth whispered another apology. "Colonel, I am deeply sorry for striking you. I had no thought but to protect her. I feared—"

He interrupted her with a faint smile. "You need not explain. I quite understand. In truth, I am impressed—your bravery in defending my cousin is remarkable, and your choice of weapon even more so."

Elizabeth flushed. "It was simply the first thing I could find that was heavy enough to be useful."

"Then fortune smiled on you—and less so on me." He chuckled softly, then winced again. "Why was the door so devilishly difficult to push open?"

"The barrels," she admitted. "We—well, *I*, rather—rolled them in front to barricade it."

"Let me guess—that was also your idea?"

"Yes, Colonel."

He nodded approvingly. "Then I wish half my soldiers had as much sense and loyalty."

By the time they reached the upper floor, his steps had steadied. In Georgiana's chamber, Darcy laid his sister gently upon the bed. Her pallor was startling against the linen, and the curve of her stomach was unmistakable. The colonel halted, his expression softening into sorrow.

"I see," he said quietly.

He turned to Elizabeth and Darcy, giving them each a curt nod. "You have done your duty well. Thank you—both of you. You may go."

They exchanged a glance, reluctant but obedient, and began to retreat toward the door.

"Wait." Georgiana's voice, though weak, carried across the room. She struggled to sit upright, one hand braced behind her. "Oh no—both of you stay, please."

The colonel's brows lifted. "I should much prefer to speak with you privately, Georgiana."

She shook her head. "It will be easier if Beth remains. She has been my dearest companion—my confidante—and, if it is not too improper to say, my friend."

"Your *friend*?" the colonel repeated, half in disbelief.

"Yes," she said firmly. "If one may be friends with servants."

He opened his mouth to protest again, but Georgiana's eyes met his squarely. "Am I not the mistress of my own home? I shall decide who may hear what I have to say. These two have proved themselves both caring and trustworthy. I wish them to remain."

For a moment, silence reigned. Then Colonel Fitzwilliam sighed, sinking onto the couch beside the fire. "Very well," he said quietly. "Tell me everything, Georgie-girl."

~~*~*

Though Darcy already knew much of what Georgiana had endured—Elizabeth had told him the worst of it—he found it nearly unbearable to hear his sister recount it in her own trembling voice. Every word seemed to carve fresh wounds upon his heart. He had thought himself prepared; he was not.

Across from him, Colonel Fitzwilliam's expression darkened with each revelation. The fury in his eyes matched the storm within Darcy's own breast, and in that strange mirror of emotion Darcy found a grim sort of comfort. Whatever else this world had altered, Richard's heart remained steadfast.

He wondered, as he had so many times in his real life, how two people as cold and unfeeling as the Matlocks could have produced a son like him. Even before joining the army, Richard had possessed a warmth and sincerity that neither parent seemed capable of. Darcy had long credited their childhood at Pemberley for shaping him—that steady companionship between cousins which had drawn Richard away from the frost of Matlock Hall—but as he watched him now, Darcy realized the truth ran deeper.

Such goodness could not be taught, not with parents like that.

It was born within him.

When Georgiana's account at last faltered to an end, she slumped back against the pillows, pale and exhausted. Elizabeth leaned forward at once. "She has not slept more than an hour since yesterday," she said softly.

The colonel nodded. "No wonder. It sounds as though the night you spent together was much like a battlefield."

Elizabeth gave a faint, weary laugh. "That is precisely what it felt like: trying to sleep on the hard ground, no fire, never knowing if or when the enemy might strike."

Georgiana opened her eyes, managing a small smile. "Even so, the scullery was better than my rooms. At least I was not alone."

Elizabeth's expression gentled. "You have been very brave these last weeks, my dear. Braver than most women would ever be."

"It is only because of you, Beth," Georgiana murmured drowsily. "Before you came, I had given up. I spoke to no one, I stayed in bed for days... but you made me believe there might still be hope."

Elizabeth smiled, brushing a stray curl from the girl's brow. "And as much as I celebrate you leaving your chambers, I would now like to see you back *in* bed, if you please. You must rest if you are to keep up your strength."

The colonel gave a short nod. "You can sleep soundly, my dear. No one will enter this house unnoticed. It may be wise for us all to take what rest we can while we wait for the scoundrel to return."

Georgiana's eyes were already closing before he finished speaking. Within moments she had drifted into sleep. The colonel rose quietly, gesturing for Darcy and Elizabeth to follow him into the corridor.

"It seems," he said with a faint smile, "that I owe the Smiths more than I first thought."

"You owe us nothing," Darcy replied gruffly.

Elizabeth shook her head. "Indeed not, sir. We would hope another might do the same for one of our sisters in such circumstances." Her voice softened. "But I fear that so long as Mr. Wickham continues his dissolute ways, she may again find herself in danger."

"I concur," the colonel said. His tone hardened. "And I have a few ideas on how to prevent it."

"What are they?" Darcy demanded.

The colonel studied him for a moment, and Elizabeth's heart leapt in alarm, fearing Darcy's eagerness had betrayed him. But when the colonel's eyes flickered to her face, his expression only softened.

"You need not fear my censure," he said quietly. "I am not my parents. I have seen enough on the battlefield to know that courage and honor belong not to birth alone. My cousin trusts you, and your loyalty goes far beyond that of a hired servant or companion. I would not normally discuss my plans with those of your station, but in this case, I believe I shall make an exception. Georgiana has been fighting this battle far too long, and I will gladly work beside those who stand with her."

Then, with a glimmer of humor, he added, "Besides—it is your fault my brains are scrambled, so I expect your assistance in devising a strategy."

Elizabeth flushed, while Darcy's lips twitched in spite of himself.

Together the three descended to the lower floor. The house was still and dim, the hush before morning fully broke. In the drawing room, Mrs. Reynolds sat before the fire, her knitting in her lap and a look of apology upon her kind face.

"Colonel Fitzwilliam," she said quickly, rising as they entered, "I must beg pardon for not being present when you arrived. I was up the entirety of the night keeping watch, and when I learned Mr. Wickham had not yet returned, I thought it safe enough to lie down for a few hours."

"Quite understandable, Mrs. Reynolds," he said gently. "You have no need to fear reprisal. You have been with Pemberley since long before my cousin was born, and I know you only have the estate's best interests at heart. In fact, I am here to enlist you for our council of war— we could use your expertise and good sense."

"Mine, sir?" she asked in astonishment.

"Indeed. My cousin may soon be a mother, but she is still little more than a child in many ways. A woman of experience and sound judgment will be invaluable."

Mrs. Reynolds's eyes filled with earnest purpose. "Then I am at your service, Colonel."

The colonel inclined his head. "Excellent. Let us begin."

He motioned for them to take their seats. Elizabeth sat on a comfortable settee, and Darcy eagerly took the place next to her. He knew that it was not entirely appropriate, even for a *married* couple such as themselves, but he could not resist being near her. The hours spent in fear for her safety made him wish for nothing than to continually reassure himself of her well-being. He brushed his knee against hers, felt her warmth through the worn fabric of his breeches, and the tightness in his chest eased at last.

"I know we are all quite exhausted—myself and William here especially—but we do not know when Wickham will return," the colonel began, his voice steady despite the bandage around his brow—though Darcy had no idea where it had even come from. "I should like to have a plan in place. Once that is finalized, we should all follow Mrs. Reynolds's good example and rest as long as we can."

"We should also eat," Mrs. Reynolds said, "as none of us has broken our fast."

"That," he agreed, "is the most sensible suggestion I have heard all night."

Arrangements were quickly made for a tray to be brought. As Mrs. Reynolds busied herself giving orders, Darcy leaned back and closed his eyes. He still held Elizabeth's hand, their fingers loosely entwined between them. The faint scent of lavender clung to her hair, and he breathed it in as if it were the only thing anchoring him to this uncertain world. Her thumb brushed across his knuckles in a small, unconscious motion—so gentle it might have been imagined.

For the first time since that terrible evening began, his body surrendered to fatigue. His head tipped back against the cushions, and he dozed lightly until the sound of clinking china roused him again.

The tray was set before them—a modest breakfast of bread, cheese, and strong tea. The early light brightened the drawing room windows. After the first few grateful bites, Elizabeth spoke, her tone thoughtful.

"The law is against us, I fear. Legally, Mr. Wickham is the master of Pemberley, and Georgiana is his wife—pregnant with his child. She might flee, of course, but he could compel her return through the courts. Besides, she would not wish to abandon her family home."

Mrs. Reynolds nodded, adding, "She is perhaps two months from her confinement, and travel would be not only uncomfortable, but it would also be dangerous."

The colonel frowned. "Then we must think beyond the law. A man like Wickham makes enemies wherever he goes. It would not surprise me if one of them were to shorten his career—permanently."

Elizabeth sighed, though a small, reluctant smile curved her lips. "My husband has been of the same mindset, though he tends to prefer a duel—or even a brawl."

Darcy turned toward her, his eyes glinting with mischief that only she would recognize. "A man must meet his talents where they lie, Mrs. Smith," he said softly. "Though I admit, I have been told my aim is rather good."

His chest swelled when he saw her cheeks pinken, and she shook her head in silent reproach. The colonel's laughter rang out, hearty and genuine for the first time that morning. "I think I like you, William," he declared, clapping Darcy on the shoulder. "Any man who can jest after a night like ours is welcome in my company."

Darcy only smiled, though his hand lingered at Elizabeth's side beneath the folds of her gown. Instead of pulling hers away, she intertwined her fingers with his, and he silently sighed in contentment.

The colonel leaned forward, elbows braced upon his knees. "We must assume Wickham will return before nightfall. He will expect the household to be as he left it—obedient and silent. Our advantage lies in that expectation."

"He will be very angry," Elizabeth said. "His pride was quite wounded when William bested him and no one responded to his orders to summon the magistrate."

"I am surprised he has not returned by now," Darcy added. "I was certain last night that he would arrive long before I even reached Matlock."

Elizabeth's hand squeezed his at this reminder of the danger. "As was I," she whispered.

"Perhaps we could use his anger and pride to our advantage," Mrs. Reynolds suggested.

"It would certainly make him careless," the colonel replied.

"But whatever we do will not be a long-term solution," Darcy said. "We need something that will prevent him from causing any more damage… and my wife will not allow murder to be an option."

This last was said with a wicked grin and a small wink towards Elizabeth, causing the colonel to laugh perhaps a bit more than the jest warranted.

He is as exhausted as I am.

"What about prison?" Elizabeth said once the humor had subsided.

"He has not broken any laws," Darcy reminded her. "Even with his attempts with you, that would not be enough to put him in the gaol—not for long, at least."

"If what I remember about Mr. Wickham is correct"—she gave Darcy a significant look—"then he must have quite a few debts. Could they be purchased and combined, then used to put him in debtor's prison?"

Darcy gaped. *The woman is a genius,* he thought, just as Colonel Fitzwilliam exclaimed, "My dear, that is brilliant!"

"I know it will take time to gather his vowels, and it would mean a significant amount of money to be able to purchase them all…" Elizabeth's voice trailed off.

"That would be no trouble for my father," Richard said, waving a hand. "The only issue will be what to do in the meantime until enough evidence can be gathered."

The room fell silent as everyone contemplated the situation. Elizabeth suddenly grinned and said, "Perhaps I could hit him over the head with a bottle of wine, and then we lock him in the stables or the cellar for a month or two?"

Darcy was not entirely certain if she was serious or not, but there was no time to ask her. As she finished speaking, the faint but unmistakable sound of hooves coming up the long drive drifted through the still air.

Four heads turned towards the window, frozen, listening—the rhythmic beat grew louder, approaching the front of the house.

Mrs. Reynolds was on her feet in an instant, moving swiftly to the window where she had been keeping watch. She pulled back the curtain just enough to peer out, her posture rigid.

A breathless pause followed before her shoulders relaxed. "It is not Mr. Wickham," she said, relief flooding her voice. "The man is too scrawny by half."

The others exhaled as one. The colonel rose nevertheless, his hand resting on the butt of his pistol. "Best see who it is, Mrs. Reynolds. We can take no chances."

She gave a brisk nod and hurried from the room. The muffled sound of a door opening, followed by low voices, reached them. A moment later, Mrs. Reynolds reappeared, ushering in a man Darcy recognized at once—the innkeeper from Lambton, Mr. Whitlow.

"Colonel, sir," Mrs. Reynolds said, her face pale, "you are going to want to hear this."

Chapter 27

Elizabeth watched as the thin innkeeper shifted nervously upon the threshold, twisting his cap between his hands. His eyes darted from one face to another before settling at last upon Colonel Fitzwilliam.

"Sir, I was asked to bring you news—though Heaven help me, I would rather be anywhere else than bearing it."

Colonel Fitzwilliam leaned forward, his tone brisk but not unkind. "Then speak, man. Out with it."

Mr. Whitlow cleared his throat. "Last night I was at the tavern across from my inn. I do not often join their games, but with the weather turning, there are fewer travelers. We pass the time playing for pennies, no more." He gave a nervous glance at Mrs. Reynolds, as if uncertain how such talk would be received in Pemberley's drawing room.

"Go on," she said gently. "No one will think ill of a man for keeping company on a cold night."

The innkeeper nodded gratefully. "Well then—about an hour before midnight, Mr. Wickham came in. He had been drinking elsewhere, I think, for he was loud and unsteady. He called for ale, teased the serving girls, that sort of thing."

Elizabeth's stomach twisted. Even after all she had seen, it chilled her to hear his name again.

"No one dared confront him," Mr. Whitlow continued, lowering his eyes. "You know how it is. He holds sway over so many livelihoods in these parts. The girls laughed it off, but they were frightened. They may serve in the tavern, but they are good girls, sir."

The colonel made a sound of impatience. "I can well imagine it. Get to the point, if you please."

"Yes, Colonel. He saw us playing and insisted upon joining. We tried to discourage him, but he would not be denied. He sat himself down, wagered heavily, and lost almost at once. After the third hand, he slammed his cards on the table and accused us all of cheating."

Elizabeth could picture it too easily—the flushed face, the sneer, the arrogance.

"What then?" Darcy asked quietly.

Mr. Whitlow hesitated. "It angered one of the men—Mr. Harris, who owns the mill. He told Mr. Wickham to watch his tongue. The magistrate was there as well, and he tried to calm them both, but Mr. Wickham would not have it. He began to shout—terrible things, sir. He said the whole county was against him, that everyone conspired to keep him down, that he was the godson of George Darcy and deserved better than to rot in this cursed corner of England."

The colonel's expression hardened. "And then? Was he arrested?"

"No, sir," Mr. Whitlow said, his voice faltering. "He was not arrested."

"Then what?" the colonel pressed. "Was he thrown out? Beaten? Sleeping off his drink somewhere?"

The innkeeper looked down at his hat. His fingers twisted the brim until it nearly tore.

"He is dead."

The word hung in the air like smoke.

Elizabeth gasped. The colonel's head snapped up, and Darcy's chair scraped sharply against the floor as he rose.

"Dead?" the colonel repeated, his voice low and disbelieving.

Mr. Whitlow nodded, his throat working as he swallowed. "Aye, sir. Dead. I saw it myself."

The silence stretched as Darcy lowered himself back into his seat. Then the fire gave a sharp crack, startling them all. The colonel was the first to recover.

"Explain yourself," he ordered quietly. "What happened?"

Mr. Whitlow wet his lips. "After the quarrel, sir, no one sided with him. The magistrate warned him to mind his tongue, but that only made him worse. He ranted that we were all cowards conspiring to ruin him. He said he would not stay another hour in this godforsaken backwood county, that he was meant for better company. He boasted that he would return to London where he was known and respected."

Elizabeth's fingers clenched together in her lap. She could almost hear Wickham's voice in her mind, the hate and vitriol she had witnessed from him the day before blending with the innkeeper's words.

"And then?" Richard prompted again.

"He was told to leave," Mr. Whitlow replied. "So he did—stormed out into the street, cursing us all. I followed to be certain he did not cause trouble. The magistrate and Mr. Harris must have thought the same as me, for they came along, too. He grabbed the reins of his horse, which seemed to almost not be very well-trained."

"It was not," Darcy said grimly. "I am not certain where he procured the animal, but he rode it to Pemberley when he came back from who-knows-where. When he left last night, I was half expecting the animal would throw him—it was difficult to manage, even if its rider were more experienced."

Mr. Whitlow nodded. "That would be it, then. The horse was restless when he mounted. Mr. Wickham jerked the reins, and I think he spurred too soon. The creature danced sideways, half-reared, and Mr. Wickham just… well, he just lost control of his anger, I guess. He began to whip it—hard. The more he struck, the more it fought him. It finally reared up and kicked its front legs, then crashed down and bucked, throwing Mr. Wickham from its back."

Elizabeth and Mrs. Reynolds gasped. "Is that what killed him, then?" Elizabeth asked.

"Yes, Mrs. Smith. His neck was broken. Clean, like a snapped twig. He did not suffer long."

Elizabeth felt as though she might be ill. No one spoke. Mrs. Reynolds' hands trembled where they clutched the back of a chair. The colonel exhaled slowly, the sound heavy in the still room.

"Well," he said at last, "that saves us the trouble of deciding what to do with him. It seems the Almighty has settled the matter."

Elizabeth closed her eyes, uncertain what she felt—shock, relief, or guilt that any relief could exist at all.

The colonel rubbed a hand over his brow. "Well, William, we are fortunate indeed. He has spared your wife the from the necessity of preventing one of us from killing him."

Darcy shot the colonel warning glance.

The colonel raised a hand in apology. "Yes, yes—poor form, I know." Turning back to the innkeeper, he asked, "Will there be an inquiry? The magistrate will not leave it at that, surely?"

Mr. Whitlow shook his head. "There will be none, sir. The magistrate was present when it happened. He saw Mr. Wickham's fall himself. He said it was an accident and that nothing more needed to be done. The body has already been taken to the undertaker's."

Elizabeth drew a steadying breath. "Then it is truly over."

Darcy's eyes softened as they met hers. "Yes," he said quietly. "It is over."

"I will go inform Georgiana," Richard said, rising from his chair.

"No, not yet," Elizabeth said firmly. "She has had too many shocks already."

"Yes, let the dear girl sleep," Mrs. Reynolds agreed.

"Very well," replied the colonel. He rubbed the back of his neck, and Elizabeth could see the weariness settle over him like a weight. "Truthfully, we should all do the same. There will be enough time later to decide what steps we should take next. For now, let us rest."

Elizabeth rose, feeling the exhaustion in every limb. The tension that had held her upright through the long night drained away, leaving her hollow but lighter than she had felt in days. "A sensible plan at last," she murmured.

The colonel gave her a faint smile. "A soldier learns to sleep when the battle ends, even if the smoke has not cleared."

One by one they parted—Mrs. Reynolds to the servants' wing, the colonel to the guest chamber prepared for him, and Darcy and Elizabeth to the quiet refuge of their room. The morning sun had risen high in the sky and shone in through the windows as they walked along the corridor, but to Elizabeth it felt as though the dawn had only just come.

For the first time since that terrible night began, she felt safe. When they reached the small chamber that had been given to them, Elizabeth closed the door behind them and stood still for a long moment. The house had fallen silent. The only sounds were the whisper of wind along the windows, and the quiet seemed almost unreal after the chaos of the past day.

She crossed to the narrow bed and sat down heavily. Her limbs felt heavy, her eyes burned, yet her mind would not rest. Every nerve still hummed with memory—the echo of hooves on the gravel, the crash of splintering wood, Georgiana's frightened face. It was over now. Truly over. Mr. Wickham was dead.

Relief washed through her in slow, unsteady waves. It seemed impossible that the long night was truly ended—that the danger which had shadowed every hour might now be gone forever. Her body trembled as though it had only just remembered how to feel.

Darcy moved about the room without speaking, lighting a candle and drawing the curtains against the pale light. When he came to lay down in bed beside her, she looked up at him.

"He cannot hurt her again," she said quietly.

"No," he answered, but his voice held a note she could not name. There was relief there, and sorrow as well.

She wanted to ask, yet she was too weary to form the words. Instead, she reached for his hand and held it between both of hers, feeling the warmth of him seep slowly into her cold fingers. The simple contact steadied her at last, and she closed her eyes.

For the first time in many days, there was no need to listen for footsteps or fear a shout from the hall. The silence of safety felt almost as fragile as glass.

~~*~*

Darcy watched Elizabeth's head droop against his shoulder, her lashes heavy with sleep. For her, the end of fear had brought peace; for him, it had brought only weariness and a strange, aching regret.

He should have rejoiced that Wickham could not harm anyone again. Instead, he felt hollow. Memories flew through his mind of a laughing boy with sun-browned hair and quick wit, the companion of his youth.

How much promise there had been then—how much good might have come of it, had he chosen differently. It was a wasted life, and Darcy could not help but mourn the friend that had died long before the man.

Elizabeth stirred, her hand tightening over his. "What shall we do now?" she murmured, her voice thick with fatigue.

"I do not know," he said truthfully. "My mind is too clouded to think."

She gave a small sound of agreement, half sigh, half whisper, and leaned against him once more. He wrapped an arm around her shoulders, drawing her close.

The room was dim and the air in the room was warmer than usual. The steady rhythm of her breathing lulled him, and the heaviness in his eyes would not be denied.

At last, together, they drifted into sleep.

~~*~*

Elizabeth awoke to the afternoon light pressing against the curtains. For a moment she could not recall where she was, only that the room felt still and unfamiliar. Then the sound of a knock at the door brought everything back—the night before, the news, the strange relief that had followed.

Mrs. Reynolds's voice carried through the panel. "Mrs. Smith, ma'am—Mrs. Georgiana is awake."

Elizabeth stirred, glancing toward Darcy. He was already watching her, his dark eyes heavy with fatigue but softened by something that looked very like peace.

"I have an idea," she said quietly, pushing back the coverlet.

He smiled faintly. "I am grateful that you always have ideas, for I am often at a loss. An emergency upon an estate is simple enough. Matters of the heart, however, are an entirely different campaign."

The warmth in his tone spread through her like sunlight. "Then it is well one of us has some experience," she replied gently, rising to dress.

They went down together to the dining room, where lunch was being served. The smell of tea and warm bread met them at the door. Georgiana sat at the table, pale but composed, her hands folded in her lap. Colonel Fitzwilliam was beside her, a cup of coffee in his hand. Both looked up as Elizabeth and Darcy entered.

"Come, sit with us," the colonel said, motioning to the empty chairs. "Now that your friend is here, Georgie-girl, there is something you should know. It may be unpleasant, but you deserve the truth."

He hesitated, his eyes flickering to Elizabeth. She understood at once.

Elizabeth reached across the table and took Georgiana's hand. "My dear, there has been an accident," she said gently. "Your husband is dead."

Georgiana blinked, her face blank for a moment. Then she looked to her cousin. "You did not—?"

"Good heavens, no!" Richard exclaimed, appalled. "It was not my doing."

Elizabeth shook her head. "It was his own foolishness. He was drinking in Lambton last night and decided to ride home. His horse threw him."

Silence followed. Georgiana's gaze drifted to the window, unfocused, and then tears began to slide down her cheeks.

Darcy and Richard exchanged alarmed glances. "You cannot possibly be mourning him," Richard said incredulously.

Georgiana only wept harder.

Elizabeth touched her shoulder. "Colonel, allow her a moment. Sometimes when women receive great news—whether happy or sad— tears are the first release. There must be so many emotions within her just now. Relief, perhaps, followed by guilt for feeling that relief. Guilt, too, that had she been a better wife, he might not have gone to the tavern at all. And now, uncertainty for the future. It is a great deal for one heart to contain."

Richard studied his cousin for a long moment, then nodded slowly. "All of those feelings inside your little body, Georgie-girl? It is a wonder you do not burst."

The absurdity of the remark drew a startled laugh from her, and soon all of them were smiling through the dampness of tears.

Elizabeth squeezed her hand. "None of this is your fault, my dear. Mr. Wickham made his own choices, and now he has paid their price. The question is what must happen next."

Georgiana's expression crumpled once more. "But what can I do now? My husband is gone, and I cannot own property. I shall fall under my uncle's authority again, and now with a child. The child will inherit, but if my uncle petitions the court, he might take it from me. I have no power at all."

Elizabeth took a deep breath. "Then it is fortunate that I have another idea."

Both men turned toward her. Their gazes were attentive but wary, and her courage wavered for a moment. What if the colonel dismissed her suggestion outright? What if she made matters worse?

Still, she pressed on. "What if you had another husband, Georgiana?"

Georgiana blinked. "Another—?"

"Yes," Elizabeth said carefully. "A man you could trust. Someone who would care for you and for the child. Someone who would protect you."

Georgiana's brow furrowed. "But how could I know he was good? What if he proved just the same? I do not think I wish to marry again."

Elizabeth met the colonel's eyes deliberately. "But what if it were someone you already know? Someone whose honor is beyond question."

Understanding dawned slowly on his face.

"Who?" Georgiana asked, still staring down at her hands.

"Me," said Richard, and Georgiana's head jerked up, startled.

He rose and came to stand beside her, then knelt so that he was level with her chair. "I know I am older than you," he said quietly, "and I have been your absent guardian more than your friend. It would not be a great love affair such as one reads of in novels, but I do care for you, and for Pemberley. I flatter myself that I am a moderately good catch."

She gave a watery laugh through her tears. "But there is no money to rebuild Pemberley. We have scarcely enough now."

"Your dowry was withheld," he reminded her, "because my father and I would not consent to Wickham. That fortune remains untouched. My father will grant permission for this marriage, and when he does, your dowry can restore Pemberley and provide for you and the child."

"And your career?"

He smiled faintly. "My injury on this last campaign prevents me from being able to return to the front. They will have to defeat the little emperor without me, whether we wed or not."

Georgiana bit her lip, uncertain. He reached for her hand and held it gently.

"You need not decide now," he said softly. "Think upon it as long as you like. But with the child so near, it might be wise to marry before your confinement. It would secure you, and him."

She looked at him through her tears. "Could you love a child of his?" she whispered. "An absent father is better than an indifferent one—but I would not wish you to bear the burden."

He reached up and brushed a tear from her cheek with his thumb. "Children are the product of how they are raised, not of their sires. Otherwise I would resemble my parents, and Heaven help me if that were so. No, Georgie-girl, I could love this child. Gladly."

Her lip trembled. "You are very good, Cousin."

He smiled at that. "Good enough, perhaps, to give your family back its name. I should like your children, and all of us, to take it again—the Darcy name. Lady Anne and George Darcy made Pemberley a place of warmth and love. It is time that name stood for that once more."

Georgiana hesitated. "But will not your father be angry?"

Richard shook his head. "I will pacify him. If the child is a boy, he shall be called Fitzwilliam; if a girl, Anne Catherine, for our mothers—his sisters. That will soothe his pride."

Tears welled again, though this time they were gentler. "Then yes," she whispered. "I would be honored."

He rose and gathered her carefully into his arms. She leaned against him, resting her head upon his shoulder, and for the first time since Elizabeth had met her, Georgiana's face held peace.

Darcy pushed back his chair and stood. The motion drew Elizabeth's attention; his face was composed, but there was something shadowed behind his eyes—something that looked very much like sorrow. His gaze lingered for only a moment upon his sister before he inclined his head and murmured a quiet word of congratulations.

Elizabeth watched him go. The sound of his departing footsteps echoed softly in the corridor, and for a moment the room felt strangely still without him. The colonel and Georgiana remained close together, speaking in low tones, their faces softened by the tender uncertainty of new understanding. Mrs. Reynolds had discreetly slipped away, leaving them to the intimacy of the moment.

Elizabeth's heart swelled with affection and relief, but also with a pang of sympathy for the man who had just left the room. Darcy's love for his sister was deep, and his heart—already raw from all that had passed—must ache with a dozen conflicting feelings: pride, gratitude, loss.

She drew a quiet breath, steadied herself, and after offering one last smile to the pair at the table, slipped out into the passage to find him.

Chapter 28

Darcy stood in the corridor, the murmur of voices behind him growing faint as he moved toward the tall window at the end of the passage. The morning light lay pale upon the floor, dust motes floating in the still air. He could hear laughter—a soft, uncertain kind—from the breakfast room below. Richard's voice, calm and confident, and Georgiana's gentler reply.

He should have felt nothing but gratitude. His cousin had stepped forward to take control of Georgiana's future, offering her both protection and dignity. For the first time since that terrible Christmas night when the fae had unmade his existence, Darcy's sister was safe. Truly safe.

Yet what filled him was not peace. It was emptiness.

For months he had thought of nothing but survival—of repairing the damage his reckless wish had wrought, of setting the world to rights again. Each day had been defined by a single purpose: to protect Elizabeth and to rescue Georgiana.

Now all of it was done.

And there was nothing left.

He stared out over the frost-streaked lawns, the familiar hills of Pemberley stretching in the distance. It had always been his world, his duty, his home—but not here. Not in this shadow of a life where the name Darcy carried no meaning, and where his sister no longer even knew him as her brother.

Elizabeth's footsteps came softly behind him. "Are you well?" she asked.

He turned, forcing a smile that did not reach his eyes. "I am relieved," he said quietly. "More than I can say. But—" His voice faltered. "Forgive me. I do not know what to do now."

She frowned gently. "What do you mean?"

"Everything has been made right," he said, each word heavy. "Georgiana has her future secured. Richard will be an excellent husband, and she will be safe at Pemberley. But what is left for us, Elizabeth? We cannot go back to Longbourn—by now, your family must have discovered the deception. And we cannot remain here. I cannot endure living in my own home as a stranger. So what purpose remains to me?"

Her hand reached toward him, but stepped back out of reach.

"You should stay here. Georgiana could take care of you in a way that I cannot."

"What?" He heard her gasp, but he could not meet her gaze.

"I am truly sorry, Elizabeth" he muttered. "You have lost your family because of me. It is my fault. All of it. My foolish wish—my arrogance—has destroyed more lives than it ever mended."

"Fitzwilliam—"

He shook his head. "Please. I must go. If I stay another moment, I shall say something I regret."

She did not stop him. Only watched, wordless, as he turned and descended the stairs.

Outside, the air was cold and sharp against his face. He walked without direction, his boots crunching over the frozen gravel of the path that led toward the river. The pale sun was low above the trees, the air so still that the smoke from the chimneys hung unmoving in the sky.

He felt hollow. Every purpose that had driven him these past months had dissolved with Wickham's death and Georgiana's safety. What remained was only the dull ache of failure.

Yes, they had succeeded in saving her—but at what cost? Elizabeth had lost her family, and he had lost his. Even if they stayed, what future could they claim? Would they marry here, in this false world, and bring children into a life that was never meant to exist? Could he condemn her to that—to living as the wife of a man who no longer existed in truth?

A bleak thought settled in his chest. Perhaps he should leave. Go to the Americas, or farther still. Leave Elizabeth here, where she could remain as Georgiana's companion and friend. She would be safe, cared for, and perhaps one day she might find a kind of peace.

As for him—he was accustomed to solitude.

The river's edge was quiet, the water dark and slow beneath a veil of mist. He stared into it until his reflection blurred and vanished, and the thought came unbidden: *I have ruined everything again.*

He drew a shuddering breath, closed his eyes, and let the cold wind strike his face.

It was as though he had become what the fae had made him—an absence, a hollow man in a hollow world.

And for the first time since that cursed night, he began to wonder if he was meant to stay lost forever.

~~*~*

Elizabeth stood frozen in the corridor, the sound of his retreating footsteps echoing in her ears. For a long moment she could not move. His words still hung between them, sharp and bewildering.

No purpose. Nothing left.

Her lips parted as if to call him back, but no sound came. Then, from somewhere below, a faint creak of hinges carried upward—the sound of the front door closing behind him.

She moved at once. Heart pounding, she crossed the corridor and slipped into a small drawing room whose tall windows overlooked the gardens. She pushed the curtain aside and pressed close to the glass.

There he was—striding across the frosted lawn, his greatcoat dark against the pale morning. He did not look back. The path he took led toward the woods beyond the east terrace, the very one they had walked together so many times before.

Elizabeth's breath caught. She stood there for a moment, watching him until the trees swallowed him from sight. At first all she felt was shock—cold, heavy, and incomprehensible. But as his last words replayed in her mind, something else began to stir.

Anger.

How *dare* he say there was no purpose left? What of *her*? Did she mean nothing now that Georgiana was safe? Did he think their time together—their long nights of fear and planning, their small victories, their companionship—counted for nothing?

Her pulse quickened, heat rising in her chest. He had spoken as if all his worth were measured by what he could mend, what he could control. As if being with her were not enough, not reason enough to live and fight.

She pressed her hand against the glass, her reflection shimmering faintly in the morning light. "You foolish man," she whispered. "Do you not see what you have done? What *we* have done together?"

They had built something between them these past months—something fierce and unspoken, forged through hardship and shared purpose. Though neither had named it aloud, she had believed they understood one another.

But now he would simply walk away? Leave her behind with words of regret and ruin, as though all they had endured together were meaningless?

The anger grew, bright and burning. She turned from the window, her skirts brushing sharply against the chair by the wall. "No," she said aloud, her voice shaking with indignation. "He does *not* get to do this."

Without another thought, she gathered her shawl from the back of the settee and strode from the room. The air in the corridor was cold, but her resolve was hotter than any fire.

If he meant to lose himself again in those woods, she would find him there—and she would tell him exactly what she thought of his talk of purposelessness and ruin.

Whatever he believed, she was not about to let Fitzwilliam Darcy vanish from her life.

Not when they had finally found one another.

Elizabeth followed the path Darcy had taken through the garden and into the trees, her breath sharp in the cold afternoon air. The sun would be setting soon, and the shadows from the trees only served to increase the cold.

The woods were quiet save a few chattering squirrels and the faint rustle of bare branches above. Ahead, through the trees, she caught sight of him—his tall figure standing along the bank of the stream. Just as he had at Rosings, he was throwing pebbles into the creek with as much force as he could muster.

"Fitzwilliam!" she called, her voice ringing across the stillness.

He turned slightly, surprise flickering across his face before he looked away again. That small gesture—so resigned, so weary—only deepened her anger.

"How dare you!" she cried, striding toward him. "How dare you speak as if everything you have done means nothing! As if your life, your choices, are so meaningless that you can simply abandon them!"

He halted but did not turn. Elizabeth's fury rose at his silence.

"You speak of having no purpose left. What of me? Have I no place in your world now? Do I not count for something? After all *we* have endured—after all that we have done together—you would cast it aside with one despairing speech and a walk into the woods?"

Her voice trembled, but she pressed on. "You have risked your life for your sister, for me, for *us*! You have set right what was broken and protected those you love. And now you would tell me it was all for nothing? You foolish, foolish man!"

He turned then, his expression tight with pain. "Elizabeth—"

"No," she said fiercely, cutting him off. "You do not get to speak until I am finished."

He fell silent, his jaw clenched.

"I believed," she continued, her breath unsteady, "that we had an understanding. That we were a team—equals. I thought we had begun to trust one another. And now you talk as though I am nothing to you, as though all of this was a mistake to be undone!"

He flinched, and the anguish in his eyes nearly broke her, but her anger burned too brightly to stop.

At last, he spoke—low, bitter, almost a whisper. "You are right about one thing. It was a mistake. I wish none of this had happened. I wish I had never spoken those foolish words that morning in Kent. I wish I could take it all back."

Elizabeth went utterly still. The cold air bit at her cheeks, but she barely felt it.

"I do not," she said.

His head snapped up. "What?"

"I do not regret it," she repeated, her voice trembling but sure. "How could I? This strange, broken world has given me something no other could have done. It has given me you. It has shown me the real Fitzwilliam Darcy—proud, yes, and impossible, but good and brave and kind. I have seen your heart."

She stepped closer, her voice softening but growing no less firm. "If there is one good thing to come from this—one blessing—it is that we finally see each other as we truly are. I would rather be in this world with you, without my family, than back in the other world without you."

His breath caught. "Elizabeth… how can you say that? To give up your family, your friends—everyone that you love?"

She lifted her chin, her heart pounding so hard she could scarcely speak. "Because I love *you*."

The words hung between them, shimmering in the cold air.

For a moment he only stared at her, astonishment written plainly across his face. Then, with a sound that was half breath, half prayer, he closed the distance between them in two strides.

His hands came up to frame her face, his touch fierce and trembling. "I love you too," he whispered, the words so low she barely heard them before his mouth found hers.

The world seemed to fall away. The cold, the fear, the ache of months—all of it melted in that single, searing moment. His kiss was everything—relief and wonder, sorrow and joy, and the fierce recognition that they had found at last what neither had dared to hope for.

Elizabeth's hands gripped the front of his coat, her knees weak, her heart soaring. She rose up onto her toes without thinking, meeting his passion with her own. She could feel his heartbeat against her own, steady and real, grounding her in the certainty that whatever world they now lived in, they belonged to each other.

He deepened the kiss, causing her to gasp against his mouth. But there was no hurry, no desperation—his lips moved against hers with a kind of reverence, as though he were learning the shape of her soul. The heat of him seeped through her shawl, dissolving the cold that had lingered in her chest since he declared his regret.

She could feel his hand slide from her cheek to the curve of her neck, his thumb brushing the hollow beneath her ear. The tenderness of it undid her utterly. Her heart swelled with so much feeling she thought it might burst. Love, gratitude, release—all of it tangled together until she no longer knew where one ended and the other began.

When he finally drew back, they remained close, their foreheads touching, their breaths mingling in the chill air. She opened her eyes and found his fixed on her, dark and bright all at once, full of wonder and promise and disbelief.

"Elizabeth," he whispered, her name rough and reverent.

For the first time since that fateful night, she felt the world settle into place. She smiled faintly, tears stinging her lashes. "Fitzwilliam," she breathed.

And in his eyes, she saw the same truth reflected back—bright, certain, and utterly undeniable.

He kissed her again, softer this time, as if to memorize her. Around them the frost gleamed, and the morning light turned to gold upon the water. It felt to her as though the world itself had been holding its breath—and now, at last, had let it go.

~~*~*

Darcy's arm remained around Elizabeth's shoulders as they stood near the creek, watching the faint current curl around the icy stones. He could still feel the echo of her words in his chest, as if they had been carved there.

I love you.

For a long time he said nothing, afraid that speech might shatter the fragile perfection of the moment. When he did find his voice, it came rough and uncertain.

"You love me," he said, almost to himself. "I can scarcely believe it."

Elizabeth turned her face against his shoulder, her breath warm through the wool of his coat. "You had better believe it," she said softly, her tone half teasing, half tender.

He let out a quiet laugh, the sound still strange to his own ears. "I have imagined those words a thousand times. To hear them now—it feels unreal."

"It is as real as this," she said, pulling gently from his side and crouching near the water's edge. She picked up a small, smooth pebble and held it in her palm. "Do you remember how you were throwing these into the pond at Rosings?"

He nodded, watching her fingers cradle the stone.

"You are like that pebble," she said. "Every action you take, every word you speak, touches more lives than you can see. It was not only Georgiana you saved. You changed everything—for her, for me, for all of us. You have had an effect far beyond what you imagine."

She held out the stone to him. "Keep this. Let it remind you that you matter—that your existence has weight and purpose. It matters very much—especially to me."

For a moment, he could not speak. He took the pebble from her hand and turned it between his fingers, feeling its smooth, cool surface. Then he closed his fist around it, his thumb tracing the soft curve, and slipped it into his front coat pocket, where it came to rest against his heart.

"I will keep it always," he said quietly, patting the place where it lay.

They lingered there until the light began to fade, the mist rising once more from the river. As they made their way back along the path, Darcy caught sight of a small cluster of white snowdrops blooming beneath the trees, their fragile heads nodding in the chill breeze.

He stopped and bent to pluck one. The stem was long and slender, the petals pure and bright against the dark of his glove. Turning to her, he tucked the flower gently behind her ear, his fingers brushing her hair.

"If I am like the pebble, then you are like this flower," he said softly, "bringing beauty and the promise of spring when all else seems dark and cold."

Her eyes met his, shining, and he leaned down to kiss her—lightly this time, tenderly, a promise of the future.

They walked the rest of the way hand in hand.

When they reached the house, the windows glowed with candlelight, and the smell of supper greeted them as they stepped inside.

Mrs. Reynolds met them in the kitchen, her capable hands already busy at the hearth. "There you are," she said with a smile. "Sit down and eat while it is still warm. Enough menfolk came from Matlock this afternoon to see to things, and I have a few helpers from the village now. You two have done enough for one day."

Elizabeth smiled. "We are not so very tired, Mrs. Reynolds."

The older woman gave her a knowing look. "Aye, but you will be once you sit. Go on, then. Sup, and then get yourselves to bed. Tomorrow will come soon enough."

Darcy exchanged a glance with Elizabeth. She was smiling faintly, her cheeks touched with color, the little snowdrop still tucked behind her ear.

He reached for her hand beneath the table, lacing their fingers together as the fire crackled and the scent of fresh bread filled the room. Upon eating their fill, they climbed the stairs in silence, the faint glow of the hearth below flickering against the walls.

When they reached their chamber, she moved about quietly, setting aside her shawl and smoothing the coverlet as if afraid to break the stillness. Her movements were calm, but there was a faint, nervous energy about her—a quickness in her breath, a tension in her fingers that did not escape him.

Darcy watched her, his heart full. She had faced every peril with courage, had met fear and despair and come through it shining—and yet this simple moment, the two of them alone, seemed to unsettle her.

When at last they lay side by side upon the bed, she kept her gaze on the ceiling, her hands folded upon her stomach. He turned toward her, unable to resist the pull of her nearness.

"Elizabeth," he said softly.

She looked at him then, her eyes luminous in the lamplight.

He leaned in and kissed her—slowly, reverently, with all the quiet certainty of a man who finally knew his heart. It was not a kiss of urgency or hunger, but of devotion, a wordless promise that whatever awaited them beyond this strange world, they would face it together.

When he drew back, her cheeks were flushed, her eyes wide and uncertain.

"I know we are already considered married in this world," he said, his voice low, "but you and I know the truth. I would not dishonor you, nor cheapen what we share. Elizabeth Bennet, will you marry me? Truly marry me."

Her lips parted in surprise. "How... how can we? We do not use our real names, and it is not as if we can post the banns or afford a license."

"It would be easy enough to marry over the anvil in Gretna Green," he said. "The border is not so very far, and we can use our real names there."

For a moment she only looked at him, her eyes searching his face. Then a smile began to form—soft, radiant, full of that quiet confidence he had come to love.

"Yes," she whispered. "Yes, I will marry you."

Something within him eased, something that had been bound tight for months. He released a breath he had not realized he was holding. "I do not know what is next," he said, his voice unsteady with emotion. "But it no longer matters—not so long as you are with me."

She smiled again, and he reached up, touching the small snowdrop still tucked behind her ear. Its stem was long and pliant. Carefully he removed it, twisting it about her finger until it formed a delicate circle of pale green and white.

"A poor thing for a wedding ring," he murmured, "but it is the best I can offer until we figure things out."

Her eyes shimmered as she looked at it. "It is perfect."

He bent toward her once more, brushing a kiss against her lips— soft, tender, full of love and the promise of all that might yet be.

When they lay back against the pillows, her hand still in his, the tiny flower curled around her finger, the last thought that passed through Darcy's mind before sleep claimed him was simple and complete.

Last Christmas, she made me wish that I had never been born. And now, because of her, I cannot imagine wishing for anything less than a life beside her.

Chapter 29

Darcy awoke with a start.

For one disoriented moment, he could not place where he was. The bed beneath him felt strange and familiar all at once. He blinked, and the ceiling above him came into focus—the carved cornices, the faint crack in the plaster near the window.

His heart lurched so violently he thought he might be ill.

He sat bolt upright. The chamber tipped and steadied around him. The scent, his own blend of cedar shavings and cold ash, was unmistakable. On the small escritoire by the hearth lay a scatter of papers, the first pages of letters begun and abandoned—his own cramped hand, slashed out and re-begun: *Madam— Miss Bennet— Elizabeth—*. Each one bore the mark of agitation and temper.

He stared at them, scarcely breathing.

Rosings.

He threw back the bedclothes and looked down. The nightclothes were the same he had worn that dreadful night—the night he had tossed and turned in bed, angry and miserable over Elizabeth's rejection.

From the corridor came the sounds of the house at morning: the low burr of voices, a footman's quick tread, the thin rattle of a coal scuttle, the distant strike of a grate being cleared. His throat tightened. A tremor went through his hands.

Was it all a dream?

No, that was not possible. It was too real, too detailed.

Darcy rose and crossed to the window and pressed his palm to the glass as if he could test the reality of the world by touch alone. The landscape beyond was bright with pale winter sunlight, the lawn glittering with frost. His breath fogged against the glass. He turned back to the room again, half afraid that if he blinked, the image would change—that he would find himself once more in the strange world he and Elizabeth had shared.

But nothing shifted. The chamber remained as it had always been.

He dragged in a breath that scraped, then another. Unable to bear the loneliness of the room any longer—*when is the last time I awoke without her by my side?*—he went behind the changing screen and tore his dressing gown from his body. He dressed with hands that would not be steady, mis-fastening one button and then another, then tearing them free to start again. He crammed his feet into his boots, forced them at last to heel, and seized his coat.

When he descended the stairs, the scent of holly and evergreens greeted him, and he froze. The halls were still hung with garlands, the side tables adorned with ribbons, and in the corner of the drawing room stood the same evergreen boughs decorated with mistletoe and candlelight.

A maid hurried past with a tray. She bobbed a curtsey and smiled up at him. "A happy Christmas to you, sir."

He stopped in his tracks.

Christmas.

His breath caught. He turned sharply toward the tall clock in the entryway. It struck eight. The same day. The same hour he left Rosings last time.

A wave of dizziness washed over him. He put his hand to the newel post to steady himself. His pulse hammered in his throat. His mind seized at fragments—Elizabeth's breath warm against his shoulder in the carriage, the weight of her head upon his arm as she slept next to him.

The clean snap of a snowdrop stem. The smoothness of a pebble turning beneath his thumb. He could feel them. He could *taste* the salt at Elizabeth's lips.

"I have gone mad," he murmured aloud.

The dream—the life—they had shared—it had felt so real. Every moment vivid, alive.

He pressed his hands against his temples. "It cannot have been a dream."

And yet the house said otherwise.

He moved toward the door, needing air, needing space to think. He would go for a walk—to clear his head. Perhaps the cold would restore sense to him.

But sense did not come. Panic did instead.

If it was a dream—then what? If it truly was Christmas morning, then it had been only last night that he had proposed.

Badly. Disastrously.

His stomach twisted.

If the world had truly returned to its former state, then Elizabeth's last memory of him was of that humiliation, that dreadful speech in which he had offered his heart and insulted her in the same breath.

And she hated him.

He hesitated at the door, uncertain whether to go to the parsonage at once or to wait until later in the day. To call so early would seem desperate, even unhinged. And yet to wait felt impossible.

He stepped outside into the cold. The air bit at his cheeks, but he barely noticed it. He walked without direction, his thoughts racing.

What if it was all a dream? What if she remembers none of it?

His chest constricted painfully.

What if she still despises me?

He had nearly reached the trees before he realized where his steps had brought him. The stream that fed the small pond lay ahead, rimmed with a thin crust of ice, the surface clouded and gray. A hush rested over the little hollow as if the very air remembered secrets. He stopped at the fringe of reeds and looked down upon the water, and his heart beat so hard he thought it might break a rib.

He stopped at the bank, staring out across the thin sheen of frost. His breath clouded before him.

339

This was where it had begun—his despair, his words to the unseen fae. He could almost hear his own voice echoing through the cold air: *I wish I had never been born.*

He closed his eyes. The memories did not fade. They rose—Elizabeth in the kitchen, bare-armed and fierce with a broken bottle; Elizabeth by the river, anger bright as a brand; Elizabeth beneath his hand, soft as a prayer. The taste of her. The look in her eyes when she said *I love you.* The flower ring. The vow.

If it had been a dream, then it had been the truest one he had ever known.

What if none of it happened? The thought would not be driven away. What if she remembers nothing? *What if I am alone with these shadows, and she is left with only the memory of a proud fool who offended her?*

He forced his eyes open and stared at the water until the blur of panic steadied into focus. If it had been only a dream, then he would build the reality with his own two hands.

The resolve settled in his chest, warm and sure.

He would begin with an apology.

After that, he would do the work that proved a man could be trusted. He would return to Hertfordshire with Bingley at once. He would set his friend again upon the road to Netherfield, and he would contrive as many walks and dinners and calls as Jane Bennet's comfort allowed—quietly, honorably, with no pressure and no interference from those who did not wish it.

He would seek out Mr. Bennet with humility and hear his mind. He would put himself where Elizabeth might see him at his best and not at his proudest. He would earn, if not her love, then at least her good opinion.

And if she did not remember a single moment of the life they had shared—if it had all been phantasm—then he would build another life in its place, brick by brick, day by day, as long as breath remained to him.

His chest ached, but the ache felt clean now, like air drawn too deep on a cold morning. He looked up at the pale sky.

He smiled faintly, the cold wind stinging his face.

Dream or not, he thought, *I will make it true.*

He turned from the pond—and froze.

There, just beyond the line of birches, stood Elizabeth.

~~*~*

Elizabeth woke suddenly, her heart pounding, her body shivering.

Darcy.

She rolled over to borrow his warmth, but the space beside her was cold. Reaching out, she half-expected to find the solid warmth of Darcy's arm and the steady rise and fall of his chest—but her hand only met the smooth coverlet.

Smooth?

Her eyes flew open.

The room was not the one she had fallen asleep in. Gone were the deep oak beams of the Pemberley servants' quarters, the rough blankets on a lump mattress, and the folded garments Darcy had left at the foot of the bed. Even the air was different—cool and close, heavy with the smell of lye soap and fresh plaster.

Elizabeth sat up in confusion, staring about her. The narrow bed, the single chair in front of the washstand, and the closet with the shelves—all of it was familiar.

She was in the Hunsford parsonage.

Her breath caught painfully in her throat. "No," she whispered aloud. "No, this cannot be."

Looking around again, she hoped for some sign that might explain the impossibility. Had she been dreaming? Was she ill?

A sudden thought struck her.

Am I... am I Mrs. Collins?

The very idea made her shudder.

She drew a shaking breath and pressed a hand to her forehead, then stood and went to the corner where a small trunk stood open. Inside lay her gowns—her *old* gowns, the same ones she had brought to Kent from Longbourn. There were no newer gowns that would have indicated a trousseau. And there were certainly no caps or lace collars, which would have been a sure sign that she had married.

Turning back to the bed, she inspected it carefully. There was no second pillow, no man's coat, no books or papers that might belong to Mr. Collins. The smallness of the room, the faint scent of lavender and starch—everything spoke of a guest chamber.

A guest, then. Not a wife.

Relief flooded through her so suddenly that she nearly laughed aloud. "Thank Heaven," she murmured, collapsing back against the bed for a moment, her pulse still unsteady.

But her relief gave way almost at once to bewilderment. If she was not married—if she was still *Miss Elizabeth*—then what had happened to the life she and Darcy had built together? The memory of it was still so vivid. Lying next to Darcy at night, traveling with him to Pemberley, working as a maid.

Had it all been a dream?

The thought struck her like a blow. Two months—could a dream truly span two months? She could still recall the details with painful clarity: the cold air of the Derbyshire nights, the crunch of frost beneath her boots, the way Darcy's voice deepened when he said her name.

"No dream could feel so real," she whispered.

Yet here she was, in the same bed, the same room, as if none of it had ever been.

She rose and dressed quickly, her fingers clumsy on the buttons. She needed proof—some hint that she had not imagined it all. The house was quiet save for the faint clatter of pans below. The only light came from the kitchen, spilling into the hallway.

Elizabeth descended the narrow stairs, her mind spinning.

When she stepped into the kitchen, the familiar warmth and bustle met her—the glow of the hearth, the smell of baking bread. The cook looked up from her work, her broad face creasing into a smile.

"Happy Christmas, Miss Bennet."

Elizabeth stopped short. "Happy—Christmas?"

"Aye, miss. The snow's let up, but it is a bitter cold morning."

Elizabeth's breath came out in a shaky laugh. "Christmas."

So it was true. She was back to the very morning after that awful proposal—the one that had driven Darcy into despair.

The thought made her stomach twist. *If this is Christmas morning again...*

She pressed a hand to her lips.

He will be there. He will go to the grove. He will make the wish.

If it had all been real—if he remembered her—then he would surely already be there now, assuming she went there as well.

And if not...

She did not let herself finish the thought.

"Thank you," she murmured distractedly to the cook, who looked at her in mild confusion as Elizabeth turned and rushed back up the stairs. Within minutes she had pulled on her boots, threw her pelisse about her shoulders, and tied her bonnet with trembling fingers.

The cold struck her like a wall as she stepped outside. The fields glittered with frost, the air sharp and thin. Her breath came in clouds as she hurried along the familiar path through the grove.

Her thoughts tumbled over one another. *If it was a dream, how do I speak to him? What do I say? How can I even tell if he remembers?*

The questions echoed in her mind as she climbed the small rise that overlooked the stream.

Then she stopped.

Darcy stood at the water's edge. His greatcoat was buttoned to his throat, his hair ruffled by the wind, his head bowed as though in prayer. The same as before.

Her breath caught.

She could not move. She watched him—his stillness, his quiet intensity—as though afraid any sound would shatter the fragile moment.

He looked down into the icy water, and for an instant she thought she saw him mouth the words—*I wish I had never been born.*

"Fitzwilliam," she whispered.

He turned.

Their eyes met.

Both froze.

The world held its breath.

~~*~*

For a long moment he could not move.

Elizabeth stood across the frozen stream, her breath pale in the winter air, her eyes wide with the same astonishment that held him rooted to the spot.

He took a hesitant step forward, unsure whether she was a vision conjured by his desperate mind. She bit her lip, just as she always did when uncertain, and the small, familiar gesture pierced him like light through darkness.

He took another step. She did the same.

When she raised her hand toward him, he noticed that she wore no gloves. Her fingers trembled in the cold.

"Are your hands not cold?" he asked softly. His voice sounded foreign in his own ears, rough and low from disuse.

Then he saw it.

Around her finger—fragile, green, and impossibly real—was the flower.

The snowdrop.

The breath went out of him. He stared, unable to speak, every muscle frozen between disbelief and wonder.

She followed his gaze, looked down—and gasped. Her eyes flew up to his, wide with comprehension.

They stared at one another, the truth dawning between them like sunlight breaking through cloud.

"You remember?" he whispered, taking a step nearer.

"I do," she breathed, her voice trembling. "Do you?"

He did not answer with words.

In two strides he was across the narrow strip of frozen ground, his hands closing around her before thought could catch up with motion. The instant his mouth met hers, the world vanished.

Every ounce of desperation, of fear, of sleepless longing poured into that kiss. All the nights he had lain awake wondering if their experience together was real, all the mornings he had awakened with her—they found their release now. Her lips were soft, warm, alive beneath his, and when she kissed him back, he thought his heart might burst.

She made a small sound—a quiet, breathless sigh that undid him utterly. Her hands found his hair, sliding through it, holding him to her. He drew her closer still, the ache in him fierce and sweet, every muscle yearning toward her as though to prove she was flesh, not dream.

He pulled her tightly against him, needing her near enough that the chill of the morning could never touch her again—

—and something hard pressed sharply between them.

He stilled.

Confused, he reached down, sliding his hand between them to his front coat pocket. His fingers closed around something smooth and cool.

He drew it out and stared.

The pebble.

The same small, gray stone she had given him beside the river at Pemberley.

~~*~*

Elizabeth could hardly think. The world seemed to have narrowed to the circle of his arms and the taste of his kiss. When he drew back, she was trembling—partly from the cold, mostly from the force of feeling that still coursed through her.

Then he reached into his pocket, his brow furrowing, and drew out something small.

A pebble.

For a moment she could only stare at it, blinking in disbelief.

The smooth gray surface was unmistakable—the same pebble she had pressed into his hand beside the river at Pemberley, the one she had told him to keep as a reminder of his worth. She remembered watching him slip it into his coat pocket.

But not *this* coat.

He had worn a rough, ill-fitting coat then—one they had purchased in that small market town after escaping Pemberley with nothing but what they could carry. The coat of a tradesman, not a gentleman. Yet this pebble had found its way here, into the fine wool of his present jacket, as though it had crossed the boundary of that vanished world with him.

How is it possible?

Does it even matter?

Her mind reeled. She no longer doubted that their time together had been real, but this—this small, solid token in his palm—was further evidence that defied any explanation.

Which meant their love was real.

Her heart swelled.

Without thinking, she reached up and touched his cheek. His skin was cold, his jaw rough from the morning chill. He covered her hand with his own, his thumb tracing slow circles against her wrist before he turned her palm and pressed a kiss into it.

The warmth of his lips against her bare skin sent a shiver through her—not of cold, but of remembrance. She closed her eyes, breathing him in, letting herself simply feel.

When he spoke again, his voice was low, gentle, steady in a way that soothed her racing heart.

"Your hands are cold," he murmured. "We must get you inside—warm you up."

She opened her eyes and smiled faintly. "And here I thought you would scold me for running off without my gloves."

He gave a soft, breathless laugh—the first she had heard since waking in this world. "You would not be the Elizabeth I know if you did not ignore good sense now and then."

"Do you ever tire of saving me?"

"Never," he said simply. "Though I admit, you do make it necessary with alarming frequency."

She laughed softly, the sound mingling with the faint whisper of the wind through the trees. "Then it seems we are both creatures of habit."

"Indeed," he said, his smile deepening. "And for once, I am content to repeat myself."

He reached for her hand again, enclosing her fingers within his own. Together they began the slow walk back toward the parsonage, their footsteps crunching over the thin crust of frost.

Neither spoke for some time. The morning light was soft upon the fields, and the world felt still—suspended between what had been and what was yet to come.

As they reached the lane, Elizabeth glanced up at him, her breath forming small clouds in the cold air. "It truly happened," she whispered, half to herself.

Darcy's hand tightened around hers. "Yes," he said quietly. "It truly did."

They exchanged a look of quiet wonder, and then—still hand in hand—they turned the final corner toward Hunsford, where the first curls of chimney smoke rose into the pale winter sky.

Chapter 30

Everything was still.

The faint scent of beeswax and evergreen hung in the air, mingling with the cold breath of early spring that crept in through the old stone walls. The morning sunlight, pale and new, streamed through the high windows, striking motes of dust into gold.

Darcy stood near the altar of the Longbourn chapel, his gloved hands clasped before him, and tried to steady the rhythm of his heart.

He had imagined this day a hundred times since his return to Hertfordshire, yet the reality felt nothing like those dreams. There was no grandeur, no sweeping joy—only a quiet certainty that reached down into his very soul.

The pews were filling slowly. A few familiar voices murmured, the rustle of muslin and the scrape of shoes echoing faintly on the flagstones. He scarcely noticed them. His thoughts were turned inward—toward the woman who would soon walk through that door.

Elizabeth.

Even now, her name held a power over him that no title or fortune could rival. She had been the cause of his greatest despair, and the source of his salvation. Because of her, he had learned to live.

He glanced toward the window, where the light struck the frost upon the glass. In the shimmer, he thought of another cold morning—a stream bordered by birch trees, her breath misting in the air, her hand reaching for his.

So much had changed since then. The ache of doubt had been replaced by peace. The world felt new, yet familiar, as though he had been allowed to live it properly at last.

He could still remember that Christmas day with startling clarity. Their arrival back at Hunsford, arm in arm, had sent ripples through the quiet parsonage like a stone through still water.

Mrs. Collins had recovered first, her practical nature swiftly overcoming surprise. After a single, startled gasp, she had smiled and offered sincere congratulations. Mr. Collins, however, had not borne the revelation with such composure. He had gone quite white, stammered something about *Miss de Bourgh*, and sunk heavily into the nearest chair, fanning himself with a handkerchief.

When speech returned, it came in a torrent—his patroness' certain fury, the ruin of his own good name, the inconceivable audacity of such an engagement. Darcy had endured it in silence for perhaps a minute before advising the man, with as much restraint as he could muster, to hold his tongue—or have it held for him.

Unfortunately, the fool's predictions of Lady Catherine's reaction had been underestimated. Her outrage, when she learned of the engagement two hours after her parson did, had made even Collins' theatrics appear mild. The memory of her voice still rang sharp in his mind—every syllable dripping with disbelief and condemnation. Her fury had been such that, for his own composure's sake, he had been compelled to quit Rosings altogether.

Yet in a strange way, he owed her for that. For it allowed him to escort Elizabeth home to Longbourn without delay, there to seek her father's permission properly.

The recollection of Elizabeth's parents' astonishment nearly drew a chuckle from him. Mr. Bennet's shock, Mrs. Bennet's absolute silence—he doubted he would ever see their like again. It was, he reflected, quite possibly the only time in Mrs. Bennet's life that words had entirely failed her.

Mr. Bennet, suspecting some elaborate jest, had refused to take the matter seriously at first. It had taken Elizabeth the better part of an hour to persuade him otherwise—and longer still to secure his blessing.

Darcy's grin deepened as he recalled her final argument: her declaration that, should her father persist in denying her, she would tell her mother at once that he had refused a husband with ten thousand a year and then run away to Gretna Green—leaving him to bear both his wife's wrath *and* the loss of his most sensible daughter.

Even now, the memory made his chest tighten with affection and amusement. How clever she was. How impossible not to love.

With effort, he forced the smile from his lips; it would hardly do to be caught grinning for no reason before the altar.

He smoothed a hand down his coat sleeve, scarcely believing the steadiness of it. He had thought once that this moment would never come, that she would never look upon him with anything but disdain. Yet here he stood, waiting for her.

The murmur of conversation quieted. Somewhere near the back, the door opened, and a breath of cold air drifted through the church.

He turned.

And all thought fled.

Elizabeth entered upon her father's arm, radiant and serene, and Darcy's breath stopped in his throat. The world and every sound in it seemed to fall away. There was only her—the living embodiment of every dream he had once dared to wish.

~~*~*

Two hours later, Darcy found himself leaning back in his chair, his gaze drifting over the guests who had gathered at Longbourn for the wedding breakfast.

Across the room, Bingley was chuckling at something Jane Bennet had said. The sight of them together drew an involuntary smile from him; it was impossible not to be pleased by their happiness.

Although we must deal with my aunts and uncle, he thought to himself wryly, there are at least some good things about being back in our own world.

At Jane's side, Mrs. Bennet was talking animatedly with the Gardiners, who had travelled from London for the occasion—even though they had only recently been at Longbourn for Christmas. He had not yet spoken much with them, but he looked forward to the

351

opportunity. They seemed every bit as kind and sensible as they had been in that other life.

He let his eyes move around the table. Georgiana was there, bright and composed, listening to something Richard was saying. Her laughter rang out—light, unburdened—and his chest tightened with gratitude. She was free. Wickham was nothing more than a distant memory.

Darcy had seen to that.

As soon as he could tear himself from Elizabeth's side at Longbourn, he had written an express to his man of business in London, as well as another to his steward at Pemberley, ordering them to gather every note and obligation bearing Wickham's name.

Those, combined with the debts he had already incurred in Meryton—debts Darcy had settled in full, though not the soldiers' debts of honor, which were their own doing—were sufficient to see him confined to the debtor's prison for the remainder of his life.

Even so, Darcy had to remind himself that this Wickham was not *that* Wickham, and it would be unjust to punish a man for sins he had not committed. But the knowledge did little to ease the instinctive bitterness that name still evoked, and Darcy determined to not allow the man free of his prison.

At least Georgiana was safe now, and Richard greeted him with the open affection of family. The sight of his cousin's good-humored smile and his sister's easy contentment as they spoke with Elizabeth filled Darcy with a quiet peace unlike any he had ever known.

Not long later, a gentle touch drew him from his thoughts. Elizabeth's hand rested lightly on his arm.

"Are you ready, my love?" she asked, her bright eyes lifting to his with that look that never failed to steady him.

He looked down at her, and the corner of his eye caught the glint of light upon her ring. The finger that had once borne a fragile snowdrop now shone with a band of white diamonds and small emeralds—designed to echo the bloom itself. He had commissioned it himself especially for her, using stones repurposed from pieces among the Darcy family jewels.

"Quite ready," he told her, covering his hand with her own.

Together they made their farewells, and within minutes, they were seated in the waiting carriage. The coachman called to the horses, and the wheels began to turn, carrying them away from Longbourn toward London, where they would spend their wedding night—as well as a few quiet weeks before going on to Pemberley, where Richard would deliver Georgiana to them.

"Are you excited to see Darcy House properly?" he teased, glancing down at her. "I am amazed you even agreed to spend time there after seeing it in such a state before."

She laughed, her eyes bright with mischief. "As long as the bank does not attempt to take possession of it, I shall be quite content."

He chuckled and leaned in to kiss her, one hand rising to cup her cheek—

A pointed cough stopped him short.

They both turned sharply.

Across from them, lounging with infuriating nonchalance, sat the fae. His eyes gleamed with mirth.

"My apologies for interrupting," he said, his grin far too knowing. "I merely wished to discover whether you were content with having been returned. Tell me, Mr. Darcy—do you still wish you had never been born?"

Darcy stared, caught between outrage and disbelief. "Most certainly not," he said vehemently.

The fae's smirk deepened. "Excellent. Then my work here is done." He inclined his head with exaggerated grace. "My congratulations upon your nuptials—and I wish you as many happy Christmases together as you desire. Now—" he gave a languid flick of his fingers— "as you were."

With a faint shimmer of light, he vanished.

Darcy and Elizabeth gaped at the empty seat. For several seconds neither spoke. Then Elizabeth gave a soft, incredulous laugh.

"Well," she said at last, "if we are indeed losing our minds, at least we are doing so together."

Her laughter—bright and unguarded—filled the carriage, and the sight of her sparkling eyes and the curve of her smile drew him in once more. He leaned closer, his voice low and warm.

"He did tell us to continue as we were," he murmured.

She tilted her face toward his, her answering smile trembling against his lips as he kissed her. Her hands slid into his hair, and his arms drew her closer. The kiss deepened, unhurried but full of promise, the soft thrum of the wheels beneath them like a heartbeat.

There was nothing to stop them now—nothing but the narrow confines of the carriage and the few miles that remained between them and London. Soon they would be at Darcy House; soon there would be no interruptions, no separations—nothing between them but love.

When at last they parted, foreheads resting together, he let out a quiet breath that was almost a laugh. How strange that a single wish, once born of despair, had brought him here—to this life, this moment, this woman.

He closed his eyes and whispered against her temple, his heart full to overflowing.

"I am so very glad," he said, "that I was born to love you, Elizabeth Bennet."

"Elizabeth Darcy," she corrected him with a smile, "unless you are already regretting your choice."

"Not a chance," he murmured, once again claiming her lips with his own.

Her new name sounded like a promise, bright and enduring—and in that quiet, perfect moment, he knew just how much of a difference a Darcy could make.

Epilogue

Pemberley, Derbyshire—December 25th, 1826

Snow fell in slow, unhurried flakes outside the great windows of Pemberley. Inside, the house glowed with firelight and laughter. Garlands of evergreen and ivy twined along the banisters, and the scent of pine and spiced cakes filled the air.

Darcy stood near the hearth, his youngest daughter balanced upon his arm as she tugged at the lace of his cravat with gleeful determination. Across the room, Elizabeth knelt to help their middle son assemble a complicated arrangement of toy soldiers, while the eldest, Bennet—serious and bright-eyed at fourteen—was attempting to mediate a spirited debate between his cousins on whether plum pudding or mince pies were the superior Christmas dish.

It was a scene of cheerful chaos, and Darcy would not have exchanged it for all the peace in the world.

The drawing-room doors opened, and the familiar sound of laughter carried in. Bingley entered first, shaking the snow from his coat, Jane following with her gentle smile and a cluster of rosy-cheeked children.

Elizabeth rose, her face lighting with pleasure. "At last! I had begun to think the storm would keep you at Harcourt for the night."

"The storm dares not stand between my wife and her sister," Bingley said cheerfully. "Even nature must give way to Mrs. Bingley's good intentions."

Jane laughed softly, setting down her muff. "We could hardly miss Christmas at Pemberley. The children would never have forgiven us, even if we are here every other week as well."

The room filled quickly with the bright stir of arrivals—the rustle of wraps, the warmth of greetings, the sound of children meeting cousins with the noisy delight known only to youth.

Darcy watched for a moment, his arm around his daughter, and thought how far they had come. Fifteen years ago, he could not have imagined this: a house alive again, a family restored, laughter echoing in rooms once silent.

Georgiana, too, had come home for the holiday, radiant and serene. Her husband—Thomas Ashford, viscount of Derby—stood beside her, speaking quietly with Richard Fitzwilliam and his wife near the fire. His sister's happiness was steady and unclouded, her laughter that of a woman fully at peace.

Charlotte Collins had sent her good wishes from Kent, along with her son, who now spent most summers at Pemberley and was to attend Eton alongside Bennet Darcy the following year. The two boys were already thick as thieves, which did not entirely reassure their parents.

As for the rest of the Bennet sisters, life had settled each in her place. Mary had married a respectable clergyman in Oxfordshire whose sermons were as long as his kindness was deep. Kitty, refined by her years under Jane's gentle influence, had made a prudent match with a barrister of good standing. Lydia's situation was rather more complicated—her husband having been one of the less reprehensible officers in the regiment that once quartered at Meryton—but even that patchwork marriage had endured.

Wickham himself had died some years past in debtor's prison—trying, according to the warder's account, to seduce another prisoner's visiting wife. Darcy had received the news with no triumph, only relief that no one he loved could ever be hurt by the man again.

A ripple of laughter drew him back to the present. Elizabeth had crossed to his side, cheeks flushed, eyes bright with that same light he had fallen in love with all those years ago. She slipped her arm through his and looked up at him.

"Still lost in thought?" she asked softly.

"Merely counting my blessings," he said, his voice low.

"Have you finished?"

"Not nearly."

Her laugh was quiet and full of affection. "Then you shall have a very long Christmas indeed."

"As long as I spend it with you, I do not care."

He smiled down at her, the room warm around them, the children's laughter ringing through the hall. Outside, the snow fell steadily, softening the world to silver and white.

Fifteen years ago, he had wished himself unmade; tonight, surrounded by every proof of life and love, he could not imagine a world without any of it.

He drew Elizabeth closer, pressing a kiss to her temple as the candles glowed and the music began.

"Happy Christmas, *Beth*," he murmured.

She looked at him, startled, then grinned cheekily. "Happy Christmas, *Mr. Smith*."

And as they turned toward the fire, the garlands, and their family gathered round, Darcy thought—as he always did at Christmas—how wondrously different the world had become, all because of the difference a Darcy had made.

Thank you for reading "The Difference of a Darcy"

by Tiffany Thomas.

If you'd like to keep updated on new releases,

please sign up for Tiffany's newsletter.

No spam, ever!

www.authortiffanythomas.com

You might also enjoy reading Tiffany's other works:

A Look Behind the Mask

The Sins of Their Fathers

When Summer Never Came

A Most Beloved Sister

Fine Eyes & Beastly Pride

A Dear, Sweet Girl

Attempted Compromises

Ashes & Understanding

Companions of Their Youth

Pride, Prejudice, & Permutations

About the Author

Tiffany Thomas is a chocoholic former math teacher with Crohn's Disease and homeschooling mom of four kids. She and her husband Phillip (who is an engineer) work together on the blog Saving Talents. They enjoy spending time with their family, geeking out over sci-fi together, and saving money.

Tiffany discovered Pride & Prejudice as a teenager, and even made poor Phillip watch the six-hour version with her on their honeymoon when they got snowed in. After reading fan fiction for over a decade, she finally broke out into writing some herself, with the tremendous support of her husband.